Return to Ma

By Gretel Hallett

A sequel to 'Mansfield Park'

By Jane Austen

For everyone who ever finished a book, and wondered,

'What happens next?'

Introduction

At the end of 'Mansfield Park', Austen marries off the heroine to the hero in the approved romance novel fashion – but in this case, I have always found this solution unsatisfying. Like many readers over the centuries since 'Mansfield Park' was published, I was less than enamoured of either the heroine or the hero. Fanny Price has been much derided by many critics for her *faiblesse*; of which much is made throughout 'Mansfield Park'. She is weak, easily 'knocked up', timid, described as a 'creep-mouse', and shrinks away from anything that might be considered adventurous. As a bold and adventurous person myself, I rather scorned her – but I had not read the novel closely enough, nor thought hard enough about her situation and her character. Unlike Fanny Price, I had not been taken away from my birth family, and sent hundreds of miles away to live with relatives I had never met – Fanny is a displaced person: not a refugee, but someone who in her own words was, 'torn' from her birth family, and hoped that going home again, 'would heal every pain that had since grown out of the separation'. It seems that many readers and critics have over-looked the psychological trauma which Fanny endured at a very young age, and which is the direct cause of much of her personality and conduct in the novel.

Fanny Price is the eldest daughter of a large family living in self-induced squalid accommodation in Portsmouth. Her parents have enough money to live in a moderately genteel manner, but her father is fond of 'strong liquor', and her mother is not a competent house-manager. Mrs Price has two older sisters; Lady Bertram who lives an idle life of luxury at Mansfield Park, and an interfering oldest sister, Mrs Norris, who is the widow of the Vicar at Mansfield Park. Mrs Norris keeps a tally of how many children Mrs Price produces, and when the Price family reaches double figures, finally suggests that the Bertram family takes in one of the children, to relieve the pressure. Fanny, as the eldest daughter, is chosen, and sent at the age of 10 – she is not given a choice about this; her mother is only surprised at a girl being chosen as she had so many fine boys.

My opinion on Fanny has been ameliorated by John Wiltshire, in his very interesting psychological interpretation of Austen's published novels, 'The Hidden Jane Austen' (Cambridge University Press 2014). Wiltshire points out the permanent psychological damage done to children who are removed from their birth families (even with very good reason), and sent away to a different land or culture. He also notes that the evidence in 'Mansfield Park' points to Fanny having been neglected by her birth mother, and arriving at Mansfield Park under-nourished, and weak as a result. This sort of neglect at an early age will never be made up by the adult, and Fanny will always suffer as a result of this; see pages 96 – 97 of Wiltshire's analysis.

Wiltshire also points out that Fanny may seem weak and timid, but she is possessed of a quiet inner strength. She is firm in her religious beliefs, her sense of right and wrong, and where necessary, stands up against the stronger characters in the novel, and does not give way to their demands. She resists being sent to live with her Aunt Norris, she resists the constant urgings of her cousins to join in their play (although has to give in eventually), she resists the Crawfords' attempt to foist a gift from Henry onto her, and she resists Crawford's offer of marriage, despite pressure from Sir Thomas Bertram. All of this despite being constantly reminded of the duty of gratitude she owes to the Bertram family. The only person who seems to notice this quiet inner strength is the restless and dissipated Henry Crawford, who values Fanny for her, 'conduct, honour, and observance of decorum', and believes that she would be a faithful wife (although this would almost certainly not be a reciprocal arrangement!). Book 2, Chapter 12.

The hero of 'Mansfield Park' is Edmund Bertram. He is the second son of Sir Thomas and Lady Bertram, and is a serious-minded young man destined to be a clergyman, and to have the living on the Mansfield Park estate after his Uncle Norris's death. Instead, he has to make do with a much smaller living at Thornton Lacey, after his frivolous and thoughtless older brother, Tom, runs up debts, which have to be paid off by their father. The result of this is that the living at Mansfield Park is sold to Dr Grant, and Edmund will have to wait for Dr Grant to retire (or die) before he can take on the more lucrative post himself.

Edmund is kind and gentle to his newly arrived cousin, and slowly becomes her friend, and helps her begin to fit in to her new world, as there seems to be no thought of her ever returning home. As she grows up, she gradually falls in love with him. We may find the idea of first cousins marrying troubling, but it was entirely acceptable in Regency England: it meant that family money could be kept within the family. This was not in the case for the Bertram-Prices; as it is never mentioned that Fanny brought any money to the marriage. This cousins-marrying-to-keep-the-money-in-the-family arrangement can be seen more clearly in 'Sense & Sensibility' when Colonel Brandon's rich cousin is married to his older brother, against her own wishes. Edmund Bertram is sensible, and rather stolid; although nowhere near as unappealing as Mr Rushworth. Edmund may have gravitas, but he lacks humour and lightness; these desirable qualities are supplied in abundance by the witty and urbane Crawfords. And here is exactly where the problem with the end of Austen's novel becomes apparent for me – I would have preferred Edmund to marry Mary Crawford, and Fanny to marry Henry Crawford. Mary would have brought fun and laughter to leaven Edmund's seriousness, and Fanny would have helped Henry to attain respectability and domestic harmony.

I did at one point consider re-writing 'Mansfield Park' with this ending – but Austen makes certain that Edmund cannot marry Mary because of her immoral views, and that Fanny is excused from marrying Henry because he has an affair with Maria Rushworth, nee Bertram. These are indeed insurmountable reasons why my preferred ending cannot take place. So, the only option is to carry on the story from where Austen left it – and to imagine what might have happened next for all the characters.

My starting point for 'Return to Mansfield Park' was the many questions raised by the ending of 'Mansfield Park'. What happened to Mary and Henry Crawford, for example? They are both highly eligible, attractive people, with independent fortunes – can they put the Bertrams behind them and carry on with their lives? What about Tom Bertram? He is a reformed character by the end of Austen's novel, and it would be his duty marry well and bring more money in to the family – so who does Tom marry?

Another point of consideration is that 'Mansfield Park' is set in or around 1810, and in 1807 the British Government had passed an Act that would begin to dissolve the Slave Trade, although slavery did not become outlawed until 1833, and many wealthy and important men continued to make their money on the back of the Slave Trade. However, the growing calls in Parliament to abolish the Slave Trade would not have gone unheard by the characters in 'Return to Mansfield Park', and they would have been aware that much of their income and position is due to Sir Thomas Bertram's exploitation of black slaves on his sugar plantation in Antigua. What will Sir Thomas do about this?

Would Fanny and Edmund really be happy together – I have never been convinced of this in particular. But we will start with poor Maria Bertram Rushworth. At the end of 'Mansfield Park' she is brutally punished for her transgressions by being immured in the countryside with her Aunt Norris. This is cruel and unusual punishment indeed, and I could not imagine that she would put up with it for long – so how does Maria escape?

Reader, read on! All will be revealed!

Also by Gretel Hallett, and available on Amazon Kindle and in paperback:

'An Heir and Four Spares: A semi-original novel', a re-telling of Jane Austen's 'Pride & Prejudice'.

'Mrs Tilney', a sequel to Jane Austen's 'Northanger Abbey'.

FRONTISPIECE

"it was with infinite concern the newspaper had to announce to the world, a matrimonial fracas in the family of Mr. R. of Wimpole Street; the beautiful Mrs. R. whose name had not long been enrolled in the lists of hymen, and who had promised to become so brilliant a leader in the fashionable world, having quitted her husband's roof in company with the well known and captivating Mr. C. the intimate friend and associate of Mr. R. and it was not known, even to the editor of the newspaper, whither they were gone." (MP 440)

INTRODUCTION comprised of a section from the end of 'Mansfield Park' by Jane Austen, leading directly into the sequel, 'Return to Mansfield Park' by Gretel Hallett

Where [Maria] could be placed became a subject of most melancholy and momentous consultation. Mrs Norris, whose attachment seemed to augment with the demerits of her niece, would have had her received at home and countenanced by them all. Sir Thomas would not hear of it; and Mrs Norris's anger against Fanny was so much the greater, from considering *her* residence there as the motive. She persisted in placing his scruples to *her* account, though Sir Thomas very solemnly assured her that, had there been no young woman in question, had there been no young person of either sex belonging to him, to be endangered by the society or hurt by the character of Mrs Rushworth, he would never have offered so great an insult to the neighbourhood as to expect it to notice her. As a daughter, he hoped a penitent one, she should be protected by him, and secured in every comfort, and supported by every encouragement to do right, which their relative situations admitted; but farther than *that* he could not go. Maria had destroyed her own character, and he would not, by a vain attempt to restore what never could be restored, by affording his sanction to vice, or in seeking to lessen its disgrace, be anywise accessory to introducing such misery in another man's family as he had known himself.

It ended in Mrs Norris's resolving to quit Mansfield and devote herself to her unfortunate Maria, and in an establishment being formed for them in another country, remote and private, where, shut up together with little society, on one side no affection, on the other no judgment, it may be reasonably supposed that their tempers became their mutual punishment.

Mrs Norris's removal from Mansfield was the great supplementary comfort of Sir Thomas's life. His opinion of her had been sinking from the day of his return from Antigua: in every transaction together from that period, in their daily intercourse, in business, or in chat, she had been regularly losing ground in his esteem, and convincing him that either time had done her much disservice, or that he had considerably over-rated her sense, and wonderfully borne with her manners before.

He had felt her as an hourly evil, which was so much the worse, as there seemed no chance of its ceasing but with life; she seemed a part of himself that must be borne for ever. To be relieved from her, therefore, was so great a felicity that, had she not left bitter remembrances behind her, there might have been danger of his learning almost to approve the evil which produced such a good.

She was regretted by no one at Mansfield. She had never been able to attach even those she loved best; and since Mrs Rushworth's elopement, her temper had been in a state of such irritation as to make her everywhere tormenting. Not even Fanny had tears for aunt Norris, not even when she was gone for ever.

CHAPTER ONE:

Sir Thomas's zeal in arranging his disgraced daughter's fate was in line with the rest of his business dealings, and he treated it as he would his latest business project. Maria should not be in society, but should live as a gentlewoman. But where? He was well aware of the quite natural interest in new arrivals which animated every hamlet, village, town and even the cities in England, and it was not conceivable that Maria should be placed in Wales or Scotland. To be sure, Maria could be well hidden in London, but the temptations of such a place were too well known even to Sir Thomas for his taste, and to his distaste, he had even heard of young women cast off by their families absolutely going upon the town. Sir Thomas was too jealous of the credit of his family for such to be Maria's fate; the world should see Maria was not taken back into her family, but her actual fate should not reflect badly upon the family either. It was a delicate balance indeed and one that Sir Thomas worried his head over for many days, while Maria was in temporary lodgings with her aunt.

This puzzle made Sir Thomas realize far more than anything else could have done, just how much he had relied upon his sister Norris to arrange everything. On most occasions he was wont to blame Mrs Norris for everything, while at other times he was driven to wonder which out of Maria and her aunt was most to blame for this catastrophe which had befallen his family. But now he had to concede that she had a capacity for organization and information which far exceeded his own. There was no help to be sought from his wife; Lady Bertram had been quite over-thrown by the rapidity of events which deprived her of both daughters, her help-meet Fanny, and nearly took the life of her eldest son as well. Sir Thomas explained to her, Edmund explained to her, Fanny and Susan explained to her, but she could not or would not understand why her sister Norris was no longer living at Mansfield, nor why her sister Norris was to live with Maria, nor why she herself was not to see either of them. She had paid little attention to her children while they were growing up, but was now discovering how she could not do without them after all.

Although the marriage of Edmund to Fanny had restored one daughter to Lady Bertram, she could not at first be consoled for the loss of the steadfast, uncomplaining companion who had spent so many hours by her side for so many years. Susan did her best to take Fanny's place, but she had not the same temperament, and length of familiarity to assist her. To be sure, Edmund and Fanny were only a short distance away, but Fanny could no longer be there every evening to help her Ladyship with her work. The little boy and girl were of course fine children, poor little things, but Lady Bertram could not manage them at all, and was inclined to give them too many sweet things in an attempt to pacify them, which did not agree with them, and she could not get little Eddie to leave off teasing poor Pug. So, the dear little children did not often come to see their Grandmama, unless it was with their father who managed them very well, or unless Sir Thomas was there, when they were too frightened to say a word or move. But, Edmund was so busy with his parishes, that he was not often at liberty to attend his mother and bring his children to see her; and Fanny had not been able to leave her house since the arrival of little Frances, as her health had been knocked back, and she had become very much indisposed. Lady Bertram could not at all cope with such a bewildering whirl of change about her previously cosseted life; nothing in her hitherto placid and indulged existence had ever prepared her for so many losses of all those dear to her.

As a result, her plaintive tones could be heard of an evening as she sat at her fringing, assisted by the capable Susan who endeavored always to distract her aunt with Pug's puppies or with some intricacy of their work. However placid Lady Bertram was, and however flaccid her mind, when she did fix upon something, it was with a soft tenacity, and it was hard indeed to divert her.

One such exchange will stand in place of many. Lady Bertram had quite worn herself out with fretting over Maria and Julia and Tom and wondering how Fanny did, and when Edmund would next visit, and hoping he would not bring his children for she was sure they were quite out of comfits; and she had finally fallen asleep upon her sopha. Susan had moved away to another sopha closer to the working candles so she could concentrate on the fringing, which had reached a delicate stage, when Lady Bertram awoke suddenly, and found herself apparently alone in a darkening room.

'Fanny? Susan? Where is everybody?'

'I am here, Aunt.'

'Oh! What do you do over there? Why have I no candles?'

Susan stood and gestured to the footman to move the candles closer to her aunt.

'Let me see the fringing,' asked her ladyship next, and Susan handed it to her. She turned it over and over, examining it carefully.

'I believe it is unravelling at this edge, Susan, would you look at it for me?'

There was then a short silence as Susan took the piece of fringing from her aunt again and worked the loose end back in. Lady Bertram, with no occupation for her hands or her thoughts, reverted to her former concerns about her missing children;

'Susan, I am assured that Sir Thomas has told me but I do not recall, when does Maria come?'

'Oh! do look Aunt; Pug has just pushed that puppy quite out of the basket!'

'So she has. I hope it will not get cold. Put it back with the others, Susan.'

'There! The puppy is back in the basket with Pug. Now, I have sewn that end back in, what colour shall we join on next, aunt?'

'I am sure it does not signify as Maria is not come home yet. This fringe was to be for her, but I wonder if we should give it up if she is not to come.'

'It is so pretty, aunt. Let us continue for now, and add on another colour.'

'If you wish. I promised Maria one of Pug's puppies, but she if she does not come soon, they will be quite grown.'

'Indeed they will. Do look how they already practice their walking about.'

This fretting over a daughter who could not be mentioned in company meant that Sir Thomas had decided to direct the servants to deny Lady Bertram to visitors on the grounds of indisposition, while assuring them that it was nothing serious, and her ladyship was under the care of her physician. Although Lady Bertram had not been in the habit of receiving many visitors, the loss of the few that had come formerly, as well as the loss of all her children meant that Susan became almost as important to her aunt than Fanny had been, although she still hankered after Fanny.

This social segregation affected Susan more than it did Lady Bertram; although she knew she was very lucky to be living in the luxury of Mansfield Park, and did not in any way wish to return to the cramped house in Portsmouth, Susan did at first find the loss of even limited company hard to bear. The days spent on the sofa with her aunt, the endless fringing and the concern over Pug and her latest puppies, had soon lost their initial novelty, and Susan found herself wondering whether she was fixed at Mansfield Park on Lady Bertram's sopha for the rest of her life, or if she might one day leave Mansfield Park, although she had no notion of how that might come about. What if Lady Bertram were to die? On such a melancholy and shocking extremity, what would happen to her? There was more than enough time for such reflection, in the long hours when Lady Bertram dozed upon her sopha, and the weather was too inclement to be out of doors. Susan could not know that her solitude was about to be relieved somewhat when their society was enlarged by a most welcome addition, and one who was given unlimited access to the house. This additional person was necessary because of Fanny's poor health, and Edmund taking on additional parishes. He was finding there was too much work for a parson with an ailing wife and two very young children; and he appealed to a university friend to come and assist, by taking on some of his parishes, including Thornton Lacey.

Harold Ballantyne and Edmund had been at Cambridge together, and had formed a strong bond. Harold was less serious than Edmund, but equally dedicated to his chosen profession; there was a living on his father's estate promised to him, once the present incumbent retired, or moved on to a more lucrative post. Harold was therefore at a loose end, and happy to come and serve as curate to his good friend,

Bertram. His arrival at Mansfield Park provided a welcome diversion for Susan, for here was somebody new to her, and who was, moreover very easy to talk to. As Edmund's friend, and until the house at Thornton Lacey was made ready for him, he was bidden to consider himself as quite a member of the family, and they were all in frequent company together. Once his house was ready, Mr Ballantyne remained one of the very few people not forbidden the house, and Susan came to rely on him calling at least once a day in the course of his duties, to relieve the monotony of her days.

Lady Bertram was always pleased to see Mr Ballantyne, and Sir Thomas approved of this young man, and saw no danger in him spending time with the family; as he would not betray any of their confidences. Almost every day, once Lady Bertram was dozing on the sofa, and Susan felt released for a ramble about the grounds, did she meet with Mr Ballantyne, either about his Parish business, or at leisure to dismount his horse and accompany her. She felt all the luck of this chance that should bring him so often into her path, as they conversed very easily and found many topics of conversation and opinions they held in common. Susan had to admit that she found his company most agreeable, and took care to tell him where her favourite haunts and walks were, in the hopes of accidentally encountering him there again.

Over the months that followed, more than once, Susan was aware that the course of his conversation was tending into some odd unconnected questions about her pleasure at living in such a beautiful place as Mansfield Park, her love of solitary walks, her opinion of the Bertram family's pursuits, and whether she thought she was fixed there for life, or whether she would consider living somewhere else one day.

'You cannot have too strong an attachment to Mansfield Park, Miss Price,' said he one day. 'You have not always been living here.'

Susan was surprised, but replied that her attachment to Mansfield Park was based on a strong gratitude towards her Aunt and Uncle for opening up their home to her, but that she knew she also had a home at Portsmouth with her mother and father.

'Indeed,' he replied, looking thoughtful. 'And can you see yourself living somewhere other than here or Portsmouth one day?'

Susan wondered towards what this was intended, and made a slight reply;

'It would be pleasant to see other parts of the country, I allow; but I doubt Lady Bertram would part with me any time soon.'

'That is as I thought,' he said under his breath, and swung himself back into his saddle, touching his hat and wishing her a good morning.

As he rode away, Susan was left with a strong impression that she had disappointed him, but thinking back through their conversation, she could not think what she might have said to have had that effect. Still, it had been very pleasant to have a companion on her walk, and as she hastened back to the house in answer to a summons by a maid to attend upon her aunt, she hoped they would meet again soon.

CHAPTER TWO

Maria and Mrs Norris were in temporary accommodation for the time being; Fanny and Edmund were settled at Mansfield Parsonage, with Mr Ballantyne in solitary residence at Thornton Lacey, Julia and Mr Yates were occasional visitors, and Tom was away again visiting friends, Sir Thomas joined the ladies straight after dinner, as there was no other man for him to talk to in the dining room.

'Mr Ballantyne does not join us this evening?' he asked, looking about the room, and Susan gave the negative.

'It is a pity that Lady Bertram is too much over-set for visitors at the present, but I do not count Mr Ballantyne as a visitor,' Sir Thomas said gravely to Susan in an under-tone as Lady Bertram dozed on the sopha between them. 'He is more like one of the family, and I know Lady Bertram is always glad to see him.'

'Indeed, I believe it would be injurious to my aunt's health should we receive visitors from outside our family circle,' Susan replied. 'She is much given to speculating on where Maria is and how she is to live if she does not come here.'

'I am hopeful that Mr Ballantyne's presence might distract Lady Bertram from her concerns over Mrs Rushworth,' said Sir Thomas. 'I have given him an open invitation to attend any family dinner when he is free to do so, and hope that his presence will provide a suitable diversion from your aunt's concerns.'

This fretting on his wife's part over the loss of all their children, and the lack of society, had finally forced Sir Thomas to realize that he could not put off his decision about Maria's permanent residence any longer, and also that he had no idea where she could be placed. He came to the conclusion that his need for a permanent solution over-ruled his reluctance to treat with his sister Norris, and so without sending ahead to warn of his coming, he arrived, after dark, at the house he had initially engaged in a small near-by town to house his daughter and her aunt.

Mrs Norris was delighted to receive her brother and set about immediately to make him welcome and to fuss around him, offering him the best chair in the small sitting room she always sat in of an evening because there was no need for the large drawing room to be heated and cleaned just for her, and Maria always went up to her own sitting-room after meals, before deciding another would be more comfortable after his journey and then a further delay was occasioned by her leaving the room to fetch herself the refreshments that Sir Thomas had already declined as she did not like to disturb the servants so hard-working as they were and entitled to time off and she hoped she was not so much above herself as to have forgotten how to bring a drink and some little cakes which she had been showing Cook how to make earlier and she was so grateful because they used so little butter and were most economical while being very wholesome and she was always looking to save Sir Thomas money in whatever way she could. And she was gone to the kitchen, before Sir Thomas could prevent her.

He sat in silence, waiting for what felt like an inordinate length of time. Then, at the precise moment Sir Thomas decided he could not wait any longer for Mrs Norris to return, and determined to leave the room to seek her out, she returned with a plate of cakes;

'Oh! Sir Thomas, what an age a kettle takes to boil, and cook had banked the kitchen fires up, and I had to get them going again. But no matter, I will sit by the fire and bring the hot water just as soon as it boils, for I know how much store you set by fresh tea, with the water boiled just so, and Harrington understands that so well at dear Mansfield Park, and I am just about getting the servants to understand the importance of the correct temperature for tea here. Now you help yourself to one of the little cakes, or no, stay! Let me help you, for they are a little crumbly, and I see you have on your light colour clothes, and I would not wish any more work on poor Mrs Craig at Mansfield Park with having to get any stains out. I expect the kettle will have boiled by now, here are the tea things, all arranged by dear Mrs Rushworth, and so well to hand, I will not keep you a moment longer.'

Before Sir Thomas could protest, she was gone again, returning in a few moments with her hand wrapped up in a cloth and a kettle of hot water, and set about making the tea with a constant flow of observations about her scalded hand, which she did not at all regard in comparison to his journey there to see them both, which must have been most disagreeable to him, having to leave his fireside on such a cold night as this, and she would build the fire up directly for him, she did not need such a blaze herself, as she always dressed warmly, and had quite a horror of a large blaze as it used up so much coal, and what a blessing coal was to be sure; in her little country parsonage she had only burned wood, but here in a town, coal was so readily available, although she had made sure the coal-man gave her his very best price, as she was always careful of Sir Thomas's money, so generous as he had been with their allowance, and she was determined not to take advantage or spend a penny more than was absolutely necessary.

All through this, Mrs Norris was looking down at the tea-things, busily occupied about making the tea, and finally she looked up to hand Sir Thomas his cup, opening her mouth to begin another self-effacing monologue, but was instead struck dumb by Sir Thomas's grim silence. Instead, she pulled forward the chair she had previously refused to allow him to sit in as it was the least comfortable in the house and sat down on it herself; only to jump up again immediately and head for the door.

'Mrs Norris!' Sir Thomas thundered. 'Pray be seated!'

'But you will want to see Maria,' Mrs Norris said, as she exited the room. 'It is very selfish of me to assume you have come to bring me news of my dearest sisters or my beloved nieces and nephews, of course you will want to see dear Mrs Rushworth. I will dart upstairs at once and fetch her, it will not take a moment and I do not regard the three flights of very steep and narrow stairs at all an inconvenience, even without a candle on the landings, for I will not allow candles to be left untended when there is so much wood in this house …'

Sir Thomas was forced to put down his tea cup and vacate his comfortable chair to intercept Mrs Norris before she reached the stairs, and to lead her firmly back into the room.

'I do not wish to see Mrs Rushworth at present,' he said, handing Mrs Norris into a chair opposite his own and settling himself down with great solemnity and purpose.

This was all most unexpected and disconcerting to Mrs Norris and temporarily silenced her.

Sir Thomas regarded her sternly as though to discourage further outbreaks. He looked around the shabby small room with its meagre fire and felt a sense of shame that he had not, so far, provided better for his daughter and her aunt. The fireplace was quite adequate for a larger and more luxurious blaze, and there was ample provision of material with which to keep it well fed, but as Mrs Norris had informed him, she would not hear of it being kept up in this way, and so only a very small fire was set each day, and tended to sparingly by Mrs Norris herself. Servants, as Mrs Norris firmly believed, were not to be trusted with making up fires, and she was sure Sir Thomas would agree, although he kept up very good fires at Mansfield Park, for the servants were to be trusted there to be sure. The luxury of the large well-tended fires at Mansfield Park, Mrs Norris had frequently made use of in order to make her own supply of wood last even longer, but such considerations could not be in force in her current situation as Sir Thomas was paying for everything.

'Are you comfortable here, madam?' he asked, well aware that he had just given Mrs Norris another opportunity to express her gratitude for his generosity, which she did at length, and which did soothe his injured pride a little at least. When she eventually ran out of benefits to enumerate, Sir Thomas asked how they passed their days and whether any body had recognized either of them.

'No indeed,' Mrs Norris continued eagerly. 'For we do not go out except in deepest mourning and with the two footmen, which does discourage impertinent curiosity and I have not permitted any intercourse at all with anybody we have seen. The servants are all very loyal to you, my dear Sir Thomas, and would not breathe a word, not that they know there is any word to be spread, for I have told them that Maria is recovering from a severe illness and bereavement, and they are not to speak to her, except for her own maid, of course.'

Sir Thomas rather thought such a sight as two heavily veiled women guarded by two large footmen, would be more likely to excite impertinent curiosity, than the opposite, and it determined him even more to settle his daughter and her aunt in a country location where exercise might be taken without such dramatic precautions. As to Mrs Norris's attempt at disguising Maria's disgrace under the title of invalid or widow, it was absurd, for even servants could read newspapers or listen to gossip, but he decided to pass over this and proceed with his main purpose in coming thither.

'I do not consider this lodging house to be suitable for my daughter and Lady Bertram's sister,' he said. 'But I find myself at a loss to determine where would be best to place you in the comfort that you both require, and yet in a location which would not give rise to speculation or interference by members of the local society.'

'As for me,' Mrs Norris said, casting her eyes down as she spoke, 'Society is not something I care for as you know, but we do need to be near a town or village for house-keeping needs. I do not expect you to concern yourself with such matters, but we must remain practical.'

'I agree,' said Sir Thomas. 'You must be placed in a convenient location, without any privations, however, it must be somewhere neither of you will be recognized, or sought out by previous acquaintance.'

There was a short pause, before Sir Thomas continued;

'I do not wish to completely crush Mrs Rushworth's spirits, but she must not be in a position where society seeks her out, or where it is difficult for either of you to avoid the attentions of well-meaning neighbours. I also wish her to have religious instruction, so that she comes to a proper understanding of her past conduct.'

'You are very wise, Sir Thomas,' Mrs Norris agreed eagerly, 'and always so careful of the esteem of your family, and considerate of their well-being and comfort. I recall that dower house you told me of on the edge of Lord M_'s estate, which you said would be just the thing. There is no dowager in residence at present and the great house stands empty too, and it is not a good thing for a house to stand empty over-long, you said you would be doing Lord M_ a great favour were you to take the house! He would have income from the rent, and the dower house would be again occupied and less prey to vagabonds and thieves. As you know, it is large enough to be a gentlewoman's house, close enough to the town for servants to be easily retained and supplies to be fetched with little difficulty. The family is not much at home, as you know, for they prefer their house in London, and the dowager has a house in Bath too, so there is little chance of visits and the rest of the country there is very quiet indeed, hardly a gentleman's residence in evidence at all, and there is a private chapel in the grounds of the great house in very easy access to the dower house and not frequented by anybody while the family is away. The Chaplin attached to the family must have little enough to do as they are never home and he does not go with them to London, or to Bath; he can give Maria the instruction she needs and I am sure it will be beneficial to the servants as well to have regular Church services and Sunday instruction. You know I always insist upon religious instruction being made available to the lower orders for their own benefit as much as anything. Indeed! it is just the most perfect place, I would not expect you to choose anywhere less than ideal, I know your generous spirit too well.'

While Mrs Norris enumerated the merits of this house he was certain that he had never heard of before, Sir Thomas was aware of a dual emotion; relief that Mrs Norris was once more taking charge of arrangements, and wonder about how she had found out it was available and how she knew so much about its situation and Lord M_'s family. It remained very wonderful to Sir Thomas that Mrs Norris should ever have it in her power to tell him everybody's news, especially as she was so out of the way here, and was not supposed to be in direct contact with anybody. However, it did not do to look a gift horse in the mouth, and so Sir Thomas decided that he had indeed found the ideal placement for Maria and her aunt.

'Very well, Mrs Norris,' he said, holding up his hand to prevent any more effusions. 'I will instruct my agent to treat with Lord M_s agent and agree a price for the house. Look to your own arrangements and I will move you both there as soon as it is possible. I hope that the house will not need much in the way of improvements first.'

'Oh no, Sir Thomas,' said his sister-in-law complacently. 'For it was completely done over for Lord M_'s mother after his father died last year, and he succeeded to the title and lands. But she did not choose to live there and is gone to Bath where there is more society, and she may take the waters with her friends; I believe she does not enjoy the best of health.'

Sir Thomas left shortly after that, as soon as the effusions he had not quite been able to prevent had been expressed in full, and Mrs Norris hurried upstairs to Maria's sitting room to acquaint her with the good news that they were to be gone from this poky house and into one more befitting the daughter and sister of Sir Thomas Bertram.

CHAPTER THREE

Maria was rather more indifferent than Mrs Norris could have wished, and so she was soon forced to take all the praise on to herself for arranging such elegant accommodations for them both, in such a country that could not help but lift both their spirits. Maria was sunk in such a gloom that she was largely indifferent to her surroundings and cared not whether they were in the town or the country, in a poky boarding house or a luxurious dower house. She was crushed indeed, but only by a sense of extreme injustice, she did not consider that she had done anything so very bad, nothing that a hundred other women had not done. At any rate, she had not been alone in her escapade, and yet she was the only one to be so punished.

Although Sir Thomas was determined to be assiduous in procuring the comforts of his elder daughter, he did not think it right to pass on family news to her. As far as he was concerned, she was no longer part of the family and not entitled to know their nearest concerns. He should have remembered, however, that his attempts at totally isolating Maria from her family were pointless as Mrs Norris had her own ways of finding out the news and telling Maria what she thought Maria needed to know. Thus, Maria knew that Julia was making the best of her hasty marriage to The Honourable Mr Yates; but in this piece of news was another source of vexation for Maria to be sure. What had Maria done that Julia had not? Julia had eloped too, but she was not exiled and in disgrace. No! Julia was married and respectable, in society and constantly at Mansfield Park, accepted by the family which had rejected Maria.

Mrs Norris had made certain that Maria also knew that the encroaching Price family had installed another daughter at Mansfield Park; Mrs Norris had been especially angry about this. Although she had been stupefied with the shock of Maria's disgrace and unable to protest Susan's arrival, she had felt all the evil of it, and mentioned it frequently as a sore grievance. Before leaving Mansfield Park forever, and despite not being in spirits to notice Susan in more than a few repulsive looks, Mrs Norris designated her a spy, an intruder, an indigent niece, and everything most odious. Another Price daughter dangerously installed at Mansfield Park! And with Tom unmarried! As if Fanny had not been bad enough, with her sly and creep-mouse ways, marrying dear Edmund in the end, when he could have done so much better with one of the young ladies of the neighbourhood, or dear Miss Crawford. And then for Sister Price to pass the cost of another daughter over to dear Sir Thomas, who was more generous than Sister Price and her over-large family deserved; paying as he did for all those boys to be schooled, and finding them apprenticeships, or buying them into the Navy! Mrs Norris was not at all done with the subject of Susan's moving into Fanny's place at Mansfield Park, and did not hesitate to let Maria know of her displeasure, although it is doubtful whether Maria attended to her, or even cared. *She* was not to return to Mansfield Park, so it mattered not at all to her if all her Price cousins were there.

Despite her aunt's vigilance, Maria did hear from time to time of Mr Crawford; her own maid who disliked Mrs Norris's parsimony and interference, smuggled her the society papers whenever Mrs Norris sallied forth alone about her marketing, or was in the offices harrying the servants. Maria knew from the society papers that her former husband was in London, and considered very eligible; the fêted darling of The Season, with many ambitious Mamas hoping to settle their daughter with him on his Sotherton estate. It was said that Miss Crawford was being paid court to by Sir Cedric L_ and the Earl of _, but however closely she read the paper however, she could not discover that Henry Crawford had married, nor that he favoured any of the young women offered up to marriage so eagerly each season; and with that she had to be content for now.

Further reading revealed that Sir Cedric L_ was Sir Cedric Cholmondley, a young man in possession of a fortune he needed a wife to spend, for he had not a single idea of how to do so in his own head, while the Earl of _ was almost old enough to be Mary Crawford's grandfather, and moreover had already had two wives, both now dead. Although both were avowedly eligible, neither seemed to Maria to be worthy of the Mary Crawford she remembered, and she wondered why Mary was not more sought after. It may be something to do with the scandal around her brother, Maria thought, although she did not know whether any body in London cared for the matter any longer. All Maria herself cared about was that Mr Crawford had not married; for while she did not like to think of his being sought after, she also did not like to think of him at his ease in London while she was to be stuck out in the countryside for the rest of her life with only her aunt for company.

Had Maria but known it, Mr Crawford was not entirely at his ease in London, and the years since their final separation had not passed entirely happily for him either. He was living with his sisters at Mrs Grant's house, and although he was still quite as well known, he was considerably less captivating. Some taint of the scandal which had ruptured Maria's marriage and destroyed her life had attached itself to him after all, and the more ambitious Mamas were rather keeping their daughters well away rather than thrusting them at him, Norfolk estates or no. While there were other eligible bachelors, Mr Crawford would not be their first choice; it was not as though he were anything especial, after all; he was not handsome nor tall, and neither had he particularly helpful connections in society, unless they happened to have a younger son in want of patronage in the Navy, and even then, it was Mr Crawford's uncle rather than Mr Crawford himself who had the patronage to offer.

To Crawford's chagrin, and as Maria had discovered from the society papers, Mr Rushworth was considered as the more eligible match by the Mamas and by the young women themselves. He was younger than Mr Crawford, and there was a certain amount of sympathy for him on account of the scandalous behaviour of his first wife. His personal fortune and estates at Sotherton further raised him in their estimation; as did the fact that his mother had already moved out of Sotherton Court, and would not be there to interfere in any marriage he might make. Society considered that Mr Rushworth himself was not at all to blame for his first wife running away; and he was still near the top of the list for ambitious mamas. The young hopefuls themselves might find him dull, if not positively stupid; but he was a man in command of a large fortune, with a grand house, and an accommodating Mama. Yes, Mr Rushworth was very eligible indeed.

And such a jewel would not remain without a suitable setting for very long; a couple of years after the distressing rupture of his first marriage, and the indignity of having to apply for a divorce, Mr Rushworth did marry again, and Maria was able to read about every detail of the costly nuptials in the society papers. He had taken his time to select his second bride, having learned a painful lesson from his first; and although the second Mrs Rushworth was not as handsome or accomplished as the first, *this* Mrs Rushworth was content to live with him at Sotherton and did not cast her eyes about her for a better husband. Moreover, her mama and his became inseparable friends, although the unkind whispered that this was because her mama had only a very small annuity, and no home to speak of, but whatever the truth of the matter, the two proud mamas were living together to great mutual satisfaction in Sotherton's Dower House, with frequent trips at Mrs Rushworth's expense to stay at Bath, and finally Mr Rushworth could relax and revel in domesticity.

As for Mr Crawford himself, the years passed, and he was finding that the girls who had come out and were being paraded for marriage each season seemed very young, very frivolous, and not as handsome as the first Mrs Rushworth, nor as sweet natured as Mrs Edmund Bertram; he did not feel he could confide in any of them should he marry one of them. Had Maria but known it, Mr Crawford's spirits were low too, for although he was not crushed and exiled, he was beginning to experience a sensation he had not experienced before; ennui, accompanied by a sense that life was passing him by, and that he was not quite so happy with his bachelorhood after all. He had played high and lost all his stakes, and he was finding life rather stale as the years passed, despite his sister's lively company and loving support.

'Well, Henry,' Mary said one morning as they sat at breakfast, and she looked over the cards which had been left for them. 'Despite my sister's absence, we are much in demand still. The Season is a little slow this year, but there is still entertainment enough for now. Where are we to go when it ends? Do you mean to visit the Admiral, or will you go to your estate in Norfolk earlier than September this year?'

When he did not reply, Mary went on, 'If you do not wish me to accompany you, it matters not to me, for my sister has said I may stay with her, even though it is very unfashionable to stay in London after June. Or I may visit Lady Stornoway, or make a stay with Mrs Fraser, for as long as I wish, as they are both to go to their country houses, and thus I will avoid being unfashionable by leaving London. But they have not extended the invitation to you, I regret. A single man is not so easy to accommodate as a single woman of good fortune.'

'I have not yet decided,' Henry finally said. 'In truth, I find none of those options to my taste. Will you not marry so that I may make you long visits in your castle or country home, or wherever you go?'

'Indeed, I will not marry for your convenience,' Mary replied pretending to be stern, 'but only for my own, and I cannot guarantee a castle at all.'

'Nay, but you must marry,' Henry said, roused at last to join in the gentle raillery. 'I would not have you a spinster at last.'

His sister just shook her head at him.

'How can you say so?' cried she. 'When you know as well as I that a single woman of good fortune will always be first in society?'

'As your brother, I advise you to curb your ambition to be first in society, and to marry for my sake. So, who will it be? Sir Cedric, or the Earl of _? Will I be calling you Lady Cholmondley, or Countess?'

'That is a difficult decision to be sure,' Mary replied playfully. 'What would best suit my dearest brother? For although I will not marry merely to provide you with accommodation at the end of the Season, I will consider your preference for a Lady or a Countess.'

'Indeed! Would you? That is most sisterly and shows real delicacy of spirit. However, Cholmondley is a dolt and the Earl of _ a dotard. I am not sure I would wish to condemn my sister to either fate after all.'

Mary shook her head again in mock disapproval, 'I do not follow your reasoning, brother. If both are in love with your most excellent sister, they cannot by definition be either stupid nor senile.'

'Is it love, Mary?' Henry asked. 'Or is it your fortune that attracts them?'

'I do not believe for a moment either of them to be in love with me,' his sister replied. 'Nor does my fortune attract them, although I am sure neither would turn it down. Both are said to be very rich.'

'So, to what do you attribute the fact that I have had these two men call on me for permission to pay you their addresses, then?'

Mary stared at him thoughtfully.

'I suppose I must attribute it to my charms alone. But now I think on it, I am somewhat concerned that you have only been approached for permission to court me by these two very unattractive men out of all the eligible bachelors in London.'

'I could put in a good word for you with Rushworth, if you like,' Henry said idly, picking up the paper again.

'Now that would indeed be doing your brotherly duty, and I thank you for it! But you are too late; Mr Rushworth has found himself a more compliant bride already.'

Henry found nothing of interest in the paper and let it fall. He was silent, thinking of Mansfield Park. 'It is a shame my sister is no longer in Northamptonshire,' he said at length, 'That was a most agreeable country. I should very much enjoy a visit to Mansfield Park again.'

'Or was it the inhabitants which made it so agreeable?' Mary asked slyly. 'For myself I confess to missing Lady Bertram and Mrs Norris, their company was so stimulating and edifying, but I suspect you of missing two younger ladies.'

'Convention would dictate I do not think of missing Mrs Edmund Bertram nor Mrs Rushworth,' Henry said ruefully.

'But Mrs Rushworth is no longer married to her own dolt,' Mary said.

'This is true, but she has not been seen anywhere, and I am supposing that Sir Thomas has secreted her somewhere away from society, and I have no idea where she might be now. I do not believe he would allow her to return to Mansfield Park; that would look too much like forgiveness, and he would not want society to think him accepting of her actions.'

'Indeed, he is very careful of his own credit in the world,' said Mary. 'Wherever Maria has been placed, it would be in a suitable lodging for a gentlewoman, even a fallen gentlewoman.'

There was a silence as both considered likely locations for such an accommodation.

'It cannot be in London, nor in Bath,' mused Mary. 'Nor anywhere she would be likely to be recognized, or have society call upon her. Does not Sir Thomas have family connections in Plymouth?'

'Portsmouth,' corrected Henry. 'If you refer to Mrs Edmund Bertram's family.'

'Ah yes, Fanny's sea-faring family,' said Mary. 'Might Sir Thomas have turned to them for assistance in concealing Maria?'

'Having met the family, I am inclined to think not,' answered Henry. 'They do not live in a style which would satisfy either Sir Thomas nor Maria's sense of what would be the right degree of comfort and luxury.'

'How do they live, then?'

'It is a large family in a small house in the centre of the town,' said Henry. 'There would not be room for Maria and a maid, I suspect, and it is not an orderly house from what I observed, although I could not say so to Mrs Bertram, when she was Miss Price, and a daughter of the house.'

'Portsmouth does not sound a likely place, then,' said Mary, 'And it is, I would guess, a lively place with many comings and goings, where she might be noticed, anyway.'

'Yes, it is certainly a very lively town, with ships in and out, and all manner of comings and goings. I agree, it is unlikely that Maria could successfully be concealed there.'

'We must look elsewhere for her then,' said Mary. 'But if we were to attempt to discover her, what then?'

Henry looked at his sister thoughtfully. He had not taken his suppositions thus far, and Mary's questions raised all manner of possibilities in his mind.

'If we did find her out, and she was still in love with you, should you marry her?' Mary asked, all seriousness.

'If I did …' Henry said, thinking it through as he spoke aloud, 'We could throw ourselves on the mercy of the Bertram family, and make long stays at Mansfield Park. If Maria were respectably married, they could not refuse to have her back in the family.'

'There is an assumption in that thought which I will not challenge,' said Mary playfully, 'but if you were able to return to Mansfield Park with your bride …'

Brother and sister looked long at each other before Mary continued, thinking aloud as she followed her brother's train of thought, 'Fanny?'

'Mrs Edmund Bertram,' Henry corrected her, mock severely, 'She must have grown tired of that milksop Bertram by now.'

'Even if she were not, you would now be her brother, and would be in daily close contact. A little light flirtation would do neither of you any harm.'

'But first, we have to find Mrs Rushworth,' Henry finished, and he stood and bowed to his sister, 'I have no doubt at all that you will find her, and right speedily.'

'Phoo, phoo,' returned she, 'I have no more idea of where to look than do you. But what are you about this morning?'

'I hardly know,' said Henry.

'In that case I advise you to take a walk and then call in at White's. My uncle is not in town, but there may be some of his acquaintance present, and there is nothing like an Admiral for gossip; they may have heard something of where Maria is placed.'

'Very well, and if there is nothing to be learned at White's, I shall go on to Button's; there may be some talk there that is of use.'

'I think it far more likely that you shall read over the newspapers again, drink coffee and talk scandal with your idle friends,' replied Maria, waving him away.

'I never talk scandal,' said Henry, 'but I shall keep my ears open for those that do.'

As Henry left the house, he thought more about his sister's scheme; should he marry Maria after all, if they were to discover her? Their last attempt to live together had not been a success; they had quarreled, and Maria had been angry with him for not offering to marry her. At that time, he had still had hopes of Fanny, but that was all over now, she was married, and out of his reach, unless he were to reconnect with the Bertram family by marrying Maria. Whichever way he looked; all roads led to Maria, she was his way forward, if he could but discover her.

And then, why not marry her this time? She was beautiful and accomplished, and would make a fine ornament in the society at Everingham; there would always be those who would remember the scandal of their elopement and shun them. But with good dinners, and large parties, there would always be enough others glad of the acquaintance of Mr and Mrs Crawford. In some circles they would never be admitted, but they would regain enough of their footing in society to be pleasing to both of them, and, Henry considered, society was undoubtedly more liberal on these points than formerly. He did not know whether his uncle would approve, but Henry was not completely reliant on his uncle's good opinion, and did not need his permission. The Admiral had always appreciated beauty, and he would welcome Maria to the family for that reason alone, even though he disapproved of marriage in general.

'And,' said he to himself, 'It seems that I must marry; the world must be peopled!'

After Henry left, Mary sat by herself at the breakfast table, her coffee and toast cooling unregarded on the table before her, and gave herself up to some serious thought. Although her natural tendency was to be frivolous, especially with serious subjects, she was also clever and worldly, and the more she thought on the possible outcomes of finding Maria Rushworth nee Bertram, the more she realized quite what it would mean to her own position in society.

Although she had made light of it to Henry, Mary was not at all happy with the thought that her hand had only been sought by two of the least attractive amongst the many eligible men in London. She could no longer hide from herself that she was approaching the years of danger, and was concerned that no more attractive man than Edmund Bertram had yet to appear to solicit her to change her name. Mary was certain that she was as handsome now as she had been when the Admiral's late wife had brought her out in to society over ten years before, and she had never suffered with any ill-health to dim her bloom.

However, she was beginning to comprehend that she too had reached a crossroads, and that a decision would soon have to be taken on which way her future would lie. Although not thinking highly either of men, or matrimony, marriage still had to remain her object; it was the only possible future for a well-educated woman, even if she did have her own fortune. Mary knew that marriage would not guarantee her happiness, and also that she did not need to be preserved from want by marrying, and so she pondered each possibility in turn.

If she were to marry, she could choose between the two offers she had currently in hand, or she could reject them both and hope to find somebody more to her taste. However, this way was fraught with difficulty; and Mary knew she would not wish to marry a man in need of an heir, for nothing would suit her less than being a mother to a large family, and losing all the freedoms she had enjoyed in her life so far. Added to which, from what she had observed amongst her own suitors, as well as amongst her brother's friends, the eligible bachelors were considerably less intelligent than she, and she would have to subdue her own nature in order to suit her husband's lesser wit.

Of the two men currently soliciting her hand in marriage, the Earl already had his heir, a wastrel son who nonetheless would inherit, and so he may not insist upon a family, added to which he was much older than her and might be expected to die soon, leaving her a rich widow. However, there were an incalculable number of years before his convenient demise to be got through, and Mary was not at all certain she could stomach being his wife.

As for Sir Cedric Cholmondley, he was a much younger man, and would definitely be in want of an heir; and many of the same objections applied to him, without the certainty of an earlier demise. The more she thought on it, the less Mary was finding matrimony to her taste at all, and the more inclined was she to dismiss Sir Cedric completely; he had not called on her, nor sent her any presents or letters recently. Mary nodded decisively; Sir Cedric was no longer to be considered as a potential husband.

Next, if she were not to marry, there were other options open; her sister Mrs Grant would be very happy to share her life and her home with Mary, and they would deal very well together. But it would be a life on a smaller stage than Mary had been accustomed to; Mrs Grant was much loved, but only amongst her very small circle, and had a few close friends, many of whom were the relicts of clergymen, and although all were comfortably situated, none could be considered to be in society. Mary knew enough of the world to suppose that invitations from Lady Stornaway and Mrs Fraser, and her other friends, would soon dry up. Unknowingly, Mary had reached the same conclusion about her friends as had Edmund many years before; Mrs Fraser was a cold-hearted, vain woman, who married entirely from convenience and was unhappy in her marriage due to her thus becoming less affluent than many of her acquaintance, and especially her sister, Lady Stornaway. As for that lady, she was a determined supporter of all that was mercenary and ambitious, and would certainly not continue to offer friendship to a confirmed spinster, no matter her personal fortune. Therefore, should Mary choose not to marry, her only society would be provided by her sister's friends. She loved her sister dearly, but a life spent in the company of her sister and her sister's friends would not supply the excitement and variety Mary so craved.

If Henry did not discover Maria, or should Maria decline to marry Henry, then his devoted sister could spend her life at his side, managing his households at Everingham and in London, and entering into such society as the country provided, as well as accompanying him anywhere else he wished to go. But if Maria were discovered and did marry Henry, then there would be no place for Mary at Everingham, except as a spinster sister to be pitied and patronized by the more fortunate married woman. Maria would be mistress of Everingham and the London house; and Mary would not want to live in her shadow, or be thought less important than she.

There was one more possible direction for Mary to take, but even she was not sure if she were modern enough to consider it. 'If I were a Princess, I would escape the censure of society, but even though I have a fortune which would enable me to set up a home, and live very comfortably on my own,' said she to herself, 'it might mean putting myself out of society all together, and if there is one thing I cannot do without, it is society.' And, frankly, she concluded, there would be little advantage to her in living alone when her sister offered a comfortable home for her convenience.

She allowed herself a moment of annoyance that none of her close acquaintance had been thoughtful enough to have an intelligent and attractive brother in want of a wife with ten thousand pounds. But the servants were waiting to clear the room, so Mary rose and made her way to her own sitting room. There she sat for some time in deep thought: like her brother, she was not best pleased with any of the options she had outlined to herself. None of them suited her as well as did her life at present; but she knew that she and Henry were on the brink of a big change in their lives, and she also knew that nothing stays the same forever. A decision must be made, a direction must be chosen; but for Mary, it felt more like a sentence for transportation than a move into an exciting new life.

CHAPTER FOUR

As no objection had been raised by anybody to Sir Thomas's plans to secure the dower house on Lord M's empty country estate, in due course, with suitable secrecy, and with considerable parade, Maria and Mrs Norris were moved into their permanent seclusion. Sir Thomas had been assured that the dower house had been refurbished as befitted a gentlewoman's residence, and it had proved to be so. The house was both comfortable and elegant, with sufficient rooms, bed-chambers, and offices to accommodate a sizeable household, and there was nothing wanting to be done to prevent his daughter and sister taking the house immediately.

It had been agreed between Sir Thomas and Mrs Norris, that their names would be given as Mrs Raworth (a young woman, recently widowed, and in the deepest mourning as well as much afflicted with the after-effects of the Smallpox, especially about her face), and Mrs Morris, her aunt, who had agreed to live with her during her self-inflicted seclusion in the countryside. Mrs Norris did not think that she would remember a complete change of name, but Morris was close enough to her own name for her to manage, and Maria did not care what name she was given, for almost nobody would have the opportunity to use it.

Although not expecting to mix in a wide circle of local society, Mrs Norris soon discovered that there were very few families of suitable standing for her to ingratiate herself with either in the immediate environment about the Champford Hall estate, or in Champford itself. Over the first year of their seclusion, she left cards with the name, 'Mrs Morris' engraved up on them, with the vicar at Champford, but there were no other families of suitable standing that she could discover. She called on the Vicar's wife in due course, whilst about her marketing in the town. Her poor niece, Mrs Raworth, so disfigured by the small pox, and in impenetrable mourning for the loss of a young and much-loved husband, did not accompany her, and it was made clear that she was not in society. Her nerves were quite overturned and only the peace and quiet of the countryside was supportable to her; she could not bear any liveliness or company at all. But her aunt, now, that was quite a different thing; Mrs Morris was very willing to accept any and all invitations issued by her new acquaintance, especially if it meant she did not need to order dinner, for Maria hardly ate a thing.

One of the earliest and most promising of her new acquaintance was Mrs Southworth, the housekeeper at the Great House. She was a most superior servant indeed, and in her hands were all the resources of the Great House, which Mrs Norris subjected to so many courtesies that Mrs Southworth was persuaded to present her with many delicacies and receipts. Mrs Southworth was also able to give Mrs Norris a tour of all the public rooms at the Hall, although she could not be persuaded to show Mrs Norris any of the family rooms, despite all Mrs Norris attempted by way of supposition, question or bare-faced request. Mrs Norris also sought out the gardener to put him right on many aspects of his planting, and was rewarded with a number of curious specimens which he had been quite unable to nurture.

Despite all this activity on Mrs Norris's part, those called upon by their new neighbour, Mrs Morris, were soon happy to allow her to retire to the company of her inconsolable relative, and leave everybody else in the peace and company they had enjoyed prior to her arrival amongst them. Mrs Southworth took steps to avoid her once she realised that her newest neighbour was an accomplished spunger, and Mrs Norris soon took to complaining to Maria that Mrs Southworth was not all together to be trusted, as she had discovered the servants were allowed wine at the second table, and Mrs Norris was certain she had seen housemaids in white gowns. The gardener was less fortunate in being mostly out of doors, and it was far harder for him to avoid Mrs Norris when she took her walks across the park, but even he had a shed he could retreat into if he saw her coming in time.

This loss of even a restricted society meant that Mrs Norris threw herself into managing her new household, even to the point of accompanying the servants on their afternoon off to ensure they behaved as befitted servants of Sir Thomas, and attending the local markets in person to harry the shopkeepers into discovering greater bargains. Maria was not permitted to accompany her, and this meant that Maria's maid was also denied her afternoon out with the other servants;

'Everybody is to go, except for Sarah,' Mrs Norris said to Maria every week. 'Sarah shall stay and attend upon you. It is not right that you should be in the house alone.'

This was clearly unfair to Sarah, who would pout and flounce, but did not dare to protest, and Maria was too indifferent to her maid's plight to attempt to intervene. Sarah was instead permitted an afternoon off on Sundays, when another maid was deputed to attend on Mrs Raworth, should she be required, and Sarah would walk about the grounds or sit in the servants' hall, and complain to all the other servants about Mrs Morris. They had not much sympathy for her, as they too suffered under Mrs Morris's parsimony, suspicion and tyranny.

Mrs Norris herself, as the widow of the vicar of Mansfield Park, also considered herself authorized to busy herself about the few poor of this new Parish, secure in the knowledge that in her grasp was the very generous allowance Sir Thomas had made for his daughter's comfort, and she decided that a very little of that could be used for the relief of the poor. Had the parish poor been numerous or necessitous, Mrs Norris would have remembered that it was the duty of the local landowner to succour them; and that it was not the place of a visitor to interfere with this time-honoured and natural process.

As it was, to her delight, Mrs Norris discovered that she would not have to spend a single penny of her own, and now that her entire living expense was covered by Sir Thomas, she was able to increase her own fortune considerably by saving all of her money.

However, this energy and desire to be useful had caused Mrs Norris to be Maria's downfall once and would prove to be so again, as she gradually became a familiar sight in nearby Champford. The servants had all been hired at great expense and charged with the necessity to keep quiet about their employers, but such silence is difficult to maintain in the face of curiosity, particularly from family members and close childhood friends, and slowly the strange story, with embellishments, began to seep out.

Even in the depths of the English countryside, it is not possible to go completely unnoticed, and despite all of Sir Thomas's precautions, speculation about Maria and her aunt started to spread abroad, and after the manner of such stories, they changed as they spread until they had all the excitement of a horrid novel. A beautiful young woman, heavily veiled at all times, allowed no visitors, attended only by her aunt and servants, clearly wealthy, but never leaving the house and garden. An older man visited in great state in a chaise: possibly a lover? He staid only a few hours, and all the shutters were closed as soon as he entered the house.

Both Sir Thomas and Mrs Norris would have been speechless with indignation and astonishment at the speculation running rampant through the small secluded neighbourhood. And even people in small secluded neighbourhoods have friends, acquaintances and relatives in towns or cities, and they in turn have correspondents and intimates in other towns and cities and thus it was that after a few years, the stories and rumours finally made their way to London, and to the ears of a certain well-to-do idle gentleman, one Mr Burnell, who in turn brought them to his good friend, Crawford.

It may have taken more than four years, and she knew nothing of it, but Maria's supposed life-time of seclusion, with Mrs Norris only for company, looked likely to be coming to a premature end.

Sir Thomas was as unaware as his errant daughter that any further disaster could befall his family from any action of hers. As far as he was concerned, she and her aunt were permanently settled now, well away from any society, and in a place where they would not be discovered by accident or design. Life at Mansfield Park settled back down into its usual quiet, sedate pattern, and Sir Thomas turned his attention to the next loose end to be tied back in; Tom, and his want of a bride. He had the very woman in mind; it just remained to wait for her to return to England, and he was in correspondence with her mother on that very matter, and for Tom to return to Mansfield Park at the same time.

Despite Sir Thomas's caution, Mrs Norris soon discovered the news that Sir Thomas was tentatively arranging a bride for Tom; which meant that he was safe from the designing Susan Price, at least. Mrs Norris contrived to be especially proud of this news and announced it to Maria as though it were a particular triumph of her own, as if she had personally introduced the idea of the fortunate young woman to her brother-in-law. To Mrs Norris's mind this trumped the failure of her brokering the match between Maria and Mr Rushworth, even though she had no idea who the lucky young woman might be!

However, this was just speculation still; it would take something in the nature of a miracle for Tom to marry at all; he was far too indolent to shift for himself in such matters. It was his father who had decided it was time that Tom settled down with a wife, and as Tom was now fully recovered from his brain fever, Sir Thomas quietly and efficiently reviewed his fellow plantation owners and their families and settled upon a suitable young woman. As her family had no title, he was confident they would look with favour upon their daughter becoming the next Lady Bertram, and he had been quietly promoting links between the two families since his visit to Antigua with Tom.

Following the disaster of Maria's marriage, which he could have prevented, had he not been governed by expediency, and motives of selfishness and worldly wisdom; Sir Thomas decided that he would not insist upon Tom marrying Miss Fairhaven, but would invite her and her mother to Mansfield Park, and let nature take its course. He was confident that Tom would be too lazy to seek out a suitable bride for himself even amongst his friends' families, and that Miss Fairhaven's being accepted by the family would find acceptance in his son as well. There was nothing to do now but to wait for the new year, when the young lady and her mother intended to return to England for good, but just as Mrs Norris had her own ways of finding out the news, so did the London society papers.

CHAPTER FIVE

Despite being November, it was a fine morning, and Henry accompanied Mary on her daily walk to the nearby park, despite objecting to her bringing her very spoiled lap-dog with them. This tiny animal was the latest fashion amongst the ladies in Mary's circle, and despite its size had a most unpleasant temperament, and frequently bit anybody within reach, except Mary. She was quite devoted to it, but her brother was much less enamoured.

"Must you bring the dog along?" he asked in distaste, as the tiny animal nestled in his sister's arms.

"Frou-frou needs fresh air as much as you or I," answered Mary.

'Well,' replied her brother, 'it cannot need much, for it is so very small. Could you not just hold it up at an open window every now and then?'

Mary did not answer, and he continued;

'And I am persuaded that it gets more than enough exercise in chasing the servants about. My sister tells me that more than one has threatened to leave on account of it; even servants object to being growled at and bitten, you know.'

Mary just lifted Frou-frou to her face and it licked her rapturously, its tail wagging from side to side in exstasy. Henry sighed;

'Well, if the dog must come, then it must come. At least you do not need to be followed about by that sour-faced maid of yours if I accompany you to the park.'

'Fontaine disapproves of you, which is why she looks so sour at you,' said Mary with some amusement; she had not thought Henry had noticed her maid's dark looks at him.

'Disapproves of me?' echoed Henry. 'Firstly, how dare she have any opinion of me, and secondly, what is there to disapprove of, may I ask?'

'I cannot tell you.' Said Mary setting the tiny dog on the ground as they entered the Park. 'It is beyond my imagination how anybody could disapprove of my brother.'

'Which is just how it should be,' said Henry, and they started to walk up the central path of the park, bowing every now and then to acquaintances, and looking about them with pleasure at the tranquil scene. This tranquility was interrupted by a shout, and both of them turned to see who was making the disturbance. A figure in the distance was coming towards them and shouting, 'Crawford!', and as it drew nearer, they could see it was an acquaintance of Henry's. He was running very fast towards them, calling out to gain their attention, and waving a newspaper in the air above his head.

'Upon my word, Henry,' said Mary, 'Mr Burnell is showing a pretty turn of speed for a man I never saw walk when he could ride, or run when he could take a chaise. His figure is not at all suited to be a runner.'

'I cannot think what can have prompted such a devotion to exercise,' answered Henry. 'But he will be upon us soon, and no doubt all will become clear.'

'I would not presume upon such a hope when it comes to Mr Burnell,' said Mary pertly. 'He is not the most organized in his thoughts and speech.'

There was no time for any more aspersions to be cast on poor Mr Burnell's person as he was nearly upon them, and had slowed down to a walk, panting and mopping his forehead, before addressing Henry directly.

'I say, Crawford, you're connected with the Bertrams of Northamptonshire, are not you?'

'Good day, Mr Burnell,' Mary interjected, holding out her hand. "It is a fine day, is not it? Do you take your exercise in this park every morning? I have begun to frequent it during this fine weather, as it affords many winding paths and excellent vistas, and although I cannot call it picturesque, there is much welcome shade from the trees when the sun grows too hot. I see though that you are endeavouring to improve upon nature by the vigour with which you run.'

'Mary,' said her brother mock severely, 'Mr Burnell does not know whether yours is a serious enquiry, or whether you are joking. He does not know you so well as I. You will forgive my sister, Burnell, she has a lively wit at your expense.'

Frou-frou objected violently to this addition to her family party, and began to growl and worry at the young man's highly polished boots. He attempted to evade the dog's attentions without kicking out at it, suspecting that do so would not be taken in the right spirit by its owner.

'Oh, I say, sorry Miss Crawford, a good day to you, indeed it is a very good day, this your dog? Jolly little fellow. No, not been to this park before, called at your house, and the maid said you were walking here, so I came after you. Lovely day indeed, glad you are enjoying the - the – distances and – paths. Just wanted a word with Crawford, if you would be so good as to excuse us?'

'Well, before I leave you to discuss your weighty matters,' Mary said, taking pity on Mr Burnell, and picking up her little dog. 'What is it that you have heard about the Bertrams of Northamptonshire? For I am also intimately acquainted with that family.'

'Heir to the estate getting married, in the paper,' Mr Burnell said, holding out the society pages to Mary. Mary took it and scanned the columns, wondering how she had managed to miss this momentous piece of news in the paper that morning. Tom getting married! She could scarcely take it in.

'Henry, I shall sit on that bench there and look over the paper,' Mary said, 'When you have finished with Mr Burnell, please to return for me.'

As the two men walked on down the path with Mr Burnell talking non-stop and gesticulating wildly all about him, Mary set Frou-frou down on the ground again, made her way to the bench and sat down. Despite what Mr Burnell had said, there was less of an announcement, and more of a speculation, couched in very allusive language that a marriage was being arranged between a certain plantation owner's heir with an estate in Northamptonshire, and a young Miss newly out, who was (or so it was believed) a sugar heiress of Antigua. Most interesting, Mary thought and cast her thoughts back to her first visits to Mansfield Park; she had been so sure she would prefer Tom over Edmund, for it was only natural that she should prefer the older son and heir, but it had not proved so to her chagrin. Tom had shewn no interest in Mary whatsoever, nor in any other woman that she could discover. He was wholly taken up with his many friends, and with the horse-racing, and the gambling that abounded at horse races. Indeed, he had mostly been absent during the time that Mary and Henry had been staying with her sister and Dr Grant. It was as well that Mary had not fallen in love with Tom, for she had realised he was not the marrying kind. Instead, she had fallen in love with his brother, but most unfortunately Edmund had indeed been the milksop of Henry's condemnation. Not only had he gone into the Church against Mary's express wishes, but he had thrown her over completely when Maria eloped with Henry.

All that étouderie was over now; Henry and Maria were separated, Edmund had married Fanny, and Dr and Mrs Grant's decampment to Westminster, before his timely death, meant there was no longer a reason for Henry and Mary to return to Mansfield Park.

There was a small sore spot on Mary's heart however, whenever she thought of Edmund. He had piqued her interest, challenged her sense of self, disapproved of her attempts to ameliorate the situation their brother and sister had caused, and had then turned away from her into a life she could not countenance for herself. Mary was not accustomed to men rejecting her, and as she stared unseeing at the society pages, she realised she still had some anger towards Edmund for his intransigence. Surely, if Henry were able to carry out his plan and find the missing Maria, it would throw Mary back into Edmund's way again too. Mary found that she would very much like to see how he liked being a country parson, and how his marriage had turned out; surely Fanny would have children by now? The lack of news from Mansfield Park had never seemed to be vexing before, but now Mary found that she was wild to hear how they were all getting on, and what was happening in that remote part of Northamptonshire. And, although the life of a country parson's wife was still not amongst her list of possible futures, Mary wanted to make Edmund smile upon her once more, and remember how to regret the loss of her.

A growl from Frou-frou at her feet preceded a voice from somewhere above her bowed head, and broke into her reverie;

'Upon my word, Miss Crawford, you are away with the fairies!'

Mary looked up to see the Earl of _ bending solicitously over her.

'You are here alone?' he continued, looking about him in concern, as though Henry, or her maid, were concealed behind a tree.

'No indeed, my Lord,' Mary replied, rising to drop him a curtsey, and extending her hand to be bowed over. 'My brother walked out with me today and is just over there, with Mr Burnell. I was taking a rest to look over the paper. Henry will return to escort me home shortly.'

'It would be my honour to escort you home if you do not wish to wait for your brother,' the Earl said. 'My carriage is at the gates.'

Frou-frou objected just as violently to the Earl's presence as it had to Mr Burnell's, but somewhere in the recesses of its tiny mind was the suspicion that the Earl would not scruple to kick out at it, and so it contented itself with barking and snarling from behind its mistress's skirts at him. Mary scooped up the little dog, which carried on growling at the Earl from this elevated and safer position, and weighed up her options. If she were to accede to his request, another marriage proposal would almost certainly be made in the privacy of the carriage, but if she turned down the Earl's request to escort her home, and waited for Henry, the Earl might think her not interested in marriage, and might not renew his addresses when they next met. If she should decide her best choice was to accept him, he was certain to request an early wedding day, and Mary would not then be able to assist Henry with the rather delicious schemes with regard to the Bertrams. All of this passed like lightning through her brain, but before she had to make a final decision, Henry turned, saw the Earl with his sister and hurried back towards them to make his bow.

'Indeed, you are all consideration and condescension,' Mary said. 'But here you see is my brother, and my sisterly duty bids me return home under his protection.'

The Earl leaned just enough in to say quietly, 'I would you had a wifely duty to me instead.'

'Fie, my lord,' Mary returned, just as Henry arrived, a little out of breath and bowed to the Earl, who despite being thwarted in his aim to get Mary on his own in his carriage, was nonetheless looking rather pleased with the results of his little flirtation.

'My apologies, sister, but Mr Burnell kept me longer than I intended. If you will excuse us, my Lord?' They all bowed, and Mary made sure to look back at the Earl over her shoulder as they left the Park; it did not do to burn all one's bridges, after all.

The family at Mansfield Park had no concept that their continuing health and happiness was of any concern of the Crawfords; indeed, it is unlikely they gave the Crawfords much thought at all now that the immediate crisis with Maria was over. Life at Mansfield Park had moved on in their absence, and the years had blended one into another with no more excitements than are usually provided by family life. Susan was now grown up, and had settled into her sister's role as her aunt's main comfort and stay. Sir Thomas's concerns over Maria, and over Tom's lack of interest in marriage, had pushed the realisation of his niece's needing to be brought out to the back of his mind for the present. Sir Thomas decided that now Maria was settled, he had the time to take Tom's future happiness into his own hands, as there was no indication that Tom had thought to do so for himself. And so he had re-opened a correspondence with the recently widowed Mrs Fairhaven of Antigua, with the intent in mind to invite her daughter, Agnes, to visit her homeland, and hope that Tom would remember having met her previously, and events would take a natural course from there. As it turned out, Mrs Fairhaven and her daughter were being encouraged to return to England by her son, as the climate was less suitable for ladies, and, which was probably more to the point, there were no young men suitable for Agnes to consider as a husband. England would provide greater variety of men from which to make a suitable choice – not that her daughter's matrimonial prospects was specified by Mrs Fairhaven as her reason to return to England. As far as she was concerned, it was all about the heat, and as there was a family house in London, it would seem the ideal time to return to England, and make visits to friends and relations there. Sir Thomas replied to her letter and issued her an invitation to come straight to Mansfield Park upon her arrival into England. A reply eagerly accepting was received in due course; Mrs Fairhaven being as keen to settle her daughter's future as Sir Thomas was his son's, and she also could see the future benefits of combining their estates in Antigua through marriage, although the reason given for accepting the invitation was that their house in London would need time to be made ready for their arrival; servants had to be hired, and the rooms aired.

Thus the newspaper's hinting on the subject of Tom Bertram's forthcoming engagement, which had sparked such interest in Mr Burnell and the Crawfords, was mere remote speculation, not fact. Tom was not engaged to anybody; the forthcoming union with the sugar heiress alluded to in the society paper, came simply from the double fact of his inheritance being in the sugar plantation his father owned on Antigua, and the impending arrival in England of the neighbouring plantation owner's widow, and heiress daughter, Mrs and Miss Fairhaven. Society was behaving itself unnaturally well so far that Season, and there was very little scandal to be sniffed out, so the papers were having to make the most of a very little when it came to news.

CHAPTER SIX

Tom had regained his health after his fever, and he was naturally young and strong of body. At first it seemed that, although he had regained his health, he would not regain the thoughtlessness and selfishness of his previous habits, his suffering had indeed done what nothing else could; it had taught him to think: and the self-reproach arising from the deplorable event in Wimpole Street, to which he felt himself accessory by all the dangerous intimacy of his unjustifiable theatre, made an impression on his mind which, at the age of six and twenty, with no want of sense or good companions, was durable in its happy effects. It seemed to everybody that Tom would finally become what he ought to be: useful to his father, steady and quiet, and not living merely for himself. However, like many sea changes made after a severe shock, it did not all-together last; and Tom was soon something like the old Tom again; restless, much given to visiting friends, and avoiding his responsibilities at Mansfield Park, although he did not return to the race tracks, and he was much more careful of his own health. The fact that all of his friends had vanished and left him when he fell ill had also had an effect upon him, making him less trusting, and a little more particular about who he considered to be a friend.

The effect on his brain of his illness was clear when Edmund married, and Tom said he wished Edmund had been his father's heir. He could not have known it, but his sentiments were an echo of those expressed by Mary Crawford in her letter to Fanny many years before when he had fallen ill with a brain fever, and as such, gave Edmund even more of a shock to hear them from his brother's lips.

'Perhaps it would have been better for the whole family if I had not survived the brain fever,' said Tom determined to scourge himself as much as possible, but to this Edmund could not agree.

'No, indeed, you must not think like that. None of us knows what God has planned for us, and we must live each day in His service, and doing His will.'

'You must allow that you would make a far better Sir Edmund than I will ever be Sir Thomas in my father's place,' continued Tom. 'And you would join with my father in his enterprises in Antigua; I know how much he relies on your judgement rather than mine.'

Edmund did not know quite how to respond to this rare moment of introspection on his brother's part; but no reply was required, for Tom went on;

'And Fanny would become Lady Bertram! Nobody deserves it more than she, after all those years with my Aunt Norris.'

To this Edmund could agree, Fanny had indeed suffered under the implacable and crushing rule of his Aunt Norris, but that lady was now gone, and Fanny was happy in her own home, with no overbearing aunt to disapprove of her.

If Tom had not the strong faith of his brother, there was nothing to be done anyway; he had survived the brain fever and the die was cast; Tom was to be Sir Thomas in due course, and his younger brother was settled with Fanny at the Parsonage. Edmund did not know, for Tom had never told anybody, but his time in Antigua with his father had given him a disgust of plantation ownership, and he was avoiding staying at home too often partly because he did not want his father to ask him to go back out to Antigua to assist the agent on the Bertram plantation. Had Tom been the sort of man who debated politics in the coffee houses, he would have known that the winds of change were blowing strong over the transatlantic slave trade, and the trading of slaves by British ships was already at an end, and the use of slaves on plantations was coming to an end. Tom did not know this until he visited his friend Hallett in Devonshire; there the Government's intervention in the slave trade and the effects it would have on their trade and income, was a matter of much debate, as the Halletts had long been slavers.

Tom's friend, Hallett, lived in a small port town, and his father was much engaged with improvements to the docks in order to facilitate the transatlantic liners. He had a younger brother who was expected to make a good marriage, and step into his father's shoes as Vicar of Axmouth in due course. There were numerous cousins at a nearby vicarage, where the Reverend Comyns worked hard to cover up the deficiencies of Axmouth's absentee Vicar, and never complained. If he hoped that one of his daughters might marry their cousin, or their cousin's rich friend, he was likely to be disappointed. Tom had never been one to seek out a bride, although he cannot have been unaware that his father was manoeuvring around him, looking for a woman suitable enough to become the next Lady Bertram. However, being Tom, he ignored this, and carried on with his visits to his friends; although he could no longer be persuaded to bet upon the horses, and his spending remained very nearly within the very generous allowance his father made him.

There was little in the way of temptation for a young man of fortune in Axmouth, even if Tom had still been the careless gambler of his recent past, but Mrs Hallett had been determined to give her son's friend as much entertainment as a small society could provide before he left with her younger son for Bath. The Comyns family was the most come-at-able, although she kept a wary eye on the daughters, not wanting one of them to raise her eyes to her younger son. It was fortunate that her eldest son John's wife was lively and had a wide circle of friends, relations and acquaintances who could always be prevailed upon to take part in an impromptu Ball, or attend a family dinner.

'You do not come with us to Bath?' asked Tom to his good friend John as they sat with his younger brother Richard, and their father after a very good dinner one evening.

'No, my wife does not care for Bath,' replied John. 'She would rather I took her to London. But Bath is a good enough place for Richard to find himself a suitable bride.'

'With no expectation that my father will act for me as he did for you, I must shift the best I can,' answered Richard, idly.

'I have done my duty by my eldest son,' said Mr Hallett. 'And he has done his duty to his family in his turn.'

'It was my pleasure, sir, I assure you,' said John, with a wink at Tom and Richard.

'And now, my youngest son must look to his own fortunes.'

'And have you hopes of finding a future Mrs Richard in Bath?' asked Tom.

'I have hopes of a Miss Shaw,' said Richard. 'I have met her there several times, and she is both sensible and good natured. Her father is a military man, and she brings with her a fortune of so many thousands as are usually called ten.'

'A point of considerable dignity,' said Tom. 'I wish you success.'

'Shall I ask if she has a similarly endowed friend for you?' enquired Richard.

'No, I thank you,' answered Tom, endeavouring to make light of it, 'You younger sons are the privileged ones, you may marry where you chuse, or not marry if you chuse not to.'

'Do not you wish to marry?' asked Mr Hallett. 'You are the heir, and it is your duty to your father, as it was John's to his.'

'I accept that, sir, I thank you, and I know my father wishes me to marry soon. I suspect he has already picked out a suitable bride for me. After Bath, I will have to go home and face up to my responsibilities.'

'So, we are for Bath,' said Richard, raising his glass and saluting his father and brother, 'To give poor Tom here some diversion before the guillotine of Hymen drops upon the back of his neck and severs him from all enjoyment.'

Tom laughed, but his heart was not all together easy. He knew there was no way of avoiding this future, but also that he had little stomach for it either. Despite Richard's attempts to turn the subject, as he could see it was making his friend uncomfortable, his father had no such sensibility, and continued questioning Tom;

'Your younger brother is married, is not he?' asked Mr Hallett.

'Yes, sir, he married my cousin, Fanny,' said Tom.

'And have they children?'

'Yes, sir, a son and a daughter.'

'So if you do not wish to marry, cannot the boy become your father's heir?' asked John.

'Or if you marry but do not have a son, your father will have to look to your brother any way,' added Richard.

Tom made some slight answer and finally managed to turn the subject;

'Shall we join the ladies?'

The four of them left the dining room for the drawing room, where Mrs Hallett was playing a delightful country dance on the piano, and Mrs John was taking turns about the room dancing with an imaginary partner. The arrival of her father, husband, brother and their friend was a delight to her, and she pressed them into dancing at least one set each with her before the evening ended.

CHAPTER SEVEN

'Now, how do you propose we begin our campaign to discover the current whereabouts of Mrs Maria Rushworth, formerly Miss Maria Bertram?' Mary asked the following morning at breakfast.

'I would answer,' said her brother, 'but I suspect you already have some notion of where to start.'

'Indeed I do!' cried Mary. 'But I do not at all relish being so much of an open book to you. Is a sister not to have her secret ways without a brother guessing them?'

'I may have guessed that you have a plan, but I do not in the least know what the plan is,' Henry assured her.

'Julia Yates, nee Bertram, is the first move of my plan,' said Mary, 'Maria's much-loved younger sister. Eloped with and then married that dolt Yates after the failure of her sister's marriage.'

'I do recall Julia, and all of those events,' said Henry, 'but I do not see how this forms into your plan. You were never a friend of Julia's, that I was aware of; and you have never been in company with her since we were all last at Mansfield Park together.'

'No, I was not a particular friend of Julia's, and it is strange indeed that we have not happened to encounter her since we were all last at Mansfield Park,' Mary agreed. 'I am supposing that she is at the Baron's house in London, but our lack of contact over the last few years will not stop me presuming on prior acquaintance and writing to her. If I can get an invitation to visit, or persuade her to come here, she may tell me where Maria is to be found, or she may not. It is worth a try, and will be our first step in reconnecting ourselves with the Bertrams.'

'Remind me never to underestimate you, my dear sister,' said Henry, rising and folding up the newspaper by his plate.

'Certainly I will,' returned his sister. 'And remember that you had your chance with Julia, but she was not enough of a challenge compared with Maria, and you rejected her and broke her heart. Yates must be a very poor alternative to Mr Henry Crawford.'

'As to that, I have no information,' said Henry. 'I have never been in company with the Honourable Mr Yates either since we last met at Mansfield Park. But you are right as always; if I had been content with the conquest of Julia Bertram, I could have had a standing flirtation with Mrs Rushworth, and Mrs Edmund Bertram, whenever we met at Mansfield Park, and our lives would all now be very different. However, it is not in my nature to repine, and what is more important, I will be back by dinner.' He bowed and left the room.

Mary opened her campaign to reconnect with the Bertram family, by carefully composing an artless and affectionate letter to Julia, Mrs Yates:

My very dearest Mrs Yates, or may I call you Julia? There can be no quarrel between us, we were always such friends you and I. It may be old news to you, but I would still like to offer you my most sincere congratulations on your nuptials, and I will give you just a hint that I may soon be joining you in the lists of Hymen. But hush, no more for now. Am I to begin instead by congratulating you on a happy event? I have been scanning the newspapers daily for such wonderful news, but have seen nothing of you. As for my own family, I am certain you will have heard of my sister's happy news? Not the same one that I suspect you may be experiencing by now, but the happy loss of her husband, and I am sure you will agree with me that it was a most happy loss for her. She has been quite revived by her widowhood, and is very content in town, where we live most comfortably together with my brother. Since my brother Grant had the bad taste to leave Northamptonshire for Westminster, our only source of sadness is being starved for news of dear Mansfield Park. I feel sure you must spend a good deal of your time there with your dearest parents and brothers. How fortunate you are to be sure! Mansfield Park remains my ideal of a country house; if I were ever to establish a country seat, Mansfield Park would be my model. And I consider its inhabitants are surely to be classed amongst the most fortunate in all the land.

By the bye, the papers are full of the speculation that Tom is to be married! What good fortune for your family, and to a sugar heiress too! Shall I say how sweet this news is to my ears, for it gives me a glimpse, the merest glimpse into the place closest to my heart. Ah, how I cherish the happy memories of all our romps and escapades, such a joke as we had with 'Lovers' Vows' to be sure! And how could I forget that day we spent at Mr Rushworth's estate? Such a fine house and garden, although the owner was rather less pleasing to the eye: you must agree that Maria had a happy escape there, did not she?

Henry joins me in sending our sincerest wishes to you, he is often with me, and shall I whisper that he is a missing a certain young woman of our mutual acquaintance? We have heard nothing of our dearest Fanny, or Mrs Edmund Bertram as I must now call her. How is she? You must be in constant correspondence with everybody at Mansfield Park; do I pray you, ask her to write to me, she need not stand upon ceremony; we were such friends!

Pray, pray write to me yourself, Julia, my dearest Mrs Yates, or call if you are at your London house. Or do not stand upon ceremony, and pray do visit me here and tell me all the news. I send my very best wishes to your excellent father and mother, and your most industrious Aunt Norris. I shall be in agonies until I hear from you.

Mary Crawford

After waiting just long enough to be slightly insulting, Julia replied with equal sincerity and warmth.

My dearest Miss Crawford, for dearest you will always be to me. I am indeed most happy with my caro sposo Mr Yates, and we do indeed pay long visits to my mother and father at Mansfield Park whenever we can be spared by the Baron and Baroness. Seeing Mr Yates with my father is such a pretty sight; my father quite dotes upon Mr Yates as another son and Mr Yates is so respectful to my father and always asks his opinion upon everything to know what he is to think. There is no such happy event for us as you allude to, but I am delighted to hear that you may be married soon. I hope you will send me a piece of the wedding cake to remember you by.

How I envy you the leisure to write such a long letter. Lord knows we married women have little enough time for writing letters; the housekeeper has been wanting me this half hour, and I am to *accompany the Baroness to The Exchange. I shall be brief and you will forgive me, such friends as we are. I am in town, but much engaged with Mr Yates's family. I cannot recall seeing your name in the arrivals and I am all astonishment that we have not chanced to meet: I expect we move in different circles. My fondest love to Mrs Grant and to yourself. Do call at any time, do not be denied, I will always be at home for you.*

As ever, your friend, Julia Yates

'There,' said Julia to herself as she sealed the letter, and rang for a footman to take it to the post. 'That should put an end to any such attempts to encroach upon me. How does she dare to bring herself to my attention after what her brother has done? Does he not think he has done enough damage to my family already? And, does she think that I can ever countenance her or her brother again, if I wish to retain my rights to visit Mansfield Park? And as for her brother hankering after Fanny; the very thought! She is a married woman now! And married to my own brother! Does Miss Crawford think that I would play pander?'

There was nobody that Julia could speak to about this within her own family, and she never took counsel from her husband about anything. But in this case, she was certain that she had acted correctly, and that she had saved her family from further contamination from the Crawfords.

Julia's letter was duly delivered and presented to Mary. She read it through shaking her head. There was no help to be had there, so Mary tore the letter up and dropped it into the bin. It was time to explore other avenues.

CHAPTER EIGHT:

The next piece of the puzzle of Maria's disappearance and her current location dropped suddenly into the Crawfords' laps, in a most unexpected place. After the failure of Mary's attempt to reconnect with Julia Yates, and Henry not finding anybody with any information to add to that they already had in the clubs or coffee houses, they had put the puzzle to one side, in order to attend Mrs Grant at Weston's, a new warehouse. There was talk of many new and exciting fabrics, and both women knew it was important to be there to view the coming season's colours and styles. Henry was happy to escort them, and advise them, having excellent taste in muslins, which was of great comfort to his sisters, who knew they could rely upon him to guide them in the best direction. The warehouse was busy, and there were so many people before them, that there was not a person at liberty to attend to them, and they were obliged to wait. Mrs Grant met with a friend, and was drawn off by her to advise upon her own choice of fabrics, so Henry and Mary sat down near a counter to await their turn.

They had not been there long, when Henry, happening to look up, saw an acquaintance of his own, and waved to attract his attention. Mr Jones was delighted to see him, as he had gossip to pass on, even though he had no idea that his news would affect them so nearly, or assist them in their schemes to return to Mansfield Park.

'I say, there you are Crawford, I called on you but was denied.'

'Jones, you will remember my sister, Mary?'

'Oh yes, of course, how de do, Miss Crawford?'

'I am just as well as the last time we met, thank you, Mr Jones,' Mary replied, holding out her hand for him to bend awkwardly over.

'Oh, but I say, Crawford, have you heard the latest?'

'No indeed, Jones, do tell me, what is the latest?'

'A real-life Sleeping Beauty to be sure. Were not you at Button's this morning? No, I recall you were not, or you would have heard all the news for yourself.'

'Do you tell us the news, Mr Jones, for we are no nearer being served by these assistants, there is such a shocking crowd, and they are terrible slow at serving,' said Mary, nonetheless keeping a sharp eye on the people before them to be served.

'Well, you must know Parsons is to inherit after all as his cousin has died, and every shop-keeper in London is lining up to be paid; his debts are said to be beyond anything! Parsons has had to flee to the country to avoid them, as he does not yet know how much he is to inherit, and the talk is that his cousin has run through all the money and the estate is up to mortgage. Sutton is gone into the spunging house after his father refused to pay his gaming debts, and Adams is to go into Parliament if he can get a Borough; but I think you already knew that.'

'But what of the Sleeping Beauty?' asked Mary, endeavouring to keep Mr Jones to the point. 'You have told us nothing of her.'

'Sleeping Beauty? asked Henry, 'Yes, what the d–l do you mean by that, Jones?'

'Mr Jones wishes to tell us a children's bed-time story, Henry,' Mary teased.

'A bed-time story, at this time of the morning? I have no notion to what you refer, sister; I never heard of this Sleeping Beauty before.'

'That is because you paid even less mind to our governesses than did I,' answered Mary.

'Certainly, I recall governesses, many governesses, they did not last long under the same roof as my uncle, but I am convinced they never told me bed-time stories.'

'Indeed, they did!' cried his sister. 'And had you paid attention, you would recall the story of a beautiful princess enchanted to sleep for an hundred years, never mind why for now, and who was rescued by a prince. But it was just a child's story, there never was a real Sleeping Beauty.'

'No, no, to be sure, it's true, as I live and breathe,' Mr Jones insisted. 'I had it from my sister, lovely girl, not quite out yet, will be at the next ball, Mother says I must introduce you, will have ten thousand at least, anyway, my sister has a friend and this friend's brother has married a rich woman with a maid, and this maid has this brother you see and he's getting married, and his intended is a chambermaid at an Inn some place in the middle of nowhere, and she's told him about a mystery woman locked away in the countryside nearby with her wicked stepmother, never allowed out, always heavily veiled. You would not think it possible in England, now would you? Sounds more like something the ladies are always reading in those novels of theirs. I know my sister is always on the look-out for the latest horror coming out of London.'

There was quite a lengthy pause when Mr Jones finally ran out of words. Mary recovered first.

'Upon my word, Henry,' she exclaimed playfully. 'Mr Jones has found you a veritable triad of unhappy women, not just one Sleeping Beauty!'

'Three women, Mary?' Mr Crawford queried. 'How do you reckon three women from Jones's absurd tale?'

'To be sure! There is indeed one Sleeping Beauty, although by Mr Jones's account, she is already awake, if heavily veiled, one Rapunzel locked into a tower, and one Cinderella with a wicked step-mother.'

'Oh! I say, that's d_d clever, Miss Crawford!' Mr Jones exclaimed. 'I had forgot all those other stories!'

'And do you intend to be the handsome Prince dashing to their rescue, Mr Jones?' asked Mary.

'No, not I,' Mr Jones declared stoutly. ''Tis said she's horribly disfigured from the pox.'

'Well, maybe tis better she stay where she is, then,' Mary concluded. 'For nobody wants to see a disfigured woman.'

They made their adieus to the garrulous Mr Jones as an assistant was now at liberty to attend to them, and Mary began to look through the new fabric swatches, holding each one out for Henry's opinion, but it soon became clear that Henry was deep in thought, and not really giving the fabrics the attention they merited. Normally, he would have been most attentive, and given his opinions very swiftly, but Mary could not get a 'yes', 'no' or 'maybe' out of him. She cast several impatient glances at him which were not detected, and eventually made a few choices without his assistance, but decided to defer the most important purchases until her brother could attend properly again.

'Henry,' she scolded, 'your mind is not at all fixed on fabric today, so I will defer my purchases. If you will go and find my sister, we will see if she has made her purchases and is ready to go home. I declare we have been here for hours and you will be wanting your dinner.'

Henry bowed and left to seek out Mrs Grant, returning shortly with her full of apologies for having left them to go with her friend, and on viewing the few purchases Mary had made, was full of praise for Mary's taste and selection of fabrics. She had not made her own purchases, having been all this time at the service of her friend, and Henry promised to bring them both back the following day.

'I hope they will still have some of the sarsanet,' said she in the carriage. 'And Mrs Hinchliffe had a length of the most exquisite muslin with Vandyke edging, which I hope they will not run out of before I can return, oh! and lace, there was some silver Belgian lace there, the like of which I have not seen for many a year. This new warehouse has so much better stock than the others, I do declare!'

'I am truly sorry for taking you away from all these delights, sister,' said Henry. 'Shall I order Dawkins to turn the carriage about and take us back?'

'No indeed!' said Mrs Grant, 'I shall be quite content to return tomorrow, and it will give me time to review my wardrobe and see what I need ahead of next season. And I must speak to Mrs Hunter about dinner; you must be hungry, my dears?'

Mary waited until Mrs Grant was gone to speak to the housekeeper about dinner, before turning to her brother and asking;

'Henry, tell me what it is you are thinking of, for you were paying me no mind at all at the warehouse. Do you think Mr Jones's contacts have discovered Maria?'

'I do not at all know,' replied he. 'Jones has doubtless got the tale wrong; he is as addlepated a fellow as I ever met. I daresay there is nothing in these idle reports or they have been much exaggerated as they passed through the coffee houses.'

'Nonetheless,' said Mary, 'It is an odd report, and one which I think would bear further investigation. I suggest that you seek out Mr Jones and ask if there is any more that he can tell you.'

'Very well,' said Henry. 'But do not hold out much hope, for he is a foolish rattle, and moreover has never once asked me if he may pay you his addresses, despite being unattached, and in possession of a fortune of his own, which makes him even more of a dolt than Cholmondley!'

'Talking of Sir Cedric Cholmondley,' said Mary, 'he has not called upon me for at least a week now, and I think he no longer wishes to pay his addresses to me.'

'Then he is an even bigger fool than I had first thought,' said Henry warmly, 'I do not all know what he is about. Maybe somebody will know something when I go to Boodle's tomorrow; he is a member too.'

'Well, enquire discreetly, I beg of you,' said Mary, 'I would not want him to think I cared one straw whether he liked me or no.'

Mrs Grant returned at that moment, and the subject was dropped between Mary and Henry in all the excitement of talking over the purchases Mary had made, and Mrs Grant's own recalling of the enticing fabrics she hoped to purchase on the morrow, and her hopes for longer sleeves in the coming season.

CHAPTER NINE

While Maria was not a Sleeping Beauty, nor a Cinderella or Rapunzel, she was a very much in danger of becoming a damsel in distress. With each day, month and year which passed in sleepy rural seclusion, she sank a little deeper into lethargy. While her aunt's reaction to their banishment was to throw herself into activity, Maria's was to remove herself more and more from even the daily business of the house. The days all passed for her in a dreary procession, with Sunday being the only day when she left the house to walk across the Park to the little chapel where Mr Ricket gave his sermons. On all other days she submitted to being dressed by her maid, and sat silently at table while her aunt ate and talked and planned, and took a silent walk about the garden with her maid in attendance. She did not miss her parents or her brothers and sister, nor did she care about Mansfield Park or Mr Rushworth's estate at Sotherton. What she felt the sore lack of was the gaiety and excitement of London society, the privilege and power of having a large income at her disposal, and the freedoms afforded a married woman by society. All this had been missing at her childhood home, and all this she had tasted all too briefly in those heady early days of her marriage, before the reappearance of Mr Crawford had thrown into sharp relief all her discontent with her husband.

All the excitement and privilege had been ripped away from her so suddenly and completely once she had left Rushworth's house, and had quarreled so finally with Henry, and parted from him too. She had not the capacity for self-reflection, she was incapable of truly understanding or repenting of her actions, and she did not conceive that she had done anything so very wrong at all by leaving her husband and throwing herself into Henry's power. She had long harboured a resentment that Henry had not spoken to her father when he was at Mansfield Park; had he made her an offer then, it would have saved her from having to go through with the marriage to Mr Rushworth. And she resented his comparing of her with Fanny Price, always to her own detriment, and then his blaming her for his loss of Fanny which he said had resulted directly from his liaison with Maria. There was also the resentment that he did not offer her marriage after persuading her to leave Rushworth, and it was all these resentments combined which had spilled out into the many quarrels, which had led to their final separation.

In the quantity of lonely hours at her disposal, Maria did come to one great realization; that she had misplayed her hand. Her distaste for her husband had brought about so complete a breach, and had led directly to her current seclusion. Had she been more clever, she should have been able to manage a husband and a lover, as did so many of the new acquaintance she had made in London. But Mr Rushworth really had been insupportable; such an embarrassment in public, making scenes and trying to forbid her to visit her friends or attend their parties without him, and never understanding the jokes and lively chatter around him. And his mother! Insupportable! With her maid acting as spy, and *she* acting as though her son were still unmarried, and *she* were the mistress of the house, and Mr Rushworth behaving in his mother's presence like a little boy, instead of a married man. And then Henry had been so very attentive when he returned from Portsmouth, so very determined to have her as much under his power as she had been at Mansfield Park; that she had not been able to resist him. He had really pricked her pride with all his talk of Fanny's perfections, and Maria had been determined to have him all to herself for once and for all, but in the heat of their quarrels he had declared he would not marry her, even after Rushworth divorced her. This had been the final straw for Maria; she had left him to return to her father, who in turn treated her like a leper, and sequestered her like a Nun.

Subsequent to this realization, Maria reached another; if she had been more clever, she could have wheedled and caressed Henry into marrying her once she was free of Rushworth. It had just been so galling to hear Henry talk so much of Fanny, but she should have kept her temper, waited for her freedom, and then persuaded Henry to marry her. It was a relief that there was no child resulting from either her marriage or her liaison with Henry, but did her father really mean her to waste away all her youth and beauty in this nun-like seclusion?

Such were Maria's reflections while she submitted to all Mrs Norris's fussings and to wearing the heavy black veils over her drab black clothing on their daily walks about the garden. She was too down-hearted to even flirt with the rather nervous young clergyman who attended daily for prayers and religious instruction, and whose name she had not even learned. She did not speak to the servants, except to the maid engaged to attend upon her, and to that girl she only spoke to give orders. No-one called, except her father, and he did not want to see her. Despite the heaviness of her spirits, Maria was young yet, and could not be completely crushed. It was a beautiful country she had been exiled to, and there was some interest in colluding with her maid to obtain the London newspapers, and in keeping that a secret from her aunt. The maid had incurred Mrs Norris's wrath over some transgression that Maria was not interested in enough to enquire, nor to intervene to save her place, and she had been given notice.

However, Mrs Norris could not turn her from the house, nor replace her until Sir Thomas's next visit; and so the maid stayed on, resentful against Mrs Norris, and happy to assist Maria in obtaining forbidden newspapers, hoping that her mistress would intervene and prevent her being sent away.

Mrs Norris herself, totally unaware of Maria's thoughts and manoeuvres, had recovered more rapidly than her niece from the shocks she had been dealt by Maria's elopement and their subsequent disgrace and exile. There was much to do in the house, servants to be harried and spied upon so that they were kept about their duties at all times, and shopping trips to the town where there were all manner of luxuries obtainable with the generous allowance from Sir Thomas, not that Mrs Norris was at all interested in luxuries for herself, no indeed, she was more than content with the simplest and plainest of food, which was definitely the most nourishing for herself and her unfortunate niece, but she was not too old to be interested in the variety of goods from all over the country available in the shops in this town so far from London, there was no harm in looking, and should a friend visit, Mrs Norris wanted to be sure to have some dainties to offer, as it did not do for guests not to be offered the very best of what could be had, and she was always determined to do her very best by any friend or guest who came.

Then there were the trips in to the village for Mrs Norris to show what a rich and beneficent patroness she was to the poor with gifts which were accompanied by intrusions into their homes and advice about how to live even more frugally on a small income. Lord M_ may have been an absentee landlord, but he had appointed a good land agent in his stead, and this man ensured that the tenants' cottages were well maintained, and that they had all the modern conveniences which could be provided for them. Despite the care with which the poor kept their houses, Mrs Norris, alighting from her carriage at their front door, and insisting on seeing into every room, was always able to detect any dirt, and was certain that the poor people were grateful to her for bringing it to their notice, for nobody wished to live in a dirty house, after all.

While Mrs Norris was busy about her various concerns, and Maria was languishing at home, barely speaking to anybody, neither of them had the slightest notion that Henry Crawford was endeavouring to track down the source of his friend Jones's information about the young woman kept in a fairy tale fastness in the depths of the British country side.

Despite Mary's hopes, Jones did not have any further information than he had already divulged to Henry and Mary, even upon Henry's further application. He merely repeated what he had already told Henry, who carried it home to discuss further with Mary.

'In answer to your earlier question, my dear sister,' said he, 'I am coming around to your opinion, and I do think that there is a very good chance that this Sleeping Beauty is Maria. It would be just like Sir Thomas to send her away from Mansfield Park, but to keep her in the style of a gentle-woman. He may be an old stick-in-the-mud, but he has his standards, and keeps to them.'

'Let us review what we know,' said Mary, sitting at her writing desk with a pen and paper to hand. 'Tell me again how Mr Jones heard about this mysterious woman.'

'If I have the chain of communication correct,' said Henry, 'then it goes something like this; Jones's sister's friend's brother married a rich woman with a maid, and this maid has a brother who is getting married to a chambermaid at an Inn, and Jones was able to tell me that it was in somewhere called Champford, although I have no idea where that is, or even if Maria is there, or somewhere close by. I have no knowledge even of what there may be close by! It seems quite hopeless to me.'

'Not at all,' said his sister briskly, finishing her writing. 'There are three, nay four avenues of further enquiry I can see at once.'

'And what are they?'

'I shall apply to Mr Jones's mother to pay her a visit, and I am certain that Miss Jones will be there too; she is not yet out, so you are not able to talk to her, but I may. And she may have some further information, or be able to put me in contact with somebody else who has. As for what you might do first, I suggest you ask about at your club, and in the coffee houses amongst your other acquaintance to ascertain if anybody else has heard anything. If this man who married a rich woman is currently in London, he may know something that would help you narrow down your search.'

'And thirdly? You said that you could see three possible avenues of enquiry. Or was it fourthly? Did not you say there might be a fourth line of enquiry?'

'I think there might well be. But let us continue with thirdly; find out where in all the country is Champford, and go there yourself. There is bound to be an Inn for travelers, and Inns are great places for local gossip, and nobody thinks anything strange of enquiries being made there, or of strangers asking for stories of local interest. If Maria is anywhere in that country, somebody will have heard the story, and may even know more nearly where she is living.'

'These are all excellent ideas, but what was your fourth, after all?'

'My fourth is to send your man to locate this fortunate manservant who has inherited all and intends to marry, and see if some common freemasonry can get us the information we require, if he has not yet left London, that is.'

Henry stopped pacing the room, and bowed low to his sister.

'Mary,' said he, 'If you were not a woman, you have the brains to run this country!'

Mary stood and dropt a curtsey in reply, 'I am indeed fortunate to have a brother that truly esteems me.'

'You are the cleverest person I know,' said he simply.

'I take that as slightly less of a compliment when I consider that you know men such as Mr Jones, and Mr Burnell! But to work. I shall write to Mr Jones's mother, to ask if I may call upon her, and you? What shall you do first?'

'I shall send Dexter out to enquire about this manservant, and then go myself to ask about at my club, and at the coffee houses for a man who has married a rich woman recently,' said Henry. 'Although I do not expect much success with such little information.'

'I do not like to contradict my own brother, but I would rather expect that a man who has the good sense to marry a woman of fortune, may well be much talked of, and you will be able to find out her name.'

Having been so firmly rebuffed by Julia Yates, Mary was relieved to receive an early reply from Mrs Jones and a warm invitation to call the following morning. Mrs Jones had indeed been delighted to receive Mary's note; a visit from the sister of one of London's eligible bachelors could only have one meaning; that her son had done as he promised and mentioned his sister (and her fortune) to Mr Crawford. Mrs Jones was comfortably certain that Miss Crawford was coming to see whether her daughter was a suitable bride for her brother. In this she was much mistaken, but everybody must be allowed to dream.

Setting out together the following morning to pay their visits, Mary and Henry parted at the door to Mrs Jones's house, and Henry promised to return to escort her home once he had been to Button's. Mary knocked and sent in her card before being admitted to a very old-fashioned morning breakfast room, crammed with heavy dark furniture, and with the blinds let down, amongst which gloom she could just make out two women, who rose to make their curtsies as she entered.

'Mrs Jones, how kind of you to receive me,' said Mary, shaking their hands and feeling along the furniture to sit down on an uncomfortably over-stuffed chair. 'It is my greatest regret that we did not meet sooner, your son is a great friend to my brother.'

'I have heard George speak of Mr Crawford often, Mama,' said Miss Jones importantly. 'They are indeed great friends.'

'Then I am most happy to make your acquaintance, Miss Crawford,' said Mrs Jones happily. 'My son is a great comfort to me. I hope your brother is a great comfort to you?'

'Indeed he is,' said Mary.

'He is not yet engaged to be married, then?' enquired Mrs Jones, ignoring her daughter's shocked exclamation of, 'Mama!'

'No, he is not, ma'am, I regret that he is no friend to matrimony at present.'

'I am always encouraging George to marry,' sighed his mother, 'but he says he is still looking about him for a suitable woman.'

'You must make your house too comfortable for him to consider a wife,' said Mary, 'Henry says that my sister's house is so comfortable that he has no need of a wife.'

'But your sister is not there with him when he is at Everingham?' asked Mrs Jones, revealing that she had been diligently researching the Crawfords ahead of this visit.

'No indeed, ma'am,' said Mary, smiling to herself. 'If I do not go with him, my brother visits his house at Everingham quite alone.'

'Maybe when he does marry, he will want to be at Everingham more often, do not you think so, Miss Crawford?' asked Miss Jones.

'It is a possibility, or I may keep his house for him as I do in London,' said Mary.

'Surely he would want you to also marry well, my dear Miss Crawford?' said Mrs Jones.

'I am assured that he does, but we deal so well together, that I confess I have not yet accepted any offers. But Henry has had applications from suitable husbands for me, and in return, I look about for a suitable wife for Henry.'

'Finding a suitable wife is most important for a man, and for all of his friends,' said Mrs Jones, sighing heavily.

'Does this subject trouble you, ma'am?' enquired Mary.

'Indeed it does, my dear Miss Crawford,' cried Mrs Jones, eager to share the latest gossip with this important visitor. 'For we have heard terrible news of the brother of a friend of Miss Jones's.'

'I am very sorry to hear it,' said Mary, 'has your friend's brother contracted an unfortunate alliance?'

'Indeed he has, Miss Crawford. It is very shocking!' cried Miss Jones, who had been waiting for a chance to join in the conversation again.

'George assures me it will turn out for the best,' said Mrs Jones, with another heavy sigh. 'But until we know which way it is; I cannot let Miss Jones visit her friend.'

'That must be quite a difficulty for you,' said Mary, turning again to Miss Jones. 'If you are not able to visit your friend because of this unfortunate alliance?'

'Oh! Yes,' cried Miss Jones. 'You understand me, but Mama is keeping me away from Clarissa in case her brother and his bride should visit at the same time as I am there.

'My dear, I have explained, oh, so many times that you must understand we cannot be too careful. Not being out just yet, we cannot let any scandal touch you, even through your friends.'

'I do understand that, Mama, although I cannot think what Clarissa's brother is about to marry as he did.'

'You must not mind that, for he had pockets to let and she is very wealthy, even if she is so much older than he, I can only hope there is some affection in the case, but it is just that her - situation - is as yet unknown to me, and I cannot risk you meeting them at Clarissa's house until I have found out more.'

Mary was looking all interest, so Miss Jones was emboldened to explain.

'You see, Miss Crawford, my friend Clarissa's brother has married a widow with a lot of money.'

'That is very fortunate for him, to be sure,' answered Mary. 'Does he love her very much?'

'No, indeed,' said Miss Jones, 'for despite mama's sensibility, I cannot think that he could care three straws about her; she is an old woman and he is a man in the prime of his life, although he is not at all handsome, or I might have - .' There she stopped, rather confused, realizing that it was not correct for her to say she would have set her cap at Clarissa's brother herself.

'Then I am sorry for the lady,' said Mary. 'It must be galling to her to be married just for her money. What is her name?'

'Well now she is Mrs Gently, but before that she was Mrs Pickle!' and Miss Jones laughed heartily on imparting this information.

'Do forgive Catherine,' said Mrs Jones, frowning at her daughter. 'She finds Mrs Gently's former surname most comical.'

'I can understand Miss Jones's mirth; it is a most comical name,' agreed Mary.

'How shaming to be named after a food stuff,' said Miss Jones, and Mary wondered if she had ever given any thought to the fact that her own surname was hardly one of any distinction.

'And her husband was in The City,' whispered Miss Jones, as though someone might overhear.

'Was he?' cried Mary. 'And now this city widow, this Mrs Pickle, is Mrs Gently after marrying your friend's brother?'

'Yes, you have it. Charlotte is most upset about it, but her brother tells her she must not mind, as he now has enough money to make a settlement on her, which she could not have had before. Her family has no money, at all, although her father is a gentleman, or we could not be friends.'

As both their minds were running upon matrimony that morning, Mrs Jones said, 'And there is more, I do declare! Oh! My dear! Tell Miss Crawford that strange story about Mrs Pickle, I mean Mrs Gently's manservant inheriting a fortune and quitting service to be married, of all things. I do not remember the details, but you had it all from Charlotte.'

'Mrs Gently's manservant inherited some money when her first husband died, and is now marrying? Is this in consequence of Mrs Gently re-marrying? Did she turn him off after her first husband died?' asked Mary, hoping that she was finally arriving at the purpose of her visit.

'It is not Mrs Gently's manservant who inherited and is to marry, mama,' said Miss Jones severely. 'Do attend! And I do not think Miss Crawford would be interested in such a tale.'

But Mary continued to look all attention, and Miss Jones was emboldened to carry on with the tale, as she had always hoped to do.

'Well, you must know Miss Crawford, that Mrs Pickle as was had a friend in the city, I do not remember her name, or maybe Charlotte did not tell me, anyway, it was her husband what died around the same time as did Mr Pickle, and he left his manservant enough money to be independent and in consequence of that the fellow intends to leave service and marry!'

'I am not sure that I all together follow you,' said Mary. 'Was it Mr Pickle or this friend of his which left the money to the manservant?'

'Oh! his friend, to be sure. Mr Pickle left all of his money to his wife, so Charlotte said.'

'That was very correct of him,' said Mary. 'But is it so very – unusual for a man to leave his servant money?' asked Mary, certain now that she had the correct person. 'And is it known to whom this manservant intends to marry? I hope he has not raised his eyes to his master's widow?'

'Oh! No!' cried Miss Jones in horror. 'It is some maid or servant or some such, that he marries, Charlotte did not know her name, and I did not ask, of course, for I care not what a servant does,' she added with scorn, 'it is not at all important to me.'

'He was a most superior manservant, I understand,' said Mrs Jones apologetically. 'And very much deserving of the money, for he assisted Mrs Pickle's friend all throughout her husband's last illness, and was most devoted to him.'

'And was Mrs Pickle, I should say, Mrs Gently's, friend left with nothing by her husband, if he gave all to the manservant?'

'Oh! no,' exclaimed Miss Jones, who had far more information about the case than her previous disclaimer of interest would warrant. 'Mrs Gently's friend has the business, and his fortune, and the manservant was given ten thousand pounds, so Clarissa said.'

'Ten thousand pounds? Goodness! He is a most fortunate fellow indeed!' said Mary, considering the difference between this man's future and her own; on the same amount he could live independent on that money, but she could not.

Before she had time to ask anything more, the maid came in with refreshments, and the talk turned to Miss Jones's hopes for her first ball, and then to her sending the maid running upstairs to bring down her new gown and asking Mary's opinion on whether she should wear a string of pearls, or a citrine riviere collet given to her by her father, and which was an heirloom that she would one day inherit. And then whether a single ostrich feather was enough, or would she be putting herself forward if she were to wear two?

Mary gave her opinion for the pearls, with the citrine riviere collet to be worn at the next event, and just one ostrich feather with the new gown.

There was no more conversation of any interest until Henry was announced, and Mary rose to take her leave.

CHAPTER TEN

After leaving Mary to tease the information they required from Mrs and Miss Jones, Henry had dismissed Dexter to ask about for the manservant, and himself walked on to Button's, his current favourite coffee shop. There he found that there were several pieces of news in circulation; and one of them was exactly as Mary had predicted, there was much discussion about a Mr Gently, of genteel but impoverished stock, who had recently married a Mrs Pickle, a city widow left a fortune by her husband who had been in trade. There were a great many witticisms at Mr Gently's expense, and the new Mrs Gently's former surname, former husband's profession, and her person (being more than twenty years her new husband's senior), were all highly profitable sources of amusement to the idle rich in the coffee house. There was much fishing for jokes in the bottoms of the coffee cups, and many were dredged up and passed around. Mr and Mrs Gently were not the only rich source of gossip; Henry heard one man call out to anybody who happened to be listening that Chummers was to marry some girl who was just out, and another man joined in to add that Miss was said to have fifty thousand pounds, although she was not thought to be handsome or accomplished. In all the hubbub, Henry lost the thread of that conversation, and instead heard others commenting on the latest gossip from Westminster, and a minor scandal in the Royal household.

The jokes were still being passed around as more men came in and were loudly hailed with the latest news, until Crawford sickened of it at last, and took his leave.

He had his information; the new Mrs Gently was his target, and he turned his steps thither, to pay his wedding visit to the new bride. On the way there, Henry had time enough to consider whether this was a good idea, or not. He would never have been in company with the former Mrs Pickle, and while her marriage to Gently may have elevated her to the status of a lady, her manners may not have been equal to the task. By the time he was sending in his card, Henry was regretting his impulse visit, but he need not have been concerned.

The new Mrs Gently was a large, slow woman who reminded him very much of Lady Bertram in her placid acceptance of the fact that she had never before met this young man who had come to visit her. Her manners were perfectly correct, although she could never be said to be elegant, but there was nothing in her appearance or manner that could give him any disgust of her. What he had seen of the house as he followed the footman to the morning room showed a real delicacy of touch, and everything was done with great good taste, and in the latest fashion. There had been a deal of money spent, which backed up the information from the coffee house that the new Mrs Gently had brought a fortune to the marriage, and Mrs Gently herself was dressed in fabric that Henry estimated at considerably more per yard than Mary had ever paid, although she had resisted the temptation to dress in the latest fashions, and kept instead to the styles of her youth.

As Henry entered to make his bow, a younger woman, more fashionably but equally tastefully attired, rose and dropt a small curtsey, and then sat down again without saying a word. The butler announced him, and Mrs Gently held out a hand to indicate he should sit beside her.

'I do not believe we have met before, Mr Crawford,' Mrs Gently said comfortably; 'Are you a friend of my dear Gently?'

'Yes indeed, ma'am,' Henry said mendaciously. 'We were at Cambridge together. Will you introduce me?'

'Of course, do forgive me,' Mrs Gently said, checking the card Henry had sent in, before continuing. 'Mr Crawford, may I present my niece Julia Waldegrave.'

Henry rose and bowed and said he was honoured, and Miss Waldegrave inclined her head in acknowledgement, but did not speak.

'Would you ring for refreshments, my dear?' Mrs Gently asked her niece, who rose and rang the bell and then gave orders to the servant who appeared, before sitting down again and picking up her work.

'Oh, and, Tiller? Please bring me some of those little cakes as well,' Mrs Gently added. 'My cook makes very good rout cakes; I do hope you like to eat rout cakes, Mr Crawford?'

'Indeed I do, ma'am,' said Henry.

'They are a favourite of my dear Gently, so I always order them,' Mrs Gently continued in her slow way. 'I am expecting my dear Gently home at any moment, and I do hope you will stay to meet with him, Mr Crawford, he is always happy to see old friends from before our marriage.'

'Nothing would give me greater pleasure, ma'am,' said Henry, wondering how he should introduce the questions he had come to ask before the happy husband returned and failed to recognize him as an old university friend.

A servant carried in the rout cakes, and Mrs Gently's attention was soon given over to making her selection from amongst them, a task she took very seriously indeed.

'Now, aunt,' said Miss Waldegrave. 'Remember what Doctor Amis said about not eating too many rout cakes?'

'Oh! I pay no attention to such fellows,' said Mrs Gently, dropping Mr Crawford a surprisingly sly wink, and putting more than half the rout cakes on to her own plate. 'My dear Gently says they are very wholesome, and I always take his opinion on everything.'

The appearance of a second servant with the hot water for Miss Waldegrave to mix the tea, seemed to provoke some transfer of thought from mind to mind, causing Mrs Gently herself to raise the vexed question of servants.

'Do you have much trouble with servants, Mr Crawford?' asked she once the door was shut behind her own.

'I cannot tell you, ma'am. Certainly, I am not aware of any trouble with the servants. My sisters are the ones to ask.'

'Oh! you live with your sisters, do you?'

'Yes, ma'am.'

'And they have not mentioned any trouble with servants to you?'

Miss Waldegrave spoke for the first time as she busied herself amongst the tea caddies;

'I do not suppose gentlemen to be much interested in the servants, Aunt, so long as they go about their duties. When you discussed this with Mr Gently only this morning before he went out, he gave it as his opinion that it did not matter as long as they did not neglect their duties.'

'Indeed I do recall my dear Gently saying that,' Mrs Gently agreed. But like Lady Bertram, she did not let go of an idea until she had worked all the way through it first. 'But my dear, they cannot do their duties if they go off to be married.'

'It is not one of our servants who is to go off to be married, Aunt,' said Miss Waldegrave, with the weary air of one who has explained this several times previously.

'Then whose servant is it?' asked her aunt.

'It is your friend's manservant, Aunt.'

'And what has he to do with me?'

'He is your maid's brother, Aunt, but he is not in your service.'

'Then why is it a problem?' asked Mrs Gently.

'I do not believe it is a problem to you, Aunt, for your maid will not be leaving with her brother. But your friend Mrs Channing is to lose her manservant, just after losing her husband, and she has been complaining everywhere about it. The fellow had been running her household for her and her husband for many years, and she says she will not know what to do without him.'

'So it is not a problem for me, or my dear Gently? We are not to be incommoded by a servant leaving?'

'No Aunt.'

'Well, that is good for I very much dislike having to find new servants. It takes them so long to learn our ways and begin to do their duties as I wish, and if they are new to serving, it can be very vexing indeed to wait until they are properly trained.'

Henry could see that this exchange could easily become prolonged, so he sought to shorten it by asking, 'And is Mrs Channing's manservant the brother of Mrs Gently's maid?'

'Yes, you have it!' cried Miss Waldegrave.

'A gentleman's mind is so much clearer on these matters, I find,' said Mrs Gently, 'My dear Gently explains everything so clearly to me, just as you have done, Mr Crawford.'

'I am happy to have been of service, ma'am,' said Henry, surreptitiously checking the clock and realizing his fifteen minutes was nearly over. 'But I must not trespass upon your time any longer. Please do give my kindest regards to Gently when he arrives, I am sorry to have missed him. If it is agreeable to you, I shall ask my sister Mary to call upon you, and I will then call upon you on my own account in due course as well.'

'That would be most agreeable, Mr Crawford,' said Mrs Gently, and Miss Waldegrave rang for the footman to show him out.

On his way to collect Mary from the Jones's house, Henry walked with triumphant step; he now knew that the intended groom had been in the service of a Mr Channing, and wondered if Mary's enquiries had yielded similarly useful fruit. As he walked, he cast his mind about, but could not recall a Channing amongst any of his acquaintance, and then realized the Channings were probably former city friends of the new Mrs Gently, which would mean Henry would almost certainly have never encountered them in society.

He also wondered about Miss Waldegrave; the name was familiar, but he could not recall the family immediately. He wondered if she were a niece of the Pickle family, but her surname was definitely familiar, and she had had the air of a gentlewoman, despite being Mrs Gently's niece. She was clearly out as she was in company with her aunt; maybe somebody would know something about her, and whether she was to have any fortune, especially as it was unlikely the Gentlys would be having any children of their own.

And then there was the news of Cholmondley to think on too – the 'Chummers' referred to in the coffee shop; Henry was not at all sure whether he should mention what he had heard to Mary. After all, Cholmondley had approached Henry to ask if he could pay his addresses to Mary, but that had been nearly a year ago now. As far as he could recall, Chummers had been assiduous in his attentions towards Mary over quite a few months, and in such a way that others may well have noticed. Certainly, Mary had never given her brother any indication that she would ever consider him as a future husband, and may well have told that to Cholmondley himself, but it did not seem to have prevented him calling upon her almost every day. Now it seemed he had forgot all of that in the light cast by a younger woman who would have fifty thousand pounds. To be sure, Mary's treatment of Cholmondley would have deterred a more sensitive man; she had always treated him with faint scorn, but as far as Henry knew, Chummers had never stood accused of any sensibility in all his life to date, and did not appear to have been put off by Mary's manner.

Ultimately, Mary would find out about Cholmondley and his new fiancée, as it would be in all the newspapers, and she would certainly see it for herself, but Henry did not want to be the person to tell her beforehand. He decided that he had not heard about Chummers's perfidy, and that he would be guided by Mary's reaction when she read the news. It may be that she would be relieved that he was no longer paying her suit, and that would clear the way to her accepting the Earl of _.

Henry was not kept waiting at Mrs Jones's house, and Mary introduced him to Mrs Jones. That lady was delighted to have had two visitors in one morning, and chose to believe that Henry calling for his sister in person was more confirmation that he was interested in her daughter. Miss Jones herself could not speak to him, and stood very quietly behind her mama, the very picture of a demure girl who was not yet out. She may not speak, but she could look, and Henry caught her giving him swift appraising glances, while he said all that was proper to her mother. Finally, he bowed to Mrs Jones and as Mary guessed that he had some news for her, she did not linger over her farewells to Mrs and Miss Jones.

When they turned the corner of the street, they stopped and looked at one another.

'Gently?' asked Mary.

'Channing!' replied Henry.

'There is too much clatter and confusion here for us to understand each other well enough,' said Mary. 'Meet me before my sister comes down to dinner, and we will exchange our news.'

CHAPTER ELEVEN

Henry and Mary hurried through their dressing in order to meet up before dinner, but found their tête-à-tête anticipated by Mrs Grant, who never took long to dress. Her husband had from the first been very impatient over any delay in dinner for something as frivolous as dress, and this had caused her to change with considerable dispatch, and she was never behind-hand in coming down stairs. She was to find that her brother and sister had much to acquaint her with; and a life-time of practice had made Mrs Grant a very good listener, and a most satisfying person to tell the whole story of their investigations so far to.

Dexter had reported to Henry that he had investigated as far as he could in the time at his disposal, but had not discovered either the manservant himself, nor anybody with any knowledge of his name, so Henry had instructed him to go out again the following day, with the extra information he had gleaned himself. To his sisters, Henry recounted his visit to the coffee house, his discovery of the newly married Mrs Gently, and his subsequent visit to her and the new names which had come out of the visit; Mrs Channing, and Miss Waldegrave.

Mrs Grant had been listening with keen interest, and here she said, 'Did Mrs Gently say what relation she was, and did you gather Miss Waldegrave's name in the course of conversation?'

'Mrs Gently introduced her as her niece, and called her Julia,' said Henry.

Ah! Then I am indeed able to assist you, for I know exactly who Miss Waldegrave and Mrs Gently are!

Henry and Mary looked at her in surprise, and she laughed.

'My dears, it is an old, old scandal, long before your time. I was but a girl myself, but I remember it very well.'

'Then pray tell, sister,' said Mary.

'It was while I was at school, and you two were still tormenting governesses.'

'And Henry was not listening to their bed-time stories,' interjected Mary wittily.

Henry laughed, Mrs Grant shook her head fondly, and continued;

'I remember over-hearing my parents talking about the Waldegraves and my father shaking his head and saying they were in financial difficulties, although it was not news as they had been for several generations because of spendthrift oldest sons, and a complete lack of knowledge about how to make or keep their money. However, when I was a girl, their difficulties reached such a pitch that when the eldest Miss Waldegrave came out, her father was able to do nothing for her. She was not handsome nor clever, and with no fortune, no man would even look at her. Miss Waldegrave took matters into her own hands, and her parents cast her off and never spoke of her again. I do not at all know where or how she met Mr Pickle, but meet him she did and they were married, for she was of age and her father could not stop the match. It was said that her new husband was very wealthy indeed. *He* wanted to be able to say his wife was a Waldegrave, and *she* wanted to be married and was not over nice about who to. But it was a happy marriage as far as I know, and he has left her all his money, and not even in trust. Over the years, despite their coolness towards him, Mr Pickle helped the Waldegrave family to get back onto an even footing with their money, and provided dowries for all the girls, and places in the city for any of the sons who wanted one, or bought them commissions in the Army or Navy. He was most generous, but they never acknowledged him in public.'

'So, the Mrs Gently I met was formerly Mrs Pickle, and was born a Miss Waldegrave?' said Henry.

'To be sure. And this Miss Julia Waldegrave must be the daughter of one of her brothers. I recall there were several brothers.'

'That is why Mrs Gently and her niece had such the air of a gentlewoman,' Henry said.

'Then Mrs Gently is back where she started, only this time married to a gentleman,' said Mary. 'What an extraordinary story to be sure! And it is not so very widely known, as Mrs Jones did not know that she had once been a Miss Waldegrave. I suspect Mrs Gently will be back in society once that piece of news comes out and everybody remembers who she once was. I expect she will go back into society as she will be looking for a husband for her niece.'

'And did she know anything of a servant marrying in Champford?' asked Mrs Grant.

'Yes indeed, sister. She was most put out about the elevation of a servant to independence not through her first husband's generosity, but that of a friend of his; a Mr Channing, whom I assume is also a city man as I have never heard that name before,' said Henry.

'Now we are getting somewhere,' said Mary with satisfaction. 'This Mr Channing died, and left his manservant enough money to leave service and marry.'

'Yes, that was it exactly,' said Henry, 'but do tell us what you have discovered from Mrs Jones?'

'I have not much to add to your information,' said Mary, 'but I have set in train enquiries of my own, by asking Hawkins to enquire from other coachmen as to where Champford is, and I hope he will be able to bring us that information soon. And here is dinner announced!'

However fortunate the Crawfords had been in their enquiries to date, Dexter continued to draw a blank on the fortunate manservant's current whereabouts, but he did discover the man's name, which was Andersen, and that he was believed to have already left London to begin his independent life, and to marry. Hawkins had better luck, and within a few more days he was able to tell Mary where in the country Champford was to be found, and that there was a large coaching Inn there with many travelers coming and going all day and night.

With this name now in their possession, Mary and Mrs Grant looked over a map book and discovered that Champford was not so far from Mansfield Park as could not be travelled there and back in a day, but it was too far from London to be so reached. If Henry were to undertake the journey, he would need to be gone for several weeks, especially if his enquiries took time to track Maria's location down.

'And so do you think that Maria is discovered?' asked Mrs Grant, sitting down again and picking up her work.

'No, I am not completely certain that she is yet,' answered Maria.

'But you suspect that she is at Champford?' asked Mrs Grant, finally giving up even the pretence of working. In truth, she had barely put in a stitch since her brother and sister came to live with her. They were such stimulating company compared with what she had been accustomed to with her husband, and she enjoyed watching and hearing them together – it was better than a play! And they were so clever! Mrs Grant had never felt herself to be as clever as her brother and sister, but they always treated her with the utmost affection, and she loved to hear them plan their next escapades.

'With all the information we have been able to gather, it is more likely than not that she is in the same country, and that Champford is her nearest town,' answered Mary. 'But it may still be difficult to find exactly where she is concealed, if Sir Thomas has stipulated secrecy, and the servants do not tattle as they should in order to assist us.'

'And will you and Henry go there to seek out Maria?'

'I will not go,' Mary said. 'But I think that Henry should go, if only to find out for certain whether it is Maria, or whether it has all been a wild goose chase.'

'I hope it will not turn out to be a wild goose chase,' added Mrs Grant. 'But even if it should prove to be so, it has all been most entertaining, has not it?'

'Indeed it has, my dear sister!'

'And what then, if it is Maria? Will Henry bring her back here, do you suppose?'

'As to that, I know not,' said Mary, thoughtfully. 'She may not wish to come. Last time they were together, they quarrelled most terribly, and agreed to separate.'

Mrs Grant knew not how to reply to this, and after a moment Mary went on;

'But you, my dear sister, would you be happy to receive Maria here if she did agree to come?'

'Yes of course,' said Mrs Grant happily. 'You can I can chaperone her until she and Henry are married, and then her family cannot object to her being here, and everybody will be pleased, I am certain.'

Mary was not at all certain, but she smiled at her sister's goodness, patted her hand, and went to tell Henry the news about Champford. If he was to go there, many arrangements would need to be made beforehand.

CHAPTER TWELVE

As Champford had most obligingly been discovered in the next county to Northamptonshire, Mary set her considerable intelligence to discovering more about the country thereabouts. This entailed asking all their acquaintance if they knew anything about Champford and its surrounds, and eventually the name of Lord M_ came to her attention. Lord M_, as Mrs Norris had known long before Mary, was an absentee landlord, as his lady preferred to be in London, and he himself was on the fringes of the Prince Regent's circle, and much given to spending his time following the Regent about on his visits.

'I suspect that the most likely place for Maria to have been concealed is in a small village which serves the great house of Lord M_,' said she to her brother.

'But the Yardleighs are even now in London, my dear,' said Mrs Grant, whose knowledge of the society papers was proving invaluable.

'Ah, but if there is a dower house,' said Mary. 'And if we were to discover that the Dowager Lady M_ was not in residence, it would be an ideal lodging for Maria.'

'Again, I am able to assist you,' said Mrs Grant. 'For I know that there is a very fine dower house on the estate, and that the Dowager is not in residence. Her son took possession of the estate a year or so ago, but his mother did not choose to reside in the dower house, even though he had it all modernized with the greatest of luxuries for her.'

'How very ungrateful!' said Henry.

'The glazing alone cost hundreds of pounds, and there was all new furniture and drapes. I even heard talk that a new ice house was dug right beside the house as she was very fond of ices.'

'But despite all these wonders, his mother did not choose to live there?' asked Mary.

'No, she went to her own house in Bath, which was an inheritance from her mother, and did not pass down to her son, and she has remained there ever since. I understand she is not in the best of health, and likes to take the waters every day.'

There was a silence as all three considered this new information.

'Hawkins tells me he has discovered that the country about Lord M_'s estate is mostly set to farming, and that, aside from Champford, there is not another town of any size for miles about, and no other families of note than the Yardleighs,' said Mary. 'I would be reasonably certain that that this is where Maria has been placed.'

'She cannot be living alone, my dear,' said her sister. 'Sir Thomas would never allow his daughter to live alone. He must have engaged a chaperone for her.'

'As to that, I have no information at all,' said Mary. 'But you are correct in your supposition, sister. Sir Thomas would not allow his daughter to reside alone. We may assume he has engaged some dragon or Gorgon to guard her, and you will need to employ all of your charm Henry, to gain access to Maria.'

Henry just bowed in acknowledgement of his charm, but his thoughts were not with Maria, but with another woman who had intrigued him, and he was beginning to wonder whether he would ever be content with marriage to Maria after all, and whether all this effort to secure a bird so far away was worth it, now that there was another bird much more readily to hand.

This bird so readily to hand was, of course, Miss Waldegrave. After that very first visit to pay his respects to the newly-weds, while seeking information which might lead him to Maria, Henry had found that Miss Waldegrave intruded on his thoughts, and he decided he must see her again, if only to reassure himself that this interest was fleeting, and based on nothing but a sense of the novelty of meeting her just the once, and later finding out who she was.

He could not go to the house again until Mary had paid her first visit, and Mary was most provokingly busy about her own concerns, but his luck held; he and Mary encountered the new Mrs Gently and her niece out taking the air in her carriage;

Henry noticed them first, and pointed them out to Mary, and just as they were wondering how to attract their attention, Mrs Gently most obligingly looked in the right direction.

'Oh look, my dear, there is Mr Crawford,' said she, and Miss Waldegrave turned to look, and smiled, so Henry brought his own barouche to a halt, stood and bowed.

'Mrs Gently, Miss Waldegrave, how very pleasant it is to encounter you on this lovely morning. May I present my sister Mary to you?'

The ladies all bowed and said how charmed they were to make each others' acquaintance, and promised early visits, and family dinners. Through Henry's and Miss Waldegrave's promptings, these invitations were confirmed and carried out, and a very pleasing intimacy arose between Mary and Miss Waldegrave, giving Henry, under the pretence of escorting his sister, the opportunity to spend a not inconsiderable amount of time getting better acquainted with Miss Waldegrave.

Thus was Henry's search for the missing Maria almost forgotten in this heady new acquaintance; there was something about Miss Waldegrave which recalled Fanny to Henry. True, the resemblance was not in any way physical, or even in temperament; she was dark, where Fanny was fair. She was lively, where Fanny was reserved. She was tall and stout, where Fanny was short and slight. She was, in truth, in character far more like his sister than she was like Fanny; but Miss Waldegrave had something of Fanny's steadfastness and high principles, and Henry felt sure he could confide in her just as he would have been able to confide in Fanny. They met almost daily, and Henry was well on the way to being much in love with her.

Henry's and Mary's attentions were greatly appreciated by Gently himself, whom Henry did finally meet, as they meant that the marriage was becoming acceptable in society, and that he and his bride would not much longer be shunned. And it proved to be so; where the Crawfords had led, others followed, and Mrs Gently was soon receiving visitors, keen to ingratiate themselves with a former Miss Waldegrave, who was now a very wealthy woman.

Despite this set-back in their search for Maria, the Crawfords were now in possession of greater knowledge of the area she lived in than was Maria herself. She had never roused herself to ask any questions of her Aunt Norris as to exactly where in the country they were now residing, and as they had travelled there in a closed carriage, she had not seen any of the country they passed through on their way. Had she asked, she would have probably been told that she did not need to know; that no-one except Sir Thomas knew where they were, and that she must pay more attention to the Chaplain than she had been in the habit of doing so far.

The Chaplain in question was a nervous young man with a stammer. He had the air of a saint or martyr of old, being very thin in his person, with an ascetic looking face. It was well-known that he never ate meat, and he fasted regularly; that aside from communion, he never took wine and that he prayed incessantly; he had never been married and shewed no inclination to do so, and there were no young ladies in the neighbourhood other than the Vicar's family in nearby Champford to tempt him into changing his mind on the subject of matrimony. Mr Pagan, the Vicar of Champford had several daughters, whose lively and uninhibited manners distressed Mr Ricket so much that he only visited their Papa when he could be assured they were otherwise occupied. If anything, they were confirmation to Mr Ricket that marriage would not suit him in the slightest.

Unfortunately, Mr Pagan was the only other religious in the immediate area, and he and Mr Ricket met at least once a month to shore up each other's faith, and to discuss what could be done to alleviate local suffering. In this, Mr Ricket had the least to contribute, as Lord M_'s land agent, and the recently arrived Mrs Morris, between them left him nothing to do. However, he was hoping to gently guide Mrs Morris's charity towards the more deserving families in Champford. Mr Ricket believed that Mr Pagan would not stoop to gossip, and had no compunction about consulting him on the new arrivals at the Dower House, and in particular the instruction which would most benefit Mrs Raworth. And as Mr Pagan was a genial family man much devoted to his wife and daughters, he passed on such information as he felt could not hurt anybody to his family. Thus it became known that Mr Ricket had been requested to give instruction to a distraught and pock-marked widow at the Dower House. His daughters thought it the most romantic thing in the whole world, and wondered if they would fall in love, and she would finally shed her widow's weeds, and take up his charitable work about the area. They secretly thought Mr Ricket rather a poor excuse for a man, compared with the heroes of the romances that their father did not know they borrowed from the local Lending Library. With men of this ilk with which to compare all possible suitors, they had not the least interest in Mr Ricket for themselves, and so did not begrudge him to this poor disfigured widow they were never to meet.

Nothing could have been further from the truth, had they but known it. Mr Ricket was singularly unsuited to the moral instruction of a woman of Maria's character; not through any viciousness of his own, but due to his own unworldliness, and there was absolutely no possibility of either of them being in love with the other. He was a distant cousin of Lord M_, and one for whom his Lordship had some sympathy and patience; they had grown up together, and Lord M_ had very early on realized his cousin's unfitness for anything but the most quiet occupation, well away from the hurly-burly of modern life.

Before closing with Lord M_'s land agent on the Dower House, Sir Thomas had interviewed Mr Ricket and had been very pleased with what he saw. The young man had the air of one who was above all worldly pleasures and pursuits, and was fervent in his faith; moreover, he was in no way a vivacious man, and would certainly not appeal to Maria. Sir Thomas engaged him to give Maria the moral and religious instruction he considered her to be so lacking given her recent behaviour, and impressed upon Mr Ricket the seriousness of his task, and the need for consistency of message and frequency of application. So, Mr Ricket came once a day to spend an hour in a room with a heavily veiled Mrs Raworth, her maid, and at first, her aunt, Mrs Morris, and all the other servants. This was in addition to the entire household walking across the park twice every Sunday to hear him give his sermon, and to say their prayers in the Chapel.

If all of this was not daunting enough for the shy clergyman, Mrs Morris had been quick to tell him that she was the widow of a very devoutly religious man who had dedicated his life to interpreting and elucidating the obscurer passages in the Gospels, and who had even been on a visit in the Holy Land in his own youth. Mercifully for Mr Ricket, Mrs Morris soon discovered that he had no more to teach her, owing to her dear husband's instruction, and that such frequency of religious instruction was not in the servants' best interests for it led to a shocking neglect of their other duties. It has to be said that the other servants were greatly relieved to be allowed to stop attending the daily sessions with Mr Ricket; never before had their duties seemed so enjoyable when compared with an hour in his company!

Sir Thomas had been obliged to tell Mr Ricket exactly in what way Maria had sinned against the Christian principles, which caused that nervous young gentleman to regard her with horror every time they met, but as Maria scarcely even glanced at her instructor, she did not notice. Mr Ricket had no personal experience of any of the sorts of sins that Maria had committed, but he duly consulted Mr Pagan, and between them, they prepared him diligently for his instruction with selected readings from the Books of Genesis, The Book of Kings, and the canonical Gospels, and he conscientiously did his best to lead this particular sinner back to the light of God's grace.

As Sir Thomas had hoped, there was nothing in Mr Ricket's looks or address to excite Maria's interest at all; she made slight response to any question that he asked, and as far as he could ascertain under all the veiling, she took full part in the services which he provided; responding, standing, sitting, and kneeling as required.

However, as for the content of Mr Ricket's moral instruction lessons, Maria could not have told anybody of what they consisted, even an hour after she left the room each day, for she simply did not listen. She had become an adept at appearing to respond appropriately while her mind was fixed quite elsewhere.

CHAPTER THIRTEEN

Despite becoming convinced that Maria was to be found at Champford, it was some weeks yet before Mr Crawford was able to set out for Champford, to see if the next piece of the puzzle could be slotted into place.

He had not been inclined to set off earlier at least partly because of Miss Waldegrave's many charms, as well as a very valid concern that he was about to be set upon a wild goose chase. However, by the beginning of January, he had just about made up his mind to at least visit Champford, discover that they had been wrong in supposing Maria to be concealed there, and come home with a clear conscience to continue his pursuit of Miss Waldegrave. Just as preparations were nearly complete, he was prevented from leaving after Mary found the notice in the newspaper about Cholmondley's intended marriage to an heiress with fifty thousand pounds, and there was other bad news for her too.

'Oh! Henry!' she cried, holding out the paper towards him. 'See what is here!'

'What is it?' he asked in alarm, all manner of visions crossing his mind; the Admiral dead! Miss Waldegrave to be married! Coutts bankrupt!

'Sir Cedric Cholmondley is to engaged to be married, and the Earl of _ has died! That is all my chances of marriage gone in one day!'

Henry took the paper his sister held out to him and scanned through the notices. While he had known about Cholmondley for some time, and wondered privately why it had taken so long to be put into the newspaper, the Earl's death was news indeed.

'If I had married him when he first made me the offer,' said Mary, 'I would now be the dowager Countess of _, with property and income to add to my own fortune.'

'If his son has not gambled them all away by now,' said Henry.

'I had not got so far as to ask you to look into his finances,' said Mary, 'but it is too late now.'

'It is vastly vexing, for there would have been time for me to visit you at the castle after all, and you would not have had to be a wife long either,' said Henry.

'No, indeed. I am also most vexed upon both counts; I assure you. And I am no longer surprised that I have not seen the Earl for above a month.'

'What about Cholmondley?' asked Henry, 'Did he ever make you an offer? I can call him out if he did and now is to marry somebody else.'

'There is no need, Henry. He never quite got that far, and even had he made me an offer, I had quite made up my mind to refuse him, as I told you. There has been no betrothal, Henry, no announcement in the newspapers; there has been no breach of promise.'

'He did write to you, I recall?'

'Yes, indeed. I had a lot of letters and pretty speeches from him with nonsense about my eyes and hair, and how his life would be worthless without me. I read some of his more absurd poems about my various attributes aloud to you in the evenings.'

'Ah yes, until you reminded me, I had successfully put those out of my mind; they were truly terrible,' said Henry. 'Well, some of his praise of you was certainly justified,' he went on, 'and I cannot imagine this Miss _ will be anything compared with you. The loss is on his side alone.'

Mary said nothing, and Henry continued;

'Let me fetch my sister, she will know how better to comfort you, if it is comfort you are in need of. Do you wish me to postpone my visit into Champford?'

'Not on my account, Henry,' said Mary, looking up with an effort. 'But I would be glad if you would ask my sister to attend me.'

Henry rose and bowed, leaving the room to look for Mrs Grant, and then summoned Dexter to postpone the hiring of horses, and packing of cravats for the journey into Champford.

When he returned to the sitting room it was clear that there had been a few tears, but also that Mary was quite resolute in her decision that he should continue with his own plans, that she would do very well with her sister to comfort her, and that she had lost nothing by this defection of Sir Cedric's and wished him a long and happy marriage with his heiress.

When, finally he could delay his visit into Champford no longer, Henry set out rather later than he had originally planned to discover whether the Sleeping Beauty of Mr Jones's imagination was indeed the same person as the Maria of his own past. Although Henry's own desire to discover Maria and insinuate himself back into the good opinion of the family at Mansfield Park had lately rather faded, it was still with a sense of his life taking the next step forward that he set out, expecting to be several days on the road.

In the event, the journey went without incident, and on riding in to Champford, they easily discovered the Maid's Head Inn fronting on to a busy market place. Dexter took the horses through to the stabling block, where he soon entered into animated conversation with the grooms, and Henry walked through the front doors to bespeak them both accommodation.

To his surprise, the Inn was very busy, and there were no rooms within doors for servants; but Dexter could be accommodated with the grooms, and Henry paid for a room to himself, and ordered food and hot water to be brought to his room, and he sauntered forth in the meantime to see what delights Champford might have to offer a London gentleman. There was little enough compared with what he was accustomed to; but the people of Champford were very satisfied with their lot in life, and with the variety of goods on offer at their market. And there was an agricultural society show to demonstrate improvements in farming about to take place with many ingenious engines on display, which explained, in part, the Inn's busyness.

When Henry returned to his room, Dexter was waiting with the hot water and food, and had unpacked Henry's bags.

'If I recall correctly, Dexter,' said Henry, 'There was a maid servant at the end of the chain of enquiry I have been pursuing. A maid servant who was to marry a manservant who had just inherited an independence when his master died. See if she is yet at this Inn, or if she is gone already, I expect it will be much talked of by the other servants.'

It did not take Dexter long to discover that the maid servant was indeed still being talked of with much envy by the other servants, and he brought the story to Henry, who passed it on to his sisters in a letter.

'*My dearest sisters,*

I have not been idle since arriving into Champford. It is a busy town, and I am put up at the Maid's Head. Please forward any letters to me here, as I am expecting to be in residence for several weeks. Dexter has discovered the story of the maid servant and the manservant who inherited from Mr Channing, and I set it down here for you, without attempting to reproduce Dexter's individual syntax and vocabulary.

The manservant's name was Andersen, and he and his sister, Anne were born and brought up in Champford by respectable parents; which must be what Mrs Gently meant when she told me he was a 'most superior young man'. He received a good education, and was intended to go into his father's business. However, the Andersen parents mismanaged their finances, and left their children with nothing when they died. Both children entered into service after their parents' death; Andersen took a place with a family, and his sister found employment at the Inn.

In time, both rose in their positions, the son to manservant, and the daughter managing the Inn's other servants, until both decided they could do better for themselves if they took service with rich families in London, and so left Champford to seek their fortunes. And it appears that they were both successful in doing so; Andersen becoming manservant to Mr Channing, and Anne taking up employment as maid to the former Mrs Pickle. But I see I am neglecting the other half of this most affecting tale; the young woman to whom Andersen has returned to rescue from drudgery. Why it is a very parallel to my own endeavours to discover and rescue Maria from her fastness! Was not there a children's story of a young woman rescued by marriage from drudgery, Mary?

Where there is or no, this young woman, who was indeed a maid servant at this very Inn, had been a childhood sweetheart of Andersen, and bosom friend of his sister, and, when the Andersens left to go to London, he promised to return and marry her one day, when he had earned enough money to keep them both. For some reason, which quite escapes me, she believed him, and kept herself aloof from all other offers against his return. This I gather from Dexter was the account of the head groom, who had set his own heart on this girl, but who could not weaken her resolve to wait for Andersen.

And her faith in him was justified; for return he did, and they are now respectably settled in a house somewhere in the neighbourhood. I have sent Dexter to find them, and enquire if there is anything more they may know about Maria, as it appears the report of her may have originated from Andersen's new wife initially, as I believe her to be the maid at an Inn who was at the end of the line of communication we first had from Jones. I will continue to enquire, and will also take a ride out to inspect Lord M_'s estate; the housekeeper may admit me and housekeepers know everything which happens in their neighbourhoods, as is well known.

Thus has my search for Maria commenced, although it may appear to you that Dexter is actually doing all the work. For now I end, as I must give my full attention to a really splendid repast, the praise of which should bring me into the good books of mine host, who in turn may have more information about our sleeping girl in the tower with the long hair, or whatever the story was that you told me, Mary. I declare I have no recollection of ever being told it before!

I shall write again when I have more to tell.

Your loving brother

Henry'

'There!' said Mary to her sister, folding the letter up, 'Henry is arrived, and begins to enquire. Or at least, sends Dexter to enquire. And we must await his next communication. Are there any letters for Henry that I can enclose for him in my reply?'

'None that I am aware of,' answered Mrs Grant. 'He has only been gone a few days.'

'Then, if you are at leisure to attend me, there is something else I wish to consult you about, my dearest sister.'

Mrs Grant was happy to be at leisure to advise her sister, and looked all attention, so Mary told her of her own concerns about the newly affianced Sir Cedric Cholmondley and his unguarded protestations of devotion prior to his engagement. As Mrs Grant was well aware, Sir Cedric was a lumpish and rather absurd young man, much given to outbursts of enthusiasm, but what neither of them had realised was that he had nonetheless harboured genuine feelings for a woman so very different from him; her vivacity, intelligence, and good humour had indeed captivated him. For the whole of the previous year, he had poured out his feelings for Miss Crawford, chiefly in poetry, containing exstatic descriptions of her facial features, and deportment, as well as clumsy references to her sparkling wit. She had kept the letters not because she harboured any reciprocal feelings, but for their sheer absurdity; and before she discovered he was to marry somebody else, had delighted in reading aloud passages from them to her brother and sister in their rare evenings at home alone.

'I do recall the letters,' said Mrs Grant, 'but did you ever reply? I cannot think that you ever replied.'

Mercifully, Mary had not written any replies to any of these absurd letters, nor had she acknowledged their receipt in any way; in fact, she had never even written Sir Cedric a note to confirm a time or date he could call upon her, and for that omission she felt greatly relieved when the announcement of his engagement to another was made. There were no notes from her that might be used to hold her up as a laughing stock or as a jilted lover. There was no evidence in his hands of any involvement with Mary at all, whatever he may have told his friends and family. However, his own letters, cards and notes to Mary were quite another matter.

'My dear sister,' said she. 'You are quite right; I did not send him a single line. But you will recall how absurd those letters from Sir Cedric Cholmondley were? And how you and Henry enjoyed me reading aloud extracts from them this past year?'

'Indeed I do,' returned her sister. 'Although I did not always agree with you and Henry that they were absurd; in point of composition, his letters were not completely defective, and I thought them often well expressed.'

'And yet they were absurd!' cried Mary. 'I could not respect a man who fell in love with a woman for the beauty of her eyebrows, and committed such adulation to poetry! Even you, the most partial and loving of sisters, would not admit that my eyebrows were anything out of the ordinary way.'

'To write in such a way is not new,' said her sister. 'But I can see why you might think it absurd; I grant you. And although I have never considered your eyebrows as anything more than in the appropriate place upon your face, I am convinced that they are as perfect as the rest of you!'

Mary kissed her sister affectionately.

'You are the best of sisters!' said she. 'However, no matter how perfect my eyebrows may be, it is no longer appropriate for me to keep odes to them penned by a man who is affianced to another.'

The reason for Mary's consulting her dawned on her sister. 'Oh! I see! Apart from the praise of your eyebrows, is there anything else in the letters that would cause him embarrassment now he is engaged? Did he make you an offer?'

'No, he stopped just short of actually declaring himself either on paper or in person, thankfully,' said Mary. 'But I do not wish to keep these letters now that he is to be married. What shall I do? Burn them, or return them to him under a plain cover?'

Mrs Grant looked perplexed;

'I have not the least idea what to advise you, Mary,' said she at last. 'What does Henry say?'

'I have not been able to ask him,' said Mary. 'And I do not want to keep the letters until his return. He will have other things to think of, and it may be some weeks before he is with us again.'

Both women stared at the packet of letters on the table between them.

'I think it best to return them,' said Mrs Grant at last. 'He will know what to do with them; I expect he will destroy them as he will not want his fiancée to think he once cared for another woman.'

'I do not in the least think he cared for me,' said Mary. 'From the tone of the letters, he was dazzled by me, but not really in love, or he could not have given me up for another woman, even for fifty thousand pounds. Not that I would have seriously considered marrying him, even had he made me an offer.'

'As to that,' answered Mrs Grant, her mind wandering on to a parallel subject, 'I cannot at all understand why you are not wed yourself, Mary. You are so very attractive, and lively, and you have a good fortune of your own. I had hopes once in Northamptonshire, but …'

'As did I,' Mary interrupted hastily. 'But they came to nought. And I suspect that the sparkling wit that Sir Cedric mentions so often, and rhymes with 'submit' and 'flit', and once even 'grit', by the by, is enough to put off the slow minded bachelors in London who prefer their wives to be dim and pretty, with big fortunes.'

CHAPTER FOURTEEN

Mary and Mrs Grant put all Sir Cedric's communications into one packet, and sent them with no accompanying note, to his London address. That they thought was the end of the matter, but they had reckoned with Sir Cedric's stupidity, and his fiancée's jealous vigilance. For Sir Cedric had actually been much more in love with Mary than she had given him credit, and all that had stopped him from making her an offer was the disparity in their ages; she was older than him, and when he went to speak to his parents about his wish to make her an offer, they had told him to forget her and seek out a younger bride. Sir Cedric had done as his parents advised, but he could not stop himself from comparing his former passion for Miss Crawford with his feelings for his future wife; and not in his new lady's favour.

'I know a woman who plays the harp like an angel,' said he wistfully one evening after Miss Payne had twice plunged noisily through her entire repertoire on the pianoforte, and he had not been able to doze after a splendid dinner as was his preference.

'Oh?' said she, and the tone of her voice should have warned Sir Cedric from any further disclosures, but he was too rapt in his memories to notice, and continued;

'Yes, indeed. Played the harp like an angel, sang beautifully too.'

Miss Payne did not sing.

'What a paragon she must be,' said Miss Payne sweetly. 'Was there anything else she could do so well?' Any married man would have recognised the tone and steered the subject smartly away, but Sir Cedric was not yet married, and did not see the danger.

'Witty, very witty. I could not understand the half of what she said, but the sparkle in her eyes as she said it, was worth being thought a dolt, and having to get her to explain what was meant by it.'

Miss Payne knew herself not to be witty, but her eyes were certainly sparkling with anger by this point, and she forbore to question her beloved any further in case any more invidious comparisons were made, instead turning back to pound out her feelings on to the keyboard of the pianoforte.

'Miss Payne plays the piano divinely,' said her fond Mama, leaning over to confide in her future son. 'Her piano master said that he had never heard anybody play quite like her.'

Sir Cedric was not able to agree that the playing was divine, but fortunately his future mama-in-law did not require his agreement to continue admiring her daughter's performance.

Thus it was that the future Lady Cholmondley found out that there had been Another before Sir Cedric made her his offer, and she put herself on the look-out for any attempt by that paragon of a woman to lure Sir Cedric back. This vigilance extended to instructing his servants to forward on any letters received by Sir Cedric to her own home, where he was spending the majority of his time now, and where they would be living after their marriage until Sir Cedric's parents could be persuaded to retire to a Dower House on their estate. Miss Payne's foresight was rewarded when Mary's packet of letters was delivered to Mr Jones's London house, from where it was taken as instructed directly to Miss Payne's house by an obedient servant, and put straight into her hands.

Something about the size of the packet, the elegance of the paper, even the hand-writing of the direction, immediately gave Miss Payne a strong suspicion that this packet was from Sir Cedric's former love. Furthermore, the size of the packet indicated to Miss Payne that her fiancé's partiality for this woman of so many virtues might have manifested itself in letter writing, although she had yet to see him with a quill in his hand herself. In Sir Cedric's fortuitous absence, his fiancée felt herself entirely justified in opening the packet and was rewarded for her jealous vigilance when a quantity of letters written by Sir Cedric himself tumbled out on to her table.

Mary had not thought to erase the direction on the letters, as it did not occur to her that anybody other than Sir Cedric would see them; and so Sir Cedric's fiancée now knew the name of the paragon she had been compared with and found wanting. Miss Payne was not in the least in love with Sir Cedric; but she wanted to be Lady Cholmondley, and live on his estate (once vacated by his parents), and have a London house and a large income, and she did not at all care to have written evidence of her future husband's previous love. That Mary had returned the letters was a point in her favour, to be sure, but Miss Payne did not know whether the other half of this fervent correspondence was currently being treasured by Sir Cedric at his own home.

Her next move was clear; she must go to his house, and either demand that he destroy any letters from Miss Crawford, or search the house in his absence, and find them for herself. The second option was less dignified, and would expose her to the censure of his servants; and so she decided to visit him, suitably chaperoned by her fond mama, and watch him burn any letters from Miss Crawford that he might have kept. This course of action having been decided to her own satisfaction, she turned her attention to the letters themselves, wondering just what it was that had required Sir Cedric to write so many letters to this Miss M_ C_.

Pushing the letters about on the table top, she selected one at random, and opened it. Although she knew they were from Sir Cedric to Miss M_ C_, and might reasonably be expected to be love letters, she could not in all her wildest imaginings have foreseen that her fiancé had stooped to rhyme to express his devotion.

The poem now revealed to her astonished gaze, ran thus:

*To Miss M_ C_*
She, whom all the world should know
Doth twin perfect eyebrows grow.
They float, like to two gentle doves,
Above two eyes I confess to love.
Each hair lies straighter than a quill,
Beside brother hairs, smooth and still.
Black though they be, t'is true,
Glossy as a blackbird wing,
In shades from jet to inky blue,
The sight of them makes my poor heart sing!
I can but gaze, and weep and sigh,
And hope to see them bye and bye.

Miss Payne was at first astonished: and then she became very angry. Unlike Mrs Grant, she found the poem to be wholly defective in composition, and had taste enough to know that this wooing was very badly done indeed; but her anger was chiefly directed at Sir Cedric for not writing such poems to her! She was now his accredited fiancée, and so far he had written her nothing but badly scribbled notes to confirm his attendance at their family dinners, or with paltry excuses for his non-attendance, such as having run out of cravats! She stood and walked slowly over to a looking-glass to examine her own, clearly inferior, light brown eyebrows, and to wonder briefly if she should attempt to darken them. Then she returned to her desk, and picked out another letter at random.

In this, Sir Cedric had turned his poetic efforts to capture Miss Crawford's elasticity of gait; but as he spelled it 'gate', his puzzled fiancée took some time to discover its meaning. As she opened more and more letters, there were revealed many more poems in the same vein, each focusing on a different aspect of Miss Crawford's character or person; each as bad as the others. Furious, Miss Payne gathered them all up and secured them again, before stowing them away in her desk against a moment when she could confront her fiancé. Until then, she decided to consult her dearest friends about this shocking discovery; and thus Mary's disappointment in love became widely talked of amongst the ladies of Miss Payne's intimate circle.

As we know, such stories rarely stay within the circle they were first intended for, and soon the matter of the letters and poems was more widely known, with Miss Payne presented as a victim, Sir Cedric as an innocent dupe, and the Miss he wrote his poems to was branded a dangerous woman for easily taken-in men to be around. Although Miss Payne was very careful never to name her former rival for Sir Cedric's affections, his attentions to Miss Mary Crawford over many months had not gone unnoticed by society. It became gradually clear to Mary that something had gone amiss with the return of Sir Cedric's letters, by the way she was greeted and treated by other women. There was a sort of snicker arising all around her, and knowing looks were exchanged on the edge of her sight; cards were no longer being left daily at her sister's house requesting their attendance at all the smart parties, and her own invitations were refused.

Until her brother could return to defend her, Mary found herself wishing that there was some way she could leave London, as she had confidence that by the time she returned, the matter would all be forgotten. Sir Cedric would be married, and gone to his country estate, and society would have moved on to the next light amusement. Unfortunately, all her friends were currently in London, or sent back excuses as to why she could not stay with them at present, such a shame, visitors in every bed chamber for months to come, and empty endearments, meant that Mary had to stay with her sister, and wait for her brother's return.

Now that she had the evidence of Sir Cedric's forlorn former passion in her own hands, Miss Payne had to ascertain whether Miss Crawford had been as equally indiscreet in her admiration of Sir Cedric as he had been of her. Whilst it was unclear to Miss Payne just what qualities Miss Crawford might have found in Sir Cedric to praise in prose or poetry, she was determined that he should not have those letters as a keep-sake of his former passion.

Accordingly, she and her mother presented themselves at his London lodgings at a time carefully calculated to find him on the brink of leaving to pay the daily visit to her that Miss Payne had insisted upon since their engagement. He was all astonishment to see her and his mother-in-law-to-be being shown in by his man, but as Miss Payne was to discover, his conscience was clear – there were no letters from Mary in his possession. Instead, Miss Payne and her mother watched as Sir Cedric burned all his letters to Mary Crawford one by one in the fireplace, and showed them his desk in which there was a confusion of unpaid bills, but no letters from anybody at all, with which they had to be content.

CHAPTER FIFTEEN

Dexter returned to report to his master that the new Mr and Mrs Andersen had not been at all welcoming to him; they clearly wanted to put their servant days well behind them now that they had an independence, and were not inclined to receive a manservant as a visitor. However, he had been able to talk to a servant of theirs, who said that there was much talk in the neighbourhood of the lady who was being kept away from public view, and that the ladies in the vicarage knew all about her.

Accordingly, Henry waited on Mrs Pagan at the Vicarage, introducing himself as a man looking for an estate of his own in the neighbourhood.

Mrs Pagan received him with great interest; visitors of his degree not being frequent, and with hopes that he might take one of her daughters off her hands, and install her at his new estate. In this hope Mrs Pagan was but the latest in a long line of Mamas to be disappointed, but for now she had hopes of Mr Crawford. Miss Pagan was in caps, but Miss Catherine was out and her four younger sisters were hoping she would marry soon, so that they could make their own come-outs in turn. Miss Lucy, Miss Anne, Miss Elizabeth, and Miss Elinor had long been petitioning their parents for their own share of society and amusement, claiming that it was very hard upon them to be denied this because Miss Pagan and Catherine had not the opportunity to marry. It did not, they concluded, promote sisterly affection or delicacy of mind. Mrs Pagan supported them in this wish, and pointed out privately to her husband that Miss Anne was rightly considered a beauty, and that should she marry well, it would throw other rich men in her sisters' way. But there was nothing come of any of these petitions; Mr Pagan was old-fashioned, and insisted upon only one daughter out at a time, while Mrs Pagan endeavoured to console her younger daughters with the practical observation that they had not the money to bring more than one out at a time anyway. Poor Miss Anne had to hope that it would not be many more years before she could be brought out, and that she would not lose her looks in the meantime.

'And so, you are come into Champford looking for an estate to purchase, Mr Crawford?'

'Yes, Ma'am. London is well enough during the season, but at other times it is oppressive to the spirits, and I am much taken with the country hereabout. Do you know of anything suitable which may be available to purchase?'

Miss Pagan entered with hot water for the tea, there not being a maidservant fit to serve a visitor of Mr Crawford's calibre; the Pagans could afford a cook and a kitchen maid, but no manservant, and Mr Pagan did not keep his own horses.

'I regret that I cannot recommend anywhere that I know of near Champford,' said Mrs Pagan, watching her daughter out of the corner of her eye to make sure she did not take too much tea out of the caddy. 'Unless the Yardleighs were to quit Champford Hall. No, really, there is nowhere to match it close by.'

Miss Pagan handed Henry his tea, and then they were joined by Miss Catherine, with a small plate of rout cakes, which she handed around cheerfully.

Henry accepted one, merely to ingratiate himself, but found to his surprise that it was really very good indeed.

'I declare, Ma'am, this is the best rout cake I have ever tasted. My compliments to your cook.'

Mrs Pagan bowed her head graciously, but forbore to inform Mr Crawford that the cook in question was Miss Pagan; their own domestic not having skill or patience for such delicacies. All the Misses Pagan had to turn their hands to domestic duties, including cooking, as there were not servants enough for all the work.

The conversation became about Henry after that, with both the Misses Pagan eager to hear all about life in London, and about his sisters. Finally, Henry was able to turn the conversation back to Champford Hall.

'I believe the family to be in London at present, ma'am?' he said to Mrs Pagan. 'Does the housekeeper admit visitors to see over the Hall?'

'Oh yes,' said she. 'The family is seldom at home, but there is a very superior housekeeper called Mrs Southworth, who I am certain would show you the principal rooms if you sent your man to make an appointment.'

'And what of the estate?' asked Henry. 'Does the family not return to tend to the estate?'

'They have not been back these five years,' said Mrs Pagan. 'Although they do not neglect the estate, they have a very good land agent. The estate workers are well looked after, and there is even a priest who lives on the estate to tend to their spiritual needs as well.'

'Mr Pagan is not the vicar for the Champford Hall estate?'

'Oh! No,' Miss Pagan said, pleased to be able to give Mr Crawford some information. 'Mr Ricket does the duties for the servants and estate workers, and for the ladies in the Dower House.'

Henry felt certain that he had arrived at some very important information, but he did not wish to seem over-eager, so he asked;

'Would that be Lord M_'s mother and her servants?'

'The Dowager Lady Yardleigh lives in Bath,' said Miss Catherine, knowingly. 'And the house is let to a very mysterious lady indeed!'

'Now, Catherine!' warned her mother, 'Mr Crawford is not come here to listen to gossip!'

'Sorry, mama,' said Catherine, not at all abashed. 'But it is just like a horrid novel, really it is!'

'Firstly,' said her mother in stern tones, 'I cannot understand how you would know what a horrid novel is like, and secondly, it is unchristian to speculate in such a manner about people we have not met, and know nothing of.'

'Yes, mama,' said Catherine, and subsided into a chair.

There was a little silence, and then as there seemed little chance of the Misses Pagan being permitted to tell him any more about the mysterious occupant of the Champford Hall Dower House, Henry took his leave, with many compliments to Mr Pagan, regrets at having missed meeting him on this occasion, and promises to return for a family dinner when he would be sure to be at home.

As Henry left the Vicarage, he reflected that he seemed to be making a habit of late of visiting families when the man of the house was absent. The thought first amused him, and then was succeeded by the remembrance of the last time he had eaten rout cakes; and this memory in turn gave rise to a little melancholy at the thought of Mrs Gently and Miss Waldegrave waiting in their sitting room, and him not coming to visit them. He had made his apologies to them before he left London, saying he had business to attend to in the country and would be back soon, when he hoped to have the honour of calling on them again. This permission was graciously given by Mrs Gently, and rather more enthusiastically by Miss Waldegrave, and Henry wondered what she would think if she knew his actual destination and purpose in leaving London at this most interesting time in their relationship. Mrs Gently was unlikely to speculate on either, or possibly even notice if he never came to see them again.

Henry returned to the Inn, confident that he was on the right track at last, and wrote again to his sisters:

'My dearest sisters

I have made some progress, although Dexter has once again been rejected by a fellow manservant. The fellow Andersen and his wife are set up in a snug little cottage on the outskirts of Champford, but are now above their company, and would not allow him over the threshold; it seems they no longer wish to associate with servants on an equal footing. In the brief conversation he managed to have with them before being ejected, neither would admit to having any information about Maria. However, not all servants are turned snob, and a maidservant of theirs was rather taken with Dexter and followed him out with some ruse or other to tell him that the ladies at the Vicarage might have information of use to him; so accordingly, I bent my footsteps thither.

The vicar's family is the highest in Champford, but they live in a very low way indeed; I cannot think the parish brings in enough to support a married man with quantities of daughters. However, before Mama stopped them talking, the Misses told me there was a mysterious woman at the Champford Hall Dower House, so that is my next destination.

Your loving brother

Henry'

Leaving Dexter to continue his enquiries amongst the serving classes, Henry explored about the country side by horse, and quickly located Champford Hall. It was indeed the grandest residence in the country, and he admired the well-kept fields and villages, and saw evidence of enclosure, as well as woodland for game. There was much he could have learned from the land agent to put into practice at Everingham, and he toyed idly with schemes to offer high wages to lure away Yardleigh's land agent, and dismiss Madison. But he decided against calling in to interview the housekeeper in case she alerted the priest to his presence, and if the priest were a visitor at the Dower House, he might carry the information there. Instead, he located the Dower House, with the assistance of a passing carter, and observed it from as great a distance as he could. However, there was nothing to see but servants going about their business; there was no sign of the house's occupants.

That evening, Henry reviewed his progress. He had been in Champford for two weeks already, and had not yet positively located Maria. He decided that one more week would be reasonable to continue the observation of the Dower House, and if there were no glimpse of her, then he would consider his duty done, return home, and make Miss Waldegrave an offer.

Henry took up his station near the Dower House each successive morning, and as far as he was aware, none of the inhabitants had noticed his presence. His patience was rewarded a few days later when from his station nearby, Henry could see some servants gathered outside the front door, and a coach and cart already to horse, waiting to leave. To his very great surprise, Mrs Norris came bustling out, and scolded several of them back in again, before coming back outside with armfuls of wraps and baskets, and, even at a distance, Henry could hear her scolding them all for their tardiness.

CHAPTER SIXTEEN

Maria's maid, Sarah, was standing in the hall-way, deeply unhappy at being left behind again, and giving one of the housemaids some small commissions to transact for her in Champford. Unusually for someone so self-absorbed, Maria on passing through the hall-way had noticed Sarah's petulance at being left behind every week, and on this day decided to intervene.

'Sarah had much better go with you, aunt,' she said. 'I have the bad headache and will go to bed. She will not need to attend upon me while I sleep, and you will all be back by the time I awake.'

'Very well,' Mrs Norris replied distractedly, too busy with arranging everyone else's wraps and belongings for the outing to have the energy to protest. 'Sarah, get your things for you are to come too this time, but do not expect to come next week, for Mrs Raworth may well have need of you and it is not right that she is left here alone.'

As Sarah flew gratefully to collect her wraps, Maria made her way up to her bedroom, and Mrs Norris chivvied the other servants outside to where the horse and cart was waiting for them, and the barouche was waiting for her. She did have a moment's uneasiness about leaving Maria alone against Sir Thomas's instructions, but she argued herself out of it by reminding herself that he was not due to visit, that nobody else had ever called on them, and that Maria was to go to sleep and would not venture out of the house. Her reasoning continued with; it was also a very quiet house, not near to any other habitation except the Great Hall, and there was nobody there that might visit except Mr Ricket, and he knew it was the servants' day out, and would not come. So, assuring herself that all would be well, she ordered the coach to set off, with the servants' cart following behind. Thus, with a bang of the front door, Maria was alone for almost the first time in her whole life.

Outside in the lane, hidden behind a tree, Mr Crawford watched the party exit and had recognized Mrs Norris immediately. There was now no doubt that he had found his quarry. He briefly wondered why he and Mary had not thought that Mrs Norris might be the dragon engaged to guard Maria during her exile, then he dismissed the thought as something to add to his next letter home, and watched the carriage and the cart disappear, before leading his horse up the sweep. As no servant came to take his horse to the stable, he supposed all the outdoor servants were also gone with Mrs Norris, so he tied the reins to a pillar and knocked at the front door.

Upstairs in her own sitting room, Maria heard the knock with great surprise. As Mrs Norris had reasoned to herself not ten minutes earlier, nobody had ever attempted to call at the house, and her father did not usually knock as he had his own key to the door. Also, her aunt would not have gone if Sir Thomas were expected to visit. Maria had never been completely alone or had to answer a front door in her entire life, and it was with a sense of double novelty that she walked down the stairs and opened the door.

Henry pretended a very pretty surprise, but Maria was shocked to the very core at the sight of him, standing where she had never thought to see him, and fell fainting into his arms. This was a very promising start indeed. Henry caught her up, noticing as he did so that she weighed far less than the last time he had held her thus, and a small stab of pity pierced his heart. He carried her into the hall-way, and kicked the nearest door open with his booted foot, hallooing as he did so. No servant came running at the noise, so he laid Maria on the nearest sopha, and looked in a nearby cupboard for a restorative.

Hearing a noise behind him, he turned around to find Maria sitting up on the sopha, looking at him with wide eyes huge in her white face. 'Henry! What do you do here? How did you find me?'

Henry handed Maria a glass of brandy, which she drank in one go, still staring at him as though she expected him to disappear as suddenly as he had appeared. Sitting himself down beside her, Henry took great pleasure in outlining all the different stages of his discovery of her whereabouts, and if he glossed over the part his sisters had played in the scheme, we will not judge him too harshly. He was finding all the reward for his cleverness in the widening of Maria's eyes, and in the colour returning to her cheeks amidst her exclamations of surprise and admiration.

Henry made sure to leave long before Mrs Norris and the servants were expected to return, but the visit had been well worth it. Maria was just as much under his power as she had been before, but now there was no inconvenient husband or father to protect her. She herself seemed softened, and not at all angry with him as she had been before. He found his feelings towards her really had changed; he actually felt sorry for her, locked away in the depths of the countryside with only her aunt for company for so many years, while had had been living at his ease in London.

It had been agreed between them that he would call again the following week when Mrs Norris and the servants took their afternoon out, and Henry had decided to himself that he would unveil his plan for their second elopement to Maria at the same time. She did not appear to be looking beyond next week's precious visit, but Henry was determined to play Prince Charming to the hilt, and to rescue her from this fastness. If marriage was the only way to do this, then marriage it would have to be.

Henry considered the idea as he rode his horse back to the Inn at Champford, and handed it into Dexter's care; and he could see little disadvantage in it. Sir Thomas would give Maria her settlement, and then the newly-weds could express contrition enough to be re-admitted privately into the family, even if Sir Thomas's pride would not allow them back into the local society around Mansfield Park. Then Fanny would have to smile upon him as he was now her brother.

London was another matter all-together. Rushworth was in town with his new bride, but Henry thought it would be rather a good joke if he and Maria were to appear in society as a married couple. There was also the estate in Norfolk to consider; maybe it was time to settle down and live there, and play the part of the local squire. On his rare visits to Everingham, Henry had found the countryside soothing to his spirits; there might even be a child, a son to inherit after him; the Admiral would be glad to see the inheritance was secure. Although he was no friend to marriage, even the Admiral had to admit that a wife was necessary for the production of a legitimate heir.

Furthermore, in marrying Maria, Henry might hope for an assistant, a friend, a guide in every plan of utility or charity for Everingham: a somebody that would make Everingham and all about it a dearer object than it had ever yet been, and keep him fixed there. He could consult her about Maddison; about improvements to tenants' cottages, about everything! And from what he knew of Maria, she would not hesitate in giving her opinion and advice, unlike Fanny, who always shrank from any such appeal. For the first time, Henry was aware of a small resentment against Fanny; a disappointment in her, that he had not felt before, allied with a growing certainty that Maria would be a better mistress at Everingham than Fanny could ever have been.

Moreover, society about Everingham was small, and he was certain that the local families would welcome Maria; the scandal could not have touched them so far from where it happened. Henry made a very good dinner, confident that this time everything would work in his favour, and there would be no more scandal.

He wrote again to his sisters;

'My dearest sisters

I have found our Sleeping Beauty! As you suspected, my dear Mary, the Dower House outside Champford Hall is the location of Maria, and the dragon guarding her is none other than our old friend, Mrs Norris. Luckily she is no better a guardian of her niece than she was when she encouraged the match with Rushworth, and I was able to see Maria alone, after Mrs Norris took all the servants out of the house for the afternoon.

If you are still happy to receive Maria into your house, my dear sister Grant, I will propose to her that we leave for London as soon as we can be assured that she will not be prevented, and will come straight to you. If she chooses to come with me, I will take rooms for myself elsewhere, so that all the proprieties are preserved. Even if Maria does not wish to marry me, I think it my duty to rescue her from Mrs Norris at least.

Oh, and I must tell you, Dexter has been working hard on our behalf to locate Maria, and came to me this evening all proud to have made the acquaintance of her maid, and to have discovered the ladies who live at the Dower House on the Champford Hall estate. Poor fellow! He was most downcast when I had to tell him that his was old news, and that I had already discovered our quarry at the Dower House. Still, if the maid is loyal to Maria, we have an ally in the house now, and that can only be good.

I will inform you when we leave Champford. I suspect I shall have to leave soon in order to save Dexter from all the maids he has been wooing to breach of promise point, or he will no doubt be pursued by all their fathers, and I will have to buy them all off or lose him to the most persistent!

Until then

Your loving brother

Henry.'

CHAPTER SEVENTEEN

Mrs Norris harried all the servants back in to the house in time for a light supper. Maria made certain she was discovered in her bed by Sarah, and had to be gently roused to partake of some refreshments in the breakfast room. Even that one visit by Henry had given Maria a new lease of life, for it gave her hope that her incarceration was nearly at an end. The revival of her lover's interest, and the hope of freedom had such an immediate effect that Maria had quite come back into her bloom. This did not go unnoticed by her Aunt Norris, who attributed the revival of her niece's spirits to the healthy country air, the good plain country-grown food, and the spiritual guidance she had been receiving regularly from Mr Ricket.

Had she known that the guidance Maria had been receiving was physical, rather than spiritual, Aunt Norris would not have remained so sanguine, nor would she have continued with her weekly outings to the local town.

Maria did not listen any more to her aunt than she did before, but she was triumphant. Henry had not asked her to elope, but his reappearance had given rise in her mind to the hope of a second elopement, and this was the vindication of all her suffering over the years of exile with Aunt Norris; she was confident this time the elopement would be followed by marriage. She was determined to forget that the last time they had attempted to live together, it had ended in disappointment, with her wretched because he would not marry her. This time they would be married, and all the bad temper and feelings of hatred that she had harboured towards him were swept away in the exultation of his reappearance in her life. She did not ask herself why she thought he would propose now, having refused to marry her before, but she would not think that it had anything to do with the fact that Fanny was married to Edmund. Nothing mattered but that Mr Crawford would be her husband, and she would be restored into society, with a respectable marriage, an estate of her own, even if it was in Norfolk, and with all the privileges of rank and status returned to her. She would hold her head very high, and forget the misery of the past.

Aunt Norris had never known her niece so compliant, and cheerful.

'Well, Maria,' said she over breakfast one morning, 'I must say that this country air agrees with you most wonderfully. You have quite got back your bloom. I am sure that Sir Thomas will agree when he comes, that I have looked after you very well, and that you are quite restored to yourself again. However, I do not take upon myself all the credit for your looks; the air in this country is very good indeed, and you have been taking your daily walk about the garden. I told you it was most healthful exercise to take, and would bring some colour back to your face, and I notice you have started to eat a little more too. Although the food we eat here is plain, it is both wholesome and nourishing, and I have hopes that Mrs Southworth will allow us into the kitchen garden again this summer, where there is far more fresh vegetables than the Hall could want just for their staff. No, no, it would be of benefit to them to share; as plants need to have their produce picked, or they will rot in the ground, and I cannot abide waste of any sort. Also, Mr Ricket has been coming every day as I promised Sir Thomas, and I am certain that the instruction you have been receiving from him has also helped with your looking so well again.'

Maria smiled, but said nothing, and life went on as before, except that now she had a delicious secret from her aunt, but also that the days went much more slowly until Henry could come again on the day of the servants' half day out.

The problem that Maria was wrestling with while her aunt engaged in self-congratulation was that each time Mrs Norris and the servants went to Champford, she could not keep pretending to have the headache in order to be left alone, but she would have to come up with some other scheme to prevent Sarah from being left behind. If Sarah went with the other servants, and a male servant was left to satisfy the proprieties, Maria could easily send him out into the grounds to perform some tasks well away from the house; and Henry would be able to visit unseen again. Accordingly, she introduced the idea to her aunt at breakfast that morning.

Mrs Norris was always distracted on the morning of the servants' half day out, as she took it upon herself to arrange every last detail, and consequently it was easier for Maria to make her suggestion than it might have been on an ordinary day.

'Aunt,' said she, 'it is very good of you to take the servants yourself into Champford each week. It cannot be easy for you to arrange all of this.'

'Well, my dear Maria,' said Mrs Norris, both distracted by the thought of all that had to be arranged, and pleased that her niece had noticed how much trouble it was to her. 'I do not at all regard the trouble to myself, as you know. I am only sorry that you are not able to come with me, there are some shops in Champford – still, I am able to carry out any small commissions you may have in the town, things which we are not able to obtain locally, although dear Sir Thomas does bring some necessities and luxuries every time he visits, but you do not see him my dear. I would not say that I think him in ill-health, but the journey is wearying to a man of his age, and no doubt he is tired by the time he arrives, and I think his visits will become less frequent now that he is satisfied that we are well settled here. Still, the servants must have some time off from their duties, they do work hard, but I am thinking always of the credit of our family, and do not think it at all wise for them to go into the town unsupervised, and so I do not consider the inconvenience to myself at all having to accompany them, I assure you. However, now that you are so much better in your health and looks than you were this time last week, I will tell Sarah she must stay here with you again in case you have need of her.'

'Indeed Aunt, you are very careful indeed, and most considerate,' replied Maria. 'But Sarah has only had one outing into Champford where the other servants go every week. I have nothing for her to do for me today, so I am happy for her to go too. I have some reading from the Bible that Mr Ricket bade me pay attention to, and I shall be well occupied until your return. Or perhaps one of the men might be left instead? There is always work for them to do out of doors, where they would not disturb my reading.'

Mrs Norris thought about this briefly. Her dislike of Sarah, and her reluctance to give the maid a treat she felt she did not deserve, won out, however, and she said;

'No indeed, Sarah shall not go, my dear. It is not right that you should be left alone. I did not mind it last week, for you were ill and took to your bed, but this week you are below stairs, and somebody may call. I cannot leave you without a servant, and you will not be able to walk out into the garden either if Sarah does not stay.'

'Very well, Aunt,' said Maria, not wishing to arouse Mrs Norris's suspicions by any further resistance.

While Mrs Norris ordered the carriage and the cart to be brought round, and began to assemble the servants in the hall, Maria went upstairs to her own sitting room. She rang for Sarah and told her that she was not to go this time, and gave her some little chores to do about the rooms. Sarah was very upset for she had greatly enjoyed her previous outing, and had been very much looking forward to spending another afternoon at the Inn in Champford where she had met a man who had been most flatteringly interested in her, and the things she had to tell him about her employers. However, there was nothing to be done, so she tidied away the very few things that Maria had left out, and listened to the sounds of Mrs Norris harrying all the other servants out to the waiting cart, while the coachman handed her into the waiting carriage. Maria was standing by the window watching the departure, and both women could also hear Mrs Norris scolding the servants under the pretext of not wanting to inconvenience the coachmen and the horses, such noble beasts to be kept waiting in such sun, and the coachman in his great cape too, it was not right that he … the rest of the harangue was lost in the sounds of the horses beginning to move.

As soon as the sound of horses' hooves had died away, Maria turned to her maid and said, 'I have changed my mind; I do not need you to attend on me today. You may go into Champford after all. Here is some money to pay a carter to take you. I expect you back before the other servants; there is no need to trouble Mrs Morris with bringing you back.'

Sarah gratefully seized the purse her mistress held out to her, and hurried upstairs to fetch her wraps. It was easy to find a carter heading into Champford for market day, and Sarah arrived very shortly after the other servants, but was careful not to be seen by any of them. As the carter had waved away her offer of payment, and told her what time he would be going back again when he was done, Sarah had the luxury of more money than usual to spend, and hurried off to the Maid's Head to meet up with the valet she had met the previous week. His name was Robert, and he was staying at the Inn with his gentleman. He was waiting in the Inn's yard, hoping she would come, looking out for her and was most interested again to hear what she had to say about Maria and Mrs Norris, and the comings and goings of one Sir Thomas.

Sarah had quite made up her mind that Sir Thomas was one of the seducers of young women that she had read about in the novels she had taken secretly from the bookshelves in the library at the Dower House. She had plenty of time to read as Maria had not required much in the way of attendance, until these last two weeks, when suddenly she had started to spend many hours in front of her looking glass, and calling on Sarah to concoct various preparations to brighten her complexion. It did not take much more than this for Sarah to realise that something had changed, and that whatever it was had happened recently. Sir Thomas had not visited for several weeks, however, and Maria had not received any letters; but nonetheless, Sarah was convinced that he was the cause of her mistress's altered behaviours.

Sarah was not much in Maria's confidence, but she liked to think she was. Still, there was plenty of other speculation and supposition to share without this, and Robert was again most agreeably interested in all that she had to say about her mistress, and the Dower House, and the visits by the mysterious Sir Thomas, and they passed a second most enjoyable afternoon. Sarah missed meeting up with the carter for the return journey, and Robert offered to escort her part of the way back to the Dower House in a hired chaise instead. She had had to walk the last half a mile, but still arrived back at the Dower House before Mrs Norris returned with the other servants. Before they parted, Sarah told Robert she had hopes of being again in Champford the following week at this time, and he bowed over her hand, and said he would be waiting impatiently for the days to pass. It was all most pleasing.

CHAPTER EIGHTEEN

The week passed slowly to Maria, but pass it did, and on the morning of the servants' afternoon out, she told her aunt that she had some errands for Sarah in Champford that she did not wish to burden her aunt with, knowing how much she had to do already. These were things Sarah understood, and could carry out for Maria but which would be onerous for her aunt to attend to. But Mrs Norris had not been easy in her own mind since she had left Maria alone a sen'night previously;

'No, my dear,' said she. 'If Sarah is to go, although I do not agree that she deserves to, then one of the housemaids must stay with you instead. I promised dear Sir Thomas to keep you safe, and I shall keep you safe, no matter the inconvenience to myself. If Sarah is to stay, then give your commissions to one of the other maids to carry out for you; she can have little else to do with the time, and it will give her some respectable occupation to keep her out of any trouble.'

There was nothing Maria could do but hand her list of requirements over to one of the other maids, bow to her aunt's dictum to keep Sarah at home, and then give over her not inconsiderable intelligence to putting Sarah out of the house in time for Henry's arrival with a task that would occupy her until he left again.

Knowing that Henry would appear as soon as Mrs Norris and the servants were gone, Maria told Sarah to go across to the Hall and ask Mrs Southworth for some receipts that had been promised to Mrs Morris, and to take the opportunity to look in their kitchen garden in search of some herbs she wished to use to make a new preparation. Maria deliberately chose unusual herbs which would require Sarah to ask one of the Hall's gardeners to assist her in discovering, as they were quite out of the usual run of herbs gathered from the Hall's herb garden for the Dower house's use. However, as this was something Maria had never asked her to do before, Sarah was instantly suspicious; so she pretended to leave, but instead concealed herself in the hall-way closet. The hope of discovering Sir Thomas making a secret visit was enough to sustain her through the disappointment of not being able to meet up with Robert in Champford; she wondered if she could write to him, and ask him to visit her at the Dower House instead. They could meet out of sight in the extensive grounds, and she could tell him what had occurred when she had been left at home by Mrs Morris.

Only a few minutes after Mrs Morris and the servants left, Sarah heard footsteps come creeping down the stairs. She could not see much from her position in the closet, but she could hear the front door open, and heard a man's voice – a man who did not sound in the least like the Sir Thomas who visited Mrs Morris, and whom Maria greeted as, 'Henry!'

There was then the sound of two people mounting the stairs together, and then a door shut and there was silence.

Heart thumping, Sarah let herself out of the closet and walked as quietly around the house as she knew how. Whoever this 'Henry' was, Maria had taken him straight up the stairs. Sarah crept quietly as possible up the stairs; there was nobody in Maria's own sitting room, and the only door which was closed on this landing was Maria's bedroom door. Sarah crept as close as she dared, but the doors were thick, and she could hear nothing; so she crept back down stairs again to Mrs Morris's parlour, which looked out on to the front as well, and there was a gentleman's horse tethered to the front gate, bold as brass!

Sir Thomas always came in a carriage, and Mrs Morris always made such a pother about the horses being taken round to the stables, and the coachman, and the footmen being taken in to the kitchen, where they sat in state, eating and drinking stolidly, and refusing to answer any questions. So, this 'Henry' was not another name for Sir Thomas it seemed. Conscious of the time, and not knowing how long this Henry would stay above stairs with Maria, Sarah hunted through Mrs Morris's things for some information about Sir Thomas – Sarah knew that it was his money which kept them all in this house, and wondered if he knew about this 'Henry' visiting Maria.

Sarah had other motives for wanting to alert Sir Thomas to Henry's visit, the chief amongst them being to revenge herself upon Maria, who had done nothing to stop Mrs Morris from telling Sarah that she was to be turned off without a character following Sir Thomas's next visit. She was in the hopes that Sir Thomas would be grateful to be informed of this visitor, and might take Sarah into his own employ, or give her a pension which would enable her to live independently of service, and possibly even to marry. And here Sarah gave full rein to her imagination, and saw herself in service no more, like the Andersens she had heard about in Champford, in her own cottage, free from demanding employers. However, time was moving on, and Sarah needed to find the information leading to Sir Thomas before Maria and Henry came back down the stairs again, and Maria asked where were the receipts she had been sent to fetch, and the herbs she had been asked to pick?

Finally, she found a letter from Sir Thomas to Mrs Morris, addressed to 'My dear Sister Norris', which puzzled Sarah, and giving an address, which Sarah memorized before putting the letter back where she found it. Why did Sir Thomas think Mrs Morris was called 'Mrs Norris', unless it was just a trick of his hand-writing to turn an 'M' into an 'N'? Sarah could not think of another solution to that puzzle, so she carried on searching for any information she could find about anybody called 'Henry'. There was nobody of that name in any of Mrs Morris's correspondence that Sarah could discover, but there were many references to a 'Mrs Rushworth' which puzzled Sarah as well – who was this 'Mrs Rushworth' who featured so much in Mrs Morris's and Sir Thomas's correspondence? The more she thought about it, the more the name of Rushworth was awakening a vague indistinct memory, which the more she tried to grasp at, the more elusive it became. Where had she heard the name 'Rushworth' before?

Sarah knew where Maria had all the society papers hidden, but there was no time to look them out now; she put the problem to the back of her mind, and quietly left the house by the kitchen door to walk across the park to seek out Mrs Southworth, and to find a gardener to direct her to the location of the herbs Maria had specified.

Later, when Maria and Mrs Morris were at dinner, and Sarah was not required to attend them, and was supposed instead to be preparing Maria's bed chamber, she pulled out the pile of society papers and began to look through them. It took her a while, but finally she found a paper from some four years ago with a reference to a Mr R, who was said to be still in London and looking for a new bride, after his previous bride had quitted his house with the *well known and captivating Mr C, the intimate friend and associate of Mr R*. Although the names were not given in full, Sarah suspected that this was important, and so she continued her search, being rewarded with the report of a Mr Rushworth's marriage, and veiled references to his first wife having left him for another man, although she remained unmarried and out of society.

Rushworth was not a name in common usage, such as her own surname of Smith, and so Sarah concluded that she had found the right person. She put the papers back in their concealed place so that Mrs Morris would not discover them, and as she rushed around arranging everything how Maria liked it to be, she was attempting to puzzle it all through. If Mrs Raworth was in fact Mrs Rushworth, and the two names were very similar, then it appeared she had left her husband's protection and run away with his friend. How she had ended up here, Sarah could not begin to imagine; had she but known it, she had the means now to expose Maria, in exactly the same way as the maid-servant of Mrs Rushworth senior, had done previously. But Sarah's reasoning could take her no further; she did not know how the Mrs Rushworth who had left her husband's protection had become the widowed Mrs Raworth, or even whether her suspicions were correct. There was nothing to do now but endeavour to join the other servants on their next half day out to Champford, and consult with Robert; he would know what best to do.

CHAPTER NINETEEN

While Maria was renewing her intimacy with Henry Crawford, her father had allowed himself to become comfortably certain that was all was so well and settled in Champford, that he need not visit quite so often. Instead, he turned his attention to the next matter; that of his heir's marriage, and to welcoming Mrs Fairhaven and her daughter to Mansfield Park. His coach being sent to meet them, they arrived on a clear January afternoon, in great comfort and style, with a hired chaise full of luggage and servants following on behind. Their servants and the luggage being dealt with by Mansfield Park's own efficient servants, the two ladies were shown in to Lady Bertram's parlour. As they were announced, Lady Bertram actually rose up from her sopha to give her hand to Mrs Fairhaven, and Susan and Miss Fairhaven made each other very pretty curtsies. Susan rang for tea, and Sir Thomas came in from his study to express his gratitude at their arrival, pleased that his less agreeable duty to his sister and daughter could now give way to a much more agreeable duty as host.

'Oh! Sir Thomas! Lady Bertram!' cried Mrs Fairhaven, turning from one to the other. 'How kind, how very kind it is of you to invite us to make our stay with you while our house in Wimpole Street is being made ready for us. Well, I say our house, it is of course dear Agnes and John's house now, I am just a poor widow dependent upon my children for my daily crust. Most of the servants have stayed in London to get the house ready for our return, while we came on here at your kind invitation, and what a sweet little room this is! Agnes! Does not it remind you of the small breakfast parlour at *The Great House*?'

Susan looked in surprise at Mrs Fairhaven and then around at the size of the room they were all still standing up in, for no-one had got a word in to invite the guests to sit down. Agnes rolled her eyes expressively and replied;

'No indeed, Mama. This is a far larger room. I do not think I have been in such a large room in all my life.'

'Oh! Do you think so? Well, I must agree with you then, for you know your own mind best, I am sure. Now that I look about me more, I can see that it rather resembles the second drawing room at *The Great House*.'

Sir Thomas now stept forward to stem the flow of comparison, and made Mrs Fairhaven his best bow. She coquettishly extended her hand and he bent over it, before inviting them both to sit down. Mrs Fairhaven he conducted to the sopha next to Lady Bertram, who exerted herself further to enquire;

'Have you come far today, Mrs Fairhaven?'

'Oh! Yes, to be sure! Ever such a long way! Although only from Bristol today. Agnes, how far is it to Antigua? Oh, she is talking to Miss Price. Well, Sir Thomas will know how far it is and what the journey is like, of course, so fatiguing, I do not recommend it; I do not believe you to have been out to your lands in Antigua?'

Sir Thomas leaned forward to say the climate was not thought healthy for Lady Bertram, and that he and his eldest son were the only members of the family to have visited their plantation in Antigua.

'Ah yes, dear Tom, where is he?' asked Mrs Fairhaven, looking about as though she was expecting Tom to be concealed behind a sopha, or standing in the corner with the footmen. 'Such a gentleman; Agnes and John were very pleased with him in Antigua, I assure you. Such good manners, and so attentive.'

'He is a good boy,' said Lady Bertram comfortably. 'You know he nearly died, of course."

Mrs Fairhaven was very shocked;

'Was that after his visit to Antigua? There is all manner of ills that befall white people out there. It is quite shocking, and one reason dear John was so insistent that his sister and I come to live in England, even though it will be very hard for him to manage on his own now, and I did offer to stay and send Agnes back on her own, but he insisted. But dear Tom so ill! How did it happen?'

'Tom had a fall from a horse, and did not take care of his health,' Sir Thomas said quickly when she paused for breath.

'Oh! The poor dear boy! I am always telling John to take better care of himself, but men are not so good at making their health into a priority, are they, my dear Lady Bertram? Tom needs a wife to look after him,' said Mrs Fairhaven with a glance over at where her daughter was deep in conversation with Susan Price.

'And are you looking out for a house in this neighbourhood?' asked Lady Bertram, quite missing Mrs Fairhaven's hint.

'Mrs Fairhaven is here because her house in London is not ready for her after being shut up for so long, my dear,' said Sir Thomas.

'Ah, that is it, I remember you told me.' Said Lady Bertram, picking up Pug and losing interest in the conversation.

'Yes indeed,' said Mrs Fairhaven, 'I have not been to our house since, oh! ever so many years ago. Dear Sir Thomas invited us while the servants open it all up again, and get it aired and cleaned for us. Then I do hope you will come down to London to stay with us in Wimpole Street. You would be most welcome, I assure you.'

Sir Thomas bowed in acknowledgement of this invitation, although he could not like the reference to Wimpole Street, and instead led the conversation around to the conditions on Antigua when Mrs Fairhaven left, and made minute enquiries after all their mutual acquaintance there, glancing from time to time with approval at the pretty sight of his niece talking with Miss Fairhaven in a window seat.

Miss Fairhaven had managed to draw Susan away from the others by asking her to say what that sweet building was which could be seen out of the window across the park. Although once at the window, Miss Fairhaven's attention could no longer be captured by the view, and her thoughts turned instead in quite another direction.

'I gather that you are Lady Bertram's niece, Miss Price,' said she.

Susan agreed that she was.

'And have you always lived with your uncle and aunt?'

'No, I came to live here when I was fourteen.'

'I am so pleased to make your acquaintance; you must tell me all about yourself. There are very few white people out in Antigua and no other young women my age left now. All my friends left Antigua to move back to England when we were quite children, and it takes letters weeks to go back and forth, and it is quite dependent upon the ships and the tides and such like. I shall be able to write to all my friends much more easily now that I am to settle in England. It is indeed a relief to be out of Antigua at last, Miss Price. The heat there is beyond anything; Mama and I were really suffering when John insisted we come to England, and it is what drove all the other families away, I assure you. I cannot call England *home* yet, for I have lived all my life in Antigua. Where did you live before you came to live here, Miss Price?'

'In Portsmouth.'

'Portsmouth! I have never heard of it. Is it near here?'

'It is a port town above a hundred miles away on the south coast.'

'I do not know of it, but we sailed into Bristol,' Miss Fairhaven said. 'Is that near Portsmouth?'

'No, it is quite some distance from there.'

'And do your parents still live in Portsmouth, Miss Price?'

'Yes, they do.'

'If it is a port town, were you ever aboard a ship?'

'No, never.'

Miss Fairhaven looked surprised. 'Well,' said she, 'I find I cannot recommend it. The motion is enough to upset the stomach, and there is little room to walk about. When we ventured up on to the deck, there was so much ropes and the like under-foot that it was hard to take our walk, and so many sailors running about in all directions, and ordering us below again, that it was most provoking. The cabin my mother and I had to share was barely big enough to turn about in, and there were none of the comforts of home. We were aboard a month; I cannot think how the sailors can bear it to go back and forth across the oceans for as long as they do.'

'I will ask my father when next we meet,' said Susan.

Miss Fairhaven visibly drew back. 'Is your father a sailor?' she asked in some alarm.

'He is a retired naval officer,' explained Susan. 'He retired after eleven years active service at sea.'

'He has no command at present? How does he occupy his day?'

'He likes to go down to the docks to see the ships come in, and he spends time with his fellow officers who are at present ashore for want of employment at sea.'

'And your mother?'

'She is much engaged with her house and family.'

'I suppose you know that we left my brother in Antigua? John is such a good brother to me, do you have a brother, Miss Price?'

'I have six brothers.'

'Six! Heaven!'

'And I had three sisters,' Susan added, rather enjoying watching the look of surprise on Miss Fairhaven's face. 'One of them died very young, and another is married to Edmund Bertram, our cousin.'

'Ten children! And did you have a governess?'

'No, we did not.'

'Ten children and no governess! Your mother must have been quite a slave to your education and care! I know Mama was quite fagged out by my brother and I, although we always had a governess, and a nursery maid!'

Susan looked across at Mrs Fairhaven, prosperous, plump and comfortable next to Lady Bertram on the sopha; and assured Miss Fairhaven that it was not so for her own mother. In fact, Susan could not recall her mother teaching her anything at all, but she did not say so to Miss Fairhaven.

'Are all your brothers and sisters still at home?'

'No, two of my brothers are at sea; my eldest is just made a first lieutenant; my sister, Fanny, as you know is married to my cousin Edmund, and they live close by at the Parsonage. As for my other brothers, Sir Thomas has been most generous in paying for their education, and finding placements for them all once they finished school. Betsey, the youngest of us all, is the only one left at home now, and she is full young yet to be thinking of her future.'

Miss Fairhaven was silent for a moment while she considered this. Mr Price might be just enough of a gentleman by virtue of his profession, and Mrs Price was sister to Lady Bertram, but the children had clearly gone down in the world if they were sent out to work, and she was not at all certain that Miss Price was someone it would be in her own best interests to know. However, she was the only other young woman in the house, and was clearly a favourite of Sir Thomas and Lady Bertram, to say nothing of being a cousin to Tom Bertram; all of which were points in her favour. Miss Price's brother being a first lieutenant was another a point in her favour; Miss Fairhaven had seen enough of the chain of command aboard a vessel to know that first lieutenants were important gentlemen, just a step below a Captain. Miss Price's sister Fanny had married well: so, with such a brother and sister, Miss Fairhaven decided she could sink the rest of the children.

All of this passed like lightning through her brain, and she decided that Miss Price would have to do, until a more eligible friend should appear in the person of one of the daughters of the house.

'Now to more important matters,' went on Miss Fairhaven, glancing about her in a stagey manner, before leaning forward and lowering her voice. 'Tell me of the society hereabout, particularly the young men; are there any handsome beaux? Are any of them sensible enough to be paying you their addresses? I declare I have never seen such a delicate complexion as yours; tell me do you use Gowland, or some other preparation of your own devising? I know that I am very brown from the sun in Antigua, although Mama did her best to keep my complexion white with sunshades, still it was very hard to stay out of the sun all of the time.'

Susan could not like this turn of conversation, but while she was thinking of a polite way to reply in the decided negative about young men and face cream; Miss Fairhaven, who was more of a talker than a listener, soon plunged on again.

'Oh! And my dear Miss Price, reassure me I beg of you, that there is an Assembly Rooms nearby. How I long to attend an Assembly and dance every set! We had no Assembly Rooms in Antigua, we had to dance at *The Great House*, but I have heard of Assemblies forever from my friends in England, and they sound heavenly!'

Susan was able to give a decided negative to this enquiry; there was no Assembly Room within easy distance of Mansfield Park. Miss Fairhaven looked a little put out, but soon continued;

'In that case, I am persuaded that Lady Bertram must give many a Ball here. The rooms are so commodious, and perfectly suited to dancing. Are there regular Balls held here, Miss Price?'

Again, Susan was unable to satisfy her questioner on this score;

'Lady Bertram has given very few Balls.'

'Well,' Miss Fairhaven said, 'I dare say she has reached the age where – well, I will not say so for she is a very handsome woman for her age, Tom has her looks, I am happy to say, but she will not be Lady Bertram forever, and maybe in the future, things will be very different, I shall say no more for now.'

And she looked very mysterious, and smiled and nodded, certain that Susan knew to what she was alluding. Susan would not understand her, and was very glad of a diversion caused by the maids bringing in the tea things, followed by Miss Fairhaven's own maid, bringing her a shawl. This maid had accompanied her all the way from Antigua, and her likes had never been seen before in all the country around. Susan could see all the other servants openly staring at Miss Fairhaven's maid, and pitied the poor girl so far from home, and amongst such different people.

Although Susan too had left her family to come to Mansfield Park, she had been older at the time of leaving Portsmouth than had her sister Fanny, and she was a much stronger character as well, so that the separation from her family had benefited her, far more than it had Fanny. Susan was not so much at a loss as Fanny had been when first she came to Mansfield Park, and she had benefited from Fanny's help and guidance until her marriage, where Fanny had been quite alone. Still, Susan knew what it felt like to be far from home, and in a place so very different from the one she had grown up in.

Lady Bertram was looking helplessly at the tea caddies and then around the room for Susan, so she seized the opportunity to excuse herself to Miss Fairhaven, with her impertinent questions and suppositions unanswered, and go over to assist her aunt. In truth, Susan was very glad of the excuse provided to move away from Miss Fairhaven; their conversation had resembled more of an interrogation, and there was something about Miss Fairhaven that Susan could not like. She was uncertain what it was that was repulsive about this young woman, but certainly the close questioning had not endeared her to Susan.

Miss Fairhaven followed Susan across the room, but to Susan's relief, seated herself by her mother, and waited for the maid to bring the tea to her. Then she dismissed the girl. There was no confidential conversation to be had while the Mansfield Park servants were yet in the room, and so the ladies contented themselves with genteel enquiries as to how each of them took their tea, on the relative merits of tea and coffee, and which was preferred by every one of their separate acquaintance, and family members. Mrs Fairhaven vouchsafed that she hoped to drink more chocolate now that she was home, back in England, for the climate in Antigua was not conducive to chocolate drinking, although tea was very much drunk everywhere and by everybody, she assured the present company. She did not wish them to think that society in Antigua was in any way backward compared with England.

Susan enquired whether the climate in Antigua was suited to the growing of tea, but as to that, Mrs Fairhaven had no information to give. Miss Fairhaven gave it as her opinion that tea was grown in India rather than in the Caribbean, and this was seconded by Sir

Thomas, who added that coffee came from Africa, chocolate from the southern Americas, and sugar from Barbados and Antigua.

'Which put all together gives us the most enjoyable choices of refreshment!' declared Agnes, and even Susan could find nothing to disagree with in that.

After all had drank their tea, and the tea-things had been cleared away; Mrs Fairhaven reverted to her question of the whereabouts of Lady Bertram's eldest son.

'I do hope you are expecting Tom to come home soon, Lady Bertram?'

Lady Bertram looked helplessly at her husband for the answer; and realizing that she had no idea where her son was, Sir Thomas coughed to get Mrs Fairhaven's attention and said;

'Tom is visiting friends in Devonshire, Mrs Fairhaven, we are expecting him every day. I do hope that you and Miss Fairhaven will be at liberty to stay with us until Tom arrives?'

'Oh! Certainly we will, is not that why we came, Agnes? We are both looking forward to seeing Tom again so very much, and I carry so many greetings and messages to him from all of his acquaintance in Antigua, and even a letter from John! And he never writes to anybody.'

Agnes blushed prettily, and agreed with her mother. Susan could see Lady Bertram looking from her husband to Mrs Fairhaven, and then to Agnes, with a dawning suspicion of the reason for their presence in her home.

CHAPTER TWENTY

Later, as she went up to dress, Susan reflected on the visitors. Mrs Fairhaven seemed kind enough although prone to being a little tactless, but she was still puzzled as to what was it about Miss Fairhaven that she found harder to like? A knock at the door heralded Miss Fairhaven's maid, who had come to see if she could be of help to Miss Price, Miss Fairhaven always dressing quickly, and she was already gone downstairs, and had sent her maid to assist Miss Price.

Susan was startled by this attention, but seized the opportunity to get to know the girl a little bit.

'I am not in much need of assistance, as I am dressed, but I am very grateful to Miss Fairhaven for sending you. Perhaps if you could help to dress my hair?'

The maid came over and started to arrange Susan's hair into a style she had not yet attempted herself and which was most becoming. Susan thanked her most sincerely, and attempted to draw her out a little, watching the girl's serious face in the mirror. However, it was not easy to get much more than one-word answers; Susan was uncertain whether this was reluctance to talk about herself for fear of being thought forward, or for fear of Miss Fairhaven's disapproval; or whether the girl did not have sufficient command of English to express herself more fully. But under gentle questioning, Susan discovered that the girl was a native of Antigua, her parents having been brought over from Africa to work on Mr Fairhaven's plantation. Her father had died, but her mother and brothers and sisters were yet alive and working in Antigua. She herself was happy not to be working on the plantation, but had found the journey to England frightening, and England's weather too cold for her, as she had been accustomed to the heat on Antigua.

She gave her name as Camba, and Susan noted a curiously defiant lift of the girl's chin as she said her name, but Camba could not be drawn any further. As the maid finished, and stepped back, Susan turned her head from side to side to admire what Camba had done with her hair.

'Oh! How prettily you have dressed my hair! How clever you are! Thank you, Camba!'

Camba dropt Susan a slight curtsey and Susan left her tidying up the dressing table as she made her way down to dinner.

As Susan came down the stairs, Edmund was just coming in through the front door to join them for dinner, and to pay his respects to the visitors. He now came forward to make his bow to his cousin, and to compliment her on her looks, which he said were much improved.

'And there is something different,' he added, looking very seriously at her. 'I cannot think what it is, but you do look different to usual.'

'I think it is my hair,' Susan said. 'Miss Fairhaven kindly sent her maid to help me.'

'She has indeed done it very well,' Edmund said, 'It is quite striking; I cannot see how it is all held in place, but those little curls there, and the way it is swept up, I must remember the detail of how it looked to tell Fanny when I go home.'

'Fanny is not come?'

'No, she is not recovered enough to leave her bed today. I left her resting, and the physician is sent for. I thought it best I came as Tom is not here at the moment. Why he must be forever away at some friend or other's house, I do not know!'

Susan was a little uneasy about Edmund's manner of talking about his wife; he seemed weary, but not overly concerned. It was true that Fanny was more often indisposed than not these days, and maybe it was something very minor this time, but even so, Susan could wish for more solicitude from Edmund. She wondered whether to enquire further into Fanny's particular symptoms, but Edmund was holding out his arm to escort her and there was no more time to ask.

Miss Fairhaven, who had been sitting quietly on a sopha playing with one of Pug's puppies, jumped up and came forward to meet them, and Susan introduced her to Edmund.

'I am very pleased to meet you, Mr Bertram,' she said. 'You are the very likeness of Tom! I am sorry not to meet with your brother here; I had quite depended upon it.'

'You met my brother out in Antigua, did not you, Miss Fairhaven?'

'Indeed I did! He and your dear father were frequent visitors to our home on the plantation. Tom and my brother, John, became very good friends.'

'My brother is blessed with such happy manners as to enable him to make many friends very easily, and he is dedicated to keeping those friendships alive with frequent visits,' said Edmund.

'He is away with friends at the present time?'

'Yes, down in Devonshire. You may know the family; they are the Halletts of Lyme Regis? Although I believe they have a house in Axmouth.'

'I do not know it at all,' said Miss Fairhaven. 'Have you any knowledge of Axmouth, Miss Price?'

Susan denied any knowledge other than that it was on the south coast of England.

'And is Axmouth then a port town?' enquired Miss Fairhaven.

'I believe so, why?'

'They all seem to end with the word 'mouth'; I have heard today of Portsmouth, and Weymouth, and now Axmouth. And then I recall we sailed into Bristol from Antigua; should not the port have been called *Bristolmouth*?'

Susan started to laugh at the joke, but Edmund replied very seriously;

'Axmouth is named after the river Axe where it comes out into the sea, while Bristol is a port-city on the River Avon, and there is indeed an Avonmouth further down the river where it flows out into the sea. Axmouth itself is one of the smaller ports, Miss Fairhaven, I do not believe the transatlantic ships dock there as they do in Bristol, but the Halletts have been long settled there.'

'I do not believe I know the name of Hallett either,' began Miss Fairhaven, and then noticing that Sir Thomas was approaching, called out to him gaily;

'Dear Sir Thomas, do come and tell me if I should know of the Hallett family of ... where was it?'

Sir Thomas approached gravely and bowed slightly before saying, 'Lyme Regis, I believe, although some of the family are settled at Axmouth in a fine new house called Stedcombe. I do not believe you would have met them, Miss Fairhaven, as they trade into Barbados, not Antigua.'

'And it is to this very same Hallett family that Tom makes his visit?'

'To one branch of the family,' said Sir Thomas, 'but we expect him home any day. I have written to inform him of your visit.'

Sir Thomas looked around and then said;

'Is Fanny not come?'

'No, sir. She is once more indisposed.'

Susan again waited for the concern and enquiries into Fanny's health, suggestions for her treatment, and predictions on how long her recovery might be expected to take; but none came. Instead, Edmund turned to Miss Fairhaven;

'My wife begged that you and Mrs Fairhaven would consider yourselves as quite friends already, and dispense with ceremony to visit her as soon as you are able. She is very sorry not to be here to make your acquaintance this evening.'

Miss Fairhaven bowed her head, and said something pretty, and then Edmund asked if she would introduce him to her mother. They moved away from Susan and Sir Thomas towards where Mrs Fairhaven was sitting with Lady Bertram.

'Well, Susan,' said Sir Thomas, when they were safely out of hearing, 'What think you of Miss Fairhaven?'

'She is most charming and considerate, sir,' replied Susan somewhat mendaciously. 'She sent her own maid to assist me at dressing.'

'Did she? Did she indeed? That was most thoughtful, although it prompts me to remember that you are in want of a maid of your own now that you are quite grown up,' said Sir Thomas, turning to look where Miss Fairhaven was performing the introductions between her mother and Edmund. 'I am not the best person to decide upon a lady's elegance or otherwise, but do you think her a lady in every sense of the word?'

'Certainly,' said Susan. 'Do you intend her for my cousin, Tom?'

Sir Thomas frowned a little at her directness, but replied, 'I would not presume to arrange a match for Tom, but Miss Fairhaven being here might incline him towards her, and they have much in common. Mrs Fairhaven and her daughter are to settle permanently in England now, and it would be a most eligible match for them both.'

'He is a friend of her brother too, I hear,' said Susan.

'Yes, all the young people kept very lively company together when Tom and I visited Antigua, although Miss Fairhaven was not out at the time, if I recall correctly, but the customs were a little different out there, less formal than they are here, and so she was very much of the company, and attended all the evening dances and dinners, as well as the picnicking parties.'

'And if Tom is to choose for himself, has he mentioned any eligible daughters in the Hallett family, or amongst his other acquaintance?'

'I have not heard Tom speak of any particular young ladies in Devonshire, although there may be some cousins in a nearby Vicarage, but I do not know enough of the family to give you correct information.'

'We shall have to wait until Tom returns, then,' said Susan, and at that moment dinner was announced, and everybody went through to the dining room. Mrs Fairhaven was quite transported by the room, and remembering her *faux pas* in Lady Bertram's sitting room, she complimented Lady Bertram on the size of the table, the number of chairs, the place settings, the candelabra, until Susan became quite impatient with her. Sir Thomas and Lady Bertram did not seem to notice anything amiss in Mrs Fairhaven's praise; Sir Thomas pointed out some little arrangement which recalled something he had seen at the Fairhaven's home on Antigua, and she declared herself very pleased that he had remembered and attempted to replicate it. Susan tried to catch Edmund's eye, but he was looking grave, and listening to something Miss Fairhaven was saying as they took their seats next to one another.

Susan was sitting between Mrs Fairhaven on one side, and Edmund on the other, both of whom were talking to the person on the other side of them, and she had some moments during the soup for private reflection. It was possible that Sir Thomas's hints about his hopes for Miss Fairhaven and Tom may have been meant for her as a veiled warning not to set her cap at Tom herself. He may have feared that one alliance between cousins might have led to another; but he need not have feared on Susan's account. She had no intention of marrying, not yet at any rate, besides she suspected that Tom had little interest in marriage, and none at all in her; although he must know that the heir to Mansfield Park had a duty to marry. To be sure, Miss Fairhaven was a most convenient bird in the hand, unless there was an eligible cousin in the Vicarage at Axmouth to throw Sir Thomas's scheme into disarray?

As dessert was set on the table, and declined by Mrs Fairhaven and Agnes, Susan managed to alert Lady Bertram to rise and lead the ladies out into the Drawing Room.

CHAPTER TWENTY-ONE

Mrs Fairhaven walked out with Lady Bertram, and Susan found her arm taken by Miss Fairhaven, so she thanked that young woman for sending Camba to help her with her dressing for dinner.

'Camba?' said Miss Fairhaven in surprise. 'Do you mean my maid, Miss Price? That is not her name! Her name is Abigail.'

'She told me it was Camba,' said Susan in some confusion.

'I expect that she thinks that is her native name in Antigua, but it is not so at all. I must tell you, Miss Price, that the plantation workers have some terrible superstitions, and some quite dreadful practices that would horrify you if I were to tell you of them,' and here Miss Fairhaven gave Susan a sideways look, quite clearly inviting her to push for the horrid details, but when Susan did not give her any encouragement, Miss Fairhaven was obliged to continue without. 'The workers and servants give themselves such strange names because of the – rituals, I suppose I must call them, that they brought with them from their native lands. Mr Aylmer was always most concerned to bring them all in to the light of God's grace and save their souls, and my father insisted that all our plantation workers and servants were properly baptized before they could work for us. So, I know for certain that her name is Abigail.'

'Was Mr Aylmer the governor of Antigua?' asked Susan, as they walked towards the drawing room together.

'Oh no!' cried Agnes, 'Mr Aylmer was our priest; Mr Elliot is the Governor of the Leeward Islands.'

'And the Leeward Islands is near to Antigua?'

'Antigua is part of the Leeward Islands,' Miss Fairhaven said rather severely.

Susan thanked her for the information, and once they reached the drawing room, it seemed Miss Fairhaven had no further corrections to give to Miss Price, and instead devoted herself to helping Lady

Bertram wind up some wool. Susan sat down by Mrs Fairhaven, and endeared herself to that lady by asking about her life in Antigua.

'Tell me about Antigua, Mrs Fairhaven; I have never been further from home than Mansfield Park, but you have been half way around the world!'

'Well, my dear, Antigua is one of the Leeward Islands; Bermuda and Bahama are not, as you know in the West Indies, but Barbados is.'

'There were maps and charts in my school-room days, but I do not recall the details to that degree, I regret. I suspect I have never called any of them anything before in my life! Were you born in Antigua?'

'No indeed!' said Mrs Fairhaven, sounding shocked at the question.

'I beg pardon, ma'am, I did not mean to offend you,' said Susan hastily.

'Oh, no, Miss Price, I am not at all offended. My father purchased his estate shortly after his marriage, but my mother did not at all like the heat in Antigua, and the slaves on the plantation frightened her, and so she insisted upon him hiring a man to manage the estate, and returning with her to England. I was born in Bristol, where I lived with my parents until I met Mr Fairhaven at a ball in the Assembly Rooms there.'

'And then you went out to Antigua with Mr Fairhaven to his estate?'

'Yes, we combined our estates after I inherited my parents' estate. My brother died when he was very young.'

'I am sorry to hear that. I had a sister who died very young too.'

'It quite broke my mother's spirit; she was never the same after he died, and followed him to the grave soon after.'

Susan began to see that Mrs Fairhaven was not so silly as she had once thought her; there was a thinking mind beneath the breathless chatter and the excessive admiration.

'The house on Mr Fairhaven's estate was in much better repair than the one on my estate, so we lived there, and it was at that house we had the honour of the visits by Sir Thomas and dear Tom.'

'And is your house there called '*The Great House*'?' Susan asked.

'No indeed. That was the house on the *Sarah's Hope* Estate, the largest on the island, and where they would hold the balls for the young people. My house is called *Jemima Joy*; my dear husband insisted on renaming it after me once we were married.'

'And that is your own house on your parents' plantation, or your husband's?'

'I do apologize, it seems that I am confusing you, Miss Price! My parents built a small house on their plantation, called '*The Rose Arbour*', although my mother never could get her roses to grow there, the gardener *said* he did his best, but I do not think he *understood* roses, there not being any in Africa where he came from. My husband's house was larger and in better suited to our family by the time we married; and he renamed the house *Jemima Joy* as I told you. There was quite a craze to name houses for the owner's wife or daughter.'

'That is a very pretty compliment indeed,' cried Susan. 'Tell me more about your home on Antigua. Are the houses there very different to England, or are they much the same inside?'

'Well, my dear,' began Mrs Fairhaven, looking around to make sure that her daughter was not listening to disagree with her again. 'It was said by everybody who saw it, that it was the second-best house on the island after *The Great House* at *Sarah's Hope*. We had a large hall, and two parlours, a dining room and drawing room, entirely fitted up and furnished with the latest fashions from England. There was Mahogany everywhere, and mirrors in the hall, although we did not give balls there as everybody went to *Sarah's Hope*.'

Susan began to suspect some rivalry between the two estates, but she continued to look interested, and Mrs Fairhaven was encouraged to continue with her description of the house.

'My dear husband told me our hall was between thirty and forty feet long but I did not measure it myself. I know it was a very great room, with windows cut down to the ground on one side, all glazed. He would not tell me the cost of bringing the glass from England, for he said it was a very great extravagance, but well worth it for the pleasure it gave me to look out across the gardens.'

'And I believe you said the heat was unsupportable, ma'am?'

'Indeed it was!' cried Mrs Fairhaven, leaning back in her comfortable chair, and fanning herself as though she could still feel it. 'Although the house was situated quite high up a hill, which provided some shading at the back where we had the bed-chambers, and close enough to the sea for a cooling sea-breeze. But outside of the house, Miss Price, the heat was all together unsupportable, and made life very difficult indeed. I am happy to be back in England, and to know I do not need to return to Antigua ever again.'

Before Susan could ask for any more information about Antigua, the men came in and Susan was called to the tea and coffee table, where all talk was between Sir Thomas and Edmund, with Miss Fairhaven inserting sparkling and witty comments, which both men frowned at and ignored. Sir Thomas was enquiring minutely into the affairs of Edmund's two parishes, continuing a discussion which had begun at the dinner table, and although Miss Fairhaven had no idea of whom they were talking, this did not deter her from attempting to join in the conversation. Susan was quite diverted watching Miss Fairhaven's attempts to form part of the conversation, but had to turn her attention to her aunt and Mrs Fairhaven, and dispensing the tea and coffee. Mrs Fairhaven asked if she might have chocolate, and a maid was sent off with the request.

When Edmund came to Susan for his cup of coffee, she was able to ask more after her sister, and the two little children who had arrived so close together, and who might be suspected to be the cause of Fanny's almost constant indisposition. Although Fanny had never been robust, before her marriage she had made some progress with her health, but the arrival of two children very close together had knocked her right back.

'Eddie and Fran seem always ailing,' Edmund said wearily. 'Both are fretful and do not sleep or eat well enough for my liking. They are not so healthy as I and my brother and sisters were as children, and seem to have one ailment after another.'

'Has Sir Thomas's physician been to see them today, and Fanny?'

'He is in almost daily attendance,' replied Edmund, 'and I am very grateful to my father for meeting the very great expense.'

'What does the physician suggest for their comfort?'

'He has given them medicines to strengthen them, but it does not seem to be doing them much good. Eddie is always sick afterwards, and Frances turns away her head and screams if he attempts to give her the physic.'

'And Fanny?'

At this Edmund smiled;

'You are a very close questioner, just like your sister!' said he.

'I am sorry, Edmund,' said Susan, holding out her hand to him. 'I will talk to Fanny tomorrow if you would rather not talk of it now.'

Edmund pressed her hand silently in thanks.

'Fanny will be very pleased to see you, and says you always calm the children down when you come. They are very fond of their Aunt Susan.'

'And I am very fond of them. But one more question if I may?'

Edmund bowed in assent.

'What of you?' asked Susan. 'You look tired.'

'I have many cares about my parishes,' answered Edmund, 'and the children cry during the night loud enough to wake me and will not settle. However, Ballantyne has taken over many of my duties while we wait for Fanny to improve.'

'I wonder whether a visit to the seaside might help,' put in Mrs Fairhaven unexpectedly. Susan and Edmund had quite forgotten she was also sitting there quietly near the tea things. 'I have heard of the many benefits of the sea air and sea bathing in England from visitors to

Antigua. Of course, we could not go in to the sea off Antigua, it was too rough, and full of sharks.'

'Sharks!' exclaimed Susan in horror.

'Yes indeed my dear,' replied Mrs Fairhaven. 'They took fishermen if they fell from their boats, and children if they ventured too far into the water as well.'

'How shocking!'

'It was most shocking indeed my dear, but they were only natives, none of the white people was ever taken by the sharks, for we took better care of ourselves not to go out in small boats, or swim in the sea. But for your dear wife and children, Mr Bertram, I have heard that the sea in this country is most beneficial to health, and that there are no sharks in the oceans off England.'

'It is a most happy thought indeed, madam,' answered Edmund, 'I will go directly and speak with my father about such a scheme. It may well be the very thing that Fanny and the children are in need of to set them up and restore their health.'

He bowed and moved away to seek his father.

'I am very pleased to have been of assistance with my advice,' said Mrs Fairhaven, giving Susan the impression that her advice was not usually much attended to by her own family. 'Now my dear, tell me all about your family.'

CHAPTER TWENTY-TWO

Before joining the ladies in the Drawing Room, Edmund and Sir Thomas had continued a discussion which had begun prior to the Fairhavens' arrival, and between them settled what Sir Thomas was to tell Mrs Fairhaven about Maria. Sir Thomas had found himself torn between not wanting to reveal his family's shame, and realizing that if he did not give them the story himself, they might soon hear a greatly exaggerated version from other more hostile sources. Certainly, by the time the Fairhavens went from Mansfield Park to their house on Wimpole Street, they could not help but hear of it, as Maria had left Rushworth from that very same street, and if Mrs Rushworth senior was visiting her son, she was one of the most hostile sources the Fairhavens could ever hope to meet. Sir Thomas could have wished that the Fairhavens had a house in almost any other part of London, but Wimpole Street was where they were to settle.

From the first airing of the topic, it was Edmund's considered opinion that Mrs Fairhaven was entitled to know about Maria, and that it would be her decision how much of that to pass on to her daughter.

'I doubt, sir, whether it would deter Miss Fairhaven from marrying Tom, should she have a mind to, but we do not wish Mrs Fairhaven to hear any false report which might alarm her or give her a disgust of our family, and cause her to forbid any union between her daughter and Tom.'

Sir Thomas concurred, and so on the morning after the Fairhavens' arrival, he requested the honour of an interview with Mrs Fairhaven in his study, and solemnly acquainted her with the barest details of Maria's elopement, leaving it to her to tell her daughter as much as she considered the girl needed to know. Mrs Fairhaven was surprised by Sir Thomas's confiding this sorry tale to her, and agreed that it was most shocking indeed, but that it did not affect her very great respect for the Bertram family, and her good impressions of Tom, his father, his brother and his mother. She further agreed to give Agnes an expurgated version, so as not to shock her; however, Agnes was much less easily scared or shocked than Sir Thomas and her mother would ever have imagined, and soon filled in the blanks in her mother's account for herself. It was not hard for her to imagine exactly what had happened, and what she was not being told, given the books she was accustomed to reading under plain covers, and her diligent reading in the society papers. The disgrace that Maria had inflicted upon herself and her family did not signify at all to Agnes, for *she* would be Lady Bertram in due course, and Maria would never be admitted to Mansfield Park again. This scandal could have no effect upon *her* and would not deter her from her goal to manoeuvre Tom into a proposal just as soon as he returned home. Added to which, it was such a delicious scandal that she could not help sharing it with her dearest friends in their frequent, and much under-lined correspondence; the resumption of which she had taken much enjoyment in, for letters passed so much faster to and fro now, and Sir Thomas franked them all for her, without even being asked!

The subject of Miss Fairhaven's much under-lined correspondence was at that moment preparing to elope for the second time; she was not at all at a loss how to do it, having had practice; but she did not want to be a laughing stock in a London whose fashions had almost certainly moved on since she was last there. Although she could not arrive in London without any gowns at all, Maria was determined not to go out into society until she had ascertained the latest fashions and had gowns made up for her from the best warehouses. Before any of that, she had first to make her escape from her aunt, and from Champford.

The week had never before passed so slowly. Sarah waited on Maria, who mostly ignored her; and Mr Ricket came daily, and Maria insisted Sarah attend her during his instruction. Sunday came and went and finally it was the day for the outing to Champford. All the servants were gathered outside ready to go in the cart including Sarah, who was hopeful that Mrs Morris would over-look her and she would be able to take all her information and questions to share with Robert. But it was not to be; Mrs Norris spent so long fussing about something she had forgotten, that it gave time for Maria to come down the stairs and notice Sarah outside.

'Sarah had much better stay here today, Aunt,' she said, to Sarah's horror. 'I have some mending for her to do.'

'Yes indeed,' replied Mrs Norris, 'for she does not deserve another day out in Champford, the way she has behaved. Next time the master comes Sarah, you are to go away with him, and Mrs Raworth will have a new maid.'

Sarah dropt a sulky curtsey, and followed Maria back up the stairs to her sitting room. She waited to be told what it was Maria wanted her to mend, but Maria was over by the window, peeping out to watch the carriage and then the cart leave.

'Now,' Maria said to her. 'We have little time. Go and pack whatever belongings that are yours into this bag. Be careful to take nothing else, and then come back here to pack my gowns into my trunk.'

'Are we leaving, Madam?' asked Sarah in astonishment.

'Yes,' replied Maria, 'But it is not for you to know where we are to go. You are to pack as fast as possible, and then come away with me.'

Sarah flew away upstairs and swiftly gathered her very few belongings, pushing them into the bag that Maria had handed her, then she dropped her bag in the hall way, and ran back upstairs to see Maria staring helplessly at all her gowns and jewels which she had strewn across her bed.

'I do not know what to take,' she cried, 'for I do not know what the fashion is presently in London! But,' she continued viciously, 'I will not take any of these!' And she pulled out all her black gowns and veils and threw them on to the floor.

So, thought Sarah, we are to go to London, as she began picking out the least unfashionable gowns from amid the pile, and folding them into a large travelling trunk. If we are to go with this 'Henry', I hope he has brought a carriage this time, we cannot all travel on his horse, and with this great big trunk too. When we get to London I should be able to find Robert, as his gentleman is from London and they must go back there one day.

Sarah had no concept of how big London was and how difficult it would be to find one servant amid the many there, but hope is great motivator, and so she chose gowns and packed with alacrity, looking forward to this new adventure in her previously unadventurous life.

Their preparations were almost complete when there came a knock at the front door, and Maria flew down the stairs to open it. Sarah, still folding and packing Maria's gowns and stowing her jewels in a strong-box to be carried separately, heard nothing for a moment, then a murmur of voices, and then finally booted feet walking heavily up the stairs.

To her astonishment, and then delight, Robert walked into the room, but his surprise was in no wise equally as great as her's; he had known all along who she was and exactly what her mistress's connexion was with his master, but Crawford had paid him well not to tell anybody about his mission.

This discovery made Sarah even more excited about the elopement; not only would she avoid being sent away in disgrace, but she would be with her own lover, in London. She followed Robert down the stairs and watched Maria's trunk being loaded on to a very smart carriage indeed, before being helped in by Robert, who gave her a quick wink before the closing the door and taking up his own station at the back. Inside was the 'Henry' whose voice Sarah had only heard before, and her mistress;

'Sarah, this is Mr Crawford, who is to be your new master,' Maria said, and then ignored Sarah for the rest of the journey, except to give her orders when they stopped to change the horses, and to take refreshment. Sarah no longer resented this; she sat back in her seat in more luxury than she had ever travelled before, clutching her mistress's jewel case, and marveling at the direction her life had taken.

At every coaching inn and over-night stop, Robert was sent in ahead to announce that 'Mr and Mrs Crawford' were arrived, and to bespeak rooms and refreshments. Maria was content with just being called 'Mrs Crawford' for now; she was all sweetness, and compliance, determined not to cause any quarrel until her marriage lines were in her hands, an announcement was placed in the newspaper, and Crawford's ring was upon her finger.

CHAPTER TWENTY-THREE

At the Dower House, you may imagine the astonishment, alarm and then terror felt by Mrs Norris on her return from Champford to discover that Maria was gone; but I cannot expect any body to feel at all sorry for her. Once more her niece had slipped through her fingers, and she could not begin to comprehend what Sir Thomas's reaction would be, nor did she have any idea where Maria might have gone. As a parting gesture, Maria had stuffed her hated veiling roughly into the fireplace, which had set it smouldering; causing thick black smoke to roll through the whole house by the time Mrs Norris and the other servants returned.

As they alighted from their conveyances, many thought the house was on fire, as smoke could be seen billowing out of a window which had been left slightly open, and blanking off all the other windows. Mrs Norris sent the men servants in first to see what had happened, and when she was certain the house was not on fire, entered herself to make her terrible discovery. She ran screaming through every room in the house before she was satisfied that Maria was gone, and having swallowed too much smoke, she was found collapsed in Maria's bedroom, carried outside and laid upon a sopha that one of the men had brought out.

For a while, everything was chaos. The house had to be opened right up to let out the smoke, and the servants busily carried out all of the furniture that they could manage – but eventually they noticed that Mrs Morris was lying silent and still upon the sopha. They gathered around her, unsure what to do. She had loomed so large in their daily lives for so long, and had always been telling them what to do, when to do it, and what to think about all matters domestic and private, that none of them had any initiative left to take action without her direct orders.

Finally, the cook had a happy thought and sent the boot boy to find Mr Ricket; he was a gentleman, he should know what to do, and could take charge of the situation. Mrs Morris would not argue with that gentleman being sent for, Cook was certain.

The boy ran off across the Park, and soon returned running behind Mr Ricket's horse. Somewhat to his own surprise, Mr Ricket rose magnificently to the occasion. He sent for a Physician to attend to Mrs Morris, directed the rest of the servants to begin stowing any rescued furniture in a barn, and then sent a footman ahead to speak to Mrs Southworth in order for accommodation to be found for everyone for the night at Champford Hall. It was not possible to convey such a large household to his own small house on the estate; there were far more rooms and many more servants to assist at Champford Hall.

The Physician arrived and examined Mrs Norris. Under his direction, she was lifted gently into the carriage, and conveyed at a funereal pace to Champford Hall. Normally, this would have delighted her; for she had been longing to get inside the family rooms at the great house, but at this very moment she was feeling completely crushed, and really very ill, and could not take advantage of this supreme opportunity at all.

After every body had been suitably disposed of at the Hall, Mr Ricket, presuming upon his status as a friend of the family at the Dower House, and upon his reputation as a man of the cloth, visited Mrs Norris in the magnificent bedroom which had been opened up for her comfort.

'How are we now, Ma'am?' he asked, sitting solicitously by her bedside. 'Dr Fidler will return again later today to see if there is anything else he might offer to assist you in your recovery.'

Since being carried into the bed-chamber, Mrs Norris had been in a sleep brought on by Dr Fidler's potions, but now that she was awake, she cast about her for some explanation of where she was, and why Mr Ricket was sitting by her and asking how she did. Then she remembered: Maria!

'Where is my niece? Where is Maria?' she asked, sitting up in terror.

'As to that, ma'am, be easy. Mrs Raworth was not in the house when you returned, so she was not hurt by the fire.'

'Has she returned since?' asked Mrs Norris, a faint hope dawning.

'Not that I am aware of, ma'am,' answered Mr Ricket. 'Has she perchance gone to visit a friend? It will be a shock to her to return and find the house full of smoke, and nobody at home. It may be wise to station a footman with the carriage there to redirect her on her return.'

'Mr Ricket,' Mrs Norris said, unable to join in his sanguine hopes, 'My niece visits no body! There is no time to lose. I believe Mrs Raworth may have been stolen away, and we must seek her out at once.' She began to try to struggle out of the bed, but Mr Ricket held up an imperious hand;

'Stolen away, ma'am? No, no, that is not at all possible. We are so very remote here, and such things do not happen in the quiet English countryside with friends upon every side. No indeed! Depend upon it, Mrs Raworth has gone for her walk, and lost track of the time or was invited in to take tea with an acquaintance, and has staid to dinner. In all the confusion at the Dower House you have quite understandably missed seeing a note arriving from her to tell you of her delay in returning home.'

Mrs Norris shook her head at this willful blindness, but Mr Ricket had another thought before she could speak;

'Ah! One thing which might assist us to discover her whereabouts; is Mrs Raworth's maid amongst the servants?'

Mrs Norris did not know, and so Mr Ricket rang to enquire. No, Mrs Raworth's maid was also missing.

'There!' said he in triumph, 'Mrs Raworth is out walking with her maid, and they have wandered further than usual, or mistook the time. I am assured we will find them at the Dower House, wondering what has happened and where the rest of you are gone to.'

In vain did Mrs Norris attempt to protest that Maria's gowns and jewels were gone; Mr Ricket would not listen, and instead insisted on her taking some more of the doctor's potion, which would soothe her and help her to rest and recover.

Once Mrs Norris fell asleep, Mr Ricket ordered one of the footmen from the Dower House to return there with the carriage to intercept Mrs Raworth, and bring her to the Hall.

However, when night fell, the carriage returned, and the footman reported to Mr Ricket that there was no sign of Mrs Raworth or her maid. Reluctantly he sent for an Express to attend him on the morrow, and sat down with a heavy heart to pen a note to Sir Thomas Bertram in which he reported that Mrs Raworth appeared to have gone missing, but that he was sure there was no cause for concern.

It was the urgent sound of a horse's hooves outside her window which awoke Mrs Norris the following morning, and she rang for a maid to go and enquire whether a letter had arrived for her from Maria. The maid did not return with any letter, and instead Mr Ricket himself came in to the room in response to the maid's enquiry.

'Good morning, madam!' said he cheerfully. 'I expect that you heard the horse? Do not concern yourself about the Express, there is no message arrived, but one sent. I have sent to Sir Thomas Bertram to assure him that while we do not know where she is yet, I am certain Mrs Raworth can have come to no harm.'

Sir Thomas! While there remained a vestige of hope that Maria might return, Mrs Norris had pushed the thought of Sir Thomas aside. But now that no hope remained, terror at the thought of what he might do, what he might say, caused her to fall back on her pillows in a swoon so profound, that Mr Ricket rang for a maid to attend her urgently, and was further relieved when Mr Fidler, the surgeon arrived.

That worthy medical man later reported to Mr Ricket that Mrs Norris had suffered a brain seizure which had left her only able to move one hand, and she did not talk beyond repeatedly saying, 'Sir Thomas'; he had been unable to calm her and feared she would do herself more damage if she were not soothed directly. Mr Ricket cheerfully assured the surgeon that the matter was all in hand; and went himself in to Mrs Norris's room again to reassure her again that Sir Thomas would be receiving the letter soon, and she was not to worry any more: her niece would be discovered somewhere perfectly safe.

CHAPTER TWENTY-FOUR

Edmund had offered to escort Mrs and Miss Fairhaven to the Rectory where they were to meet Fanny. She was still indisposed and unable to leave the house, so they were to come to her instead. Susan joined the party, and they drove across the Park to the Rectory in Sir Thomas's carriage, with Edmund riding alongside.

Fanny was not yet able to leave her bed, so everybody crowded into her bed chamber, where she was sitting up amongst the pillows, and looking really very unwell indeed. Edmund bowed and said he would leave the ladies to become acquainted and would order refreshments to be sent up, and Susan undertook to make all the introductions.

After the arrival of refreshments, over which Susan presided as Fanny had not the strength, all the talk was by Miss Fairhaven, with occasional interjections by her mother, which she either corrected or ignored. Miss Fairhaven was all complaisance, and compliments to Fanny about the Parsonage, as well as full of praise for Mansfield Park, Sir Thomas and Lady Bertram, and coyly phrased concerns about Tom's absence. Fanny was left in no doubt that Miss Fairhaven intended to marry Tom on his return, but she turned the conversation gently around to their lives in Antigua, and to John Fairhaven, still there and working his plantation. Susan did not attempt to join in the conversation, having heard all about Antigua already, but spent the time quietly watching her sister, in the hopes of seeing that the visit had raised her spirits or aided her recovery.

'Well, we shall take our leave for now, Mrs Bertram,' said Mrs Fairhaven once all had drank their tea. 'And leave you to your rest. I do hope we will see you again soon at Mansfield Park.'

'Thank you,' replied Fanny, 'I am much better than I was, and the physician assures me I shall soon be out of bed and back about my business. I am expecting him to call and check on me soon.'

'You do have more colour than last time I saw you,' said Susan, as she bent to kiss Fanny on the cheek. 'I shall see Mrs Fairhaven to the carriage, and wait downstairs for Mr Hibbs.'

Susan escorted the Fairhavens down to where Sir Thomas's carriage had waited to take the ladies home again.

'There is no need to wait for me,' she said. 'I am hoping to hear from Mr Hibbs in person how he thinks my sister is and how long her recovery might take. I will walk back across the park to join you again back at the house.'

Susan waited until Mrs Fairhaven and Agnes were settled in to Sir Thomas's carriage, and set off back towards the house. However, before she reached it, she noticed a figure striding down one of the paths, which was clearly not Edmund, so she set off into the garden to intercept the man, hoping it was Mr Hibbs. She took a parallel path which she knew would intersect with the path the physician had taken, when she heard the man's voice hail Edmund. Susan moved a little faster towards them, intending to make her presence known, but it was too late, and they were already talking on the other side of a hedge.

'Mr Bertram, I am glad to have met with you,' said the voice of Mr Greville, Mr Hibbs's apothecary and very much the up and coming man in medicine locally.

'Have you come to see Mrs Bertram?' Susan heard Edmund reply, after the initial greetings and mutual assurances of good health had been exchanged, and Mr Greville gave the affirmative to Edmund's question.

'How do you think you will find her today? I am persuaded there is some improvement from yesterday.'

'I am not so sanguine, Mr Bertram. Two children in one year has left Mrs Bertram very weak, and she is not at all what I would call robust for a woman of her age.'

Susan caught her breath, and thought to herself that Fanny had never been robust; she had always been knocked up far more easily than Susan herself.

But Mr Greville was continuing a little lower still, and it was harder for Susan to hear what he was saying. There was something that

Fanny must not attempt, but Susan was not sure what that could be, and then she heard Mr Greville say;

'I cannot answer for her surviving another.'

Behind the dividing hedge, Susan did not have the usual fate of those overhearing conversations they were not intended to hear, but what Mr Greville said next was too quiet for her to hear, even though she listened as hard as she could. His concern touched her very nearly, as it applied to her beloved elder sister, and she wanted to know what it was that Fanny should not attempt, or would not survive. She waited for Edmund to reply, but it was some time before he said very quietly;

'I would do anything for Fanny, anything to ensure her health and survival, you may depend upon it, Greville.'

'Then we understand each other,' replied Mr Greville. 'Come with me to talk to Mrs Bertram.'

Susan heard the two men turn and start walking away from her towards the house, and she wondered whether to walk along on the other side of the dividing hedge and meet up with them, or whether to go in the opposite direction and walk back across the park to Mansfield. But a cold hand seemed to grip her heart, and she sat down very suddenly upon a bench. Upon reflection she was satisfied with Edmund's response to Mr Greville's concerns; after the lack of interest in Fanny's health that she had witnessed the other evening, she had begun to fear that Edmund's love for Fanny was sinking into indifference in the face of her continued indisposition; but from what Edmund had said, it appeared it was not so. Despite this relief, there was the continued worry over her sister's health, and she still felt herself very unequal to walking back into the house or across the park. A period of quiet reflection was needed; she could not entertain the idea of losing Fanny; her sister, her confidant, her friend, and the only person here in Northamptonshire that was from her own family.

Mr Greville and Edmund rounded their side of the hedge, still in close conference, and Edmund happened to glance down the parallel path to see Susan sitting in some distress upon the bench. He encouraged Mr Greville to go in to Fanny, saying he would join them directly, and hastened down the path to assist Susan.

The Bertrams coach with the Fairhavens was still outside the Parsonage, as Agnes had seen a gentleman's horse, which was not the one Edmund had ridden over on, tethered outside the parsonage. She wanted to see who this gentleman might be, and persuaded her mother to order the coachman to wait for Miss Price; and so they were still there when the owner of the horse, Mr Greville, approached.

Agnes was leaning out of the carriage door looking at Mr Greville with undisguised interest, and he bowed as he passed them.

'I wonder who that can be, Mama,' said Agnes, 'he has quite an air to him.'

'A pity he did not stop so that we could ask him if Miss Price is to join us or not,' said Mrs Fairhaven. 'We cannot keep Sir Thomas's coach waiting for much longer.'

At that moment, Susan and Edmund came up the path, and Edmund seeing the Bertram's carriage, led Susan towards it, and handed her in.

'If you would be so good as to escort Susan home, madam? She is rather done up for today,' he said, and Mrs Fairhaven agreed eagerly.

'But do tell me first, Mr Bertram,' asked Agnes, 'Who was the gentleman who passed us just now and went into your house?'

'That would be Mr Greville, our local apothecary, who is assisting my father's physician in the care of Mrs Bertram and my children.'

At the news that this handsome young man was a mere apothecary, Agnes drew her head back into the carriage, and said, 'Let us take you home, Miss Price. I am afraid that you are very ill indeed?'

'No, I thank you, I am just a little tired, I would usually pay very little mind at all to a walk back across the park, but today I am grateful for the carriage still being here. Thank you for waiting for me, we must go now, I am certain my aunt will be missing me.'

Agnes called out to the coachman and he whipped up the horses to carry the ladies back to Mansfield Park. Susan sat quietly with her face turned away from the other two, trying to get her thoughts and countenance in order before she encountered her aunt, or provoked any more impertinent questions from Miss Fairhaven.

Susan was still discomposed at dinner over what she had overheard pass between her brother and Mr Greville, and almost more so by her own imaginings over the parts she had not been able to discern, but she had no time to repine, for she must support her aunt, and Mr Ballantyne was to join them for dinner for the first time since Agnes and Mrs Fairhaven had arrived.

CHAPTER TWENTY-FIVE

Mr Harold Ballantyne had made quite an addition to their family circle in the absence of Edmund, who was much engaged with his own family in the evenings. Added to that, Ballantyne was a kindly person, interested in every body's concerns, and made himself indispensable to Lady Bertram with his good manners and ready agreement to play at cards with her, and he did not object to Pug shedding hairs on his clothing. He could not have known it, but he was to become a favourite of Mrs Fairhaven's as well, reminding her sentimentally of her own son, far away in Antigua. Although Mr Ballantyne was nothing like her son in looks, height, profession, voice, or any other characteristic, he was the only young man of her new family circle, and therefore took her son's place in her imagination.

At dinner, Sir Thomas was seated next to Mrs Fairhaven, while to Susan's lot fell Lady Bertram, whose conversation was more of a comfortable monotone, and who seldom required any response. On the other side of the table, Agnes was drawing on all her charm to entertain Mr Ballantyne with tales of her time in Antigua and the travails of their journey back to England, tales he appeared to find most absorbing. Sir Thomas appeared in the drawing room after dinner only to excuse himself as there was some business he had to attend to, but he sent in Mr Ballantyne who looked to see if he could sit next to Susan, but Lady Bertram had got her working on an intricate piece of fringing that she had got into a muddle, Mrs Fairhaven was on Susan's other side with Pug, who had taken a great liking to her, asleep on her lap. Agnes was therefore the only one at liberty, and so he sat beside her and they carried on their conversation about Antigua.

Susan watched with some alarm. She had been unhappy with Agnes's monopolising of Mr Ballantyne during dinner, and was even more unhappy when she saw him apparently head straight over to sit next to Agnes. Agnes herself was delighted with what she considered this new conquest, and in Tom's continuing absence determined to spend as much time in Mr Ballantyne's company as she could; but as she was always with Susan, this did not give rise to any comment or concern from her mother or Sir Thomas. This apparent competition for Mr Ballantyne's attention prompted Susan to realise that she had found Mr Ballantyne to be very agreeable from the first moment of being introduced to him; and for the first time in her life, she began to wonder whether there might be somebody who could tempt her into matrimony; he was certainly everything that she had ever looked for in a husband, but now that Agnes was staying at Mansfield Park, Susan could not be certain that she was the first in his attention. Added to which she was not able to spend as much time with him as she would have liked as Agnes was determined to engross him completely, and was a most determined talker, and always with Susan now when she took her walks about the Park. Susan noticed with a little sadness, that Mr Ballantyne joined her less frequently now that Agnes was always there too.

'Mr Ballantyne is quite a flirt of mine,' said she one day, peering about the Park as she and Susan walked out. 'I wonder if he will join us today?'

Susan did not know whether she hoped he would, although it would give her pain to see Agnes impose upon his good nature, or whether she hoped he would stay away for very much the same reason. But Agnes required no reply, for she was prattling on about how very agreeable he was to be sure, although so tall, she almost thought she should stand upon a stool to be at the same height when she talked to him. Or maybe she could ask him to take her riding, for the difference in height would not be so much when they were both seated upon a horse, and she had hoped to learn horse-riding now that she was returned to England, it had not been at all possible in the heat and terrain of Antigua, although the men did ride horses about the estates. What did Miss Price think? Did she think Mr Ballantyne might be persuaded to teach her how to ride?

Whatever Miss Price thought was interrupted the sight of the man himself, coming towards them on his horse.

'Oh!' cried Agnes in delight. 'And here he comes! I knew he would not miss a walk with me today!'

Mr Ballantyne reached them before Agnes had time to do any more than compose her features into a modest smile of self-congratulation at her latest beau, and prepare herself to the conquest of all that remained unsubdued of his heart, trusting that it was not more than might be won in a few more of these congenial walks about the estate.

He dismounted and bowed to them both, asking after their health, but Susan had no time to reply, as Agnes answered for both of them, and then very familiarly took Mr Ballantyne's arm, attempting to lead him along with her, endeavouring to leave Susan to walk behind, as though she were a servant.

However, her scheme did not work, as Mr Ballantyne stopped and turned around to hold out his other arm to Susan.

'Would you do me the honour, Miss Price?' he asked, and as Susan stept forward to take his arm, he added gaily, 'Now we are charmingly grouped, and would appear to uncommon advantage were there anybody to see us!'

Agnes looked thunderously at Susan, who pretended not to see, and the three of them walked about the park, with Agnes talking exclusively to Mr Ballantyne and ignoring Susan, and Mr Ballantyne good-naturedly attempting to include Susan in the conversation. The effect to an onlooker would have been most comical, and after a while, Susan's ill-humour was replaced with amusement at Agnes's transparent endeavours to exclude her and engross him. One turn about the park was enough for the gentleman, and he excused himself to the ladies with talk of visits to his parishioners, and a promise to join them after dinner that evening.

That evening as they waited for the gentlemen to join them in the drawing room, Agnes's thoughts returned to Mr Ballantyne.

'Do you know what his prospects are, Miss Price?'

'He is the son of a neighbour,' answered Susan. 'He and Edmund were at Cambridge together and are very good friends.'

'And do you know if he is to inherit?'

'I believe he is the third son.'

'Oh,' said Agnes, looking disappointed. 'A third son, you say? He has older brothers?'

'Two, and six nephews besides, I believe,' said Susan.

'And has he no parish of his own?'

'No,' Susan said. 'He is come to assist my brother who has much concern about his wife and children and needs another pair of hands about his own parishes.'

She decided not to tell Agnes about the living which was promised Mr Ballantyne, nor that he was in truth the third son of Lord Belvedere, Earl of _, and instead watched as that young lady transferred her attention back to being charming to Sir Thomas on his appearance in the drawing room. It appeared that Mr Ballantyne's attraction had diminished in direct proportion to his finances, and although Agnes was not deterred from joining Susan on her daily walk, her first object was no longer whether Mr Ballantyne would join them or not, for which small mercy, Susan was very grateful.

CHAPTER TWENTY-SIX

Tom Bertram had been away from home for some months with his friend, Hallett in Axmouth. There had been shooting parties, and dinners with friends and relatives, and finally a ball got up to amuse young Mr Bertram, which some of the Halletts' cousins, the Comyns, had attended. It was held by everybody to have been a very good evening indeed, as nobody had been left without a partner at any of the dances.

Tom and Richard were late down the stairs the morning following the ball.

'I hope our little ball last night was to your liking, Mr Bertram?' inquired Mrs Hallett, as she gave orders for a late breakfast to be served the two young gentlemen. 'Had you enough partners for your taste?'

'Yes, indeed, I thank you, ma'am,' answered Tom with a bow. 'It was all most agreeable, I assure you.'

'We have not much society here in Axmouth,' Mrs Hallett continued a little plaintively. 'Nothing compared with Mansfield Park, I am sure, but I hope we did our best to find enough young people for your amusement.'

'Mansfield Park is more remote from society than Stedcombe, I assure you, ma'am, and I have wanted for no amusement or attention since I have been here.'

'I am very pleased to hear it; and hope you will return whenever you have a mind to, and make us another long visit.'

Tom bowed again, and after Mrs Hallett had supervised the servants bringing in the sorts of meats and drinks she supposed young men would need after their exertions on the previous evening, she left them to eat in peace.

The day following, they were for Bath, to further Richard's hopes of Miss Shaw, and for Tom to continue avoiding returning to Mansfield

Park. This avoidance was not to last for much longer, however, as a letter from Sir Thomas, which had arrived in Axmouth the day after Tom's departure, now followed him to Bath, and was brought in by Richard's manservant the morning after their arrival.

'Oh Lord! Here is my father's hand again,' said Tom, throwing the letter down beside his plate, after skimming through the contents.

'And what does he want this time?' asked Richard.

'The same as the previous letters,' replied Tom. 'He wants me to come home and marry some girl from Antigua.'

'What? A slave girl?' asked Richard.

'Lord! No! Some girl he introduced me to when I was out there last. Her brother was a good friend of mine, you have heard me mention John Fairhaven, Richard?'

'It is his sister that your father wants you to marry? Does not he think you can find a wife for yourself? Why not ask one of my cousins? I am persuaded that Sophy would oblige you in order to be the next Lady Bertram.'

'Sophy?' asked Tom. 'Who is Sophy?'

'My cousin Sophy Comyns, from the Vicarage; she was at the ball and we dined with the family several times. You must recall!'

'Oh! I recall there were several young ladies at the Vicarage, and more at the ball. Which of your cousins was she?'

'The one who's out, of course. You danced with her at the ball before we left.'

'I regret I do not recall in sufficient detail to distinguish which was your cousin,' Tom said. 'All the women there looked alike to me; certainly they were all dressed the same.'

'Sophy is the only one of my cousins that you could have danced with and the only one that you could marry, as she is the only one who is out.'

'I do not understand all these outs and not-outs,' said Tom. 'I was discussing it with my brother once, and we both agreed we could not understand it at all.'

'Well, Sophy is certainly out, for she came to the dance, and her sisters are not because they did not.'

'But I was introduced to at least four of your cousins when we went there to dine.'

'Ah, they can dine en famille, just not go out to balls.'

Tom shook his head at this, and returned to his father's letter.

Tom was not ignorant of his father's manoeuvres; and well aware that, as the heir to Mansfield Park, he would have to marry sooner rather than later. Sir Thomas had thought himself very subtle indeed in the careful phrasing of his letters urging his errant son to return home. In this latest letter, he had carelessly mentioned that Mrs Fairhaven and her daughter were to come to Mansfield Park while their house at Wimpole Street was made ready for them. Tom would remember Mrs Fairhaven from Antigua? Her son and daughter had inherited equal halves of their father's estate, and Miss Fairhaven accompanied her mother back to England. Although he had made no explicit reference to Tom's bachelor state, or that Miss Fairhaven was equally unblessed by matrimonial arrangements, the implication was very clear to Tom.

Now that his friend Hallett had come up to the mark with Miss Shaw, and was about to join the lists of Hymen, and with most of Tom's other former friends, like Yates, there already, he decided that the game was probably up for him too, and he may as well accept this bird in the hand, and finally end his father's anxiety over his future.

'I suppose I shall return home,' said Tom, ringing for his valet. 'From what I can recall, Miss Fairhaven was well enough, and I shall have to marry. I have no objection to my father's scheme.'

'I hope you will phrase it a little more delicately for Miss Fairhaven than that,' said Richard. 'She will not like to think that she was just a well enough scheme! You can learn how to make compliments to young ladies by listening to me talk to Miss Shaw.'

'Nay, I have no joy in being a fifth wheel, and chaperoning is for her mother, not for your friend.'

Tom spent the rest of the day making the necessary arrangements, and on the morrow bid farewell to his good friend Hallett with every best wish for his future happiness, and set out for home.

Two days later, he cantered up the driveway, and giving his horse to the groom, made his way into his mother's sitting room, where she was dozing on the sopha next to Mrs Fairhaven.

'And here is dear Tom at last!' cried Mrs Fairhaven, quite startling Lady Bertram awake.

'Who is it?' she asked in the heavy tone of one half-roused, 'I was not asleep.'

'Oh dear, no, ma'am,' said Tom, bending over her extended hand. 'Nobody suspected you. I am come from Bath just this very moment.'

Lady Bertram smiled up at him, "I feel quite stupid. It must be sitting up so late last night; I recall some body playing the piano and singing, although I cannot tell you what the song was, still it went on a long time, and we were all very late above stairs. Tom, you must fetch Susan to do something to keep me awake. Perhaps we might play at cards, Mrs Fairhaven?'

'How lovely to see you again, Tom,' put in Mrs Fairhaven, pleased to have the distraction of his arrival, for she had been quite in danger of joining Lady Bertram in dozing off.

'Ma'am,' said Tom, bowing over her hand. 'It is most agreeable to meet with you again here. We will have much to talk over of Antigua later, and you can tell me how my good friend Fairhaven does out there. For now, if you will excuse me, I must tell my father that I am arrived.'

'And you must see Agnes,' cried Mrs Fairhaven. 'She and your cousin are out walking in the garden, but she will be so happy to see you are come at last.'

'Indeed, ma'am,' said Tom, 'If my father can spare me, I will go and pay my respects to Miss Fairhaven and to my cousin, Susan.'

'And tell Susan to come,' added his mother. 'I find I cannot work, she must bring me some cards and set them up for me.'

Tom bowed and went to seek out his father in his study. Sir Thomas had been alerted to his son's arrival, and was coming out on purpose to seek him, and so they met in the hall.

'I am most pleased to see you home again, Tom,' said his father gravely. 'I hope that you had a good visit with your friends in Devonshire. Have you paid your respects to your mother and Mrs Fairhaven?'

'Yes, sir, I have,' answered Tom.

'Good, good,' Sir Thomas hesitated; he did not want to push his son into marriage in case it later turned out as badly as his sister Maria's, but he also very much wanted Tom to marry, and was hoping that Tom would reach the same conclusion about the reason for Miss Fairhaven's presence in his home.

'My mother has asked me to fetch my cousin Susan to her,' Tom said, 'I understand she is out walking with Miss Fairhaven.'

Sir Thomas said, 'Well, I would not dictate to you your business, but Miss Fairhaven would be an asset to our family; she is quite one of us already.'

There was a pause, as they looked at each other; and for a moment each understood the other perfectly.

'Very well, sir,' Tom said. 'I shall renew my acquaintance with Miss Fairhaven if you will excuse me?' and he bowed and left his father in order to seek out the young woman herself in the garden.

CHAPTER TWENTY-SEVEN

Susan and Agnes had been walking for some time in the garden, as Agnes's lively temperament chafed at too much sitting indoors with Lady Bertram, and she was much better suited to being out of doors and taking her exercise. As she could not do so alone, she always invited Susan to accompany her, and Susan was nothing loath as there was always the hope that they might meet with Mr Ballantyne, even if she would then have to share him with Agnes.

Agnes saw Tom first, and called out, waving prettily to attract his attention. Catching Susan's look of surprise, Agnes said, 'Do not be alarmed, my dear Miss Price, I am not acting improperly. Tom and I are such old friends. He was forever with us in Antigua, and I consider him quite another brother to me.'

Susan had time to wonder how this sisterly feeling would translate into wifely feeling should Tom make her the offer his father intended him to, and then Tom was upon them, and she had to pay attention to what he was saying.

'Well met, Cousin Susan. My mother is asking for you. Something about cards, I believe?'

'I will go to her at once, if you will excuse me? Shall I send out your maid, Miss Fairhaven?'

'No, no, no need for that. Miss Fairhaven and I are old acquaintances. Shall we take another turn, Miss Fairhaven?'

Agnes took Tom's arm, and they set off down the path again. Susan went in to Lady Bertram's sitting room, with a pack of cards, and set them up for her to play with Mrs Fairhaven. Supervising Lady Bertram's cards left Susan plenty of time to play with Pug's puppies, wonder how Tom and Agnes were going on in the garden, and to explain to Lady Bertram what her next move should be.

While Susan soothed away Lady Bertram's concerns over her next move, Mrs Fairhaven's cards were not absorbing enough to prevent her being at leisure to dream of the day she could refer to her own daughter as 'Lady Bertram', whilst fondly imagining a tender proposal scene between Tom and Agnes in the garden. It quite brought back to her Mr Fairhaven's proposal, and she sighed sentimentally.

Out in the garden, still in view of the morning room windows, Agnes opened the attack straight away as it was uncertain how long they would remain out of hearing, or when Sir Thomas might appear and join them. Despite her bold words and actions, Agnes had a very healthy respect for Sir Thomas's importance. And she had her own reasons for wanting to marry Tom as swiftly as possible; to date she had been in England a whole month already.

'Well, Mr Bertram,' said she, 'here we are at Mansfield Park together! I did not expect this when last we met in Antigua. But I am very glad to be here now, and I am hoping to get to know my new country; I should very much like to travel about England. I hear that the horse racing here is very fine and much better than anything we could do on Antigua.'

This was talk Tom could join in with;

'I used to be very fond of the horse racing, Miss Fairhaven. I remember attending the races in Antigua with your brother.'

'Ah, it was just a few of the local families, Mr Bertram, nothing compared with what I hear of the races at Newmarket, or Cheltenham, but you can advise me on whether I am correct or not in my assessment.'

'To be sure it was not such a big meeting in Antigua,' agreed Tom. 'But I do not attend the races any more, Miss Fairhaven.'

'Oh! that is sad news indeed. I do so love horses, Mr Bertram, although I have never owned one of my own. I did not have the opportunity to ride out in Antigua, there was no-one to take me out on a horse as my brother and father were too busy about the plantation, but I would love to learn to ride.'

There was a pause and as Tom did not take the hint, Agnes continued a little more forcefully.

'Would you teach me how to ride, Mr Bertram? Then perhaps we could ride together, one day ...' She tailed off delicately, intending to let Tom know that she was well aware of their parents' plotting to marry them, but Tom was as deaf to her hints as his mother had been to Mrs Fairhaven's.

'Well now, Edmund's your man for teaching. He taught Fanny, his wife, you know, to ride all those years ago. She was a poor little thing, always knocked up so soon, but the horse-riding really bucked her up a treat.'

Sensing that he was venturing into dangerous waters by comparing the much more robust Agnes to shrinking violet Fanny, he hastened to lessen the damage.

'I am convinced that you would have a much better seat than Fanny, and you are so much more healthy and stout than ever she was.'

'Thank you, Mr Bertram,' Agnes replied. 'I am much recovered indeed after returning to England from Antigua. The heat was too much for me.'

'I remember the heat,' agreed Tom, and they took another turn, talking of Antigua and of John Fairhaven, who was still there, working his own plantation.

It is not the place of this work to spy upon Tom Bertram's proposal to Agnes Fairhaven; suffice it to say that somehow, for he had no natural aptitude for the task, at some point over the next few days, Tom proposed to Agnes and was accepted. Both families were delighted, and Agnes pressed for an early date; declaring that their house in Wimpole Street would soon be ready to receive them, and she did not wish to impose upon Lady Bertram's kindness, and stay over long at Mansfield Park. Edmund was engaged to read the marriage service over the couple, and Fanny promised to be in the best of health for the occasion. Susan was to accompany Agnes as her Bride's Maid, while Mr Ballantyne confessed himself honoured to stand up with Tom as Groom's Man. Following his severe illness, Tom had no friends to call upon who were not already married, but he and Ballantyne had swiftly become firm friends. Tom had been delighted to find another young man at Mansfield Park to play at billiards with, and ride out with, and while Mr Ballantyne was more lively than Edmund, he would not lead Tom astray, and Sir Thomas too was pleased to witness their growing friendship.

CHAPTER TWENTY-EIGHT

All the arrangements were well in hand, a date had been proposed far enough ahead to allow for the Banns to be read in Edmund's church, and Agnes had recruited Susan to assist her in choosing new clothes to better suit her new status as a married woman and a Lady Bertram-in-waiting, when the peace of Mansfield Park was shattered by the most unexpected arrival of an Express.

The dreadful news of Maria's disappearance in the letter from the unsuspecting Mr Ricket, threw the whole household into disarray, as Sir Thomas made ready to leave for Champford immediately.

Sir Thomas's departure, only a few weeks before her own wedding day, sent Agnes into the depths of despair. She could not, of course, express her displeasure to Sir Thomas, nor to Lady Bertram, who might reasonably be thought to be more the loser by her husband's absence than was his prospective daughter-in-law. Her own mother was in as terrible a state of suspense as she, and much given to bemoaning Sir Thomas's absence, and so Agnes's confidante had to be Susan Price.

'Oh! why must Sir Thomas go away now?' she fretted to Susan as they took a turn about the lawns. 'And how long will he be gone? Do we have a day for his return? What if the wedding has to be postponed? Maybe we could go ahead without him, and he could give us his blessing on his return? What do you think to that, Miss Price? Shall I suggest it to Tom?'

'I do not think the wedding can go ahead until Sir Thomas returns,' said Susan. 'Tom cannot marry without his father being here.'

'Indeed he can!' cried Miss Fairhaven. 'There must be hundreds of people marry every day without their father being present! Mr Edmund Bertram can marry us, and Lady Bertram and my mother will be present, Mr Ballantyne will be here as witness, and you of course. Mr and Mrs Yates are to come as witness, we do not need Sir Thomas as well!'

Susan had given her opinion and saw no profit in repeating it or attempting to insist upon it in the face of such illogic, so she said nothing, and let Miss Fairhaven argue herself into a marriage conducted in Sir Thomas's absence.

Mrs Fairhaven was quite of her daughter's opinion. She could not see why the marriage required Sir Thomas to be present, but it was his eldest son and heir, and she acknowledged such matters were important to a father, she was sure dear Mr Fairhaven would have wanted to be present at Agnes's wedding, had he lived, and it would be the same for John, she was certain, but still, the wedding could go ahead without Sir Thomas if the rest of the family had a mind to it, as it was going ahead without John. She did not at all know why it should not be so, although as a parent, she would not wish to miss the wedding of either of her children.

'I cannot countenance any delay; Mama, you know I cannot!' cried Agnes, and appealed to Lady Bertram to say when Sir Thomas would return.

'I do not in the least know, my dear,' said she comfortably. 'He has much business in London all the year round, and has been away from Mansfield Park before now for months at a time. I wish he would not go away though; I cannot support a very lengthy absence.'

'Cannot you tell him that you require him to come home?' asked Agnes.

'I could certainly do so, but he will take no heed,' returned Lady Bertram. 'He will be back when his business is complete, no matter how long it takes.'

At this Agnes burst into tears and rushed out of the room, leaving Lady Bertram looking puzzled, and Mrs Fairhaven wringing her hands and hoping that Sir Thomas would not disappoint dear Agnes and dear Tom by staying away too long. Although she quite understood that gentlemen had business that often took them away from home, and they could not be gainsaid, she did think it odd of Sir Thomas to leave at this very moment when there was a wedding being arranged. She was convinced that his business in _shire could not be so very urgent, and could have been put off until after the wedding.

Susan left Mrs Fairhaven to her flutterings and worryings, and went to see if she could soothe Agnes. She did not immediately find Agnes, but came across Tom was pacing in the hall and looking agitated.

'What is all this Agnes is saying?' he asked. 'I cannot at all understand why we may not wait for my father's return; indeed, I cannot agree to marry until then. If I had my way, we should wait until John Fairhaven can come from Antigua to give his sister away.'

Susan thought this was an excellent suggestion, and carried it with her until she discovered Agnes in her own chamber, being attended by her maid, but the mention of waiting until her brother could come from Antigua caused Agnes to fall into hysterics, and was never mentioned again. When Agnes had finally stopped crying, and was more calm, Susan did attempt to reason with her, thus;

'There can be no reason to rush into this marriage, Miss Fairhaven,' said she. 'You are yet young, and only just come to England. You have not seen society in London, or Bath. It may be that you will want to take some time to become acquainted with your new home in London before settling down at Mansfield Park.'

As to that Agnes did not at all know; what if Tom were to meet another girl with a prettier face? For Agnes knew she could only lay claim to being a well-looking girl, she was not at all pretty, her brother often said so, and what if there was a girl that Tom met with a greater fortune than her's? Her own fortune was modest compared with what other girls could offer, even though she owned half the plantation; the changes that were happening on Antigua were causing her brother concern, just as they were dear Sir Thomas on his plantation; it may be that her fortune would not be as much as she had originally been told. No, the only answer was to be married as soon as possible, then they could settle at Wimpole Street, and then she would see as much of London society as she wished, and she was sure her dear Tom would take her to Bath at any moment she wished it, and she would not want to intrude upon Lady Bertram, nor take advantage of her kindness by living at Mansfield Park permanently at present, although she expected that dear Tom would have to spend much time at Mansfield Park at his father's service, and she would quite understand that he could not spend every moment by her side, but they must be married as soon as possible, there was no other alternative that was acceptable to her.

'You must not think that Tom would pay court to anybody else now that he has secured your hand,' said Susan, 'He has too much honour for that, I assure you.'

But Agnes would not be reassured, even when Susan pointed out that there were very few young women of marriageable age in the country around, and certainly none with as much money as she herself, changes to her plantation notwithstanding. Not even the argument that Tom had shown no interest in soliciting any body's hand in marriage before he met Agnes met with any more than;

'That is a very pretty compliment indeed, Miss Price; but I cannot give up this wedding, indeed I cannot! The Banns are already being read by your dear brother Mr Edmund Bertram, and the invitations are issued and everybody has accepted, and everything is arranged. It must go ahead!'

In the end, to avoid more hysterics from Agnes, it was agreed that the wedding would go ahead the moment Sir Thomas arrived home, and the necessary arrangements continued to be made in anticipation of a swift return. Agnes took to her room, and surrounded herself with her own maids from Antigua, who were constantly down in the kitchen making up potions, to the great disgust of Mansfield's staff, as they never cleaned up after themselves. One morning, Susan met Camba on the stairs with a preparation of some herbs with which to soothe her mistress, but there was never any report made on whether the remedies that had been so carefully prepared had helped with whatever it was that ailed her. Susan could only assume Agnes's malady was of an hysterical nature due to the wedding being postponed. A mention of this to Lady Bertram roused that lady long enough to send her own physician up to Agnes's room; but Agnes refused to admit him, saying only that she was accustomed to the remedies from her own Antiguan maids, and his physick would not suit her as well as their's.

The rejected physician took refuge with Lady Bertram, Mrs Fairhaven and Susan, and shook his head over Agnes's refusal to admit him. Despite not having actually seen her, he was willing to give his diagnosis to the other three women.

'Miss Fairhaven, I believe, is particularly susceptible to those maladies which affect unmarried women,' said he, shaking his head. 'The manner of their living, and the particular organisation of their frame, renders them more prone to nervous conditions.'

'How interesting,' murmured Lady Bertram, who had quite relied upon Mr Hibbs since her own children had been prone to all the usual childhood maladies, although she herself was seldom unwell.

'Indeed,' continued Mr Hibbs, casting about for a reason to justify his rejection. 'I gather she has been crossed in love and is not to be married?'

'Oh, not entirely, I assure you!' cried Mrs Fairhaven. 'It is merely that dear Sir Thomas's absence means that Agnes cannot marry until he returns, and she had so set her heart upon it.'

'Ah,' said Mr Hibbs, certain now that he had reached the root cause of Agnes's refusal to let him examine her. 'Disappointed love is most dangerous to a young woman, most dangerous indeed; I would never recommend it.'

At this, Susan had to rise hastily, and pretend she had heard something outside the window, in order that nobody would realise she was laughing at the absurdity of a physician ever recommending a patient to be crossed in love.

But Mr Hibbs was continuing without noticing her abrupt removal;

'I recommend the wedding take place without delay; indeed I do! For I will not answer for Miss Fairhaven's health should it be delayed much longer.'

Mrs Fairhaven gave a cry of fear at this gloomy prediction, which gratified Mr Hibbs enough to add;

'Grief, madam, unassuaged grief can lead to violent fits and convulsions, which can be fatal; but I will give you my advice which you may carry to Miss Fairhaven. She must avoid all rich or fancy foods, and eat only at meal times, never late into the evening. She must arise betimes, and not sleep in too long in the morning, and neither must she indulge in too much recreation; all of this will contribute to a most dangerous indolence.'

Then, seeing that Mrs Fairhaven was becoming really very worried by his portentous manner, he hastened to reassure her;

'However, Miss Fairhaven is young yet, Sir Thomas will soon return, and in the meantime I shall send over a receipt you may have made up which will alleviate her condition.'

Having thus justified the large fee he intended to charge Sir Thomas for his visit, Mr Hibbs graciously assented to refreshments, and Mrs Fairhaven hastened up the stairs to carry his advice to her daughter, with little success, for Agnes would have none of his potions or his wisdom.

In the midst of all these alarums and excursions, Susan had had little time to reflect upon the shock of Maria's disappearance, but when she did start to wonder about it, she could not help thinking of Mr Crawford, and wondering if perchance Maria had gone away with him again. It took several days of walking about the garden before she could begin to feel herself calming down, or get it into any kind of perspective, particularly as Agnes had taken to accompanying her and insisting upon walking very fast. After one such disturbed meditation, Susan decided that she had to talk to somebody else about this matter; Agnes was of no help at all, her talking of Maria's disappearance was only to bewail its effects upon herself, the absence of Sir Thomas, and her postponed wedding. There was always one person Susan could turn to, one person who would always listen and understand, one person who could be relied upon to put the best interpretation on everything; her sister, Fanny. She ascertained that Agnes was busy in her own rooms, and slipped out quietly to avoid being accompanied. As she walked across the park towards the Parsonage, Susan wondered what Mr Ballantyne would think of this latest news, and whether it would change his manner towards her or not. She could not help but think that if Maria had eloped with Mr Crawford, or any other man come to that, her continuing disgrace would reflect badly upon the whole family again, and should Mr Ballantyne be in the way of falling in love with her, such news might prevent him making her an offer. Such a thought dismayed her more than she had thought it would, and she could not help but wish that Maria would content herself with the home Sir Thomas had arranged for her, and would not keep causing her family such dismay. How could Mr Ballantyne's family countenance a bride whose cousin had left one marriage and then disappeared from the home she had been placed in? What would Mr Ballantyne say to his family's disapproval? Would he be swayed by their opinion, or would he continue to seek her out? As if in answer to her question, the scene enlarged and there was Mr Ballantyne riding towards her from the direction of Thornton Lacey.

The sight of him recalled Susan to her senses, and she smiled to herself; it seemed that all of Agnes's talk of marriage had affected her own brain. And she was a little disconcerted to see how far her own imaginings had carried her; in the course of their acquaintance, Mr Ballantyne may have become her ideal of how a man or a husband should behave, but he had spoken no word of love to her, and might never do. His situation as a third son might never allow him to marry; and even if he did, there was no guarantee that she would be his choice; he would probably be looking for an heiress. Generous as Sir Thomas had been to her family, Susan would never expect him to provide her with a settlement which would attract such a husband. Susan gave herself a firm mental shake, and looked up at the approaching rider; it was time to put her own wishes aside, and greet Mr Ballantyne as the very pleasant companion he had become, and instead, as he arrived, dismounted and bowed, she wondered whether to tell him about Maria, or whether to let him find out from Edmund, or Sir Thomas.

CHAPTER TWENTY-NINE

Never had the journey to Champford seemed so tedious to Sir Thomas; the hills were surely higher, the horses surely slower, and the coachman surely more cautious than he had ever been on any previous journey? Sir Thomas sat in the coach and fretted, with Mr Ricket's letter in his hands. There was little information in it, but Sir Thomas read it over and over as though he could extract more meaning that was not there. Maria was gone! Where could she have gone to? Although Sir Thomas had ensured that there was plenty of money available to Mrs Norris to keep his errant daughter secured in every comfort, he had also ensured that Maria did not have access to much money of her own. In the back of his mind had been the suspicion that she might attempt to leave her aunt should she have the funds to set up her own home, and so all the purse strings had been firmly in Mrs Norris's hands.

Mrs Norris! Here was a further source of irritation and wonder. How had Mrs Norris so erred in her management of Maria and the household as to let her leave with nobody knew who, and to nobody knew where? Once again, Mrs Norris had failed in her duties towards her niece; once again, Maria had disappeared. Sir Thomas's thoughts were very dark indeed; when he discovered his daughter's whereabouts, he was determined to ensure that she would never have the means or ability to run away again. Although he had to admit to himself that he had not the least idea how to achieve that, considering all the precautions that had been taken this time had apparently not worked. Wherever Maria was gone, she would need somebody to pay her way; he pushed the thought to the very back of his mind that she might go on to the town.

Sir Thomas's thoughts moved on to wonder what had made Maria leave? Or rather who – just as his niece before him, Mr Crawford's name came into his mind. Could it be possible that Mr Crawford had discovered her whereabouts and persuaded her to elope with him once more? He could think of no other man who might do so, unless Maria had formed some attachment to a man she had met in her exile, and apparently unknown to her aunt? Mrs Norris had repeatedly assured him on every visit that Maria met nobody, saw nobody but herself, the servants and Mr Ricket. It was not to be even considered that Mr

Ricket could have had anything to do with this – he was not at all the type, and it was he that had alerted Sir Thomas to Maria's disappearance. It was not possible that Mr Ricket would induce Maria to run away, and then write to inform her father of the fact. Sir Thomas felt he could also be assured that Mr Ricket would not have introduced Maria to any gentleman that might have induced her to leave her aunt's protection.

Despite his fretting, the journey to Champford Hall was no longer than previous journeys had been, and he arrived at last to find Mr Ricket coming down the stairs in person to greet him, and earnestly solicit him to take refreshments before visiting Mrs Morris, who kept to her own chamber.

Although chafing at the delay occasioned by this politeness, Sir Thomas was too much of a gentleman to refuse, and any way, Mr Ricket could give him all the information he required before he encountered his sister-in-law.

After all the enquiries concerning the health and happiness of all Sir Thomas's family had been answered, that gentleman was able, finally, to come to the matter which concerned him most nearly; where was Maria?

'What has been done to recover her, sir? Or to discern her whereabouts?'

Mr Ricket was proud of the action he had taken in this most troubling matter, and was happy to assure Sir Thomas that all possible steps had been taken to enquire about the neighbourhood in case Mrs Raworth had gone to stay with a friend, or had been taken suddenly ill and had to remain under a physician's care in another household. But he had to admit that, however diligently the Hall's servants and Mrs Morris's own servants had searched, there was no sign of Maria, nobody had seen her leave, and nobody appeared to know anything about her current whereabouts.

Sir Thomas asked if he could see Mrs Morris in case there was anything she could tell him; but it was clear from the first sight of her from just within the bed chamber door that she knew nothing, and could tell him even less, because her speech was so impaired. Such was her terror at beholding him, that Sir Thomas hastily left the room, calling for the Physician to be sent for, and returned to Mr Ricket in his office down stairs.

'It is evident to me that Mrs Morris is not able to furnish any further details,' said he. 'I will await the arrival of the Physician to reassure myself that she has taken no further harm at the sight of me, and then I shall be on my way.'

Mr Ricket bowed his head, and once the Physician arrived and was escorted above stairs, Sir Thomas efficiently made his arrangements to leave as soon as possible, and they waited to hear what Mr Fidler would say.

'I regret, sir,' said he. 'Mrs Morris has suffered a second seizure, which has completely robbed her of speech and she is sunk into a quiet insensibility from which I fear she may not recover.'

Sir Thomas was shocked and grieved indeed. That Mrs Norris should be so near to death! This active, interfering, bossy woman had been living as part of his own life and that of his family for very many years, and it was almost inconceivable that she might soon be taken from them.

'Can she be moved, sir?' he asked Mr Fidler, 'She might be more comfortable in my own home, with her sister and her family about her.'

'It is my opinion that Mrs Morris should not be moved, Sir Thomas,' said Mr Fidler, 'It may be that she has not long to live, and Mr Ricket may soon be called upon to administer the last rites; I cannot say whether she will die very soon or linger on in this state for weeks, or even months. Having said all that, I recollect that her constitution is very strong, and it may be that she will make a partial recovery, there is always some hope, I find. But she must not be moved from here.'

'I hope that will not cause too much inconvenience, Mr Ricket?' asked Sir Thomas, wondering how long Mrs Norris might be able to presume upon the indulgence of Lord M's family in occupying a best bedroom in their home, and during their absence.

'No indeed, sir,' answered he. 'The addition of Mrs Morris's servants to the Hall's servants means that there are more than enough hands to set to work to care for the unfortunate lady. Rest assured she will be given every attention, and I will keep you updated on her health and any progress.'

'Thank you,' said Sir Thomas, bowing to Mr Ricket. 'I must go to London, for I believe my daughter, Mrs Raworth, as she is to you, to be gone there, but I will return as soon as I may to see what more may be done for Mrs Morris, or if there has been any improvement in her condition.'

Sir Thomas left Champford Hall with a heavy heart, assured of his sister's care, if not his daughter's exact location although he was persuaded that she would be found in London, and that the Crawfords were either harbouring Maria, or would certainly know where she was to be found. In this assumption he was entirely correct: Maria was in London with the Crawfords, and as no attempt was being made to conceal Maria's whereabouts, from the number of entries in the papers about her attending the theatre, parties, outings, and what she was wearing on each occasion, her father was swiftly able to ascertain that she was at the Crawfords' home on Grosvenor Square.

Sir Thomas took refreshments at his hotel, and then set out for the Crawfords' town house, sending in his card and compliments to Mrs Grant. She received him kindly in her pretty sitting room, and after settling him in to a comfortable chair, and ringing for refreshments, expressed her surprise at his being in London.

'How timely you are arrived!' cried she. 'For dearest Maria is here and is to be married to my brother. I hope you are come to give your blessing to the union, and to attend the ceremony?'

'As to that, madam, I have no information,' replied Sir Thomas. 'Maria left the home I placed her in with her aunt, and disappeared. I have only just traced her here.'

'I am certain that she mentioned she had wrote to tell you that she was come to London with Henry, and that they were to be married,' said Mrs Grant, a slight frown marring her otherwise clear brow. Then she had a happy thought, which quite cleared the frown away; 'Depend upon it, a letter has gone astray. The Post Office is a wonderful institution, to be sure, but sometimes a letter is carried wrong, and you did not receive it.'

'I have been travelling for several days, madam,' said Sir Thomas. 'So it is possible that a letter has been received at Mansfield Park in my absence.'

'Dear Mansfield Park!' cried Mrs Grant. 'How very much I enjoyed living at the Parsonage there, and how very sorry I was when we had to leave. Although Dr Grant's new stall at Westminster was very comfortable, it was not at all the same as dear Mansfield Park Parsonage.'

Sir Thomas inclined his head gravely to acknowledge the compliment, but was determined not to let Mrs Grant imitate Mrs Norris and lead him off the path he was determined down; that of finding and speaking to Maria. However, as a gentleman, he could not pursue his own interests without acknowledging the fact that Mrs Grant was now a widow;

'I was very sorry to hear of your husband's death, Mrs Grant,' said he. 'Dr Grant was a good man and a devoted son of the Church. He was much missed by all the parish when he left Mansfield, I assure you, although my own son, Edmund has done his best to carry on with Dr Grant's example in the forefront of his mind.'

Mrs Grant raised her handkerchief to her eyes, and said it had all been very sudden for all that he had been told by his physician not to eat so much, and not such rich foods, but he could not be stopped; he was a man who loved to see a table well covered, and was so generous in entertaining his family and his friends. However, he had left her well provided for, and she rejoiced in the opportunity to be with her sister and brother here in this house in London, with all its many diversions and excitements.

The formalities finally having been dispensed with; Sir Thomas was able to move the conversation around to the real purpose of his visit.

'I am come, madam, to see Mrs Rushworth. Would you permit me to see her alone?'

'Oh! Of course! I am sure dear Maria will be delighted to see you,' said the fondly deceived hostess. 'Mary and I are standing chaperone to Maria while she is under my roof, and Henry stays in lodgings nearby.'

Sir Thomas was relieved to hear that some of the proprieties at least were being observed, and bowed in acknowledgement. Mrs Grant rang for refreshments and directed the maid to tell Mrs Rushworth that her father was here to see her. As he waited for his daughter to appear, Sir Thomas reflected upon his last interview with Maria before her first marriage, and wished once more that she had been able to tell him then that she did not wish to marry Mr Rushworth. The situation now was different to be sure, Maria was not under his roof, and neither was she any longer an unmarried woman. But he was still her father, and still had a care for her future, and he intended this interview to be very different; he hoped that Maria would assure him that arrangements were well in hand for an early marriage to Mr Crawford, but in this too he was to be disappointed.

Maria entered the room with her head held high. As far as she was concerned she was no longer a dependent daughter of the Bertram family, she was an independent woman, in charge of her own situation. As the interview proceeded, it became clear that she cared for none of her family; she wanted no help of Sir Thomas's; and she would not hear of leaving Mrs Grant's house to return to her aunt at the Dower House. She was unmoved by Sir Thomas's account of her aunt's illness. She was certain she and Mr Crawford should be married some time or other, and it did not much signify when; they were already going out into society as man and wife. Since such were her feelings, it only remained for Sir Thomas to recruit Mrs Grant to his cause in order to secure and expedite a marriage.

Maria rang for the maid to ask Mrs Grant to return, and left the room before Mrs Grant could come. That lady was surprised not to see Maria with her father when she returned, but was even more surprised when Sir Thomas said heavily;

'It appears there are no plans for an early wedding, madam?'

'Oh! well, as to that, it is true that we do not have an exact date,' said Mrs Grant. 'But Henry and Maria are making all the arrangements, I assure you. They are talking of St George's, Hanover Square, I believe, and Maria has been shopping for clothes every day in the best warehouses.'

Sir Thomas could not take comfort in such vague news, and decided to go straight to Mr Crawford to ascertain his intentions at first hand.

'Where are Mr Crawford's lodgings?'

Mrs Grant gave the address, and Sir Thomas bowed and took his leave shortly afterwards, relieved at least that Maria was somewhere in respectable company, angry that Mrs Grant was so much in her siblings' power that she could not see beyond her own indulgence towards them, and very afraid that a second rupture would occur between Maria and Mr Crawford before they could have the wedding service said over them.

Mr Crawford was not at his lodgings; his man informed Sir Thomas that his master was paying a visit to a friend, a Mr Gently, who was recently married. And as Sir Thomas had no excuse to visit Mr Gently, who was not known to him at all, he went instead to Mr Harding's house, to consult his old and particular friend. The irony of it having been Mr Harding who had warned him of Maria's behaviour all those years ago, did not escape him.

Mr Harding was always at home to Sir Thomas, and they had much to catch up on; until after enquiries into all of Mr Harding's family had been made and satisfied, and assurances given as to Lady Bertram's continuing good health, Sir Thomas turned to the reason for his unexpected visit;

'I regret it is Maria, again,' said he, knowing that, of all the people he knew, Mr Harding was the one he could trust to understand, and not judge him harshly. Mr Harding knew that Sir Thomas had done his utmost to secure Maria against the censure of the world, and to provide her with a home and everything of the best for the rest of her days. Mr Harding would not, moreover, be easily shocked by anything that Maria might have done since he had last heard of her.

Mr Harding looked all attention, and Sir Thomas was encouraged to continue.

'She has left the place of safety I arranged for her, and has once more thrown herself into the power of Mr Henry Crawford,' he said. 'I have traced her to his sisters' home, here in London, where I am intending she marry him as soon as possible.'

'You will require a Special Licence,' said Mr Harding, ringing for his secretary.
'Thank you,' said Sir Thomas, relieved that his friend had understood him so immediately, and knowing that Mr Harding would be able to easily acquire a Special Licence. Maria should and would be married right speedily, and with her father in attendance to ensure it was all done properly and finally.

'This would require that I attend the wedding too,' said Mr Harding, giving swift and precise instructions to his secretary. 'Especially as it is being issued without time for Banns.'

Sir Thomas bowed his head in acknowledgement, and once the secretary was sent off about his business, he could relax and enjoy the rest of the evening in the company of his particular friend.

CHAPTER THIRTY

Mr Crawford was indeed at Mr Gently's house; but not to see that gentleman, nor his new bride. In fact, Mr Crawford had been much at Mr Gently's house, usually managing to arrive after Mr Gently had left, and departing before his return, while lamenting his misfortune in missing that gentleman. In another household, this might have looked as though Mr Crawford wanted to be alone with Mr Gently's wife; but in this case, it was Mrs Gently's niece who drew Mr Crawford there on a daily basis. Although the excitement of discovering Maria had temporarily replaced Miss Waldegrave in his imagination as a life-partner, he had argued himself into the propriety of paying her a visit once he returned to London. Seeing her again reminded Henry how he had thought before that here was a woman who would be everything that he had ever wished for in a wife. Starting to spend time with her again had even made him stop regretting the loss of Fanny, for he believed he had finally found another woman to rival even her. As for Miss Waldegrave; she did not lack for suitors, once her aunt's ancestry became common knowledge, but she could acknowledge to herself a slight preference for Henry, and enjoyed his and his sisters' company almost more than that of her other visitors.

This renewal of their pleasant dalliance was almost over, although neither party could know it. Henry did not yet know of Sir Thomas's arrival, and Miss Waldegrave knew nothing of Maria; but her presence at his sisters' house meant that Henry was living a bachelor life, accountable to nobody, and free to visit whom he pleased. Maria did not notice, but Henry was more frequently with Miss Waldegrave than he was with her. Maria was much too busy with Mary and Mrs Grant in visiting mantua makers, and taking their recommendations to be fulfilled at the warehouses, choosing fabrics, having gowns fitted, and thinking about what she should wear for her first ball in London, her honeymoon in Brighton, and her first dinner at Everingham, to notice the absence of her lover.

A hastily dispatched servant carried the news of Sir Thomas's arrival to Henry, and on his visit to his sister's house that evening, Henry discovered that the conversation was all about Sir Thomas. The arrival of Sir Thomas gave Henry momentary hope that Maria's father would take her back to Mansfield Park with him, but Maria declared she would not go there until they were married, and properly invited, and for the first time, she asked him how the preparations for the wedding ceremony were coming along. Had he put an advertisement in to the newspaper? Were the banns being read in St George's Church? Henry prevaricated, but the noose was tightening around his neck, and he could see no way out of this predicament with any honour. He promised Maria that everything was in train, and that he was only waiting on her to complete her own purchases before naming a date. Maria's purchases were all well in train, and her wedding gowns were due to be delivered very soon, so she was content with Henry's reassurances, but he was not to be allowed to continue putting the matter off.

Henry was now in a bind of his own making. He was in the way of falling in love with one woman, while being expected to make arrangements for a wedding to another. He could not see any way out of this muddle which did not leave Maria worse off than she had been when he discovered her living with her Aunt. And it says something for Henry's long dormant conscience, that its awakening meant that he was able to put concern about Maria above his own desires.

In a moment alone, he discussed this conundrum with his sister, but neither of them could see their way through to a solution which would satisfy all parties equally. Somebody would have to be disappointed;

'And it looks as though that somebody might have to be you, my dear brother,' said Mary. 'You are not a Mahometan, or you could marry both.'

'That would be a neat solution indeed,' said Henry. 'But it will not do in England, I regret.'

'Have you spoken to Miss Waldegrave?' asked Mary.

'No, I have not, thankfully,' answered Henry. 'I hope she will not think all my attentions of recent months have been leading up to an offer.'

'I have no doubt that she would think that,' said Mary. 'Your attentions have been marked.'

'Then all I can do is not see her again until I am safely married to Maria,' said Henry with a sigh. 'But I will regret her, I am certain of it.'

'It seems to be your fate, my dear brother, to be committed by one woman, while in love with another.'

Rather ruefully, Henry had to agree.

The following morning, Sir Thomas clinched the matter by arriving with a Special Licence, and Henry had at last to name the date. With Sir Thomas's intervention, Henry's fate was sealed, and Maria never knew how close she had come to losing him all over again to another woman. Thus, Henry had to put Miss Waldegrave and her own possible disappointment at losing him out of his thoughts, and focus on the final arrangements for his wedding to Maria. Rings now had to be collected from the jeweller, Maria's gowns arrived, as did those for Mary and Mrs Grant, as well as new shirts and cravats for Henry. Mr Jones was approached to stand up with Henry as his Groom's man, and Sir Thomas informed them that his particular friend, Mr Harding would stand as a second witness with Mrs Grant.

And so it was just a week later that Henry found himself and Mr Jones, standing together at the fireplace in his sister's home, awaiting his bride. Maria looked radiant and triumphant as she walked into the room, wearing one of her new gowns and leaning on her father's arm. Sir Thomas led her across the room and ceremoniously gave her hand into Henry's hand. Maria may have had misgivings and may have protested at first about not being married at St George's, Hanover Square, but the sight of the Special Licence and the promise of a detailed account in the newspapers was enough to mollify her. Within a very few minutes, they were man and wife, and Henry had to smile at Maria and everybody else present, and assure himself that everything would now be all right.

Mr Harding declined to stay for the wedding breakfast, and left after offering his sincere wishes for a long and happy life together to the newly-weds. Sir Thomas issued an invitation to the new Mr and Mrs Crawford to visit them at Mansfield House when he could be most certain that there would be no society for them to embarrass, and after Miss Fairhaven and Tom were safely married as well.

'I am only sorry that your own family was not able to be present,' said he to Henry.

'You mean the Admiral? Gout, sir, I regret,' said Henry. 'But Maria and I will pay him a visit on our way to Mansfield Park. I hope we can impose upon your hospitality to invite my sister, Mary as well? She looks back upon our time at Mansfield Park with the fondest memories and has often expressed a wish to visit again and renew her acquaintance with Mrs Edmund Bertram as well.'

'Miss Crawford is very welcome to pay us a visit at Mansfield Park; I remember her kindness and interest in our dear Fanny very well, and I am assured Fanny will be delighted to see her again too. Will she accompany you on your visits to Brighton and to your relatives as well?'

'Thank you, sir, and yes,' answered Henry. 'My sister and Maria are close friends, and will be good company for each other, while we sample the delights of the sea-side. Then Mary will be of great assistance to Maria in settling into her new home at Everingham, whilst I am attending to my long neglected estate and business there.'

'From Mansfield Park you go on to Everingham?' asked Sir Thomas.

'We will, as I have not been there since September last year, and Everingham cannot do without me in September. I am long overdue a visit, so I will aim to arrive at Everingham at the beginning of September, and I hope Maria will be pleased with her new home. No doubt she will want to make many improvements; it has long been a bachelor residence, and needs a woman's touch.'

This was also Sir Thomas's devout wish; he did not think London society agreed with his daughter's restless temperament, and hoped that now she was finally married to Mr Crawford, she would settle down at Everingham with him, away from the temptations of the city. Neither man consulted Maria; had they done so, they would have discovered she was determined to make London her home, and have her full share of all the delights and diversions she had tasted so briefly during her first marriage, and which she had missed so sorely during her incarceration with her aunt.

For now, Maria was content to have finally made her point, and become Mrs Henry Crawford after so many alarms and deprivations. There was much to look forward to; a trip to the seaside, she was wild to see Brighton, and then she would be introduced to the Admiral, and go on from there to all their friends across the country, arriving in triumph at Mansfield Park, and finally ending their wedding tour at Everingham. This would give them the autumn months in Norfolk, and then they could return to London and take their place in society again. Yes, Maria was very content indeed.

As for Henry; his fate was sealed; he had lost Miss Waldegrave, but we cannot assume him to be forever inconsolable. Henry Crawford was not born to flee from society, or contract an habitual gloom of temper, and nor was his heart ever likely to be broken by any woman. His wife was a new Maria, infinitely more compliant than formerly, so much in good humour with him and with the world, that he was sanguine about his hopes for a comfortable home, and for no inconsiderable degree of domestic felicity. Indeed, as the London gossips remarked, he had escaped marriage for quite long enough, and he himself acknowledged that he was finally ready to settle down at last.

To be sure, the Admiral sent a letter in which he firmly reiterated all his arguments against marriage, but also charged Henry with the swift production of a son and heir, whom the Admiral rather prematurely promised to assist to a good place in the Navy. Furthermore, the Admiral advised Henry to at once set up a mistress, so that he need not be inconvenienced by a wife lying-in, and with whom he need not be ashamed to be seen out with in society. Wisely, Henry burned the letter, and told Maria that the Admiral would be delighted to receive them both on their return from the seaside. He felt assured that Maria's beauty and vivacity would assist the Admiral in overlooking her legal status as a wife.

CHAPTER THIRTY-ONE

The first that Miss Waldegrave knew of Henry's perfidy was the announcement in the paper, which convinced her more fully of his marriage than anything other than actually attending the ceremony itself could have done:

'June 5 Mr Henry Crawford, and Mrs Maria Rushworth, nee Bertram, married in the dwelling house of his sister Mrs Grant, on Grosvenor Square, by Special Licence, in the presence of her father, Sir Thomas Bertram of Mansfield Park, and Mr Aloysius George Jones, with Miss Mary Crawford and Mr John Harding of Doctor's Commons as additional witnesses. The bride and groom are to make a wedding voyage to Brighton before visiting the bride's family home at Mansfield Park in Northamptonshire, and then settling on the Crawford estate at Everingham, in Norfolk.'

Although he had made her no offer, written her no letters, and had never spoken of love; his looks and actions had daily spoken louder than any words could of his growing attachment to her, and she had felt certain he had known of her growing attachment to him in return. And here he was married! And to a woman Miss Waldegrave had never heard him even mention! This was a puzzle indeed; although the names 'Rushworth' and 'Bertram' were familiar, and a very little searching and diligent questioning of friends brought the whole scandal out into the light again. It is safe to say that Miss Waldegrave was not shocked, as she had enough experience of the world to know such things happened between men and women, but she was disappointed. Mr Crawford had not been handsome, but there had been something in his air, and in the way he talked, which had made her more than half way in love with him herself.

There was almost more pain in the suspicion that Mary Crawford had only befriended her in order to facilitate her brother's access to the family. Miss Waldegrave had been happy in Miss Crawford's friendship as she had believed it was born of genuine affection and shared interests, although she had to admit it had also been useful in allowing her to spend time with Mr Crawford. Had it all been a fiction? The Crawfords had certainly been convincing in their attentions, and in their protestations of friendship; and now it seemed that Miss Crawford had known all along that her brother was to marry the former Mrs Rushworth, and had continued with the deception right up to the very end! Nobody married on the spur of a moment; unions were always the subject of lengthy negotiation and planning in Miss Waldegrave's experience. To have concealed that from her, and to have allowed her to continue accepting Mr Crawford's attentions, knowing his honour to be pledged elsewhere, was quite unacceptable behaviour from his sister.

It was safe to talk of her disappointment to her aunt, for if she listened it was only by chance, and she seldom remembered anything inconvenient, or if she did, she never recalled the details exactly. Miss Waldegrave could only be thankful that she had only ever met with Mr Crawford in the company of her aunt, or his sister, and hoped that there had been nothing in her own behaviour which might have drawn her feelings to anybody else's notice. They had danced together a couple of times, and been out with Mrs Gently in that lady's barouche, walked with his sister in the parks, and there had been numerous dinner and other social engagements; but nothing more. For weeks following the newspaper announcement, Miss Waldegrave waited for an axe of societal disapproval of her behaviour with Mr Crawford to fall upon her head, but none ever did, and she set herself instead to forgetting him.

There was one other young lady disappointed by Mr Crawford's marriage, although her claim to his affections was far weaker than Miss Waldegrave's; that of Mr Jones's sister. She had made her come out, and had been looking forward to dancing with Mr Crawford at balls and Assemblies, to furthering her acquaintance with Miss Crawford, and to eventually becoming Mrs Crawford and enjoying all the delights that a country estate at Everingham could afford. Miss Jones had felt certain that it would all be just as she had imagined, for was not her own brother a close friend to Mr Crawford? So it was doubly provoking to see him there in the newspaper, mentioned as being at Mr Crawford's wedding to another woman, when he had not breathed a word of it to his sister! Poor Mr Jones had some anger from his mother and sister for his part in keeping them completely ignorant of Mr Crawford's marriage until they saw the announcement for themselves in the newspaper. As it had not occurred to him that his sister would harbour any hopes with regard to his friend, Mr Jones felt justly aggrieved at being blamed for his friend's marriage to another.

Miss Jones was very young, and with a reasonable fortune of her own, could be expected to soothe her disappointed heart in another man's interest soon.

Henry had not been entirely honest with Sir Thomas about his reasons for inviting his sister, Mary, along on his wedding voyage. Maria was not an inexperienced bride who might need the comfort and support of another woman at such a delicate time; Mary's inclusion in the wedding party was instead to give her a valid excuse to leave London at what had become a difficult time for her. Accompanying her newly-wed brother and sister on a series of visits was a legitimate reason for Mary to leave London, and it would not look as though she had been driven away, or that she was in any way guilty of impropriety following the foolish outpourings of Sir Cedric Cholmondley, now safely married and at his parents' country house with his new wife. Although she had achieved her aim, the new Lady Cholmondley's whisperings about her husband and his former passion had made London an uncomfortable place for Mary. However, she was certain that by the time she returned, it would all be forgot, and there would be some new scandal for society to talk over.

The day that took Henry, Maria, and Mary out of London was a happy one for all three; all three Crawfords turned their faces resolutely from London and towards Brighton, and if Maria had any consciousness from arriving there in a second husband's carriage, she certainly did not show it. Instead, she appointed herself their guide to the many delights and diversions Brighton offered, as well as recommending the Old Ship Inn for their lodgings, as it was now frequented by all the best sort of people, while the Crown, despite its fortuitous location, was in the descendant. Accordingly, they took apartments at the Old Ship, were happy to see their names recorded in the arrivals, subscribed to both circulating libraries, and set out to enjoy themselves.

All three of them were very happy with their stay in Brighton; Maria would not mention Mr Rushworth to Mr Crawford, but she was very content to finally be Mrs Henry Crawford, and to appear in public with a husband she need not blush for. After the mortifying years first with an uncongenial husband, and then spent with her aunt, deep in the countryside, Maria was completely determined never to fall out with

Henry again, and to really seize every opportunity which came her way from this moment on.

Mary found that her bloom and energy quite returned by the seaside, and feeling revived, began to form plans to stay at Everingham and look out for a suitable husband amongst her brother's neighbours, should one not appear in the Assembly Rooms and concerts at Brighton. And Henry found himself continuing to be very pleased with this new Maria that he had finally married; she continued all complaisance, and good humour, and he congratulated himself on his good fortune: Miss Waldegrave was quite forgot.

CHAPTER THIRTY-TWO

Sir Thomas's return home was a source of much satisfaction to all his family. Lady Bertram was always glad to see him home safely for despite how many times he went away every year, she would invariably say how agreeable to her it was to see him again, and hear him talk and explain everything to her, and discover how dreadfully she must have missed him, even though it was but a short absence on this occasion. She was also to discover that on his return he had both good and bad news for her.

'My dear,' said he, 'I have some good news to tell you. Maria is married to Mr Crawford, and they will be paying us a visit in August.'

Lady Bertram was delighted in this news although her chief concerns were whether the fringing she and Susan had been working on for dear Maria would be ready in time, and whether Pug's puppies would be old enough to leave their mother, as she had promised Maria one.

'I must tell you though, Lady Bertram, some sad news besides; that your sister Norris is gravely ill, and the Physician has almost given her up. There is some hope that she may yet make a partial recovery, but she is not well enough to be removed to Mansfield Park to be nursed at present. I left her in the care of Lord M_'s physician, and his cousin, who is a priest, and there is a house full of servants, so she will want for no attention, or care.'

There was a short silence while everybody present attempted to feel sorry for Mrs Norris. Sympathy was in short supply: the Fairhavens had never met her, and even Susan had very little knowledge of her as she had left Mansfield Park shortly after Susan arrived and had been in no state to show her true colours before she left. Her sister might have been expected to show some concern, but the only time Lady Bertram had ever felt seriously frightened over some body's health was when Tom had fallen seriously ill with brain fever, and she had quite worn out all her emotions on that occasion. Hearing only the best, and never thinking beyond what she heard, with no disposition for alarm and no aptitude at a hint, Lady Bertram was perfectly content despite Sir Thomas's news about her sister.

It was Lady Bertram who spoke first; 'My sister Norris is so very healthy and stout, that I have every confidence that she will soon be well and with us again. But when does Maria come, my dear Sir Thomas? I shall be very glad to see her. Shall we wait until she comes before Tom and Agnes marry?'

Agnes had been feeling great relief at Sir Thomas's return only two weeks after he set off, and had believed that this prompt return would confirm that the wedding could go ahead on the date already set; so Lady Bertram's suggestion threw her into another panic.

She could not have hysterics in front of Sir Thomas, however, and was in agony until he gave a decided negative to his wife's suggestion. Agnes could not know it, but Sir Thomas did not wish to have to introduce Maria and Mr Crawford to their neighbours and friends at his eldest son's wedding; he did not wish anybody to be embarrassed by having to meet Maria at all, although it was unlikely he would be able to keep her from the other families in the neighbourhood for ever. Still, their arriving in time for his son's wedding would detract attention from Tom and Agnes, and so he made a slight answer about their plans, and their not being able to come into the country until later in August. Greatly relieved by this, Agnes felt it incumbent upon her to make some comment to Lady Bertram upon the sad fate of her sister instead;

'I am indeed very sorry to hear that Mrs Norris will not be able to come for my wedding, ma'am, and I do hope that the physician is wrong, and that she will yet make a full recovery and come home in due course. I have never met her, yet I know how important she is to the Bertram family.'

'Very well said, my dear,' agreed Mrs Fairhaven. 'Physicians do not always know what they are about, and they do make mistakes in their diagnosis. Remember poor Obadiah?'

Miss Fairhaven ignored her mother's question, and as nobody else knew who poor Obadiah might have been, nor what sad fate had overtaken him at the hands of a physician, the parallel was not helpful, and neither lady explained how it pertained to this case either. Sir Thomas gravely thanked Mrs and Miss Fairhaven for their good wishes, and asked if all the relevant preparations for the wedding were under way, and whether the date in two weeks' time was still convenient.

'Oh yes, I thank you, sir,' Agnes said promptly and with great relief. 'I am quite ready, and all the invitations have been sent out and Mr Edmund Bertram is reading the Banns each week. Everything is in train, and everybody who has been invited is to come.'

Agnes and Mrs Fairhaven had seen to everything personally in order to prevent the wedding being postponed, as Lady Bertram could never be roused for long enough to do this task herself.

'In that case,' said Sir Thomas, 'I am minded to give a Supper Ball on the night before to celebrate both the wedding and, if it is acceptable to all concerned, to give Susan her official coming out.'

Although it had been clear to everybody at Mansfield Park that Susan had been grown up these past two years, there had not been any social events outside the family for her to attend, and so her come out had been rather overlooked until now. The remembrance that Susan was now quite grown-up, added to the relief that Tom had finally secured a suitable bride, led Sir Thomas to remember how he had given a most agreeable Ball on the occasion of Fanny's coming out, and he had almost surprised himself some time before by contemplating giving another for her sister. He had been overtaken by events before he could mention it; but now there could be a double celebration. If he had any economy in mind by combining the two, we must not judge him harshly; his estate in Antigua was going through considerable upheaval, and Tom's former debts had yet to be all repaid.

With all this in mind, and knowing that Julia and Mr Yates would be travelling up from London to attend Tom and Agnes's marriage, so that all the respectable members of his family would be assembled, and his neighbours need not be embarrassed at meeting them, he proposed his idea to Susan and Agnes;

'My dears,' he said, holding out a hand to each young woman, 'I hope very much that your friendship will allow you to share this very special occasion with our friends and local society; on the night before Agnes and Tom's wedding.'

Susan was startled but pleased that her uncle would show her such attention, and she was also relieved that she would not be the sole focus of the evening, remembering what Fanny had told her about her own come out at the ball given to her by her uncle. Agnes very prettily said that it would be an honour to share such an important occasion with her dearest Miss Price, while secretly thinking to herself that it did not at all signify if Susan was also being celebrated, as *she* would be the focus of all the envy of the young ladies in the neighbourhood who must have had their eyes on the Bertram estate and the Bertram heir.

As preparations for the wedding had continued apace despite Sir Thomas's much-lamented absence, it was not too much more work to add a Ball the night before to the festivities intended to dignify Agnes and Tom's wedding. Sir Thomas did not intend the Ball to go on late for everybody would have to be up betimes the following day to prepare for the wedding ceremony and breakfast; so it was to be just a few dances, and some supper for their nearest neighbours and friends, and for the family.

Susan had observed the extreme anxiety demonstrated by both Mrs Fairhaven and Agnes over any delay to the wedding, and privately wondered what they could be about, but she could find no answer that satisfied her. Now that Sir Thomas was returned, there could be no more need for such anxiety at least, but the very fact of their having been so anxious at the delay did cause Susan to wonder. She had the sense that there was something amiss, but did not in the least know what it might be. Dresses for all the ladies were being finished, and Mansfield Park's principal rooms were being transformed into a ballroom. Agnes had had some sentimental notion of Edmund and Fanny's darling children strewing rose petals in her path as she walked into the church, but this idea was very quietly and suddenly dropped after she met them. Little Eddie put both his hands into a whole dish of jam and proceeded to share it about the room. As Agnes fled from him in horror, he thought it was a game she was playing with him, and chased after her catching hold of her white gown with his very sticky hands, and laughing until swept away by Susan.

Agnes's maid was summoned, and helped her mistress weeping from the room, convinced her gown was ruined.

'Oh dear!' said Lady Bertram. 'That lovely gown! Still, it is so very full in the skirt that a hands-breadth may be taken out and not be missed, and such full skirts are not so much in fashion this year, I recall. And white is not a practical colour when small children are around; I remember Tom and Julia quite ruining my favourite white gown with some glue.'

Susan missed Mrs Fairhaven's reply, as she was too busy in restraining Eddie without overmuch jam being transferred to her own gown, in order to take him to the kitchen to have all the jam washed away. As she carried him out crying and kicking about lustily, a line of servants trooped past her in the opposite direction with buckets of hot water and cloths to get the jam up from the wallpaper, and the carpet, cushions and curtains.

When Susan returned with a damp and chastened Eddie, it was to find Edmund had arrived and was endeavouring to calm little Frances, who was near hysterical with all the upheaval, and so she handed Eddie to his father, took Frances from him, and suggested that both children be taken home to their mother.

'They are such dear sweet natured little things,' Lady Bertram said, in the face of the evidence, as both children were now crying lustily. 'But far too fond of jam. Their father and Susan manage them very well, and they are very well behaved when Sir Thomas is here, but I cannot get them to attend to me at all, and Eddie will tease Pug.'

That was all Susan and Edmund heard before they left the room to head back across the park to the Parsonage.

'How is my sister today?' Susan asked.

'I believe her to be a little better,' answered Edmund. 'She is very excited for our visit to the seaside, that was a very happy thought of Mrs Fairhaven; I am greatly indebted to her. I am convinced, as is my father, that a visit to the seaside will materially assist in Fanny's own recovery and in helping the children to better health.'

At this point, both children, seeing their home a short walk away, wanted to be put down and chase each other the rest of the way. Eddie ran ahead, while Frances staggered after him on uncertain legs, calling all the while for him to wait for her. Susan watched their frisks and frolics, and said;

'It seems to me that both the children are already a little stronger than they were a few days ago. I do declare that they have more energy for running about.' And thought she to herself, there is certainly little wrong with their lungs!

Edmund brightened a little;

'I believe you are right!' said he, 'Let us hope that they have both turned a corner with their health, and that the visit to the seaside will assist them to a full recovery.'

'Where do you go?'

'We are to go to a place called Great Yarmouth in Norfolk, where my father has taken a house for us.'

'What is there to do at Great Yarmouth? Does Mr Hibbs recommend sea bathing?'

'There is a fine new Bath House and Assembly Rooms, I gather,' said Edmund. 'Mr Hibbs has given me a book written by a Dr Richard Russell, concerning the use of sea water to alleviate all manner of conditions. He has recommended Fanny and the children take their dips in the salt water bath there, rather than in the sea.'

'And have they healing waters, like at Bath?' asked Susan.

'If they have, then I suspect Mr Hibbs has not heard of them as he has not recommended them. But I do not recall hearing that Great Yarmouth has any mineral springs either.'

'Are the servants to go too?'

'The children's nurse will come with us, but my father has hired local servants to attend us in the house. Our servants will be airing and thoroughly cleaning out the house against our return, as Mr Hibbs has advised me that will assist in clearing out any infections that may be lingering in the air.'

'That sounds most sensible,' said Susan. 'When do you go? I wish I was coming too; I find I miss the sea after my early years in Portsmouth.'

'We will set off after the wedding breakfast,' said Edmund. 'But it will take us two days on the road. You are most welcome to accompany us, but I fear we would be sadly crowded in the carriage with another person.'

'No, I do not wish to add to any body's discomfort,' said Susan. 'I will perhaps suggest to my Uncle that I make a visit to my parents, and I can see the sea off Portsmouth.'

'My mother will be very dull after all the excitement of the ball and the wedding,' said Edmund. 'I cannot think she could spare you, unless Mrs Fairhaven stays for longer while Agnes and Tom are on their wedding journey.'

Susan assented to this and shortly afterwards walked in to the house to visit her sister, while Edmund went on about his parish business. The children could be heard in the Nursery telling the nursemaid about their adventures at Grandmama's house, and Fanny was in her own sitting room. Susan was glad to see she was out of bed, and sitting up, dressed in comfortable clothes. Susan had much to tell her sister about Eddie's latest escapade with the jam, and of Miss Fairhaven's reaction, and both ladies wanted to discuss the forthcoming wedding, the Ball, and the family's removal to Great Yarmouth.

After finishing giving her sister all the news and hearing her excitement about going to the seaside, Susan hesitated;

'What is it, my dear sister?' asked Fanny in her gentle way. 'Something is troubling you about this wedding?'

'Yes, I find that I am troubled,' Susan said, 'but I do not know what it is that is troubling me. I cannot like Miss Fairhaven; I have spent many hours in her company, but I am not at all sure what it is that I dislike. She is everything that is friendly, and often thoughtful, and always easy to converse with, and keen to accompany me on my walks. However, despite all that, I suspect that this marriage to Tom may be a mistake.'

'I have only met Miss Fairhaven a couple of times, and she seems rather young and a little thoughtless in her manner as very young women often are who have no cares or worries of their own to weigh down their spirits.'

Susan wondered if Fanny were talking about herself rather than Miss Fairhaven, but Fanny went on;

'Tom is grown-up, he is a man, and men generally know their own minds best. If he had any doubts about Miss Fairhaven, he would not have made her an offer, nor agreed to such a short engagement. He must be truly in love!'

'As to that,' said Susan. 'I am not at all convinced that either of them is in love from what I have observed of them together. I did not think Tom would ever marry; and now that he is engaged, his behaviour is not how I imagine a lover to be at all.'

'And you have such experience of different sorts of lovers to compare?' asked Fanny in a teasing tone.

Susan coloured, but answered firmly;

'There is no body I can call to mind with such behaviour in my own experience, most of the men and women about me are married already, but –.'

'But, what?'

'Are we to believe that all the stories are wrong in their portrayal of a man in love? Tom does not look to me like a man in love; he looks more like a man who hears the prison doors slam shut behind him. He does not seek Miss Fairhaven out for confidential walks or talks, he is polite to her, but no more; they do not sit with their heads close together when we are all in company after dinner. I have not even seen him kiss her hand!'

'You have been watching them very closely?' asked Fanny. 'Are you always in company with them? Are they never alone?'

'I am in company with Miss Fairhaven most of every day, and when I am not, she is always with her mother and my aunt; she sees Tom at meal times and they go riding with two grooms, for she is learning to ride, but they are never alone. There are no stolen glances, or touching of hands, nor any attempt to be together away from the rest of the family. Miss Fairhaven behaves like a daughter of the family already, and seems quite indifferent to Tom, as if he were her brother, rather than the man she is to marry.'

'That is very puzzling indeed,' said Fanny. 'Indeed, I know not how to explain it to set your mind at rest. But it is not any of our business, as you know, and if Tom and Miss Fairhaven are happy with their relationship, then we must all be happy for them.'

'That is true enough,' said Susan, 'I could only wish that it was not Edmund that is to marry them.'

'You fear for Edmund's conscience should there turn out to be a lawful reason for them to not marry, and it is not declared to him or discovered before the wedding?'

'Yes,' said Susan gratefully, 'that is exactly my fear.'

'How about if Mr Ballantyne were to marry them? Would your fears extend to him also?'

Susan coloured again, but answered firmly enough;

'I would not wish to put Mr Ballantyne in to a position I would not ask Edmund to undertake. No, I would not wish his conscience to be likewise troubled, although he is not in my family, like Edmund.'

'Very well,' said Fanny, secretly resolving to ask her husband to find out if Mr Ballantyne had mentioned Susan to him. 'Then I will speak with Edmund, and he will speak with Tom, and between us we will set your mind at rest.'

CHAPTER THIRTY-THREE

Fanny duly mentioned her sister's concerns to Edmund, and he carried them to his brother. Susan's fears were not as much a surprise to Edmund as they had been to Fanny, as from his own observations of Miss Fairhaven, it had become apparent to Edmund that she was not everything he might have wished for in a woman who would one day replace his mother as Lady Bertram. She was lively enough, and had looks enough, and her manners were civil and engaging, but he could not help but notice that she had received little advantage from any education she may have received; her want of information in the most common particulars was evident, despite her gaiety and constant endeavour to appear to advantage. Unlike his father, Edmund was not at all certain that Miss Fairhaven was a suitable bride for his brother. So when Fanny spoke to him about her conversation with Susan, his own concerns added to those raised by Susan determined him to speak to his brother and ascertain, if at all possible, just how much Tom was in love with Miss Fairhaven, or whether he had accepted her just to please his father.

Before speaking to Tom, Edmund observed his brother more closely than before when in company with Miss Fairhaven, and it was evident to him that there was an indifference between them, almost a coldness, which did not suggest a deep attachment. And so Edmund attempted with his brother what his father had done with Maria; he asked Tom if he was determined to go through with the marriage, or if he needed a way to sever this connexion. If it were so, Edmund offered to speak to his father on Tom's behalf and have him released from the engagement, no matter how painful was the severance to all parties.

Tom was silent for a moment. He was a little disconcerted to realise that it seemed so obvious to his brother that his feelings were not engaged to Agnes. He did not dislike her; he thought the match was advantageous to the family, and thus he had been content to acquiesce with his father's wishes.

'Do you know of any reason why I should not marry Miss Fairhaven, other than your belief in our indifference to one another?' Tom asked.

'Not at all,' Edmund replied. 'I am concerned only with your happiness in the match.'

'Then allow me to set your mind at rest,' said Tom, 'I have the highest esteem for Miss Fairhaven's character and disposition and believe we will deal very well together. Marriage is not always a matter of love, as it was for you; some marriages are made for more practical reasons. I need to marry; Miss Fairhaven is known to the family, and has a fortune which will greatly assist my father in his business ventures, and her plantation is next to my father's, so there is the possibility of merging the two. I can see no reason to set her aside, and I believe we shall be as happy as my own parents have been together.'

Edmund was reassured. Although he could have wished that Tom was in love with Miss Fairhaven, Tom apparently believed that they had every chance of finding happiness together, and he was certainly clear-headed about his reasons for marrying her. Edmund could only hope Tom had not couched his proposal in such language! To enter into marriage without the prejudice or the blindness of love might well be an advantage for Tom, and even if Miss Fairhaven was also not in love, then there was much to be said for a well-disposed young woman who was already in a great way of becoming sincerely attached to her new husband's home and family. Miss Fairhaven was young enough to improve, and given the amiable and innocent enjoyments of the society and pastimes at Mansfield Park, she surely would improve, and become the asset to the family that Sir Thomas already believed her to be.

The conference ended with Tom and Edmund shaking hands, while burying their feelings under a calm demeanour, both knowing their strong attachment would lead either of them, if required, to do anything for the good of the other. Thus Tom was not offended at Edmund's concerns, and Edmund was not scornful of Tom's indifference to his fiancée; and they parted on the best of terms; Edmund to carry reassurance to his wife and sister, and Tom to pay more attention to Miss Fairhaven. The outcome of Edmund's concern for Tom was for that young man to endeavour to discover more about the woman he was intending to spend the rest of his life with.

Although between them, Fanny, Edmund and Tom had attempted to soothe away her fears of the marriage, and although Tom and Miss Fairhaven behaved a little more like lovers when they were together, Susan was not able to completely shake the slight uneasiness she felt. But there was nothing more to be done than concentrate on her own coming out at the Ball. Susan was determined to enjoy the evening, despite having to share it with Miss Fairhaven, who in her status as bride-to-be, would expect to outshine a mere coming out. Susan had smiled to herself at Miss Fairhaven's anxious efforts to ensure that her own dress had more lace on it than Miss Price's, and that her pearls were larger and in more profusion than Miss Price's simple single string. Lady Bertram had been persuaded by her husband to gift Miss Fairhaven one of the family's tiaras, while Susan was more than content with the loan of one of Lady Bertram's diamond combs.

The arrival of guests coming to stay at Mansfield Park prior to the Ball and wedding sent Agnes into quite a flutter. Although she had been preparing for this moment ever since arriving in England, suddenly these guests brought it all home to her that the wedding was becoming imminent. Julia and the Hon Mr Yates arrived several days before the wedding in a hired chaise, and Julia and Agnes immediately became best friends, and were inseparable, always whispering with their heads close together. A resemblance in the semblance of good humour and high spirits recommended them to each other, and despite their only just having made each others' acquaintance, they passed rapidly into friendship and from there into intimacy within a very few days. They were soon calling each other by their first names, and had Susan valued Agnes's friendship, she must surely have felt wounded by this desertion; *she* remained Miss Price to Agnes, who had never authorized her to call her anything but Miss Fairhaven. But it seemed that Julia's arrival meant that Agnes no longer needed Susan; the wife of the Honourable Mr Yates was a far more prestigious and useful friend and ally than a retired sailor's daughter, on top of which, Julia was a daughter of the house, not a mere cousin of the Bertram family.

Mr Yates himself was a nonentity; Susan had been in company with him a number of times before on his visits with Julia, and liked him well enough. He was an agreeable companion for a short while; his deportment and manners were good, and he always agreed with everybody; indeed he was so much in awe of Sir Thomas that he made it his business to agree with everything Sir Thomas said, and to ask his opinion on every matter before stating his own. Marriage had made him settled and rather stout, and he had quite given up on his ideas of acting upon the stage, although he referred to it wistfully when there was no chance of Sir Thomas hearing. Julia herself had not lived at Mansfield Park since Susan's arrival – her own elopement pre-dated it – but she had always treated Susan with the same slightly disdainful politeness that she had always shown to Fanny. To Julia, Susan was Susan, a cousin she did not have to be any more than slightly superior to, and she had never made any attempt to be anything more.

CHAPTER THIRTY-FOUR

With Julia engrossing Agnes, and Mr Yates and Tom renewing their friendship, Susan found herself suddenly free to pursue her daily walk alone, and to not have to share the precious time she was able to spend with Mr Ballantyne. For his part, seeing Susan alone again, encouraged him to endeavour to discover if her feelings towards him were as strong as his were towards her. He began to deliberately time his ride across Mansfield Park to coincide with her daily walk about the grounds, and on one bright morning they encountered one other in the garden, as Susan took her morning walk, in the opposite direction to the one taken by Agnes and Julia.

'Good morning, Miss Price,' said Mr Ballantyne dismounting his horse, bowing and looking about with mild concern, 'I am very pleased to meet with you. Does Miss Fairhaven not walk out with you today?'

'Good morning,' said Susan, 'Miss Fairhaven and Mrs Yates are walking in the other direction from me. They have some project about which they are very intent, and their discussions did not admit a third.'

'If you are not too tired, may I offer you my arm, and we shall take another turn together?'

Susan was assuredly not too tired to walk on with Mr Ballantyne, and they walked for a while in a comfortable silence, while Mr Ballantyne's horse cropped the grass behind them.

After several minutes had elapsed, Mr Ballantyne appeared to be making up his mind to say something, and had several false starts, before finally stopping, and turning to face Susan. He did not seem able to look her in the eye, turning his own face to the ground, before looking up in earnest appeal, and saying;

'Miss Price, you can hardly be without suspicion –.'

But at this most interesting of moments, they heard voices, and there was Agnes and Julia coming towards them along the path, and Mr

Ballantyne had first to be gallant, and then to excuse himself to the ladies and go about his business.

'Have you finished your walk, Miss Price?' asked Agnes. 'I believe Lady Bertram was asking for you.'

'Yes, I thank you, I will go to my aunt directly,' answered Susan, her thoughts still somewhat disordered by wondering what it was Mr Ballantyne had thought she had some suspicion of. Luckily or unluckily, depending on your point of view, Lady Bertram's demands that morning were light enough to give Susan enough leisure to think over her walk with Mr Ballantyne and to question his every word and gesture. Sometimes she thought he might have been about to declare himself, and at other times she scolded herself for her impropriety of thought, and persuaded herself that what he felt for her was friendship only, and that he was only going to tell her that he would be leaving soon for his promised parish. She hoped that he would ask her to dance at the forthcoming Ball, where maybe they would have more time to talk uninterrupted, and she might find out what it was she was supposed to suspect.

During the days leading up to the Ball and the wedding, there was no mention of the other wedding that Sir Thomas had supervised before returning home. Julia certainly did not want to hear that Maria had succeeded in marrying Mr Crawford at last; while Lady Bertram was quite content with Sir Thomas's promise that Maria would come soon, and did not have enough curiosity to question him about any detail of her wedding. Susan would have liked to know what had happened, but did not feel authorised to ask, but she was able to find out via Fanny after Sir Thomas told his two sons about their sister's second wedding.

'It seems terrible to think it of Maria,' said Fanny to Susan, 'But she was happy to live with Mr Crawford again without any expectation of marriage. Sir Thomas had to apply for a Special Licence, and they were married at Mrs Grant's house, not in a church.'

'That is shocking indeed,' said Susan. 'But it is done now, and there will be no more elopements or disappearances, and everybody will be happy and settled now that they have what they want.'

'I think you are the only one left to run away,' teased Edmund, who had come in to the room during this tete-a-tete.

'Be reassured, I am not in any danger of running away,' said Susan, laughing.

'No, there is too much incentive for you to stay,' said Fanny slyly.

'Indeed there is,' cried Susan, refusing to understand her, 'You and my beloved nephew and niece are here, and my aunt cannot do without me.'

Fanny and Edmund exchanged knowing glances that caused Susan's face to glow, and she hastily changed the subject.

CHAPTER THIRTY-FIVE

As she went up to dress for the Ball, Susan was surprised by the sight of Camba in the corridor outside her bed chamber, apparently waiting for her.

'Has Miss Fairhaven sent you to assist me again?' she asked, 'That is most considerate of her. I do have my own maid now, still, there is plenty she can learn from watching you dressing my hair.'

Camba did not reply, and on looking more closely, Susan could see that the girl was in some distress.

'Camba, what is it?' she asked, but it seemed that the girl had lost whatever courage she had gathered in waiting for Susan to come upstairs. She seemed to be on the verge of tears, curtseyed and started to move away. Susan put out a gentle hand to stop her; she could see that the girl had something to say, and that she was afraid to speak.

'Let me speak for you,' said she. 'Is your concern for Miss Fairhaven's marrying Mr Tom Bertram?'

The girl's eyes widened at the nearness of Susan's guess, but she still didn't speak.

'Come into my room,' said Susan, 'I will not make you speak, but I will make some guesses, and you can nod or shake your head, if that will make things easier for you?'

Camba did not reply, but followed Susan into her room and stood before her with eyes lowered, and hands crossed.

'Now,' said Susan, 'I will make some guesses as to why you are upset by Miss Fairhaven marrying Mr Bertram. One is that you fear you will be turned off for a new maid; is not that one of your fears?'

Camba shook her head, but Susan said, 'I am certain that Mr Bertram would not insist that his wife change any of her servants; he has none but his own man at present, and the arrangement of a household is more the wife's province. If Miss Fairhaven is happy with your work, I am sure she will keep you in your current place. Unless you would rather return to Antigua to be with your own family? I am certain that were you to mention that to Miss Fairhaven, she would do all she could to assist you to return.'

There was a silence, and, as Camba did not make any move to leave the room, Susan moved on to another guess as to why the maid might be worried about the forthcoming match between her mistress and Tom Bertram.

'Is it that you know something to Miss Fairhaven's discredit, which you believe means she should not marry Mr Bertram?'

Camba looked terrified, shook her head, bobbed a small curtsey and ran out of the room.

Susan did not pursue her; she sat and thought about this for quite half an hour, while her own maid moved about her room getting her gown and accoutrements ready, and wondering how she was to dress Miss Price's hair without Miss Fairhaven's maid's guidance. It was clear to Susan at least, that Camba did know something to Miss Fairhaven's discredit; a reason why it was unwise for Tom to marry her. And if Susan did not persuade Camba to speak, could she go to Tom and give him a hint that marrying Miss Fairhaven might give rise to another scandal, leading at the worst to another broken marriage in the Bertram household? She did not know whether Tom would believe her, and she did not have any evidence of any wrongdoing on Miss Fairhaven's part, and neither was she sufficiently intimate with Miss Fairhaven to ask her if there was anything to prevent her marriage, despite Miss Fairhaven's formerly frequent protestations of friendship.

She recalled her earlier conversation with Fanny; this was possible vindication for her fears, for although Camba had not said anything at all, she had not denied Susan's suppositions either. What could, or should she do now? It was altogether too late! Everything was in motion, nobody had come forward after the Banns were read by Edmund in church to protest the marriage should not go ahead, and Susan was certain there would be nobody rising from their seat to give any reason why the wedding should not go ahead on the morrow either. If Camba did know something, she would not be present at the ceremony, and it would go ahead without impediment.

It was altogether too late. Susan could not now raise her concerns again to her cousins; Edmund and Tom had both negatived her fears and now Tom must face his fate without any further interference from Susan. Tonight was for her, tonight was her coming out into society, and everybody in the neighbourhood would be there to witness! She would forget her fears, and enjoy the evening to her very utmost.

However, there was her new maid waiting for her to commence all the business of dressing in her very beautiful new gown which would do double duty both for the Ball and for the wedding on the morrow. While she stepped into this, and stood still for that to be fastened, Susan found herself hoping that somebody would secure her for the first two dances. It could not be Tom, of course, but maybe Edmund might, if Fanny did not wish to dance. There was Harry Ballantyne, but Susan did not feel she could assume he would want to dance with her; he might not wish to dance; he might prefer to join the other men in the supper or card room. She set this worry aside, and turned her attention instead to attempting to show her new maid how to replicate the way Camba had dressed her hair once before.

Susan had to own they had been quite successful between them, as when she came down the stairs, Edmund, Tom and Harry were all standing in the hall, and all three turned to her and bowed.

'Ah,' said Edmund, 'Miss Fairhaven's maid has dressed your hair again, I see!'

'It is indeed most becoming, Miss Price,' said Harry, and before Susan could protest that it was all her own work, he went on rather hurriedly, 'May I ask if you are engaged for the first two dances?'

'No, sir, I am not,' answered Susan, a little breathless under such close scrutiny.

'In that case,' said Harry, 'May I have the honour of the first two dances?'

'Yes of course, sir,' said Susan dropping a small curtsey, but her moment of attention had passed as Miss Fairhaven was coming down the stairs, and all three men had to turn back to make their bows to her.

Susan, momentarily forgotten, watched Miss Fairhaven make her way towards them, and was torn between watching Tom's expression, and her own surprise at the rather outré way Miss Fairhaven's hair had been dressed. She wondered, briefly, if this was Camba's revenge for the way Miss Fairhaven treated her, or if the maid was trying to warn Tom away by dressing her mistress's hair so strangely. Or maybe it was that the fashions in Antigua were very different, and perhaps Miss Fairhaven had not yet caught up with fashions in England to be content to appear in public with such a hair style. Tom himself was staring too, but Susan could not tell if it was in admiration or surprise; he pulled himself together enough to offer her his arm as she reached the foot of the stairs, and to make some slight compliment on her dress, which Miss Fairhaven answered at length as they walked in to dinner.

Susan found herself solicited again by Harry to take his arm, and they followed the happy couple in. Edmund walked behind them on his own, his head bowed, and his hands clasped behind his back; Fanny was not well enough to attend again.

CHAPTER THIRTY-SIX

Tom and Miss Fairhaven opened the Ball, with Susan and Harry Ballantyne standing just below them in the set, and Harry was not far from Susan's side for the rest of the evening, although he did not attempt another confidential talk with her. Despite the helpful cover of the music and chatter, there were too many other people wanting her attention, and she had to dance with everybody who asked her. Sir Thomas had noticed that Harry Ballantyne was paying his niece attentions which were marked enough to give no possibility of misinterpretation to his experienced eye, although he was delighted to observe that the young woman herself was all propriety, just as her sister had been when Mr Crawford had paid her equally marked attentions.

Given his family's propensity to choose unsuitable mates for life, Sir Thomas had quietly set in motion quiet enquiries to the young man's family to ensure they had not a bride already in mind for him, and that the living promised him would be his in due course. There had been reassurance from the Ballantyne family, as well as enquiries about Susan, which Sir Thomas had not answered, as he supposed that Ballantyne would have sought such information from Tom or Edmund. Even though he was the son of a fellow Member of Parliament, Sir Thomas was determined that should this young man should turn out to be another Hon Mr Yates, or another Mr Crawford, he would step in firmly to prevent any match. For now, Sir Thomas decided to leave well alone and see whether Mr Ballantyne did intend to make his niece an offer or not; there was no profit in worrying any further about something which may never happen.

Sir Thomas regretted that he had not been able to prevent Julia from eloping with Mr Yates, although the marriage seemed firm enough now, and Mr Crawford had twice let Sir Thomas down by his behaviour with Maria, although all of that was sorted out to Sir Thomas's approval now. But with all this history behind him when it came to the marriages of the next generation, Sir Thomas was determined not to have another member of his family disappointed in their marriage partner. That Tom might fall into that category did not occur to him, for as far as he was concerned, Tom and Miss Fairhaven had chosen each other freely, and there could be no impediment to a very successful married life together.

Susan herself was unaware of any of these manoeuvrings; she was just happy to be at her first Ball, and to be solicited for every dance; beyond that she did not let her thoughts or expectations go. Her only source of sorrow was that Fanny was not here to witness her triumph; Edmund's explanation was that Fanny had much to do before their departure to Great Yarmouth after the wedding the following day, and her health did not allow her to dance or sit up late at night anyway.

The evening ended early, as Sir Thomas had intended, and Mr Ballantyne could only press Susan's hand very warmly in farewell, and hope to have another opportunity to speak more privately with her in the near future. Susan herself went to bed with her head full of the excitement of her first ball, her hopes of Mr Ballantyne's regard, and her concerns for her sister's health. The wedding was almost forgot!

Everybody was punctual to the Church just before mid-day the next morning, and looking around, Susan allowed that everybody was in their best looks. Certainly, Tom looked more as though he were being strangled than about to become the happiest of men, but she recalled Edmund's looks at the altar as he waited for Fanny had been of a similar nature, and concluded that was how a prospective husband should look.

Miss Fairhaven did not keep Tom waiting; and Edmund opened the Book of Common Prayers and started the service with;

'Dearly beloved, we are gathered together here in the sight of God, and in the face of this congregation, to join together this man and this woman in holy matrimony; which is an honourable estate, instituted of God in the time of man's innocency, signifying unto us the mystical union that is betwixt Christ and his Church; which holy estate Christ adorned and beautified with his presence, and first miracle that he wrought, in Cana of Galilee; and is commended of Saint Paul to be honourable among all men: and therefore is not by any to be enterprised, nor taken in hand, unadvisedly, lightly, or wantonly, to satisfy men's carnal lusts and appetites, like brute beasts that have no understanding; but reverently, discreetly, advisedly, soberly, and in the fear of God; duly considering the causes for which Matrimony was ordained.'

Susan let her gaze wander around those gathered to witness this marriage. Edmund spoke well and feelingly, she thought, and she hoped that the solemnity of the occasion would impress itself upon Tom and Miss Fairhaven. Had she but known it, her uncle was also hoping that the words Edmund was saying would impress themselves upon not only the unmarried, the about to be married, but the already married as well. Edmund was continuing;

'First, it was ordained for the procreation of children, to be brought up in the fear and nurture of the Lord, and to the praise of his holy Name.'

Susan could not help herself from thinking of Fanny's children, and the effect they had had on her health, and wondering if Julia and Mr Yates were to have a child; there was no sign of one so far, and then she wondered whether it was indelicate of her, as an unmarried woman to have such thoughts. But there was no avoiding them given the content of the wedding service!

'Secondly, it was ordained for a remedy against sin, and to avoid fornication; that such persons as have not the gift of continency might marry, and keep themselves undefiled members of Christ's body.'

Edmund's voice rang out in the quietness of the church, and if there was any body to whom this applied, we may hope that they were not present on this momentous occasion.

'Thirdly,' Edmund continued, 'It was ordained for the mutual society, help, and comfort, that the one ought to have of the other, both in prosperity and adversity. Into which holy estate these two persons present come now to be joined. Therefore, if any man can show any just cause, why they may not lawfully be joined together, let him now speak, or else hereafter for ever hold his peace.'

The short silence with followed this abjuration seemed to last forever. When Edmund spoke again, Susan was aware of several people letting out a breath of relief, including Mrs Fairhaven, sitting beside her.

'No one? Well, let us continue.'

Edmund turned directly to Tom and Agnes;

'I require and charge you both, as ye will answer at the dreadful day of judgment when the secrets of all hearts shall be disclosed, that if either of you know any impediment, why ye may not be lawfully joined together in matrimony, ye do now confess it. For be ye well assured, that so many as are coupled together otherwise than God's word doth allow are not joined together by God; neither is their matrimony lawful.

'At which day of marriage, if any man do allege and declare any impediment, why they may not be coupled together in matrimony, by God's Law, or the Laws of this Realm; and will be bound, and sufficient sureties with him, to the parties; or else put in a caution (to the full value of such charges as the persons to be married do thereby sustain) to prove his allegation: then the solemnization must be deferred, until such time as the truth be tried.'

The words of the marriage ceremony, so solemn and so binding, never failed to impress Susan. There was again a silence, but neither Tom nor Agnes spoke, so Edmund went on;

'Thomas Ward Bertram, wilt thou have this woman to thy wedded wife, to live together after God's ordinance in the holy estate of matrimony? Wilt thou love her, comfort her, honour, and keep her in sickness and in health; and, forsaking all others, keep thee only unto her, so long as ye both shall live?'

Tom replied firmly, 'I will,' and Susan heard another sigh of relief from Mrs Fairhaven. Surely she had not thought Tom would pull out of the marriage at the very altar?

Edmund turned to Agnes;

'Agnes Jemima Fairhaven, wilt thou have this man to thy wedded husband, to live together after God's ordinance in the holy estate of matrimony? Wilt thou obey him, and serve him, love, honour, and keep him in sickness and in health; and, forsaking all other, keep thee only unto him, so long as ye both shall live?'

Agnes answered almost before he had finished;

'I will,' and out of the corner of her eye, Susan could see Mrs Fairhaven fanning herself as though transported back into the heat of Antigua.

Edmund next asked,

'Who giveth this woman to be married to this man?'

Sir Thomas stepped forward to indicate that he was fulfilling this role in the absence of Agnes's father and brother. He held out Agnes's hand towards Tom, as Edmund said;

'Take each other by the right hand, and repeat after me; I, Thomas Ward Bertram, take thee Agnes Jemima Fairhaven to my wedded wife, to have and to hold from this day forward, for better for worse, for richer, for poorer, in sickness and in health, to love and to cherish, till death us do part, according to God's holy ordinance; and thereto I plight thee my troth.'

Tom repeated the words loud and clear, and then they let go of each other's hand. Edmund told Agnes to take Tom's right hand in her's, and repeat after him;

'I, Agnes Jemima Fairhaven take thee, Thomas Ward Bertram to my wedded husband, to have and to hold from this day forward, for better for worse, for richer for poorer, in sickness and in health, to love, cherish, and to obey, till death us do part, according to God's holy ordinance; and thereto I give thee my troth.'

Under Edmund's direction, they let go of each other's hand again, and Harry Belvedere stepped forward to put two rings on to the Prayer Book held out by Edmund, and stepped back, his duty done. Edmund picked up the smaller of the two rings, and handed it to Tom, directing him to hold Agnes's left hand and to hover the ring over the third finger of her left hand while he spoke these words;

'With this ring I thee wed, with my body I thee worship, and with all my worldly goods I thee endow: In the Name of the Father, and of the Son, and of the Holy Ghost. Amen.'

From her position near the front, Susan could see that the ring did not fit on Agnes's finger; it stuck above her knuckle, and she spent the rest of the service trying to twist it into place. Meanwhile she made the same vow was made by her over Tom's ring, which did slide easily on to his finger.

'All kneel,' said Edmund, and there was a rustle as everybody present knelt, including Tom and Agnes.

'Let us pray. O eternal God, Creator and Preserver of all mankind, giver of all spiritual grace, the author of everlasting life; Send thy blessing upon these thy servants, this man and this woman, whom we bless in thy Name; that, as Isaac and Rebecca lived faithfully together, so these persons may surely perform and keep the vow and covenant betwixt them made, whereof these rings have been given and received as a token and pledge, and may ever remain in perfect love and peace together, and live according to thy laws; through Jesus Christ our Lord. Amen.'

Susan said, 'Amen,' with everybody else present, and was aware that Mrs Fairhaven was crying very quietly beside her. She pressed the older woman's hand in silent sympathy; she must not forget that although Mrs Fairhaven had wanted this match as much as Agnes, that she was losing her daughter, her husband was dead, and her son was very far away in Antigua. If Tom and Agnes chose to live at Mansfield Park, and Mrs Fairhaven returned to their home in Wimpole Street, she would be alone indeed.

Edmund bade everybody rise, and then took Tom and Agnes's right hands and joined them together saying, 'Those whom God hath joined together, let no man put asunder.'

Then he turned to the assembled congregation and said, 'For as much as Thomas Ward Bertram and Agnes Jemima Fairhaven have consented together in holy wedlock, and have witnessed the same before God and this company, and thereto have given and pledged their troth either to other, and have declared the same by giving and receiving of rings, and by joining of hands; I pronounce that they be man and wife together, In the Name of the Father, and of the Son, and of the Holy Ghost. Amen.'

The 'Amen' which followed this was most heartily given by all present, and there was much surreptitious clearing of throats and dabbing at eyes as Agnes and Tom knelt again for a blessing.

'God the Father, God the Son, God the Holy Ghost, bless, preserve, and keep you; the Lord mercifully with his favour look upon you; and so fill you with all spiritual benediction and grace, that ye may so live together in this life, that in the world to come ye may have life everlasting. Amen.'

Tom and Agnes were directed to sit, and Edmund sang Psalm 128, which had always been one of Susan's favourites; and everybody joined in the singing of Psalm 67, as Agnes and Tom, Harry and Edmund, plus Mrs Fairhaven and Sir Thomas went through to the side chapel to sign and witness the Register, and fill out Agnes's wedding lines.

CHAPTER THIRTY-SEVEN

Susan thought that Agnes looked very happy as she and Tom emerged from the side chapel and processed back down the aisle, followed by Sir Thomas arm in arm with Mrs Fairhaven, who looked dazed but relieved. Just three months after Miss Fairhaven's arrival in England, she had become Mrs Tom Bertram, and her mother cried with relief.

Everybody else followed them out and there were many congratulations and compliments to Edmund on the service before Sir Thomas handed Lady Bertram and Mrs Fairhaven into his carriage, and everybody else set off to walk back across the Park to the house for the Wedding Breakfast.

Sir Thomas was able to sit back in his comfortable carriage and reflect on a good morning; and to perhaps compare this wedding with his own, while thinking also of those of his other children. He had not been present at the wedding of Julia to Mr Yates; Maria and Rushworth's marriage had been set aside by law, as Maria at least had not abided by the promises she had made at the altar. Maria's second marriage had been conducted behind closed doors at Mrs Grant's house, but it was legal, and he hoped would, this time be binding on her. At least he could be certain that the marriages of both his sons stood fair to being honoured by all parties, and that there would now be no more scandal or ruptures to come.

'All four of our dear children are married, Lady Bertram,' said he in satisfaction, as they headed back to the house to greet the wedding breakfast guests.

'Indeed, my dear Sir Thomas,' said she. 'It is most gratifying to see them all so well settled at last.'

Mrs Fairhaven, to whom this remark was not addressed, but who nonetheless had an equal share in the happiness, felt herself authorised to reply likewise.

'It is so very gratifying to see young people so happy together, my dear Sir Thomas,' said she. 'Agnes is a very lucky woman to have found such a husband, and Tom will have a wife like no other, I assure you.'

'We are all very fond of Agnes,' said Lady Bertram in her sleepy way. 'She is a dear girl.'

'An asset to our family to be sure,' concluded Sir Thomas, and that was all the mutual congratulation the happy parents had time for, as the carriage had arrived back at the house.

Fanny and the children were expected to attend the wedding breakfast, and Susan set off across the park eagerly to see them before they left on their journey to Great Yarmouth. She could see Tom and Agnes ahead of her, and they were arm in arm and seemed to be talking and laughing with each other, which gave her some comfort. Then Harry walked up beside her to ask if he might escort her back to the house, and she felt herself entitled by their acquaintance and their having danced together, to take his arm.

'Upon my word, it has done me good to witness Tom's marriage ceremony being conducted thus,' said he enthusiastically. 'It was very well done, was not it, Miss Price?'

'Yes, indeed,' answered Susan. 'It is a most powerful and solemn moment in a person's life.'

'And Edmund read it so well,' continued he, 'I must model myself upon him when it comes to my turn to read ceremonies over couples.'

'How long is it before you will take your own living up?' asked Susan.

'Not long now; my father has said the living is being made ready for me. Mr Williams is to retire by the end of this year, and I have a house on my parish, so all that remains for me is to secure …'

But what he was about to say, Susan did not find out, for they were interrupted by her niece and nephew rushing out of the house to find her, in the greatest excitement.

'Aunt Susan! Aunt Susan!' Eddie cried, 'You must come and see!' While little Frances jumped up and down with the joy of their news.

With an apologetic look at Mr Ballantyne, Susan bent down to see what it was they were so excited about.

'The cake!' cried Eddie. 'Come and see the cake! It's all over white and sparkly!'

In vain Susan tried to tell the children that she had indeed seen the cake before she left for the church, but they were determined to show it to her themselves, and so with just one backwards regretful look at Mr Ballantyne, she allowed them to pull her by both hands into the house. Once the cake had been duly admired, Susan found her sister sitting comfortably on Lady Bertram's sofa, and assured herself that all was well with Fanny today, and that all the arrangements for their removal to Great Yarmouth were now complete. While everybody else mingled and admired the cake, and congratulated Agnes and Tom, Susan gave Fanny an account of the wedding ceremony, in particular how well Edmund had spoken it, and how Mrs Fairhaven had cried.

Lady Bertram finished her round of greeting her guests, and came to take up her usual position. She was delighted to see Fanny back upon the sopha with her, so Susan left them together, and walked away, hoping to have some quiet time to think about that walk back from the church. She had felt certain that Mr Ballantyne had been about to build upon his earlier attempt to ask her something of the utmost interest, but in the event, there was no time to think on it any further; for it was her place now to smile and greet guests, and ensure that the footmen and maids were amply supplying everybody with food and drink. As she neared the table where the guest of honour was enthroned in sugary splendour, Susan was amused to see that Mrs Fairhaven had taken up station next to it, in order to inform everybody who came to admire the sugar icing on the wedding cake, that it had come from her own plantation in Antigua, and that she had brought it all the way from Antigua herself as a gift for Lady Bertram.

Although amused by Mrs Fairhaven's tenacity, Susan had to admit that the cake was well worth all the praise heaped upon it, standing as it did three tiers high in the centre of the room, liberally covered in sparkling white sugar. It had soon become the absorbed focus of all the children present as well as much admired by all the adults. Mrs Fairhaven, however, was not content with everybody else's admiration, and soon took all the praise for the sugar icing on the cake into her own hands. It was just as well she had stationed herself there, for some of the children might well have attempted to push their fingers into the icing out of awe or in order to have a taste, but a swift promise that they should each have a large piece in their own hands before the day was out, deterred them.

The room became lively with all the wedding guests, and the children running about; Susan was relieved to see that Tom was now in high spirits, and Agnes was making herself very agreeable to all the guests. The wedding ring was finally in its right place with the aid of a little soap. Sir Thomas was making the rounds of the room, and Susan watched as his approach to each group caused a definite drop in the liveliness and animation of conversation. Although Susan had a lot of respect for Sir Thomas, and gratitude for his continuing care of herself and her family, she noticed how everybody became more stiff and formal in his presence, even though he always appeared perfectly genial himself. He caught little Eddie up as he rushed past, and lifted him above his head to make him laugh. This occasioned a rush of other children, all wishing to be lifted up in the same way, but Tom came forward to take the burden of rough and tumble away from his father, and Sir Thomas continued his rounds of greeting all the guests.

After a few hours, Edmund and Fanny announced their departure for Great Yarmouth, and everybody came out to see them off in one of Sir Thomas's most comfortable travelling coaches. Everybody waved, and called their good wishes for a safe journey, and Agnes became quite put out, for she and Tom were not to leave for Brighton until the following morning, when there would only be the family to see them off. However, there was nothing to be done about it, and so Agnes smiled and waved with all the rest.

It was indeed somewhat of an anti-climax when Tom and Agnes left for Brighton the following morning; their farewell audience consisted only of Mrs Fairhaven, Susan and Sir Thomas, but Agnes was gracious, and Tom said that he was looking forward to seeing Brighton, and that they would then meet up with Mrs Fairhaven at Wimpole Street, and then they were gone too, sharing a carriage with Julia and Mr Yates, who could not be spared any longer by the Baron.

Lady Bertram was very dull that morning, despite Susan and Mrs Fairhaven being in constant attendance upon her.

'How very sad it is,' said she, 'that everybody must go away. I am quite forlorn without them all. Tom and Agnes are gone, so are Julia and Mr Yates, and even Edmund and Fanny!'

'I am still here, Aunt,' said Susan. 'And so is Mrs Fairhaven.'

'Yes indeed,' said Mrs Fairhaven, but did not help by adding, 'Although I will soon be gone too, for my house at Wimpole Street is ready for me and I cannot trespass much longer on your generous hospitality, my dear Lady Bertram.'

'As to that,' said Sir Thomas, 'You are welcome to stay as long as you wish. Although I understand you will want to be at your home to welcome Tom and Agnes on their return from Brighton, that will not be for a few weeks yet, and so if you can be spared from Wimpole Street, Lady Bertram would be glad of your company.'

'Oh, I would indeed be very glad of your company,' cried Lady Bertram. 'Do not you leave me as well, Mrs Fairhaven!'

'Then I will stay a little longer,' promised Mrs Fairhaven.

'And do not forget, Lady Bertram,' added Sir Thomas, 'that Maria and Mr Crawford are to visit in the summer.' Although he was intending that they would not do so until Mrs Fairhaven were safely in her own home in London.

This was a happy thought indeed, and quite diverted Lady Bertram from her woes as she made talked happily of Maria and fringes, and Pug's puppy, which she was certain would be old enough to leave its mother by then. This topic lasted for the rest of the day, and was picked up again on each successive day until Maria's arrival.

CHAPTER THIRTY-EIGHT

The Yates and the Bertrams travelled very comfortably together as far as London, where Julia and Mr Yates were dropped off at the Yates's town house. Tom and Agnes were entreated to come in and pay their respects, and they were nothing loath. The Baron was so delighted with them, that this introduction became an invitation to stay for a few days, and Tom bowed and smirked and said they would be, 'very happy.' Agnes was ecstatic to be thus distinguished, and by a Baron no less! She could not have been more pleased with her dearest Julia for inviting her.

When they finally parted, it was with many kisses and promises of future visits, and lengthy letters, and Tom and Agnes were finally alone, and heading for Brighton.

Unbeknown to them, Maria, Mr Crawford, and Miss Crawford were already at Brighton, and had been there a few weeks already. In the interests of narrative expediency, they were all there together, and living in accommodation very close by one another, although this is not much to be surprised at, for there are not many places with apartments expensive enough to stay at, and so anybody arriving at Brighton is likely to discover some dear friends or family already in residence. That this was the case for each of them, they discovered to their mutual surprise and enjoyment, on the very morning after Tom and Agnes arrived, on taking their morning walk to register at the library and read over the other arrivals.

'Well, it seems your brother is also in Brighton, Maria,' said Mr Crawford, passing her the paper. 'And with his newly married wife, Agnes.'

'Tom married?' said Mary. 'I am all astonishment.'

'My father did not tell me that he was to marry,' said Maria. 'I hope this Agnes Fairhaven is someone we can be seen with about Brighton.'

'Let us go and introduce ourselves,' said Henry. 'If you do not wish to pursue the acquaintance, there are ways of avoiding them thereafter, and we are not staying in Brighton much longer anyway.'

The three of them walked towards the Castle Inn, where the newspaper had reported Tom and Agnes to be staying, and encountered the newly-weds coming out of the front doors for their first walk along the sea-front. There was much pretty surprise, and many exclamations of joy at this chance encounter so carefully engineered by the Crawfords. Tom introduced Agnes to his sister, his brother-in-law, and to Mary Crawford, and she declared herself delighted with all of them;

'I can see that you are dear Julia's sister too,' said she. 'You are indeed a very handsome family!'

While the ladies exchanged compliments, Henry asked Tom;

'When did you arrive? I trust your journey went well?'

'Yes, I thank you. The roads from London are kept in excellent repair,' said Tom. 'Our journey was most comfortable and speedy.'

And Maria, feeling that she ought to show some interest in her family added;

'Are you come direct from Mansfield Park? Henry, Mary and I go there in August, after visiting the Admiral and our other friends when we leave Brighton.'

'We are come from a visit to the Baron and Baroness in London,' said Agnes with great importance. 'Dear Julia and Mr Yates attended our wedding and gave us the invitation on our arrival into London with them or we would have been here last week.'

'We are all very well-met indeed!' said Henry. 'Had you delayed but a few more days, we would have passed each other on the road heading in opposite directions.'

'And you need not trouble yourselves to find out what there is to do for we can be your guides, having been here a month already,' said Mary.

'I have heard,' said Agnes, 'that the sea air is very beneficial in England, unlike in Antigua.'

'Indeed it is, Mrs Bertram,' said Mary, with apparent seriousness, 'Nobody can catch cold by the sea; nobody wants appetite by the sea; nobody wants spirits; nobody wants strength.'

'As my sister says, you are correctly informed, Mrs Bertram,' said Mr Crawford, 'It is very true that the sea air is healing, softening, relaxing, fortifying and bracing; just as is wanted, sometimes one, sometimes the other.'

'And if the sea breeze should fail,' continued Mary, 'the sea-bath is the certain corrective; and should bathing disagree, the sea air alone has been designed by nature for the cure of all ills.'

'What if I have no ills?' asked Agnes, not entirely certain whether this panegyric was to be taken seriously, or no.

'Then you will enjoy the sea air for all its relaxing and fortifying aspects, and return to London refreshed and braced for the winter!' finished Henry triumphantly.

'Then I am very happy to be here,' said Agnes with an air of finality, and turned her face to the breeze, which was doing its best to live up to its reputation for fortifying and bracing, although she did wonder whether it might not also cut up the complexion her mother had tried so hard to preserve.

On mentioning this concern to Mary, however, Agnes found her less than sympathetic.

'I used to consider sea-breezes to be vile,' said she. 'And advised many of my acquaintance to avoid them as the ruin of all beauty and health. But I have quite changed my opinion since coming into Brighton, and believe them to be most invigorating.'

'My aunt used to declare herself affected if within ten miles of the sea,' put in Henry, and Mary laughed;

'The Admiral did not believe the sea-breezes to affect anybody, and never believed my aunt, but I suspect it was being within ten miles of my uncle which affected her so badly, rather than the sea-breezes,' said she.

Now that the two families had found each other, there was to be no parting them, and the Crawfords agreed to stay for a little longer to further their acquaintance. Agnes found, to her delight, that Maria and Mary were a very good substitute for Julia, and the three women very quickly became intimate, leaving Tom to associate with Henry Crawford. As Maria was the only one who had visited Brighton before, she appointed herself their guide to all the town's delights and diversions, as well as setting herself up as the arbiter for their party of what they could and could not be seen to be doing during their visit, where were the right places to visit, and at what times during the day and evening.

Agnes made sure that Tom obtained the newspaper so that they could check that their arrival had been duly noted; Tom as the future Sir Thomas Bertram, and Agnes as his newly married wife, and a sugar heiress in her own right. Henry and Maria had kept the newspaper announcement of their own arrival, with their own recent wedding duly noted, and the fact that Henry had an estate in Norfolk. Miss Mary Crawford was also noted as having travelled with them, and there was mention of her independent fortune as well.

Mr Rushworth, Maria and Julia had taken a house at Brighton for their honeymoon, but the Crawfords and Bertrams had chosen instead to stay at hotels. Not knowing their error, Tom and Agnes had taken an elegant apartment at the Castle Inn, directed thither on their arrival into Brighton by an astute employee of the proprietor, but the Castle's star was waning, and its Assembly Rooms had already closed. The Old Ship Hotel was the place to stay now, and the more worldly-wise Crawfords had duly taken rooms there. Once Agnes discovered that she was staying at a less prestigious hotel, even though it was right next door to the Prince's own house, there was the end of all her delight in her Brighton stay. The Prince's house was undergoing renovation works, and Agnes complained about the noise from the workmen coming and going at all times of day and night. The rooms at the Castle, though elegant, she was persuaded were not so comfortable as those at The Old Ship, and the presses in The Crown Inn were something quite shocking. She was having to send her gowns to be ironed daily! Unfortunately for Agnes, there was no suitable apartment available for her at The Old Ship until another guest departed, and so she was forced to make the most of her inferior accommodation for the time being.

Another minor irritant for the whole party, was Frou-frou. Mary had insisted upon the tiny dog accompanying her to Brighton, and it had taken a violent dislike to Agnes and all the staff at the Ship, frequently biting anybody who came within range.

'I declare that dog costs more to house and feed than all three of us put together,' Henry complained to Mary, after they had to offer recompense to staff bitten by the dog, and pay for a room for Frou-frou to be shut up in when the maids were about their work in the apartments, as well as hiring a maid to feed Frou-frou, and take it for walks if it did not accompany its mistress. Altogether, Frou-frou's Brighton holiday was costing more than Henry's, Maria's and Mary's all put together.

'Frou-frou stays at my expense,' replied Mary. 'Do not concern yourself, my dear brother.'

Agnes declared herself terrified of Frou-frou, but this did not stop Mary from including the tiny dog on most of their outings.

Bathing was very much recommended; although Agnes was most put out to discover that Martha Gunn, the Prince of Wales's preferred dipper was no longer working from the beaches, having taken an honourable and well-paid retirement. Instead, Agnes, Mary and Maria would have to trust themselves to other dippers currently plying their trade on the east side of the beach, while Tom and Henry took their bathe on the west side. However, for Agnes, this operation had to wait until she could have special costumes made up for her to take her dip in; as nothing would persuade her to don the usual blue flannel costume most other women used. Tom and Henry went every day, and rather than wait for Agnes, Mary and Maria found themselves a dipper they felt they could trust, donned the blue flannel, and began to experience the delights of sea-bathing.

Maria and Mary were delighted with the sea-shells on the beach, and made all manner of plans to do some shell art on boxes as gifts for their sisters, and thought that they would be very great curiosities, but Agnes was less impressed. The shells on Antigua were much prettier – including the great conch shells, which the slaves would collect and use to decorate their huts.

'However unfortunate an association that may be,' said Mary slyly, 'We must make do with the treasures of this ocean, and I understand the royal princesses do shell art.'

With such an example before her, Agnes was persuaded to join the shell-collecting parties on the beach, and there was much talk of how the shells were to be attached to the boxes, and of patterns to lay them out in, until Agnes was quite a convert to shell art.

The Crawfords and Bertrams attended Assemblies at the Old Ship Hotel where they were witness to a new dance, a most intriguing pirouette waltz, with steps none of them had seen before.

'Look here,' said Henry the morning after the Assembly, passing The Times around at breakfast. The article he indicated was less enamoured of the new dance than they had been;

'We remarked with pain that since the indecent foreign dance called the Waltz was introduced at the English court it has now reached Brighton and stands fair to become introduced into Bath and Cheltenham as well in due course. It is quite sufficient to cast one's eyes on the voluptuous intertwining of the limbs and close compressure on the bodies in their dance, to see that it is indeed far removed from the modest reserve which has hitherto been considered distinctive of English females.'

Despite, or maybe because of, this censure, all the English females present were determined to learn this new dance in time for the next Assembly, and a servant was dispatched to discover a dancing master with all due haste to teach them the steps.

CHAPTER THIRTY-NINE

'We must make a visit to St Ann's Well,' announced Agnes one morning. 'Dear Sir Thomas showed me a book by Dr Anthony Relhan which advocated taking the waters which rise at St Ann's Well near Brighton.'

'I understand that Mrs Fitzherbert also recommends them,' said Henry.

'Is she in residence?' asked Agnes, looking around as though she expected to see Mrs Fitzherbert leaning on the Prince's arm and walking past the windows.

'Yes, her house is on The Steyne,' said Maria. 'I shall point it out to you on our next evening walk.'

'But what is there at this Well?' asked Mary. 'Do we bend over and scoop the waters from the ground in our hands?'

'No indeed,' said Maria, 'There is a wooden building, with the well in the centre of the floor inside, and a raised dais with a bench running around for visitors to sit on. A maid servant collects and serves the water. It is thought most wholesome to drink it, although it is not so convenient as the waters in the centre of Bath, as we will have to take a carriage ride out there.'

'If it is good enough for Mrs Fitzherbert, then it will be good enough for us,' said Mary.

'Well, then, we must do our duty, and drive out to drink the waters,' said Henry.

With these, and many other small pleasures and no alarms at all, their visit to Brighton was very much enjoyed by the Crawfords and the Bertrams, and moreover was drawing to a close. The Crawfords had yet many promised visits to make, and the Bertrams were to go to back to London, to the Fairhavens' house in Wimpole Street, to join Mrs Fairhaven. It may be expected that Maria would not wish to hear of Wimpole Street, but she was completely indifferent; her first marriage might never have taken place at all, and she might never have left her husband's house on that ill-fated street, for all the notice she paid to Agnes's frequent mentions of her own home there.

On the day before their departure, the weather had taken a turn for the worse, with the sun hiding behind stormy looking rain-clouds, and the wind blowing very hard onshore. Despite the blustery conditions, Mary and Maria declared they would not be put off from taking their daily walk, and Mary added that she wanted to take Frou-frou to the beach for one last time, as she found it so amusing to watch the little dog run about and bark at the waves.

Although the others had no such wish to indulge Frou-frou, they were happy enough to join Maria on her walk, and they all set out to walk along the Marine Parade. As they came on to the Parade, there was a man walking the other way, and he paused and bowed as they passed, politely drawing back to give them way. As they passed him, Mary's face caught his eye, and he looked at her with a degree of earnest admiration, which she was most certainly not insensible of. She was, in truth, looking remarkably well; her handsome features having the bloom and freshness of youth quite restored by the sea bathing and the sea air which had been at work upon her complexion, and by the animation of eye produced by being away from London and in a scene of leisure and pleasure. The stranger, having made his bow, appeared to think for a moment, and then apparently drawn by the party which had attracted his interest, turned and followed them back the way he had come.

Maria was too absorbed by Henry to notice him, but Agnes was certain his look of admiration had been aimed at her, and pointed him out none too quietly to Tom.

'He is a well-looking man,' said Tom, after turning to give the man an appraising stare.

'Indeed,' agreed Agnes. 'A very fine young man indeed. More air than one often sees in Brighton. I wonder who he is?'

Nobody was able to satisfy her curiosity on that score, and they walked on, until Frou-frou finally justified its inclusion in the party, by throwing the stranger quite in their way. The wind had not dropped, and all the party was having to hold on to their hats; then as they reached the sands, Frou-frou struggled to be put down. Mary put the little dog down and it ran at the waves, barking as though it wanted to take them on in a fight. Quite a crowd gathered to watch, as it was a most amusing sight, until Frou-frou ran too far after a particularly provoking wave, and was swept by its sudden retreat out into the sea.

It was the work of a moment, and so shocking that all the ladies present screamed. Mary ran down towards the water's edge, hoping that another wave would throw the little dog back out of the sea again, but Frou-frou did not appear for several moments. Just as all present had given the little dog up for lost, there was a collective sigh of relief as Frou-frou's tiny head appeared above the waves, but unable to hear its mistress's cries of alarm and calls to return to shore, and further encumbered by water in the ears, and a general lack of intelligence, it began to swim further out to sea.

Mary turned beseeching eyes to her brother and Tom, but neither of them was prepared to plunge into the turbulent waters after a dog they both thoroughly disliked, and Mary quite gave Frou-frou up for lost. At that very moment, the gentleman they had seen earlier now came forward, and bowed to Mary;

'If you will allow me, madam?' said he, and took off his hat, handing it, plus his cane, and his coat and waistcoat to his man who had followed on behind him. Between them, they removed his boots and he strode out into the waves. Agnes was drawn between wanting to stage a faint in order to focus every body's attention on her, and joining everybody as close to the sea as possible to watch the daring rescue. As nobody's attention was anywhere near her, she decided to watch the rescue, and keep the fainting fit in reserve for a more propitious moment.

The crowd all now pressed as close to the water's edge as they dared, and watched the gentleman first wade, and then swim strongly towards the tiny dog. As they watched, they saw him reach Frou-frou, and there appeared to be a brief altercation as Frou-frou misunderstood his intentions, and ended up wrapped firmly in his cravat, with a fold around its muzzle for safety.

The screams of the ladies, and the sight of a man striding into the rough waters, had drawn yet more people from amongst those who had braved the high winds to take their walk, as well as those whose daily business took them out on to the sands. There was rumour of drowned young ladies, but even a drowned dog was exciting enough, and there was always the chance that the brave rescuer would be swept out to sea, or possibly even some of the ladies clustered perilously close to the pounding waves; already some of the fishermen were talking of putting out boats. But although the sea was rough, it was not very deep, and the stranger had after all been able to make his way safely back to shore, with the tiny dog trussed up in his cravat.

As he returned to the shallower water, and walked out towards them, Mary rushed to meet him, and he handed the sopping wet dog to her, with another bow. His man came forward now to hand him his clothes and boots; but he was too wet to put them on. A hastily summoned physician now took charge, and commandeered carriage rugs for the stranger and for Mary, and bustled the man off to his own carriage to take him back to his lodgings. The stranger only had time to bow to Mary and ask if he might be permitted the honour of calling on them on the morrow to ascertain that neither she nor the little dog was any the worse for their ordeal. Mary curtsied, and Henry called out that their name was Crawford at The Ship. The stranger called his name out likewise, but it was lost in all the bustle and exclaiming and arrangements for Mary. A respectable looking family offered to take Mary back to her lodging, and she was handed into their carriage, wrapped in their carriage rug, with the hot brick that had been keeping the ladies warm earlier, down by her own feet. Agnes, on finding that she was expected to walk back to the hotel, decided now was the perfect time to stage her faint.

A second family came forward, eyes alight at the sight of a fainting lady, and their carriage was pressed into action, two stout fishermen being given coins to carry Agnes thither. Maria, Henry and Tom set off to walk back to The Ship, after refusing all the offers to give them lifts from other passers-by. The action now being concluded, everybody resumed their business, at a safe distance from the pounding waves, and the brave rescue of the little dog by the handsome gentleman was the sole topic of conversation for everybody for the rest of the day, and all those at leisure determined to call at The

Ship Inn the following morning, feeling licenced to do so by having taken some small part in the proceedings.

Agnes, preferring to remain insensible in the second carriage, missed an opportunity to find out the identity of the Frou-frou's preserver. Mary, although very wet and shaken, had better luck, for the Belsey family who had taken her up, knew all about the stranger. His name was Viscount Carmichael, and he was an intimate of the Prince Regent, no less.

'Such a handsome man,' said Mrs Belsey. 'And so romantic, such a tragedy!'

Mary looked all inquiry, so Mrs Belsey was persuaded to continue;

'He served with the dear Prince Regent in the army,' said she.

'The Tenth Royal Hussars,' put in Mr Belsey, with great import.

'And you may not have noticed, my dear, but he and his man was wearing black ribbands for his wife. She died recently, and they were so devoted, that he does not go into society, but lives very quietly.'

'It is said he is broken hearted and will never marry again,' added Miss Belsey, rather mournfully.

From the looks he had been giving her, Mary suspected that he was not entirely inconsolable, but she continued to look all interest and sympathy in the hopes of eliciting further information from them, and did not say anything to contradict them. However, there was no time for any more as they had arrived at The Ship, and Mary was bustled away by her maid to be seated by the fire, wrapped in flannel, and plied with hot drinks. Frou-frou was put into the hands of the servant Mary had had to engage especially to tend to the dog, as the hotel's own servants refused to feed, groom, or clean up after it, having been bitten numerous times. The tiny dog was so shocked by its sudden immersion into cold, rough water, and its unceremonious rescue, tightly swaddled by a strange man, that it was quite unable to take advantage of having been handed to the servant, and was most unaccustomedly meek.

Shortly afterwards, the carriage with Agnes arrived, and two stout footmen were summoned to carry her into the Hotel. The carriage departed before it was discovered that she did not, after all, have lodgings there, and so she was deposited on a sopha in a saloon, and a maid sent to tend on her.

Maria and Henry arrived back, having sent Tom on to The Crown, and then had to send a servant to summon him back to collect his wife. Agnes refused to walk home, and so their horses had to be put to their carriage to drive the short distance to collect her. While they were all waiting for the carriage to arrive, the physician who had taken charge of Viscount Carmichael arrived to check up on Mary and Agnes, and wagged his finger at both, telling them they should be taking extra care of themselves, but was unable to find anything actually the matter with either lady, as neither had been wetted by the rescue of Frou-frou as had Mary. On being admitted to see Mary however, he learned that she was never ill, and was perfectly well now that she was dry and warm again. Despite her assurances, he announced he would call again tomorrow, and left receipts for a sleeping draught for all three ladies, and a large bill for his services.

CHAPTER FORTY

The two families met up in the Crawfords' apartments for dinner; as Agnes continued to believe them to be much better than her own accommodations at The Crown. Tom had asked if she would prefer to dine from a tray in her own room, as the physician had told her to rest, and take care. Although there was much potential in being a pampered invalid, on reflection Agnes decided she would prefer to be much recovered, as she did not wish to be upstaged by Mary's robust good health. She also suspected the handsome stranger would form most of the conversation, and might even call upon them earlier than he had stated. Also, she was not convinced that everybody knew how much of a shock the morning's events had been to her in particular, and she intended to remind them of how delicate she was at present.

'I declare I am much recovered, and the physician does not think I have taken any harm from this morning's shocking events,' said she, as she arrived, although nobody had asked how she fared, being more concerned with Mary, who had been soaked by Frou-frou. The dog itself had now recovered fully, and had to be locked up in its own room, as it had now recovered from its immersion, and had recommenced growling at anybody who approached its mistress.

'As am I,' said Mary. 'As I told the physician, I am never ill, although Benson declares that my gown from this morning is ruined by the sea water. I have told her that if it cannot be cleaned, she may keep it for herself, and make what she can of it.'

Now the party put aside all pretence that the handsome stranger was not their first interest, and pooled their information. Henry and Tom had been making enquiries of the Inn keepers, while Mary had her information from the gossipy Belseys, and Agnes had questioned the servants at both The Crown and The Ship. To add to Mary's information was that Viscount Carmichael was staying at the Prince Regent's house, although the Prince himself was not in residence. He had been married about ten years before his wife died, and she had been one of the Colquhoun family. It was believed there were several children at some ancestral home or other, somewhere in Scotland, although nobody knew for certain. Whatever the truth, the Viscount's astonishing rescue of Frou-frou occupied all their conversation that evening, until Mary announced she was quite fagged, and wished to go to bed early, and Agnes, not to be outdone, said the same. Everybody was looking forward to the following morning, when the Viscount would call on them.

The following morning they all met again early, to take breakfast, ahead of what they expected would be a busy morning of visits. Frou-frou survived the night, to Tom and Henry's secret disappointment, and Henry found the innkeeper, bespoke a saloon for their private use, and ordered refreshments in order to best accommodate all their callers. The Belseys were the first to call, followed soon after by the Smith family who had brought Agnes to The Ship. Despite their good intentions and comfortable carriage, it was soon clear to Agnes that this was not a family which could materially add to her happiness in their acquaintance, and she was inclined to ignore them. Several other families which had witnessed the scenes on the beach had felt themselves thus authorised to call and inquire after Mary and the dog, which was clearly in fine fettle after its immersion.

'I declare the dog is a perfect example of the benefits of sea-bathing,' declared one visitor, after he was only freed from Frou-frou's attentions when it rushed away to bark at the next group of callers.

After another woman was bitten on the hand when attempting to pat Frou-frou's head, Mary handed the dog to the servant to shut back up in its own apartment, and this time Frou-frou was not to be denied the opportunity to bite the poor servant. The physician arrived to find he was not required to check on Mary's or Agnes's health, but to minister to the various people bitten by the dog instead.

The Viscount arrived so quietly, that it was only when he was bowing over Mary's hand, that most people noticed he was present, and a sudden silence fell, with everybody turning to stare before remembering their manners, and resuming their own conversations. Although the overall noise in the saloon was considerably lessened, a number of people began to move closer to Mary, hoping to hear what was being said. Had they been close enough, they would have heard Mary offering her sincere thanks to the Viscount for rescuing Frou-frou.

'I am a very selfish creature, and for the sake of giving relief to my own feelings of gratitude for your rescue of my helpless little dog, care not how much I may be mortifying yours,' said Mary. 'But we have not been properly introduced, I am Mary Crawford.'

'Viscount Carmichael, always at your service,' said he, bowing again, 'And if you will thank me, let it be for yourself alone. I take my dip daily, so the water was no inconvenience to me, and I have taken no ill from the adventure. I trust that you are quite recovered also?'

'Indeed, sir, I am never ill,' Mary assured him, and noticing that her brother, Maria, Tom and Agnes had all moved up behind her, she realised she would not have a private talk with him until they all been introduced. 'Please allow me to introduce my brother Henry Crawford, and his wife, Maria, and our friends Tom and Agnes Bertram.'

Everybody bowed and smirked and said all that was proper, and then the natural eddies of people arriving and leaving, and having to be acknowledged and farewelled, and offered refreshment, meant that the ladies had to move away, leaving the men together, and it was some time before Mary was able to manoeuvre her way back into his company. As he was as keen as she to speak again, they finally met, and were able to continue their conversation.

'And the little dog?' asked Carmichael. 'I trust it too has suffered no ill-effects from its sudden immersion in the sea water?'

'To my brother and Mr Bertram's great annoyance, Frou-frou is perfectly well, I thank you,' replied Mary. 'And I will have your cravat laundered to return to you.'

Carmichael merely smiled at this, and said;

'I am pleased to hear it, but I beg you will keep the cravat in case you are ever in a situation where you need to restrain the dog again.'

'I confess that Frou-frou does not have the most amiable disposition for a dog,' said Mary. 'But it is devoted to me, and I am very fond of it, hence my eternal gratitude for your gallant rescue.'

There was nothing Carmichael could do but bow again, and turn the subject.

'I had seen the notice of your arrival in the paper, which listed Mr and Mrs Crawford, Miss Crawford, and Mrs and Mrs Bertram,' said he, 'and I have seen you all about Brighton, and on the beach, but I did not know which of the ladies was which. I hoped very much that you were Miss Crawford, for I had heard tell that she was very handsome, and when I saw you I felt assured you must be she, for I knew there could not be two such handsome women in all of Brighton.'

'For shame, sir!' cried Mary, but she could not in all honesty be angry with such a saucy speech, for she was finding he combined the attractiveness of Edmund with the liveliness of Henry, and she was most pleased with him.

Convention dictated he could not stay much longer, and he was most regrettably unable to accept any invitations to dinner because of his mourning, but after he took his leave with one last, lingering look back at Mary, his actions and looks occupied the rest of that day and evening's conversation.

In their various conversations with their other guests, Tom and Henry had learned that Carmichael had been invalided out of the Royal Hussars after surviving Waterloo with injuries that meant it was unlikely he would serve in the army again, but which were not life-threatening. The Prince Regent had asked him to come down to his house in Brighton to over-see the planned renovations, and he was in daily converse with John Nash, and a couple of fellows who were to do the painting.

The following day was taken up with packing and making all the arrangements for their departure on the following day. Agnes did not wish to stay in Brighton without the Crawfords, and so they were all to travel together. Mary hoped Carmichael might call again so that she could tell him of her intended destinations, but he did not call that day, nor the next, and so the two families prepared to leave Brighton, with some regrets on all their parts, for it had been a most enjoyable stay. Mary in particular was anxious not to leave until she could tell Viscount Carmichael of her destination; and she consulted her new sister.

'Maria, do you think it would be improper of me to leave a message with the landlord here for Viscount Carmichael?' asked Mary as they were waiting in the saloon for their carriages to be announced.

'If you wish to see him again, why do you not pay him a visit, or send a message direct to him?'

'He is still in mourning, and we do not have an understanding that would allow me to do so,' replied Mary.

'I am all astonishment to find you so mindful of convention,' said Maria. 'But if you were to tell the landlord of our final destination, I can see no wrong in that. If Carmichael returns and asks where you are gone to, the landlord can tell him what he learned from you as to your destination.'

So Mary told the landlord that they were for Everingham in Norfolk by the beginning of September, once their visits to friends and family were complete, but he was a busy man, and not much interested in departing guests when there were incoming guests to be made money from; she doubted whether he would remember what she had said, nor pass it on to the right person should they make the enquiry.

Viscount Carmichael had indeed been intending to call again the following morning, and when prevented, on the morning after, but had been held up by enquiries from the Prince Regent, including an imminent visit to see how his works were going on, for which Carmichael would have to be present. Then the architect and the workmen discovered problems which needed decisions being taken about, and more letters written to the Prince, and by the time he was at liberty to call, the Crawfords and Bertrams were gone.

'Did they give any direction?' he asked the landlord, but that gentleman had quite forgotten what Mary had told him, in all the comings and goings at his busy inn. When Carmichael identified Mr Crawford's party as the one which contained the little dog which had bitten everybody, the landlord said that he did indeed recall the little dog, but that its party had not given any forwarding direction as they were expecting no letters to arrive for them.

Carmichael was bitterly disappointed as he left the inn. He had intended this visit to be a test of whether Mary might consider an offer from him; his period of mourning for his wife was weighing heavily, and he had determined now to marry for his own pleasure. He was much taken with Mary Crawford after seeing her walking about Brighton; he thought her looks very lovely, and was in a position not to care whether she had a fortune or not. All that had remained was to engineer an introduction which did not violate the conditions of his mourning for his wife. Frou-frou's sudden immersion in the sea was not necessarily the way he would have chosen to be introduced to Mary, but it had at least the advantage of painting him in the light of a hero, and ensuring that she was indebted to him. And now she was gone, he knew not where, and he was not at liberty to pursue her.

CHAPTER FORTY-ONE

Lady Bertram was not long in losing another of her companions shortly after Tom and Agnes's wedding. Mrs Fairhaven was determined to set a day soon to leave for her house in Wimpole Street, and Mr Ballantyne actually left, after he was recalled home by the news of the death of his great-aunt.

In Edmund's absence, Mr Ballantyne reported to Sir Thomas, and so he called on him to explain why he must leave his responsibilities at Thornton Lacey, and at Mansfield for the time being.

After explaining about the death of his great-aunt, and receiving Sir Thomas's commiserations, Mr Ballantyne's thoughts turned to his particular relationship with his great-aunt.

'I was always a favourite of Aunt Garrett,' said he to Sir Thomas, 'and I spent many of my holidays at her home. She favoured me amongst my brothers as she was the third child of her own parents, who quite shamefully neglected her until she married very well and became rich.'

'It is most shocking indeed when parents are only fond of their children when they become rich,' said Sir Thomas gravely.

'Indeed, sir. And she had younger brothers whom her parents did nothing to assist, and whom she was only able to assist after her own marriage.'

'It was most generous of her and her husband to assist her brothers. Not every sister would be so inclined to help if their parents were unable to, nor every husband so indulgent towards his wife's brothers.'

'I gather that her parents were very wealthy, but everything was for their eldest son, and no provision was made for any younger children at all, not even out of the parents' private incomes.'

Sir Thomas shook his head sadly at the improvidence of some families, and then asked;

'And so you are to leave us immediately?'

'I regret so, Sir Thomas. The funeral is in a few days' time, and under the terms of her Will, I must not only attend, but must say the words over her grave.'

What Mr Ballantyne did not tell Sir Thomas was that not only did his great-aunt's will require his presence at her grave-side, but also required him to give up his profession, and live the life of a gentleman on her estate. His aunt had been determined that she would be the one to assist this favourite nephew as she had no children of her own to leave her fortune and estate to. Mr Ballantyne was thus acutely aware that while he could no longer practice as a clergyman, he would be very rich, and was now able to marry wherever he chose.

Despite this sudden elevation in his status and income, Susan was still definitely his choice: he could not propose to her whilst in mourning, but he was determined to use this opportunity to speak to Sir Thomas and set out his intentions for his return.

Sir Thomas was pleased to hear that Mr Ballantyne wished to pay his addresses to Susan, and agreed that, as soon as the three months period of mourning for his great-aunt was passed, he would support Mr Ballantyne in his intentions towards his niece.

'Although she is my choice, I do not at all know whether she favours me, sir,' said Mr Ballantyne. 'Her manner towards me is always that of a congenial acquaintance; she had a composure of temper and a uniform cheerfulness of manner which sometimes I think is merely that of a friend, and she has no thoughts of me besides.'

Sir Thomas was gratified to hear that Susan had been conducting herself with the utmost propriety during Mr Ballantyne's attentions towards her. Although these attentions had seemed very clear to *him*, what was less clear was Susan's own opinions for he had never mentioned Mr Ballantyne's growing attachment to her, and she had not given any appearance of having noticed he was singling her out. But Sir Thomas was not about to deter Mr Ballantyne if he wished to proceed with his plan to engage Susan's affections. On the other hand, he would not push Susan to accept Mr Ballantyne if she had no mind to. He had learned his lesson from Fanny and Mr Crawford.

After Mr Ballantyne left him to make his adieus to Lady Bertram, Mrs Fairhaven, and Susan herself, Sir Thomas sat back to reflect with satisfaction on Susan's behaviour, and memory took him further back to that of Fanny. He sincerely hoped that he was not as mistaken in Mr Ballantyne as he had been in Mr Crawford, and had to own in retrospect at least, that Fanny had been perfectly correct in her refusal of Mr Crawford's proposals. Sir Thomas comforted himself with the reflection that it was much less likely that Mr Ballantyne was such another man; he had conducted himself honourably throughout his stay at Thornton Lacey, and had been a good friend to the family besides.

Mr Ballantyne found all the ladies in Lady Bertram's own sitting room. He made his apologies and adieus, and if his eyes lingered a little more on Susan, and if he held her hand a little longer than that of the two older ladies, we must not blame him. Susan accompanied him out to the front door where his horse was waiting, and held out her hand to wish him a good journey. For a moment she thought he might raise her hand to his lips, but Sir Thomas appeared to join in the farewell, and the moment passed. Mr Ballantyne swung himself up into his saddle, and was gone, leaving Susan to wonder if such looks and the firm pressure on her hand was an indication of his growing feelings for her, or whether she had imagined it.

All was quiet and very dull after Mr Ballantyne's departure; Susan took her walks in the grounds with much less enthusiasm than before. She had not realised quite how much she had come to depend upon meeting him there on his way to visit the Parsonage, or to call in upon some parishioner who needed assistance. He always had time to stop, and accompany her, while discoursing all the time on subjects dear to her heart; she had never heard him venture an opinion with which she could not heartily concur, and all his thoughts were perfectly sound. In fact, now that he was gone, Susan began to admit to herself that he was the perfect match for her, and to wish she had been a little less guarded in her responses, and a little warmer towards him. She did not know when he would return; he and Sir Thomas had said only that he would return to conclude his business at Thornton Lacey, and after that would be again living near his family home. Settling so far away from her, he might turn his eyes to a more suitable woman with a fortune, who could assist him far more materially than she ever could.

This brought about a melancholy mood which she found hard to disperse; and Fanny was not there to gently talk her into a better mind. Letters from Great Yarmouth arrived regularly and were of great comfort to her; the children and Fanny had taken their baths as recommended, and they took the children daily down to the beach for the sea air. Fanny believed it was doing them all much good and that they would soon all be very well again. With such good news, Susan had to be content, and to hope that it would not be long before Mr Ballantyne returned, and her own future could be decided one way or the other.

CHAPTER FORTY-TWO

Fanny and Edmund's journey to the health-giving coast at Great Yarmouth in Norfolk had gone as well as such journeys can for a man with a sickly wife, and two fractious children. But on their arrival at the house taken by Sir Thomas for their stay, they all found their spirits considerably lifted. They were met immediately with everything that was most agreeable; Burgh Hall that Sir Thomas had taken for them was both commodious and elegant, and set in such a superior part of the town that there was never the least inconvenience from the sea dashing ashore, or the smells of the fishing industry. The servants which came with the house were well-trained, cheerful, and efficient under the housekeeper, Mrs Dack, and Fanny found that she could preside as lady of the house with complete confidence, as it was of a size she could be comfortable in. She smiled as she remembered the terrified little girl who had first crept about her uncle's house, terrified of the size of the rooms, and afraid to touch anything in case she injured it. There was nothing in Burgh Hall to cause that fear, and she moved about it with complete confidence.

On the first Sunday of their visit, they had gone to the nearest church, and Fanny had been charmed by its construction out of the local flint stone, and surprised by the size of it, and the number of bells. The Vicar of St Nicholas, was a Mr Symonds, a large man of the middle-age, hale and hearty, and delighted to welcome a fellow of the cloth, especially one who was keen to take services in his stead. Mrs Symonds was a plain, sensible woman, even larger than her husband, and considerably his elder. Rumour, which did not reach the Bertrams, was that he had married her for her fortune, and she married him because no other man had made her an offer. As far as the Bertrams could tell, theirs was a love match, with the two of them very happy together, and entirely suited.

There were no children, and Mrs Symonds doted on little Eddie and Frances, while her husband devoted many hours to constructing ingenious toys for their amusement. Through the Symonds, Fanny and Edward were introduced to Great Yarmouth society; there were not many families, the town being inhabited mostly by fishermen and farmers, but they were welcomed by such families as there were, and for the first time in her life, Fanny felt herself equal to her company.

Other families visited, and staid a short while during the summer, and there were balls and dinners and everyone was very gay. Fanny was told that the town was much less amenable during the winter months, when all the visitors were gone, apart from a very hardy few.

For the first time in her life, Fanny felt comfortable and truly at home; she was no longer the indigent niece, taught to be grateful for every scrap of comfort thrown her way, she was Mrs Edmund Bertram, the wife of a popular priest, an intimate of the family at Everingham, and of the Symonds, and nobody at Great Yarmouth knew she had ever been Miss Fanny Price of Portsmouth, the daughter of a half-pay first lieutenant. Although the house Sir Thomas had taken for them was large, it was of far more comfortable proportions than Mansfield Park, and as it was one of the most prestigious houses in Great Yarmouth, that lustre was passed on to its inhabitants. Fanny found that she was considered as one of the first ladies in society here, just behind Mrs Symonds. Once that would have mortified her, now it gave her a quiet dignity and pride, and she enjoyed the status, and the benefits it conferred upon her.

Letters came regularly from Susan at Mansfield Park, and perhaps told her perceptive sister a little more about her heart than she might have intended. Fanny smiled at Susan's attempts to be cheerful about Mr Ballantyne's leaving Mansfield, and felt certain he would soon return. From the small hints Edmund had dropped, Fanny believed that Mr Ballantyne's interest was fixed upon Susan, and that only a little more time would be required for him to make a declaration.

CHAPTER FORTY-THREE

Just when Mrs Fairhaven was beginning again to suppose she ought to be leaving Mansfield Park for her own home at Wimpole Street, yet another circumstance occurred to fix her at Mansfield Park for a little longer. Sir Thomas had taken an interest in works being carried out in Portsmouth to install water pipes and drainage, and had been in regular correspondence with an engineer in charge of the works. He was intending to install such conveniences in Mansfield, once he understood what work was required to install them and what the benefits would be for his family and the village. One morning a letter arrived from the engineer in which he had enclosed a cutting from the Hampshire Telegraph with information about the latest developments of the ongoing project. Sir Thomas read the report, and then idly turned the clipping over to discover an obituary to one Lt William Price, formerly of the Navy, and for a moment it felt as though his heart had stopped. William dead? But on reading more closely, it was not the son, but his father who had died, and Sir Thomas breathed a little more freely again.

However, when Sir Thomas noted that the date on the newspaper was several months before, he was surprised that neither Susan nor Fanny had apprised him of her father's death. He rang for a servant to enquire if any other letters had been delivered to the house that morning. Only one for Susan, which might be from her sister, and might therefore contain the news, and so Sir Thomas asked the servant to invite Susan to attend him in his study.

Susan had been taking a turn about the gardens, reading Fanny's account of Eddie's latest scrapes, and how they had found a very welcoming congregation at a nearby church, and how Edmund had been invited to lead a service there next Sunday, when a servant came to ask her to attend her uncle at her leisure.

As she approached her uncle's study, so soon after Mr Ballantyne's departure, Susan may be forgiven for hoping that Mr Ballantyne had spoken to her uncle, and in this supposition she was entirely correct, but it was not Mr Ballantyne's hopes which her uncle unfolded to her, but a family tragedy of her own.

'My dear,' said he. 'Thank you for cutting short your walk to attend me. Tell me, have you a letter there from your sister?'

Susan held it up to show him.

'And what of family news does it contain?'

Susan told him what Fanny had written about the Bertram family's great enjoyment in their stay at Great Yarmouth so far, and added;

'But I had not read it all over before the servant came for me, so I do not know what other news there may be as yet.'

'Would you be good enough to take a moment and read the rest while you are here?' asked Sir Thomas. 'I will send for some tea.'

Although somewhat puzzled by the request, Susan supposed that her uncle had not had a letter from his son, and wanted to hear that they were all well and happy at Great Yarmouth, and be reassured that the house he had taken for them was suitable for their family, and so she sat in her uncle's study and read through the rest of Fanny's letter.

'Is there any news of your family in Portsmouth?' asked Sir Thomas when she indicated she had finished, by folding the letter up and stowing it in her reticule again.

'Oh, only of William, he has taken prizes, and has turned his hopes to being made a Commander soon. There is the prospect of a ship of his own!'

'That is good news indeed.' Sir Thomas hesitated, wondering how to break his own news to her, and surprised that no word of her father's death had reached either Susan or Fanny.

'And you have not heard from William himself?'

'No, sir, he writes to Fanny, and she passes on the news to me.'

'I regret my dear that I have some sad news to impart. It is not about William,' he added hastily, seeing the alarm in her eyes. 'And nor is it about anybody in Great Yarmouth. I can see I am alarming you; perhaps it is best if you read it for yourself.'

He passed over the clipping to her, making sure it was the right side up with the information about her father.

Susan read it through several times before the import of it became clear to her.

'My mother!' she cried, 'I must go directly to Portsmouth to comfort her. She has only Betsy left now, and Fanny is not able to go. William is at sea, and my other brothers are no longer at home either.'

'Of course,' said Sir Thomas, ringing the bell, 'You shall go as soon as it can be arranged. I will send a maid and a manservant with you, and you can go directly.'

Susan rushed to tell her aunt and Mrs Fairhaven the news, and wrote a hasty letter to her mother with a barely concealed reproach at not having been told herself, and having to find out through a stranger's chance inclusion of the newspaper clipping in a letter to her uncle. But she also said that she would be coming down to console her mother and sister, and would be there within the week. Despite the trembling in her fingers, she managed to write to her sister with the sad news, and asked Fanny to tell her brother, William, and added that she would be going down to Portsmouth herself; although she knew that Fanny was not able to come with her, she would take Fanny's love to her mother.

Mourning had to be made up for Susan and all the maids were put to creating ribbands for the servants, and for Mrs Fairhaven, who could not be expected to put on mourning for a man she had never met, and never would now. Out of respect for Susan, however, she was happy to wear the ribbands. Susan helped with the sewing, as did Mrs Fairhaven, and even Lady Bertram woke up enough to assist, and finally enough clothing was prepared for Susan to be able to go to Portsmouth suitably clad to honour her father. Sir Thomas wrote to his children, but only Fanny and Edmund put on mourning; the Yates, Crawfords and Bertrams decided they were far enough away from Mansfield Park to escape censure for not doing so themselves. Moreover, out of all of them, only Henry Crawford had met Mr Price, and their acquaintance had not been of a long enough standing to warrant a change of dress in his memory.

Susan had no fears of the journey to Portsmouth, although she would be two days on the road. The old coachman insisted on driving Susan himself in Sir Thomas's carriage to the post, from where, the manservant sent with her by Sir Thomas made all the onward arrangements of her journey. They passed through Oxford, and stopped at Newbury where a comfortable meal, uniting dinner and supper, wound up the enjoyments and fatigues of that day. Susan did not know it, but her sister and brother had passed this very way, and stayed at this very inn on their own journey back to Portsmouth. Susan did not have a brother to support her, but the manservant was very solicitous of her comfort and convenience, and she found she had much leisure to think over everything that had happened, and to wonder what she would find when she arrived home.

The next morning saw them off again at an early hour in a hired chaise; and with no events, and no delays, they regularly advanced, and were in the environs of Portsmouth while there was yet daylight for Susan, like Fanny before her, to look around, and wonder at the new buildings. There were also many roads dug up for the new watermains along the more prosperous roads, which occasioned several detours by the chaise to pass around them. They crossed the drawbridge, and entered the town; and the light was only beginning to fail as, guided by Susan's instructions, relayed to the driver by the manservant's powerful voice, they were rattled into a narrow street, leading from the High Street, and drawn up before the door of the small house where Susan had grown up.

CHAPTER FORTY-FOUR

Susan alighted and looked about her in dismay. She had not been at Mansfield Park as long as had Fanny before her own return, but it had been long enough for her to have forgotten quite how narrow was the street, quite how dirty, and quite how small and close together were the houses. The sound of a chaise rattling into the narrow street was enough to bring all the neighbours out of their houses to wonder who it could be, and to pass comments on the horses, the coachman, the dress of the passengers and to speculate on their purpose there. Susan directed the manservant to knock at the door, but there was no need; a woman had already emerged, surrounded by several small children, with a maid servant behind them all who was calling out, 'Please ma'am, I am to answer the door, it is not for you to answer the door!'

This was not her mother, and these were not her brothers! Susan found herself quite speechless with the shock of not finding her family at the house, and quite unable to assert herself to make any enquiries. Fortunately, the neighbours, having concluded their observations, speculations and remarks, and seeing nothing of any further interest, returned into their homes, closing the doors against the night. One neighbour alone remained in the street.

'Miss Price?' asked the neighbour, giving Susan a respect she would never have earned without a chaise, a manservant and a maid, as well as the quality of her clothing.

Susan thought she recognised the woman, 'Mrs Harewood?'

'Yes indeed! You poor thing, your mother is gone, and you did not know?'

'Gone?' For a terrible moment, Susan thought Mrs Harewood meant that her mother had also died.

'Yes, but this is not news for the street, come in, and take a dish of tea with me. I will tell you what has happened.'

Susan accepted, if only to get off the street, which was now dark, as well as dirty. Mrs Harewood bustled about, sending Susan's maid and manservant into her own kitchen, and ushering Susan into her parlour. Once comfortably seated, with a very welcome cup of tea, Susan asked;

'Mrs Harewood, what has happened to my family? I am come because of my father's death notice in the newspaper, but where is my mother? And my sister, Betsey?'

'Well, my dear,' began Mrs Harewood, 'I must tell you first that I do not know exactly where your mother and sister are gone to, but that if you make enquiries of a Captain Saunders, he may know where they are living now, for he oversaw your poor father's funeral arrangements, and was much at the house beforehand.'

Susan thought for a moment before recalling;

'Captain Saunders was my father's last captain before he retired from naval duties.'

'He was ashore for a while and came to look your father up. The two of them were much out at the dockyard, and spent a lot of time with fellow officers while Captain Saunders' ship was being outfitted again.'

'What happened to my father?' asked Susan. 'How did he die? Where is he buried?'

'It was one night, above three months ago,' said Mrs Harewood. 'Captain Saunders and some other officers brought your father home after a night out. There was such a to-do and a hollering in the street that it quite woke me, and I went to the window to see what it could be. I fear that your father had taken one too many bottles that night, but he was helped in doors, and the other men came out and went away. The next morning, there was Rebecca knocking at my door saying the master was dead, and the mistress was all to pieces and what was she to do?'

'He died in his sleep?'

'Well, I went next door to see what I could do to help your poor mother, and he was lying on the floor in the parlour. He had fallen out of his chair in the night and hit his head on the floor. I sent for a physician, but there was nothing anyone could do for him. I helped your mother to lay him out, and Captain Saunders came and took upon himself all the arrangements and paid for everything. He said it was his fault that poor Lieutenant Price was dead, and he would not have it any other way.'

Mrs Harewood paused to offer Susan more tea, and then resumed her tale;

'Your father was buried very properly, my dear. You need have no fears on that score. Only two days later, but everybody had been to pay their respects, and Captain Saunders gave out black bands to everybody who came. He ordered carriages for all the naval officers, and everybody who went to the grave-side was given a silver coin; you could not have asked for a better funeral for your father, my dear.'

'And how was my mother? Did any of my brothers attend?'

'Your mother and your sister did not attend the funeral, and I did not see any of your brothers, or none that I recognised anyway. There was not time to alert them, I suppose, as the funeral followed on so fast from his death.'

'And what happened then?'

'Your mother never returned to the house as far as I can tell. There was no funeral dinner held here,' Mrs Harewood sniffed at little at this, and Susan could tell that this part of the proceedings at least had not met with approval in this street. A funeral feast might set up a family for several days if there were enough cold meats and tea to be had. For her mother to not lay on a funeral feast was a grievous omission indeed. But Mrs Harewood was continuing;

'Rebecca told me the servants was all given notice straight away. I know not what became of the others, but Rebecca has taken up another place in town; I see her sometimes on the ramparts on a Sunday, but I have not seen your mother or your sister, and neither has she. The house was let again immediately with all the furniture, for your mother never took a stick of it with her that I saw.'

Susan was quiet, thinking over what Mrs Harewood had told her.

'And now, my dear, it is much too late to be thinking of enquiring after Captain Saunders. I would offer you a room here, but –.'

'No indeed, I would not trouble you for the world,' cried Susan. 'My manservant shall find us accommodation for this night, and I will commence my enquiries tomorrow as you suggest. Thank you very much for the tea, and for telling me about my father.'

CHAPTER FORTY-FIVE

The manservant was sent to bespeak rooms at The Crown, as being a respectable enough inn for Susan, and wearily she re-entered the chaise and it was directed thither. She could not know that this was the same Crown Inn that Mr Crawford had staid at when he had visited Fanny at Portsmouth, but there was enough information already crowding her head without adding that to the mix. Her father dead over three months! No letter from her mother to any of her children, as far as Susan could tell. And her mother gone from the house, and Captain Saunders the only source of information as to her whereabouts. As she thought about it by a very good fire in her bed chamber at the inn, she settled it with herself that either her mother had taken a smaller house for herself and Betsey, not wanting to stay in the house where her husband had died, or was gone to keep Captain Saunders' house for him whilst he was away at sea.

It would be a come-down indeed for a Miss Frances Ward whose sister was Lady Bertram, to be a housekeeper for a sea captain, but Susan could imagine no other position for her; either Captain Saunders had found Mrs Price and Betsey some other accommodation, or he had offered her his roof in exchange for her running his household in his absence. Mrs Price's fortune had not kept her in affluence during her marriage, and it was not to be supposed it could do so now that she no longer had her husband's half-pay to supplement her income. Still, Susan felt that as long as she could assure herself that her mother and sister were well, and safe, it would not at all signify if her mother was now having to work for a rich man.

The following morning, the manservant was sent out to enquire about the town as to the location of Captain Saunders' house, and returned very quickly with the direction. Accordingly, Susan and her maid bent their steps thither, arriving at a large, well-built modern house, which although not to be compared with Mansfield Park, was vastly superior to the house where Mrs Price had lived all her married life, and where all her children had been born.

The door was answered by a very smartly dressed maid, who studied Susan's card and said, 'If you will follow me, Miss?'

Susan followed the maid not to a housekeeper's room, as she had expected, but into a modern and well-furnished parlour, which would not have been out of place as a small breakfast room at Mansfield Park.

Mrs Price was leaning back on a sopha in an attitude which irresistibly recalled Lady Bertram to Susan, and looked up without much interest as the maid announced her visitor. To Susan's horror, her mother was not in the mourning Susan would expect for so recently widowed a woman. Instead she was in a sort of half-mourning; wearing a violet gown, with coral jewellery, and reclining in a drawing room, instead of busying herself in a house-keeper's room, or the kitchen. Susan did not know at all what to make of it, and stood, staring at her mother, wondering what to say or do.

'Susan, is it?' her mother said in a far stronger voice than any Susan had heard her use before. Indeed her mother was looking years younger, her hair beautifully dressed, and all her fretfulness quite gone. Her disposition had always been easy and indolent, like her sister Bertram's, and now that she was restored to a situation of affluence, she was more than inclined to be at leisure. Her imprudent marriage was over, and she was become what she had always thought she should have been; a woman of consequence, in her own mind at least. Now that she no longer had to do all the work about the house herself, she did none of it, and sat at her ease, dreaming on her sofa.

Some things had not changed; she was still the partial, ill-judging parent that Fanny had found her, and that Susan had come to regard her before she left for Mansfield Park. Mrs Price still had no talent, no conversation, no affection for or interest in her children, apart from Betsey, and no curiosity about Susan's sudden reappearance in her life. Indeed, had Susan but known it, Mrs Price had quite successfully persuaded herself that Betsey was her only child; so thoroughly had she parted with and forgotten all the others. Even William could not compete with Betsey, although she did occasionally bestir herself to write to him, and read over his letters with pleasure. Although she had always favoured her sons above her daughters, now that they were all settled out in the world, she was happy to forget them and live in the moment with Betsey in her new luxury.

'Mama,' said Susan, seating herself, as she had not been invited to do so, by her mother. 'Why did you not write to tell me that Papa had died?'

'Oh!' her mother said languidly, 'That was such a long time ago. I do not think of it any more. You can see that Betsey and I are most comfortably situated, and want for nothing. You may tell my sisters Bertram and Norris that I am very well set up here, and need none of their pity or assistance any longer.'

'But what do you do here, Mama? Are you Captain Saunders' housekeeper?'

'A Housekeeper? Oh! no, indeed! How can you think so? This is my home now.'

'And are you to marry Captain Saunders once your mourning is at an end?'

'As to that, I do not know. He has been everything honourable, and no expense spared as you can see. But you are come with a maid and a manservant; are you come into some money yourself? Or does my brother Bertram still pay for everything?'

Before Susan could answer this rather impertinent enquiry, there was a disturbance of voices outside the room, and then the door was pushed violently open and in came her sister, Betsey, much grown but as loud as ever. The violence of her entry, and the loudness of her voice showed to Susan that the departure of her brothers had caused little diminution in the amount of noise about the house. Betsey, it seemed, could make enough noise to make up for all their absence. To Susan's further surprise, the sudden appearance of Betsey, holding out a gown, and followed by several maids in tears, roused Mrs Price to something like animation as nothing before could do.

'Mama!' Betsey cried. 'Look what Clare has done to my gown! It is quite ruined and I must have another at once! This is fit for nothing but rag now.'

'Oh my darling, how terrible,' said Mrs Price in an accent almost approaching concerned at this tragedy. 'But here is your sister Susan come to visit us.'

But Betsey cared nothing for Susan; they had never been friends when Susan lived at home, and she had no interest in attempting to be friends now. As far as Betsey was concerned, the sudden appearance of a sister meant a dilution of her mother's attention, and could never be a good thing at all. Instead she thrust the offending gown at her mother, who turned helplessly to Susan;

'I do not at all know what is wrong with what Clare has done, my dear. Show your sister and mayhap she can advise. She is well-dressed, despite the mourning for your papa, and I remember she was always good with a needle.'

'That was Fanny who was good with a needle, not I,' Susan said, but she dutifully looked at the offending gown which had been thrown roughly towards her by her sister. It was a frothy confection of lace and muslin, and not at all suitable for a daughter supposedly in mourning for her father; but Betsey had followed her mother's example, and was not even wearing a black ribbon for her father.

'I cannot see -.' She began before Betsey snatched the dress back and threw it on to the floor.

'I want a new gown immediately,' she cried, and when Mrs Price waved a hand in what Betsey took to be agreement, she rushed out calling for her wraps as she was to go out to the mantua maker immediately.

'But you will stay a few days before returning to Mansfield Park?' Mrs Price murmured languidly, as though there had been no ill-natured interruption from Betsey.

'Thank you, I will,' Susan replied, thinking that there could be no impropriety as Captain Saunders was away at sea, but also that she would only stay long enough to visit her father's graveside, and to write to Fanny, and all her brothers to tell them of her mother's new situation, and that she and Betsey were being well cared for.

Mrs Price was able to give vague directions for the letters to all her sons, and once they were written, Susan gave them in to the care of the Post Office and just had to hope that her mother's information as to her sons' locations was up to date. She next wrote to her uncle Sir Thomas to inform him of Mrs Price's new address, although she did not mention it was at Captain Saunders' house, and she also informed him of her plans to travel home by post, unless he were able to send the carriage to meet her part way.

The inauspicious resumption of Susan and Betsey's acquaintance never improved after that. Susan did her best to set her relationship with her mother and sister on to a better footing, but where Mrs Price was indifferent, Betsey was actively hostile. Susan may have forgotten their quarrels over their sister Mary's silver knife, but Betsey's nature was more retentive of slights than was Susan's and she had not by any means forgiven Susan for the episode, even though Mary's knife had remained in her own hands. Susan's claim that it had been gifted to her by Mary on her death bed, despite being remembered as such by her mother, was enough for it to remain both Betsey's most treasured possession, and also a source of implacable resentment against her older sister.

Susan was further perturbed by her mother's and sister's entertaining of company in the evenings; she could not at all like their acquaintance, even in this superior part of town. The men appeared to her all coarse, the women all pert, everybody under-bred; and she gave as little contentment as she received from introductions to these new acquaintances. The young ladies who approached her at first with some respect, in consideration of her living with a baronet's family, were soon offended by what they termed 'airs'; for, although she wore smart pelisses, they were all a very dull black, and she did not dress any finer in the evenings. Added to which, she would not play on the pianoforte for them to dance to as she judged it inappropriate while she was in mourning for her father; all this meant that they could, on farther observation, admit no right of superiority. Susan excused herself as soon as she could from these gatherings, and returned to her own sitting room above stairs. These gatherings she felt were as ill-judged as they were unsatisfactory; not only was her mother newly widowed, but Betsey was full young to be in so much company, and the owner of the house was not at home to receive these guests. Mrs Price, encouraged by Betsey, discovered with the other young ladies, that Susan had grown satirical by her living at her uncle's house; although none of them in the least knew what it meant, it was censure in common usage, and easily given. Betsey was determined that her mother should not prefer this prodigal sister, returning in all her affluence, and constantly brought Susan's deficiencies to her mother's attention.

It was all-together a most miserable home-coming; even though Susan had not longed for her home in the way Fanny had, she had still hoped for some affection, some acknowledgement of the special ties of kinship; but it was clear to her that this was a wish on her side only, on her mother and sister's side there was none, and she was glad to know she could soon leave. Sir Thomas had replied by return in the affirmative to her letter, and reminded her of how much she was missed by Lady Bertram, even though Mrs Fairhaven yet remained at Mansfield Park, and Mr Ballantyne was expected to return any day.

Mansfield Park! Like Fanny before her, Susan was almost sick with longing to return there; to tend on her aunt who did at least value her presence, and to take her walks about the verdant loveliness of the gardens; and if another person's returning there in her own absence might hallow it more in her memory, it is not our place to speculate. That other person had indeed returned to Mansfield Park after the funeral of his great-aunt, and had done so with the sole intention of proposing marriage to Miss Price.

CHAPTER FORTY-SIX

Mr Ballantyne had discussed the matter with his father, and both agreed that as the recently departed family member was only the sister of his also deceased grandmother, there was no need to observe mourning for any longer than three months, although the women and servants were to continue wearing black ribbands for a few more weeks yet. It was therefore not inappropriate for Mr Ballantyne to be looking to marry soon, and he rode back to Mansfield Park in a state of mingled hope and fear.

His hopes were not dashed, but his fears were partially realised by the discovery that Susan was no longer at Mansfield Park, but was expected to return within the month.

A month was too long for this impatient lover to wait, and he concluded his business at Thornton Lacey, and determined to set out for Portsmouth immediately, in case that sea port should furnish many eligible young men of good looks and large fortune who might tempt Miss Price to bestow upon them her hand. On arrival at The Crown, he discovered that not only had Miss Price staid there herself on her own arrival at Portsmouth, but that she was now at the house of one Captain Saunders, with her mother and sister. Accordingly, he sent in his card the following morning, and Mrs Price was delighted to receive him. Despite her confusion at seeing him so soon, and where she least expected, Susan was able to name him to her mother as Edmund's friend, and fellow vicar at Thornton Lacey when he was shown in. He made his bow, and on being begged to be seated and take refreshment, devoted himself entirely to Mrs Price, addressing her, and attending to her with the utmost politeness and propriety, at the same time with a degree of friendliness, of interest at least, which made his manner perfect.

Mrs. Price's manners were at their best. Warmed by the sight of such a handsome young man visiting her in her new affluence, and regulated by the wish of appearing to advantage before him, she was overflowing with gratitude for what she chose to consider was his validation of her current situation and its respectability.

They talked of Portsmouth, and he deferred to her opinion about the town, and the shipping to such a degree that Mrs Price felt that she had never seen so agreeable a man in her life. She was only astonished to find that, so great and so agreeable as he was, he should be come down to Portsmouth neither on a visit to the port-admiral, nor the commissioner, nor yet with the intention of going over to the island, nor of seeing the dockyard. Nothing of all that she had been used to think of as the proof of importance, or the employment of wealth, had brought him to Portsmouth.

By the time he had given all this information, it was not unreasonable to suppose that he might now turn his attention to Susan and let her know that he was come from Mansfield Park, and that he was pleased to be able to tell her that he had left everybody there well and happy.

Susan had not been able to take her share in this conversation, nor claim her share in his attention as the sight of him had quite taken her breath away. But sitting quietly had allowed her to recover from the shame of having to introduce him to her mother under these circumstances, and become again very glad indeed to see him. She could only wish that he would not recoil in horror from her family once he was aware of the truth; this was the only time during their acquaintance that she had cause to blush for her relations, and to wish he were not a clergyman! However, on her mother being called away by some small household emergency, Mr Ballantyne was able to acquaint her with the news of his great-aunt, and his own acquisition of her estate, and his hopes for the future, at which important moment, Mrs Price returned into the room, with many apologies for her absence, and offers of more refreshment. To Susan's annoyance he had perforce to stop speaking of these most interesting subjects, and instead decline more refreshment, and hint instead at the expediency of a walk out in the fresh air.

'It is a lovely morning, ma'am, and at this season of the year a fine morning so often turns off, that I think it wisest for everybody not to delay their exercise,' said he, but such hints producing nothing, he soon proceeded to a positive recommendation to Mrs Price to take her walk without loss of time. Now they came to an understanding. Mrs Price, it appeared, scarcely ever stirred out of doors these days, not even on a Sunday any more, although she owned she used to take her walk on the ramparts on a Sunday.

'Would you not, then ma'am, allow me to persuade your daughters to take advantage of such weather, and give me the very great pleasure of attending them?'

Mrs. Price was greatly obliged and very complying, 'Indeed, sir, my daughters find themselves very much confined; Portsmouth is a sad place; they do not often get out.' Then she brightened a little, 'I do know that young women can always find some errands in the town, which they would be very glad to do, if you could escort them thither?'

'But I have not yet seen the port, nor the shipping which you have recommended to me in such terms as I cannot be happy until I have viewed them,' said Mr Ballantyne, fearing that he would never have a chance to talk to Susan alone if they went into the town about errands, and hoping that Mrs Price would not insist upon them being accompanied. 'Where would you advise me to walk to see Portsmouth at its best, ma'am?'

Mrs Price was only too happy to advise, and outlined several different ways he could walk into and about the town and the port, but on Mr Ballantyne fearing he would lose his way, added;

'In that case; go with him Susan, you cannot have forgot how to find your way about since you have been gone from Portsmouth.'

'No indeed, I have not forgot the way to the sea, mama,' answered Susan.

'And take Betsey with you, if she is within doors, or your maid if she be not,' added Mrs Price, suddenly becoming aware of the proprieties which pertained to her daughter, even if she were not concerned with them for herself.

After setting all the servants searching, Betsey was nowhere to be found indoors, and Susan wondered at her apparent freedom to be about the town without her mother having any knowledge of her whereabouts. Instead, Susan's maid accompanied them, and guessing Mr Ballantyne's purpose in taking Susan out of doors, gradually slowed her pace to fall further and further behind to render him as much assistance as possible.

The day was uncommonly lovely with a mild air, brisk soft wind, and bright sun, occasionally clouded for a minute; and everything looked so beautiful under the influence of such a sky, the effects of the shadows pursuing each other on the ships at Spithead and the island beyond, with the ever-varying hues of the sea, now at high water, dancing in its glee and dashing against the ramparts with so fine a sound, produced altogether such a combination of charms for Susan to which the addition of Mr Ballantyne was most welcome. Even without this very welcome presence, she would soon have known that she needed this walk after what had been several weeks inactivity, as her mother no longer insisted upon even a once weekly walk. Susan was beginning to feel the effects of being debarred from her usual regular exercise; she did not feel Portsmouth to be as good for her health as Mansfield Park, but the combination of Mr Ballantyne, and the beauty of the weather made up for the previous miserable weeks.

The loveliness of the day, and of the view, he felt like herself. They often stopt with the same sentiment and taste, leaning against the wall for some minutes, to look and admire; and Susan was reminded of her delight in his being as sufficiently open to the charms of nature as she, and in being very well able to express his admiration. Mr Ballantyne in turn was delighted to discern that she was far less reserved in her manner and opinions here than she had been at Mansfield Park, and in her glowing looks and smiles, began to feel more secure in his opinion of him than he had ever done before.

'You have been here a month, I think?' said he.

'No; not quite a month. It is only four weeks to-morrow since I left Mansfield.'

'You are a most accurate and honest reckoner. I should call that a month. And when do you leave again?'

'Within a few days,' Susan answered, 'My mother's situation is such that I cannot stay any longer, and I am truly sorry that you have had to witness it too.'

'I do not at all regard your mother's situation as having any bearing on your own,' he assured her. 'Thanks to my great-aunt, I am to have no profession but be a gentleman and live idly at my ease in her mansion on her estate.'

'And how shall you like that?' asked Susan, teasingly.

'I should like it very well indeed if you were there with me,' said he boldly, and when she looked up at him in surprise, the expression in his eyes left her in no doubt of his meaning, and she found her breath quite stolen away.

As she could not speak, she held out her hand and he tucked it under his arm as they continued walking, and he laid out all his plans for their future, and she felt as though she must be in a dream, a wonderful dream from which she did not wish ever to wake. They walked and talked together until Susan was quite certain that Portsmouth was the most beautiful town in the world; far more lovely than she had ever before realised, and also that it was high time to return to Captain Saunders' house.

In the unavoidable absence of Susan's father, Mrs Price, on being applied to for her blessing was only too happy to give it and be relieved of the possible future care of another child, if her brother Bertram were ever to tire of supporting her.

'I am certain that Betsey will marry well too,' said she fondly smiling at the scowling child in the corner of the room, who was none too happy at her sister's good tidings, despite her hopes of another new gown to celebrate. 'Captain Saunders regards her as quite a daughter of his own, and will give her a fortune from his prize money when she is ready to come out.'

'I am ready now mama,' said Betsey, 'if all my sisters are married, then it is full time for me to make my come out.'

'When Captain Saunders returns, then,' answered Mrs Price.

Susan was horrified at this. Betsey, by her reckoning, was still many years away from the age when even the most indulgent parent would allow her be bound into an early betrothal, let alone permit her to marry. However, it was none of her business now, and she knew that any protest would not be heeded, and so she turned to her next question;

'Will you come to my wedding mama?' asked Susan, 'And Betsey too?'

As to that, Mrs Price did not at all know. She would have to await Captain Saunders' return, as she could not leave his house unattended, and a thousand more excuses in the same vein left Susan and Mr Ballantyne in little doubt that she would not come, and nor would Betsey.

'I will write to you from my new home at Stowe Manor, mama,' said Susan, 'Once I am settled there, and I hope you and Betsey will come to visit.'

'A Manor! Well, you are most fortunate my dear.'

Betsy was less impressed; Mr Ballantyne looked very old to her, and with all the glories of Portsmouth society ahead of her, she could not find any envy for her older sister, even if she were to be living in a Manor house. She was just glad that Susan was to go away again, and would likely be too busy with her new house and family to want to return to Portsmouth any time soon.

From Mrs Price's languid response, and Betsy's indifference, Mr Ballantyne could tell they had lost whatever interest had been expressed previously, and he was even more determined to marry Susan as soon as possible to give her a family of her own to love, as there was no love for her here. In a few more wonderful days of walks, and talks, for now that Susan could speak, she was able to tell Mr Ballantyne just how much he had already engaged her affections and for how long since; their future was settled to their mutual delight, and an early wedding day was decided upon.

Sir Thomas wrote to offer his and Lady Bertram's sincere wishes for her future happiness with Mr Ballantyne, and to invite Betsey to accompany them back to Mansfield Park to take Susan's place as resident niece.

Susan handed her uncle's letter to her mother, indicating the relevant portion, but her mother begged her instead to read it aloud.

'For I find I require spectacles to read such crossings, and I will not be seen in them,' said she. 'Captain Saunders does not wear spectacles, and I have heard him say they are most unbecoming on ladies, although he does not object to a lorgnette. Do you think I should buy a lorgnette before his return?'

Susan had no option to give on this subject, but when she read Sir Thomas's offer to Betsey aloud, her mother was quite horrified; no indeed, she would not part with Betsey! Betsey was quite a favourite of Captain Saunders, and he would not hear of her going to live with her uncle and aunt so far away! What would Captain Saunders say if he were to return and find Betsey gone from the house? No, it would not do at all, Betsey must stay.

'Very well, mama, but you will not prevent me from making the offer to Betsey? She may well wish to live at Mansfield Park in my place,' said Susan, folding the letter up and placing it back in her reticule for safe keeping.

When Betsey returned from another mysterious outing about Portsmouth, she was next consulted and declared she did not wish to bury herself at Mansfield Park when there was all the excitement of Portsmouth before her, especially now that she was to make her come out, and so there was nothing to do but leave without her.

The day Susan left Portsmouth forever was one of the happiest of her life; her mother and sister bid her farewell without any hint of sorrow, soon returning to their own concerns, and she was indeed forgotten.

Mr Ballantyne rode alongside the chaise, and in a few days they were both back at Mansfield Park, ready for this next exciting new phase of their lives. As they passed into the environs of Mansfield Park, here was her Ladyship come out to meet them, looking in vain for Betsey. Lady Bertram was very glad to see Susan returned, sorry to hear she was to lose her again so soon, and could not understand why Betsey did not wish to come in her sister's place.

'It is not as though you and dear Fanny have not been happy here,' was her puzzled refrain. 'And you are to leave me soon, my dear,' to Susan, 'And then I shall have no body if Betsey does not come.'

'And I must not stay beyond this sen'night,' added Mrs Fairhaven. 'I have it from Agnes that they are returned to London already, and I should like to be back at Wimpole Street now that they have had time to settle in, and to hear how they found Brighton. I am considering making a visit there myself, and they can advise me on where to stay, and what I am to see there.'

Despite their protests, there was nothing that Lady Bertram, nor Sir Thomas, could say to prolong Mrs Fairhaven's stay; go she would and reluctantly Sir Thomas made the necessary arrangements for her removal. The day that saw Mrs Fairhaven finally leave Mansfield Park was also the day that Susan, Lady Bertram and Sir Thomas travelled to Mr Ballantyne's estate for Susan's wedding. She was very sad not to have any of her own family in attendance; her mother and sister had been invited, but no reply to the invitation had returned, and so it was supposed they had not changed their minds and still did not care to attend. The only attention Susan received from her family on this momentous occasion was a very kind letter from Fanny enclosing an amber cross from William, which had been intended for Fanny, but which she chose to pass on to her sister.

CHAPTER FORTY-SEVEN

At Burgh Hall in Great Yarmouth, Fanny had received Susan's letter giving the news of her father's death, and her thoughts naturally turned to her own memories of him, including that last visit and stay at his house in Portsmouth, prior to her marriage. The news of his death did not touch her very deeply; she had been parted from him at such a tender age, and then her return into Portsmouth had not been a happy reunion with either of her parents. But as she sat there, holding Susan's letter with the news of her father's death, she could not help but review their last encounter with a little softening in her heart.

She had travelled thither without much hope of a warm welcome from him, but she had not been prepared for him to be quite so negligent of his family, nor so indifferent to herself. She could not deny that his habits were worse, and his manners coarser than her years spent at Mansfield Park with Sir Thomas as a pattern of fatherhood could possibly have prepared her. Fanny felt now that what she had witnessed was a life wasted, a life lost to drink. Her father had not wanted abilities, but he had had no curiosity, and sought no information beyond his profession. It was a great shame that he had had to be invalided out of the Navy comparatively young; had he been able to remain on active service long enough to be made Captain, his life might have run along more ordered lines when he was finally ashore again. As it was, he talked only to his sea-faring sons about the dockyard, the harbour, Spithead, and the Motherbank; and his conversation, such as it was, was littered with profanities which he took no pains to check even when there were women or girls present.

Attempting to look further back into her life before she had left home to go to Mansfield Park, Fanny could not recall any tenderness in his treatment of herself as his eldest child. She had not had the resilience to stand up for herself amongst the growing family, or to fearlessly claim her share of her father's attention or love. Certainly, he had not stood in the way of her being sent off at the age of ten years to Mansfield Park, with no plans for her return. He had not written her a single letter, or sent her a single present; he had not marked any of the birthdays or Christmases that she had spent away from home. And when she had returned to his house at Sir Thomas's behest, he barely noticed her in his general roughness and loudness of manner, except to occasionally make her the object of a coarse joke, which had distressed her beyond measure.

Fanny decided that how she wished to remember her father was as he had appeared to Mr Crawford, even though the linking of the two caused her a little distress. Still, it could not be helped; Mr Crawford's being introduced to her father had brought out the best in him; with Mr Crawford at least, her father appeared much more attached to his daughters. With a distinguished stranger, with a man who was his nephew's friend, known to be an intimate at Mansfield Park, Mr Price's manners had not become polished, to be sure, but they had become more than passable. At the time, Fanny had been relieved to see that her father did know how to behave, how to be grateful, animated, and manly; at least out in the open air away from his home and family.

A further, more melancholy thought was that she had not had the benefit of an affectionate and indulgent father or mother in her own growing up; and the only example of parenting she had had was from Sir Thomas and Lady Bertram. Sir Thomas she had long been afraid of, although she had learned over the years to appreciate his steadfastness, and sense of propriety, and Lady Bertram had been fond of her but as one is fond of a useful companion; she had never been their own child. She had never had the love of a parent as a guide for her own parenting, and she began to wonder if she was doing all she could to be a good mother to little Eddie and Franny. It was another problem to talk to Edmund about; he could always reassure her.

As she prepared to pick up Susan's letter to see what else of news it contained, Fanny decided to herself that she would remember her father as he had been in that moment on the front at Portsmouth; a man who could meet a well-mannered stranger and react with the instinctive compliment of good manners in return.

This decided, Fanny picked up Susan's letter, and read on about her mother and sister's situation. Here was something very shocking indeed! Like Susan before her, Fanny was horrified with the idea that her mother would consent to live with Captain Saunders during her period of mourning, and without a formal arrangement of any sort between them. And that Betsey at such a young age should witness such abandoned behaviour did not bode well for her moral guidance during her upbringing. However, as she thought more about it, and how she was to present it to Edmund, she decided that there could not possibly be any real impropriety in her mother's behaviour, or she would herself be sensible of it, and with such a conviction, could have no pleasure in her circumstances.

No, it was evident to Fanny that while Captain Saunders was at sea, her mother had assumed a position in the household as his housekeeper. And it was just as well that Captain Saunders had stepped in to assist his former Lieutenant's widow, for Mrs Price's financial situation must be much impaired by her widowhood. Fanny sat down to write to Susan while these happier thoughts were upmost in her mind.

In her letter, Fanny wrote that she was very sorry indeed that Susan had had to travel alone to Portsmouth, without any support from her brothers or sister, and very sorry also that Susan encountered her mother and Betsey in such circumstances as might have given rise to misunderstandings. But Fanny was assured that it was only a sense of obligation to his former first lieutenant which had prompted Captain Saunders to take Mrs Price and Betsey under his care, she knew from William that all sailors regarded each other quite as family, and she was certain that there was no impropriety in it. Once he returned to shore, the situation would be regularised, either through marriage, or through Captain Saunders assisting Mrs Price and Betsey to a home of their own, and providing Betsey with some money so that she could make a good match.

Susan smiled and shook her head over this letter – Fanny would always think the best of everybody, there was no preventing her!

Edmund on being given Susan's letter was privately less inclined to view the situation in such a good light as his wife, but he decided that there was nothing to be done about it, but appear to agree with her, as the Price family was too far away to affect the Bertrams of Mansfield Park, if there was any wrong-doing. As a clergyman, Edmund decided instead to focus on Susan and Ballantyne's forthcoming marriage, and elevation to their own estate, and the subsequent loss of the curate of Thornton Lacey.

Edmund wrote to congratulate Harry and Susan most heartily, and to thank Harry for all his hard work in Edmund's absence about the parishes of Thornton Lacey and Mansfield. Edmund would miss his company and his assistance, and wondered if Harry knew of anybody who would be available to come in his place, until Edmund could return. As it happened, Harry did know of some body, and so a replacement was soon arranged to take on all the duties of the joined parishes, in Edmund's continuing absence.

And so Susan became Mrs Ballantyne and mistress of Stowe Manor, which was rather more daunting to her than Fanny's experience of Burgh Hall, as it was a large estate with many dependents. After the ceremony, the new Mr and Mrs Ballantyne begged Sir Thomas and Lady Bertram to stay and spend some time with them; Susan wanting advice on running the house, and Harry advice on running his new estate. But soon enough they too had to return home, as the Crawfords were due to make their own wedding visit. The return to Mansfield Park was very sad indeed for Sir Thomas and Lady Bertram. No Mrs Fairhaven, no resident niece, no sister, no child or grandchild to greet them; there was now just the two of them in the great house, and Lady Bertram became very low in mood. What to do to support Lady Bertram now became Sir Thomas's next concern; he had not thought to have run out of nieces quite so soon.

A temporary solution came from an unexpected source; a letter from Mr Rickett arrived to inform Sir Thomas that the physician believed that Mrs Norris had rallied somewhat, and was now strong enough to be moved from Champford Hall, and what was more to the point, the family was having to flee London on account of Lord M_ having inadvertently displeased the Prince Regent by being claimed as a friend by Brummel. The dowager had also decided to join the family at Champford for the first time in years, as Bath had grown stale, and both the houses were needed again. Sir Thomas arranged everything and with as much care, and as little trouble as possible, Mrs Norris was conveyed gently back to Mansfield Park, with a physician in attendance every step of the way.

Lady Bertram was pleased to see her sister, although shocked at how ill she was become. It was clear that Mrs Norris was very content to be back with her family at Mansfield Park, but she never recovered her power of speech, and spent each day lying on a sofa near Lady Bertram after being carried down the stairs. There they dozed near to one another in perfect amity until one morning Mrs Norris was found dead in her bed, and was finally reunited with her beloved husband in the Mansfield graveyard.

CHAPTER FORTY-EIGHT

It was not long after Mrs Norris was laid to rest, that Mr, Mrs and Miss Crawford reached Mansfield Park after their protracted wedding visits. They had spent a week with the Admiral, and had also made triumphant visits to many friends in London on their way back from Brighton.

Maria's reunion after so many years away from her family was muted, rather than pathetic; there was only Lady Bertram at home; and nobody was invited to meet Sir Thomas's errant daughter and her second husband. Lady Bertram at least was very pleased to see her, and for the first few days barely let Maria out of her sight, complaining gently about how everybody had left her alone, and how glad she was that Maria was come at last, she had been certain that she would come, despite what Sir Thomas had said. Maria soon found herself in possession of one of Pug's puppies and a vast length of fringing, for which she had to appear at least, to be grateful.

Lady Bertram was also pleased to welcome Henry and Mary, remembering them very well from when they lived at the Parsonage, although she had to be reminded that Dr Grant was no longer alive, and Mrs Grant was gone to live in London. Frou-frou formed an instant attachment to Maria's new puppy, to everybody's surprise, and became less hostile to everybody else now that there was something else for it to care for than just Mary. Nobody was ill bred enough to refer to the events of the recent past; Henry Crawford expressed the expected disappointment at Edmund and Fanny's absence, renewed his acquaintance with the countryside, was polite to Sir Thomas, and gallant to his lady.

All too soon, the first of September was coming up, and Mr, Mrs and Miss Crawford decamped to Everingham, and Maria was at her married home at last. There she was able to take what she considered to be her rightful place in society, for the previous scandal had barely touched the consciousness of the families about Everingham, most of whom were far more interested in their own concerns than those of unknown people in far-away London.

Here in Norfolk, Maria was welcomed heartily as an asset to a local society, which had not seen many new faces for a number of years; local families tending to marry within each other, rather than import brides. Moreover, Maria was very handsome, and when it was worth her while, had very pleasing and elegant manners and address. Her clothes were exclaimed over by the ladies, and many an alteration was swiftly ordered or carried out to bring their garments up to her standard.

And what of Mary? She had followed her brother and Maria about the country, from Brighton, to London, to the Admiral's house and finally to Norfolk. It had become apparent to her at least, that the local ladies considered her quite a spinster, although she was determined not to go into caps just yet. Her clothes were as fashionable, and slightly more daring than Maria's, given the difference in their situations, but the young ladies were not interested in Mary, and despite attending every social event they were invited to, she saw no man to compare with Viscount Carmichael. The men in society about Everingham were either much older than she, already married, or very young; and while the older men were gallant, the younger were indifferent; Mary was much older than they, and despite her fortune, could not be of interest.

'What think you, my dear?' asked Mr Crawford of his lady one morning. 'Shall we invite your brother and Fanny to pay us a visit on their way home from Great Yarmouth? They will have to pass nearby to Everingham, and it is at least a two day journey back to Mansfield Park; they may be glad to break it with a stay here.'

Maria was not in the least interested in either her brother nor Fanny, but in her new-found security as Henry's wife, saw no reason to deny him anything he proposed, and so she gave a gracious assent, and spoke so warmly of his idea, that he was assured she thought it as delightful a prospect as did he, and she sat down with every evidence of alacrity to write the letter. Mary seconded the proposal, but a turn about the grounds and some reflection revealed to her that she had no longer any particular interest in a visit by Edmund and Fanny. Rather to her own surprise, she found that that she no longer had any desire to make Edmund smile on her again and forget Fanny; another man had quite taken his place in her interest, and he was no longer an object. She began to wonder if she could instead avoid meeting him again, by making a visit to Mrs Fraser in London, although no letter had come from that fickle friend for some months. It was a matter of some sadness to her that she had left Brighton without being able to give Viscount Carmichael her intended destination, and she wondered whether his nascent attachment would survive the necessary separation of his period of mourning, and her own absence from his sight. He would be eagerly sought after should he choose to marry again, and might have his pick of all the available women who were younger and richer than Mary Crawford.

Maria's letter soon reached the Bertrams at Great Yarmouth.

'My dear,' said Edward, 'We have a letter from my sister Maria inviting us to Everingham on our journey home to Mansfield. They have been there since the first of September, and it is on our way home. It would be most agreeable to meet up with Henry again, now that he is an old married man too, and to see Maria of course; there can be no impropriety in it now, no objection to any of us meeting her that I can see.'

He passed the letter to her, and she looked over it, wondering how she could voice her objections to seeing Mr Crawford again, in such a way that Edmund would understand and agree to refuse the offered visit. She did not trust Henry Crawford, old married man, or not; and suspected him of she knew not what by making this invitation.

Of course, the letter came very properly from Maria, and was couched in empty affectionate phrases about her 'dearest brother and sister' and 'the dear little children'; in whom Fanny was certain Maria had no interest whatsoever, as she did not appear to recall their names.

But there was no time for a reasoned discussion now; Edmund was leaving, and so she smiled and wished him a pleasant walk.

'And I shall call on Symonds on my way home, he has sent a message to say that there is something he wishes to consult with me about; have you any message for Mrs Symonds, my love?'

'Oh!' said Fanny, 'My very best love, of course, and I shall call upon her myself once we have taken our walk. I may even see you there.'

CHAPTER FORTY-NINE

Once Edmund had gone, and the children were not yet brought down the stairs by their very competent nurse; Fanny gave herself up to thinking over their time in Great Yarmouth, which was now coming to an end. She had to confess it had done them all a great deal of good; the children had quite recovered their health, and she was feeling much stronger than she had done for years. The sea air, so much praised, had proved its worth; as had the frequent bathing in the sea baths, and the walks along the beach.

Fanny hoped that Burgh Hall might be available again next summer for them to pay another visit. She further wondered if Edmund might agree to an annual visit to Great Yarmouth to keep them all in the best health. All told, Fanny reflected, as she heard her children begin their noisy descent of the staircase, she was most contented here, and would very much prefer to stay. The openness of the country, the ever-changing face of the sea, the amusements of the shore, and the society, had not lost their novelty and enjoyment for her. The very air of Great Yarmouth was most conducive to her health, and she wondered whether the air at Mansfield Park might be too relaxing for her, after all, she had been living for the first ten years of her life in a seaside town; it may be that the air at a seaside town was more suitable for her than that of the countryside.

On examining her own mind, she knew that she had no desire to return to Mansfield Park, and would much prefer to remain at Great Yarmouth in the health-giving air.

'Mama! Mama!' the children burst in to the room, their rosy cheeks and bright eyes witness to the good health they had regained at the seaside. Their nurse followed them into the room, with their wraps, and Fanny assisted her to get them ready to go out.

'Are we to go to Mr Symonds' house?' asked Eddie eagerly. 'He has promised me a knife of my very own, and he is to mend Franny's doll.'

'Yes,' Fanny said, 'We will call upon Mrs Symonds, and you will wait to be invited above stairs to Mr Symonds' study, or I will tell Papa to take your knife away until you can do as you are bid.'

A letter was brought in by a maid, while the nursemaid was making the final adjustments to the children's wraps, and recognising Sir Thomas's hand, Fanny opened it to scan the contents. Sir Thomas was delighted to tell his dear Edmund and Fanny that he had concluded negotiations with Burgh Hall's owner to purchase it, in the hopes of persuading Lady Bertram to make a visit to the sea-side, and with thoughts of being able to offer family visits to Tom, and Agnes, as well as to Julia, and Mr Yates. Edmund and Fanny's letters had convinced him that living at the sea-side would be enough to cure any affliction, and raise the lowest of spirits. With no child, no niece, and no visitors to distract her, a proposed visit to the sea side might well raise even Lady Bertram's spirits. That was as much as Fanny had time to read before the nursemaid declared the children suitably well attired to go out into a strong onshore breeze, and so she put the letter quickly onto Edmund's desk for him to find upon his return.

Her own mind was in a whirl with this information. The house was more than big enough for her family to live there, and also host any of Edmund's family which wished to visit as well. And maybe Susan would visit with her new husband? And it was a port town; imagine if William's ship might put in there one day; it would be wonderful to see him again, and to introduce him to his nephew and niece. There were so many possibilities and Fanny felt that she would very much like to take some time to think about it all, but the children were tugging at her hands, and pulling her towards the front door, and she had to put the wonderful news to the back of her mind for now.

They set out for their daily walk along the sea front, heading towards the Symonds's large rambling house.

'Eddie!' said Fanny sternly as they waited to be admitted. 'Remember what I told you? You are not to run up the stairs to Mr Symonds's room. You are to wait until you are invited to go. It may be that he is busy and not able to see you today.'

'But he promised!' protested Eddie.

'Nonetheless,' Fanny said, refusing to melt at the sight of his face puckered in distress. 'You must do as you are bid.'

Eddie pouted, but did not defy this decree, and they were shown into Mrs Symonds's own sitting room. Edmund was already gone, Fanny was told, but Mr and Mrs Symonds were delighted to welcome them all, and Mr Symonds whisked the children away to his study immediately, with conspiratorial whispers of cake, and knives, and mended dolls.

'He has been waiting all morning for the dear children,' said Mrs Symonds ringing for tea to be brought and giving orders for a tray to be taken to her husband's study for himself and for the dear children. 'Now, you and I can have a comfortable coze, and I can tease you a little about the long talk Mr Symonds and your dear Mr Bertram had before you arrived. Can you make a guess what it was about?'

'I suppose that it was about the Parish,' said Fanny. 'I know that Edmund has been assisting Mr Symonds to relieve the poor, and to bring in a larger congregation on Sundays. There was also talk of a Sunday School for the children, I believe. But we shall not be here long enough to see it, I am afraid.'

'Ah, you have hit the nail on the head, my dear!' cried Mrs Symonds. 'There is more to it than that, I assure you, but it is of no use to wait for Mr Symonds to come back down to tell you, so I shall tell you myself.'

Fanny could not imagine what it might be, and was astonished that her own wishes had chimed so exactly with Mr and Mrs Symonds. For that good lady was proposing that Mr Symonds retire, and Edmund take his place as vicar of Great Yarmouth!

'My dear Mr Symonds prefers his study, with his books and his gadgets, to his work, you see,' said Mrs Symonds. 'And Lord! You should see the gadgets he comes up with to assist the maids and the cook with their daily tasks! I have money of my own, and we should want for nothing, but this living is in Mr Symonds's gift, and we do care about it. We would not want to hand it over to just anybody; it must be somebody we trust to carry on Mr Symonds' good work, and your dear husband is the very man!'

It seemed that Mr and Mrs Symonds had gone further than Fanny had ever thought in asking Edmund to take over the parish; in idle moments Fanny had wondered if the Parish might not be rich enough to support another vicar and family. But here was Mr and Mrs Symonds handing over to them entirely! Mrs Symonds assured her the living was enough for their family, and Edmund could keep his parishes at Mansfield and Thornton Lacey, and install a curate, but they would need to move permanently to Great Yarmouth themselves.

'I would not wish to give up this house,' Mrs Symonds concluded, 'and you would have to find a suitable house for your own family, but only conceive how happy we shall all be!'

It all felt like a dream to Fanny; a proper home of her own, in a place she had chosen, rather than had chosen for her, and where she was comfortable and happy! She could not tell kind Mrs Symonds that they already had a house in Great Yarmouth, for Edmund did not know about it yet. So, all that remained was for her to ascertain Edmund's views on Mr Symonds' proposal, and to tell him about the news in Sir Thomas's letter, and her own hopes for a permanent removal to Great Yarmouth.

CHAPTER FIFTY:

Fanny and Edmund spent many days discussing the offer that Mr Symonds had made them, and the news that Sir Thomas had purchased Burgh Hall, and wondering what his reaction might be to Edmund and Fanny not returning to Mansfield Park.

'Mr Castell is very popular with the parishioners, and with my mother and father,' said Edmund.

'And he is not a married man, so his needs are few; the parish can support him easily with Sir Thomas and Lady Bertram's generous hospitality,' put in Fanny.

'You and the children are so much healthier in the sea air.'

'Although we have not seen what a winter might bring, still I believe Great Yarmouth all together suits us more than Mansfield Park.'

'I have made my decision,' Edmund said, and Fanny waited with bated breath. She hoped, oh so much, that his decision would be the one she most ardently wished for; that they would stay at Great Yarmouth.

'You and the children will stay here for now,' said Edmund, taking her hand. 'I will speak with my father and Mr Castell, and hope to persuade them all that this is the best way forward for all of us. It may be that I must spend some of the year at Mansfield Park to assist Mr Castell, or it may be that I can devote myself entirely to the parish here at Great Yarmouth. I will write to you as soon as I have had the discussion with my father, and let you know what is to happen.'

'When will you leave for Mansfield Park?' asked Fanny.

'Within the week. I will call in at Everingham on my way, but will not stay more than a day or so.'

Fanny could not like the thought that Edmund would be at Everingham without her – he would be in company with Mary Crawford again! As far as Fanny had been able to ascertain, she had not married; would he feel the pull of her attraction again? Although Fanny did not wish to visit Everingham and encounter Mr Crawford again, she also did not wish Edmund to go there without her!

As Fanny could not voice her objections to either option to Edmund, she had instead to appear to be happy at his decision, and to assist him in making all the arrangements to leave instead. She almost changed her mind at the last minute, but on little Franny developing a cold, decided that she would stay and help nurse the child instead. The news of her father's death, and her own realisation of how neglectful her parents had been to her, had made Fanny determined not to let anything get in the way of her care for her own children. And, as Fanny rather severely reminded herself, Edmund was no longer an unattached man, looking for a bride; all would be well. Edmund would meet Mary as a former acquaintance, and there would be no rekindling of his former passion for her.

With this final thought, Fanny was as close to the truth of their meeting up again than she could have wished. Edmund was too tired on his arrival to do more than greet the Crawfords, thank them for allowing him to stay, assure them of his family's good health, and apologise for being unable to sit up to a family dinner.

'I intend to rise betimes to attend the early morning service at your local church,' he said as he made his bow and was shown to his room.

'Well, I suppose we ought to accompany Mr Edmund Bertram to church tomorrow?' Henry said, as they sat in the drawing room after their own excellent dinner.

'Certainly it would do us no harm,' said Mary. 'Even I give a thought now and then to my immortal soul, and it is always good for you to be seen now and then by your tenants.'

'Very well; we shall go with him, and be seen. However, I doubt you should attempt it, my dear,' said Henry to Maria. 'Even if we had horses to the carriage, the road across the park is deeply rutted after all the rain we have had. I have instructed Madison to set some men to repair it, but until then, I recommend you stay at home.'

The following morning, suitably and soberly attired, Henry and Mary accompanied Edmund to the local church. Mary claimed his arm to assist her as they walked, with the excuse that they were such old friends they need not stand upon ceremony, and besides she wanted to hear all about her dearest Fanny, or should she say Mrs Edmund Bertram?

It was all done in the most disarming way, and once Edmund would have been charmed by her manner, but he could see now that this lightness of address was merely her way, and did not denote any especial tenderness towards himself or his family.

'I am certain that Fanny would wish me to pass on to you her very best wishes,' he said. 'She and the children are at our new home in Great Yarmouth permanently now, and I shall be returning there once I have seen my father at Mansfield Park.'

'How wonderful to live at the sea-side!' cried Mary. 'We spent some weeks at Brighton, and it was divine. I declare that the sea air, and the bathing, set us all up forever.'

'It has indeed been most healthy for Fanny and the children.'

'The dear little children,' said Mary, in an uncomfortable echo of Maria's letter, for she too had no interest in them, and had not even learned their names. 'I am so happy to hear that they are in good health.'

'You are very welcome to pay us a visit,' said Edmund. 'Fanny would be very pleased to see you.'

There was no time for any more as they were by then arrived at the Church, and their attention must be on those gathered outside who were waiting to be greeted and introduced to Edmund.

As far as Edmund could ascertain, both Henry and Mary took full part in the service, sitting, standing, kneeling, and with appropriate seriousness, although the joking comments by their neighbours when they arrived had betrayed that they had not been regular communicants. The brief talk that he had managed with Mary on their walk to the church had confirmed to Edmund that he was able to view her with detachment and to realise that in giving her up, he had taken the right decision.

Mary's attention was less on the service than he realised; she was also reviewing their relationship, and discovering that she did not regret his loss at all. He had aged considerably since they had last met, and it was clear to her that his profession and his marriage were weighing heavily upon him. She could feel sorry for him; the choice he had made to leave her and marry Fanny had not answered, but there was no help for it now. If anything, seeing him again confirmed to her that she was better off as the spinster sister of the master of Everingham, than as the wife of the priest of Mansfield Park.

Edmund could not avoid a family dinner that evening, and he did not sit long with Henry afterwards. They had not much in common, apart from the time the Crawfords had spent at Mansfield, and there were too many awkward memories there for Edmund to want to prolong the conversation. Henry did not appear much altered by his marriage to Maria, but Edmund was pleased to hear him express his pleasure in his marriage, and in his newfound domestic contentment at Everingham.

When they joined the ladies, Henry petitioned his wife and sister for the indulgence of some music. Maria declared herself too tired to play, but said she would turn the pages for Mary, and the two women sat down at the instrument.

'Miss Crawford, do not you have your harp here?' Edmund asked, while the two women were looking through the papers to decide what to play first. 'I recall your playing of it with great pleasure, and I would very much enjoy hearing you play it again.'

'If it were not Sunday, I would suspect you of teasing me, Mr Bertram,' said Mary. 'I am certain that you will recall perfectly well how very difficult it was to have my harp conveyed to Mansfield; and thus you may conceive how much more difficult it is to have it conveyed to Norfolk!'

'I am very sorry to hear it,' said Edmund. 'It is a delightful instrument, and you played it so well.'

'I am gratified by your remembrance, but even Henry tells me that I may not have a horse and cart to bring it from my sister's house.'

'No you may not,' said Henry. 'Or not until later in the year, at any rate. Madison would not forgive me if I agreed to it any sooner. All the horses and carts are wanted to bring in the grass, apparently.'

'I have no wish to offend Madison, or the farmers, or to deny the importance of getting in the grass, and so I do not ask for a horse and cart for such a frivolous request,' said Mary. 'Instead, I ask my dear brother to convey it here for me as he did before in his barouche, but there again I am told of too many difficulties.'

'Ah yes,' said her brother, 'It remains a matter of horses. They are all wanted on the farm, according to Madison, and there is not a single one to hire until the harvesting is completed.'

'Not even your own horse, Henry?' asked Maria.

'The groom informs me that my horse has an injury to a hoof, which means it must rest at my expense, while I have no use of it.'

'And I am outwitted by all these horses, it seems,' said Mary. 'They have all the power hereabouts, and you must make do with my indifferent performance upon the pianoforte, I regret, Mr Bertram.'

Edmund wondered if he was meant to offer his horse to pull Henry's barouche, but decided not to hear the hint, and instead settled back to hear Miss Crawford play on the pianoforte just as well as she had once played upon the harp.

He only stayed a few more days at Everingham, in order to observe enough to reassure his parents that Maria was in good health and spirits, and happy in her new situation. A letter from Sir Thomas reached him there, forwarded by Fanny, in which he said that Tom had returned to Mansfield Park, and wished to see him. Edmund had the uneasy feeling that there was something his father was not telling him in the letter, so as not to alarm Fanny if she should read it, and determined to set out for Mansfield Park as soon as possible.

Edmund's departure from Everingham came as a relief to almost everybody; Henry was the only member of the family who did not mind if he were there or gone, although it was always pleasant to have another man to talk to after dinner. Maria was glad not to have a visitor to entertain any longer as she was becoming more tired with each day that passed, and Mary was pleased to see him go, now that she was completely indifferent to him. He had nothing to offer her that she would want, and so his presence reminded her uncomfortably of a time in her life that she would much rather forget.

Thus it was with a sense of release, that Edmund waved goodbye to the Crawfords, and left Everingham for Mansfield Park.

CHAPTER FIFTY-ONE

Tom was indeed back at Mansfield Park, and wishing to see his brother. Six months after his wedding, he returned without his wife, but with a nurse, a baby, and his man. The nurse and baby disappeared into the servants' quarters, and Tom's man commandeered several servants to help take his master's luggage up to his rooms.

Tom's arrival at Mansfield Park, although unlooked for, was not too much of a surprise; everybody supposed he had ridden home to bring the good news of his son and heir, although they were a little surprised that he had brought so new a baby with him. Maybe Agnes was too unwell to travel immediately and would join her husband and son in due course. In these suppositions they were to be very disappointed; the child currently being made the focus of attention in the offices was not Tom's son, and Agnes was not following on behind at a more leisurely pace. Tom looked almost as ill as he had done when carried home by Edmund in his fever after the fall from a horse; but he poked his head around her sitting room door to ascertain that his mother was asleep on her sopha surrounded by her dogs, and then went straight to his father's study.

There his father, shocked at the sight of him, sent the servant for brandy, and begged Tom to sit down. Tom could not sit down for a moment; he was off and out of his chair and pacing the study.

'It is good of you to come all this way to bring us news, Tom, is it of your son?' asked his father, unable to account for his own son's appearance and manners in any other way. 'Is he even now with his nurse? This follows on rather soon after your wedding, but such matters are not unknown, to be sure. Is Agnes not well enough to travel with you? I hope you are not come to tell us that she has not survived?'

'I am not come home with news about a son, sir,' replied Tom, drinking down the offered brandy in one gulp. 'And as far as I know, Miss Fairhaven is in good health. I beg you to never mention her nor her - her child to me again. Miss Fairhaven and her mother have acted very dishonestly, sir, and I will not acknowledge her as my wife, and nor will I ever acknowledge her child. It is not mine, sir! The child at present with the servants is an orphan that I rescued from a Poor House.'

Sir Thomas was very shocked, and asked if Tom was certain that Agnes's child was not his; to which enquiry Tom gave him a description of the child which made it very clear to Sir Thomas that the child was not, and could never be a Bertram.

'Miss Fairhaven has broken her wedding vows, and attempted to make a fool of me, sir,' said he to his father, with unexpected dignity. 'You would not ask me to expose myself to further insult, of that I am assured. If there is to be an heir to Mansfield Park after me, you must bring young Eddie up in the expectation of the title, or look to my sisters for sons.'

'You may want to marry again,' said Sir Thomas, but his son was firm;

'That will never be possible, sir. To divorce Miss Fairhaven would expose this family and her brother to the worst kind of scandal, and I will not permit it. I will not marry again, and Miss Fairhaven and her mother are never to be admitted to Mansfield Park while I am alive.'

Sir Thomas forbore to inquire further, but told Tom that he was glad to see him, and that Mansfield Park was his home now, and the two of them would join together to prevent Miss Fairhaven's child from inheriting, as it appeared to be beyond doubt that the child was her's alone.

It was not until Edmund arrived from Great Yarmouth by way of Everingham, and Tom was alone with his brother that the whole story could be told;

There had been, he confided, the very d_l of a fuss and pother over the impending arrival, with women coming and going, up and down the stairs at all times of day and night, and nurses engaged, and prodigious quantities of linen arriving daily it seemed to Tom. However, when he suggested that Dr Dudley be brought in, Agnes and her mother gave a very definite negative; there was a woman amongst their former Antiguan slaves who was an expert midwife, and she would be all that was required. He had tried to insist, wanting only the best for Agnes, and Dr Dudley was the best in London it was said, for he had recently brought several Duchesses and Ladies to bed successfully, but Agnes became upset, and Mrs Fairhaven said she was not to be troubled, and so he gave it up and left it to them.

On the night itself, Tom had been confined to Mr Fairhaven's study which he had had opened up again for his own use once they had returned from Brighton. A manservant kept the fire up for him, and he had his drinks and books to hand, but he could not settle with all the activity above stairs. He had paced about trying to make sense of the sounds he could hear from above stairs, and the running of feet up and down the staircase.

'Then, Edmund, I heard the sound of a baby cry, and I went to the door and looked out. I could see nothing from there, but I heard suddenly a second baby cry. The two sounds were quite distinct, it was not the same child crying twice. I could only suppose that there was twins, and I rushed upstairs without waiting to be summoned as I had been told.'

He paused, and Edmund looked at him with sympathy. It was clear that what Tom was bracing himself to say was very shocking indeed.

'When I reached the landing,' Tom went on, visibly upset. 'There was a lady, a stranger to me, standing there with a baby in her arms. At the sight of me, she attempted to cover the child with her shawl and back away into a nearby room. I asked her if this was my son and she did not seem to know how to answer. I could not insist she answer me, and so I left her standing there, and went in to Miss Fairhaven's bedchamber. She was in her bed, with several of her Antiguan women, and her mother about her; and, Edmund, she was also holding a baby, which she also attempted to conceal from my sight amongst the bed clothing!'

'So it was twins?' asked Edmund.

'No,' said Tom, 'Wait and you will hear all, I will not hide anything from you, best of brothers. Miss Fairhaven screamed when she saw me, and her mother came rushing at me attempting to push me back out of the room, telling me to go back to the study, that I would be summoned as soon as it was appropriate for me to see her daughter and the baby, but I would not go. I demanded to know what was happening; were there two babies? Why was one out on the landing? And who was the woman holding him?'

Tom paused, and then went on;

'The women all looked at one another and nobody answered me, so I walked over to the bed and looked down at the baby Miss Fairhaven was holding. She stopped attempting to hide it, and just looked up at me with defiance. It was a boy, but Edmund, it was as black as the slaves on my father's plantation.'

'How could that be?' asked Edmund in horror. 'What did you do next?'

'I left the room asking Mrs Fairhaven to accompany me downstairs to the study; I intended to ask her for an explanation. Then I remembered the other woman and the second baby, and so I sought her out. When she saw us, she asked Mrs Fairhaven if this baby was no longer required, as she could not wait about all morning. I asked her to join us downstairs as well and to bring the baby.'

Once they were all assembled downstairs in Mr Fairhaven's study, Tom had turned first to his mother-in-law.

'Well, madam?' he said.

Mrs Fairhaven was quite incoherent at first, but then it became clear to Tom that she was frightened, rather than upset.

'Well, my dear Tom,' said she, 'It is really very simple. Poor dear Agnes was startled by Joseph, the black footman, at a delicate stage, and that turned the baby quite black. I am certain that the colour will wear off soon, it is only temporary I assure you, and nothing to worry about. Babies are born with blue eyes, you know, and then they change colour if they are to be brown.'

Edmund was quite astonished by this. 'And is this likely?' asked he, 'Have there been any cases known of a child changing its skin colour in this way before or after birth?'

'No indeed,' said Tom. 'This child is clearly not mine, and moreover was born only six months in to our marriage.'

'And you had not anticipated your union?'

'No.'

'What did you say to Mrs Fairhaven?'

'I told her that I was not a fool, that the child was not mine and that I would not acknowledge it or provide for it in any way. I told her to return to her daughter, and she left the room shaking her head and continuing to protest her daughter's innocence.'

'And what of the other woman and the other baby?' asked Edmund, 'Who were they and where had they come from?'

'The second woman had been standing all this while quietly with the baby in her arms. I was certain I had never before seen her in my house, or in company with Mrs Fairhaven, nor Miss Fairhaven. So I began by asking her who she was and why she had brought a baby into my house.'

'I am Mrs Riley,' she said. 'My husband is a surgeon, and works when he can for free at the Cleveland Street Poor House. We have not been blessed with children of our own, and I believe I have been sent by God to save as many of the babies born there as I can. I endeavour to keep them alive, and to find them employment, or a family to take them in. Mrs Fairhaven asked me to procure a baby for her from the Poor House; there are babies being born there all the time, so there was a good chance of procuring one when needed. This one was born yesterday, and the mother died bringing him into the world. A summons came for me earlier today and so I collected this baby from the Poor House, and brought him here.'

'But what could be meant by this scheme?' Tom asked her.

'Mrs Fairhaven told me that she intended to substitute the Poor House baby for her daughter's baby, and that I would take her daughter's baby back to the Poor House with me. I would be given money to pay for the child's upbringing, and given a donation for our work with the poor.'

'Why did not you take the baby away before I saw you?'

'Mrs Fairhaven came out to tell me that once her daughter saw her own child, she could not give it up, and so I was waiting to hear what would be decided, when you came up the stairs and saw me.'

When Tom did not speak, Mrs Riley went on;

'I beg you will not judge me harshly, sir. Many people contract diseases and die within the walls of the Poor House, and are buried in unmarked mass pauper graves. Nearly every baby born in the Poor House will die, sometimes only one in ten babies survives, and then they often die within the first five years from want of care. I merely sought a better life for one small soul, and money to help care for the wretches in our charge. Whichever baby I take back to the Poor House, without a mother to care for him, he will most likely be dead before the week is out.'

Tom gestured to her to bring the baby over to him, and he looked down at it. The baby opened its eyes and stared back up at him from within the woman's arms. He thought that it smiled at him. And he made a decision.

'So you decided to leave the house and come home?' asked Edmund.

'Yes,' said his brother, 'I summoned my man, and the nurse who had been hired to feed the baby, and told the nurse this child would now be hers to care for, and told my man to pack essential things and summon horses for us, and a carriage for the nurse and the baby; we would all leave for Mansfield Park as soon as possible.'

'And what of Mrs Riley?'

'I told her to keep Mrs Fairhaven's money, made her another donation towards her work at the Poor House, and enough as well to give the baby's mother a proper Christian funeral.'

'That was very well done of you, Tom,' said Edmund.

'Mr Riley, the surgeon, had given his wife a piece of paper with the baby's birth date, and the mother's name at the time of her death, and she gave me that with a simple silver cross on a chain, which was all that the mother had with her when she entered the Poor House.'

Mrs Riley accepted the draft, dropt Tom a curtsey, and left the house. After she departed, Tom was left with a baby, a piece of paper, a silver cross, and the realisation that his life had been shattered and would never be the same again.

CHAPTER FIFTY-TWO

There was a moment of silence as both men reflected on the tragedy which had befallen their family.

'There is not much more to tell,' Tom said. 'It will soon be done and can be forgot.'

'There is no need to continue, if you do not wish to,' Edmund said, but Tom went on;

'Of course it took longer than I had hoped for Jenkins to organise our departure, and in that time Mrs Fairhaven returned to the study with a message from her daughter, begging me to stay, and seconding her mother's assertion that she had been startled by a servant which accounted for the baby's skin, and that it would change in time back to white. But I would not answer her and left the room to see where Jenkins had got to. When we finally left Wimpole Street, I put my wedding ring on the hall table, and left no message for Mrs Fairhaven nor for her daughter. There was nothing more I wanted to say to either of them.'

'It is shocking and grievous indeed,' said Edmund, 'That the vows she made in my church before all of us meant so little to her.'

'Miss Fairhaven, for I cannot call her Mrs Bertram, told me when we were in Brighton that we would have a son to inherit Mansfield Park, and everybody would be happy. But I will never acknowledge her child nor allow him to inherit Mansfield Park, nor will I ever live with Miss Fairhaven again as my wife.'

'What do you intend to do with the baby you rescued from the Poor House?' asked Edmund.

'I intend him to be given an education, and I will find him a position on the estate, I know not in what capacity as yet. Had he stayed in London, he would have died, Edmund. I could not have left him there. None of this is in any way his fault.'

'No, he is an innocent,' agreed Edmund, 'and his life at Mansfield Park will be a thousand times better than in the rookeries of London. You did well there, Tom. Out of all this terrible story, has come one piece of good.'

'I have done right, have not I?' asked Tom, 'I could not stay with Miss Fairhaven and her mother, when they were using me as their dupe.'

'You have indeed done the right thing,' said Edmund. 'How much of this does my father know?'

'Only that the child Miss Fairhaven bore cannot be my son, and that I will not see her again, nor permit her to come to Mansfield Park.'

Tom hesitated;

'I have told you everything Edmund, as my brother, but also as my priest. I beg that you will not tell anybody all the details; not even Fanny.'

'I understand. But what are we to tell our friends and neighbours? And what of my mother?' asked Edmund. 'She will not understand why Agnes and the baby are never to come here.'

'We will have to think of some explanation which is not the whole truth, but which everybody can accept,' said Tom, 'But at the moment I cannot think what it could be.'

They were both silent for a moment, united in their grief and shock over the terrible events at Wimpole Street. It seemed that street was unlucky indeed for the Bertram family; but something must be said which would satisfy enquiries and prevent any further questioning or concern. Mansfield Park was far enough distant from London for rumour and scandal not to reach all but those who were able to travel thither and they could only hope that the matter would not come to the attention of the local newspapers.

After much discussion, it was decided to say that Tom and Agnes had separated, and that they would not be living together again. There was no child of their union to bring them back together either; and those who heard the story may have supposed that the child had died, and the parents had been driven apart by grief. Of course, this still left an open field for the gossips, but the family at Mansfield Park now lived very quietly, without much entertaining, and the gossips soon had other richer sources to draw upon.

Despite her sons' concern, Lady Bertram was not at all put out by Agnes's staying in London, and Tom coming home to live permanently at Mansfield Park. She had not much liked Agnes, who was never interested in assisting Lady Bertram with her fringing, and moreover had refused the offer of one of Pug's puppies. Also, Lady Bertram had become increasingly accustomed to being told that one member of her family or another could not come home, and Agnes was just the latest; and it did not signify at all. As she was wont to point out, Sir Thomas had told her Maria could not come home, and then Maria did come home, and with a different husband too. And Sir Thomas had said her sister Norris could not come home as she was too ill, and then she did come home, although she was indeed shockingly ill, and had later died, but the main point was that she had come home. Now that Sir Thomas was saying that Agnes could not come to Mansfield Park again, Lady Bertram remained placidly certain that Agnes would come one day, just as dear Maria and sister Norris had done.

However, in this last case, Lady Bertram was wrong. Agnes never came to Mansfield Park again. She made several attempts to reunite with Tom; she wrote to him, but he sent the letters back unopened. She sent her mother to plead with him, but Tom refused to allow her access to the house, and she had to turn back and find an inn to stay at.

From her house in Wimpole Street, Agnes paid to have a poor house orphan buried under the name of 'Thomas Fairhaven Bertram' in the nearby graveyard. The child she had borne she brought up, not as her son; but as a foundling from her plantation workers whom she had charitably taken in. No-one except her mother, and Tom, knew that the boy was her son. The newspapers noted that Tom and Agnes were living apart, but did not know why, although there was plenty of speculation, some of it surprisingly close to the mark. Agnes appeared in public with her mother, attended by the boy in livery, and if asked about her short-lived marriage, would cast her eyes down, and delicately hint that Tom's appetites were not such that a wife should have to endure. If Tom knew about this slur upon his character, he never mentioned it, and said nothing to countermand any rumours that did reach him about his marriage, or about Agnes. He was settled permanently now at Mansfield Park, overseeing the upbringing and education of young Cleveland, and assisting his own father with the Mansfield estate, and the Antigua plantation.

CHAPTER FIFTY-THREE

All her family, friends, and relations were delighted to learn that Maria was safe and well after the arrival of her son, which was born around the same time as Agnes's; but his paternity at least was not in any doubt. There was also no more than the usual pother about his arrival into the world, and even the Admiral sent a letter to congratulate Henry and Maria, and to reiterate his advice to Henry to set up a mistress, which Henry had so far unaccountably failed to do.

Henry and Maria were now settled in Everingham, with their son, and two more sons were to join him in due course, with the family finished off by a daughter. With so many duties at Everingham to attend to, Maria and Henry gave up their house in London, and were both surprised by how little they missed the many excitements and diversions it had once offered.

It seemed that Mary alone was not settled. The arrival of Henry and Maria's son brought home to her, as nothing before had done, that she was now superfluous. Mrs Grant was to sell her house and leave London for ever to come and help with Henry and Maria's children, and there was now no home for Mary there. Just as she was beginning to think that she would start to encourage a very elderly local squire who had been creakingly gallant towards her, Viscount Carmichael from Brighton arrived at Everingham to make Mary an offer of marriage, having finally tracked her down.

He had secured permission from the Prince to desert his post at Brighton, and had made enquiries for the Crawfords in London, until he had found a man in a coffee shop who knew that the family had a seat at Everingham in Norfolk.

The family was all at home when he arrived, quite unlooked for, and to their very great surprise, Frou-frou was the first to react to his appearance in their home, by rushing forward with a great show of affection, followed by Henry to welcome him most heartily to Everingham. An invitation to stay was swiftly offered by Maria, and after making all enquiries as to their health, and admiring their son,

Carmichael was able to sit down by Mary while refreshments were being brought in.

'I see that country living suits the little dog, and that its dip in the sea at Brighton did it no lasting harm,' said Carmichael, as Frou-frou continued frisking about his feet.

'It seems that Frou-frou has quite forgiven your trespass against it in the sea,' said Mary, amused by the little dog's antics.

'But what seems to have most softened its attitude towards the whole world has been its fervent adoption of Maria's puppy,' said Henry, indicating the tiny creature curled up in a basket in a corner of the room.

'It is an ill-favoured little dog,' said Maria indifferently. 'But my mother was most insistent that I take it with me.'

'It has no use in hunting, or guarding the house, that is true,' said Henry. 'But at least it has stopped Frou-frou from biting everybody.'

'We must all be grateful for small mercies,' said Carmichael gravely.

'I do not know how long you are able to make your stay with us,' said Henry, 'But you are most welcome for as long as you can be spared from your other duties. It is a fine country hereabouts, although not as picturesque as some parts of England. Mary has been taking her daily walks about the estate and can show you the best paths to make a start on your explorations, and I have some shooting parties arranged you may wish to join in with.'

'I recommend Mary and Lord Carmichael to start with the gravel path through the shrubbery,' put in Maria. 'It is always dry underfoot no matter how wet the weather has been, and is a favourite of mine.'

Carmichael bowed and said all that was proper about having much admired the fine country he had ridden through on his way to Everingham, although in truth he had not noticed it at all, such had been his anxiety that Mary would have formed an attachment to somebody else before he could arrive!

However, the demands of society meant that it was not until several days later that Mary managed to leave the house unaccompanied, and walk about nearby until she encountered him quite by chance on his way back from the stables after his early morning ride.

'Miss Crawford, good morning! I am very happy to see you. Are you at leisure to show me Mrs Crawford's fine gravel walk through the shrubbery before breakfast?'

Mary was delighted to do so, and as they walked thither, it did not take him long to unfold his wish to enter into an understanding with her, and for her to accept. Mary had never been one to pretend to any coyness or to demand a lengthy courtship, and it was with great relief that Viscount Carmichael heard her acceptance of his offer.

In the first offering to pre-conjugal unreserve, he wanted to put the record straight about his first wife. Despite what Mary had been told in Brighton, theirs had been a marriage of convenience, not affection, and they had rarely lived together as he had spent most of their married life on active service and she had refused to accompany him, even when he was quartered in England.

'From the moment we married,' he said, 'Clarissa was always ill; and at first I had sympathy for her sufferings, and I did everything in my power to alleviate her symptoms, and bring her relief, but nothing answered. We travelled to consult all the best physicians in London; we spent months at Bath, and I would have taken her anywhere in the world if it would have cured her, war or no, but nothing I attempted seemed able to cure her.'

Mary did not speak, but pressed his arm in sympathy. While never having suffered with ill-health herself, she did know that for some people, their delicate state of health became a life-time's preoccupation.

'Eventually,' went on Carmichael, 'I was forced to concede that it was marriage to me that was at the root of Clarissa's illness, and that as long as I remained at home, she would never recover. So, I left my home and joined the Prince's Hussars, hoping that action would distract me from the disappointment of my marriage, and give Clarissa a chance to recover her health.'

'And did that answer?' asked Mary.

'No, I regret it did not. On the very few visits home I was able to make, Clarissa, having been quite well, had such a severe relapse as drove me back out of the house again.'

'So were you surprised when she did finally succumb to her illness? Was it not all imagination after all?'

'I was surprised, and I do not know whether her imagination made her illnesses a reality in the end, or not. The physicians were as surprised as I, having been confident that all their physick had brought about a complete cure. Still, that is all in the past now. I have quite worn out my desire to ride about in a smart coat and kill the King's enemies; all my hopes and wishes centre now in domestic comfort and the quiet of a private life, with you by my side.'

'And how will the ten children at your seat in Scotland feel about a stepmother?'

'What ten children are these?' asked Carmichael in astonishment.

'The gossips of Brighton gave us to understand that there were a prodigious quantity of motherless children left behind at your home. They did not know exactly how many children, and I plucked the number of ten out of the air; but they were certain of their existence.'

'There are no children, I assure you,' said Carmichael. 'Clarissa's health and her abhorrence of me did not allow it.'

'When does your period of mourning come to an end?'

'Not for another eight months,' Carmichael hesitated; 'It is a long time. I should not have asked you to bind yourself to me.'

'I do not require anybody's permission to do just as I please, and I am bound to you by my own wish.'

Once they had settled their future together to their mutual satisfaction, their talk turned to other matters;

'Now that we are engaged, will you be writing odes to my eyebrows?' asked Mary, archly.

'Certainly if you wish it,' replied he. 'I can see plenty of praise in all of your person, but why do your eyebrows merit a particular interest?'

Mary laughed, and told him about poor Sir Cedric Cholmondley's forlorn passion, and artistic inability with a pen.

'If I am ever in company with him, I shall be forced to call him out,' said Carmichael, looking as cross as was possible, given how happy he was.

'There is no need on my account, I assure you,' said Mary. 'It was entirely a one-sided infatuation.'

'On consideration,' said Carmichael, 'he has instead my sympathy, and I will not call him out for having been audacious enough to fall in love with you.'

'Why would Cholmondley have your sympathy?'

'Because I have met the new Lady Cedric, when she was still Miss Payne. And because you did not return his affection.'

'In truth, I could not,' said Mary. 'Not just for his person, but because of the poetry.'

'In that case, I will never write you any poetry,' said Carmichael. 'For I would not wish to excite your scorn, or lose your regard.'

Mary gave him to understand that even if he did write poems to her eyebrows, neither of those melancholy states would ever come to pass, and when they were able to look around themselves again, they found they had walked so far that they were quite beyond any local knowledge either of them had, and were obliged to flag down a carter for a lift back in the direction of Everingham.

The Crawfords were delighted but not surprised on their unceremonious return to learn of their engagement, and within a few days, Mary left her brother's house forever, to travel with her fiancé to his home in Scotland. There we leave her; on her way to becoming a Viscountess, and happy at last.

CHAPTER FIFTY-FOUR

Despite not wishing to further upset his father after Tom's distressing news on his return to Mansfield Park, Edmund did have to tell Sir Thomas that he and Fanny and the children wished to live at Great Yarmouth, and did not wish to return to Mansfield Park.

Sir Thomas was quiet for a moment after Edmund finished setting out his proposal, then he said;

'Mr Castell, Ballantyne's recommendation for the new curate is already established with the community in Thornton Lacey, and has been working hard in Mansfield as well. We could not do better in your absence.'

Edmund knew that Mr Castell was an older man than himself, very sensible and serious, and had already partaken enthusiastically and frequently of Sir Thomas's hospitality. However, he confined himself to replying;

'I am relieved to hear that he has your endorsement, and that you believe the two parishes will be in good hands with him.'

'He has also provided company for Lady Bertram,' said Sir Thomas. 'When his duties permit, he has been assiduous in his attentions, and she enjoys listening to him reading in the evenings.'

'I regret that our removal will deprive my mother of our company,' said Edmund. 'But my family is so much stouter and healthier for living by the sea, and I believe I can do a lot of good for the poor in Great Yarmouth.' He hesitated; 'While it seems presumptuous of me to invite you to visit your own house, I do extend a sincere invitation to you and to my mother to come and stay as often and as long as you wish. The house has more than enough room for all of us, although it is not to be compared with Mansfield Park.'

Sir Thomas bowed in acknowledgement, and said, 'Your mother has not visited the seaside for many years, and I am persuaded it would be beneficial for her health based on your reports of Fanny and the children. I shall certainly be persuading her to take up your offer of a stay.'

'I am very happy to hear it,' said Edmund, relieved that his father approved of his plans, and that he would be able to carry the good news to Fanny, that she need not leave the home at Great Yarmouth that she had become so attached to.

'I have asked Tom to join us,' Sir Thomas said. 'The future of this family will become his concern in due course.'

Tom did not keep them waiting, coming in to the summons from his father, and Sir Thomas turned to his two sons.

'We will not dwell upon Tom's situation, but it is unlikely now that he will have an heir to inherit Mansfield Park in due course. Therefore, I propose to ensure the succession falls to young Eddie, and I hope that once he has completed his education, he will return to live at Mansfield Park to learn how to manage the estate.'

'Cleveland will also be trained as a land agent to assist him,' put in Tom, and the three of them shook hands on the agreement.

When Edmund returned home, Fanny raised gentle objections to losing her son in this way, but there was no helping it; Mansfield Park needed an heir to follow Tom, and young Eddie was the only one who could step into the role.

And there we will leave the Bertrams, the Yates, the Carmichaels, the Crawfords, and the Price families to their various domestic concerns with no notion of what the following year will bring.

As we know, the wicked do not always suffer in this life in a way that would satisfy the observer. It may seem that virtue does not receive its due reward, and that vice is often winked at, or ignored. To finish Agnes Fairhaven's story; over the next ten years, she appeared with two more children, another boy and a girl, whom everybody was given to understand had come over from Antigua from her plantation, for a new life in England. Her brother's untimely death left Agnes a very wealthy woman indeed, but the Fairhaven and Bertram plantations were never merged. On Lady Bertram's death, Agnes took the title for herself, and there didn't seem to be any way to stop her, but she alone never did return to Mansfield Park.

THE END

Epilogue

I have followed the lives of the families introduced by Miss Jane Austen in 'Mansfield Park'; and introduced some of the people they met following the point at which Miss Austen left them. They cannot know that the year to come will become known as 'The Year Without a Summer'. How such a global event will affect them all, I cannot tell, although Miss Austen herself only survived through the first part of that year: it was her last.

Some websites and reference books I consulted for information about different aspects of Regency England:

https://www.fpa.org.uk/factsheets/contraception-past-present-future

https://18centurybodies.wordpress.com/2013/06/05/british-contraception-in-the-eighteenth-century/

https://janeaustensworld.wordpress.com/tag/regency-contraceptives/

https://en.wikipedia.org/wiki/Slave_Trade_Act_1807

https://janeausten.co.uk/blogs/the-austen-family/jane-austens-brothers

http://www.johnhearfield.com/History/Woodforde.htm

https://www.english-heritage.org.uk/visit/places/portchester-castle/history-and-stories/black-people-in-late-18th-century-britain/

https://www.historytoday.com/archive/history-black-people-britain

https://phorism.com/source/Jane%20Austen/1;jsessionid=AA83AF3F706EB833A6C24A41BE33A313

http://www.jasna.org/persuasions/printed/number24/fullerton.pdf

https://shura.shu.ac.uk/26464/3/Dredge_WasThereServant%28AM%29.pdf

Beach Days –in Regency England » Risky Regencies

Brighton History: The Chalybeate - St Ann's Well Gardens (7directory.co.uk)

Brighton in the Regency era | Bella Breen

https://en.wikipedia.org/wiki/Hallett,_South_Australia

Austen, Jane. The Novels of Jane Austen. Ed. R. W. Chapman. 3rd ed. Oxford: OUP, 1986.

Jane Austen's Letters. Ed. Deirdre Le Faye. 3rd ed. Oxford: OUP, 1995.

Boswell, James. Life of Johnson. London: Everyman, 1960.

Butler, Marilyn. Jane Austen and the War of Ideas. Oxford: Clarendon Press, 1975.

Cawthorne, Nigel. The Sex Lives of the Kings and Queens of England. UK: Prion Press, 1994.

Grosskurth, Phyllis. Byron: The Flawed Angel. UK: Sceptre, 1997. Honan, Park.

Jane Austen. New York: Fawcett Columbine, 1987.

Murray, Venetia. High Society: A Social History of the Regency Period 1788–1830. UK: Viking, 1998.

Stephens, Meic. Collins Dictionary of Literary Quotations. UK: Harper Collins, 1936.

Stone, Lawrence. The Family, Sex and Marriage in England 1500–1800. UK: Penguin, 1977.

Tucker, George Herbert. Jane Austen and the Woman. London: Robert Hale, 1994.

Vickery, Amanda. Behind Closed Doors: At Home in Georgian England. Yale University Press, 2010

Vickery, Amanda. The Gentleman's daughter: Women's Lives in Georgian England. Yale University Press, 1998

West, Jane. A Tale of the Times. London, 1799.

A Word About Sex

Despite all my best efforts to write in the spirit of Jane Austen, although I can never emulate her style; sex will intrude into 'Return to Mansfield Park'. I just can't prevent it under-pinning all of the action, but I can keep it under the covers, although it will be marginally more overt than in my previous two Austen Fan Fictions*. And I'm not being overly anachronistic here; sexual tension runs high in all of Austen's novels, despite criticism to the contrary. As an Eighteenth-Century Spinster, Austen was conventionally considered not to know anything about sex. Certainly, there are no descriptions of sex acts, and Austen shuts the bedroom doors gently but firmly on her couples at the start of their wedded bliss; but it's definitely there, permeating each novel, and motivating many of her characters, particularly the unmarried ones. Austen herself knew perfectly well what was going on behind closed doors; five of her brothers married, and produced between them over 30 children, killing all of their first wives in the process. In a famous quote from a letter, Austen points out that if married couples slept in separate bedrooms, there would be far fewer children - https://libquotes.com/jane-austen/quote/lbj8x1w

This knowledge is clearly demonstrated in Austen's creation of the rather wonderful Mrs Jennings in 'Sense & Sensibility'. She voices what Austen knew would happen if Lucy Steele were to marry Edward Ferrars on the small living offered him by Colonel Brandon; 'Then they will have a child every year! and Lord help 'em! how poor they will be!' (Vol 3, Ch 2)

Which brings me on to contraception. By modern standards, contraception was fairly crude in Regency England; but it was available. Condoms, some made of pig intestines, were on sale in larger cities, but men only used them with prostitutes to avoid venereal diseases. Had they used the contraception available to them in their own marriages, many hundreds of thousands of women would have been spared the lifetimes of constant pregnancies, and the dangers of repeated child-birth, which killed so many of them. From a liberated twenty-first century woman's point of view, it is astonishing that men did not use the condoms which were available, or encourage their wives to use any form of contraception which may have been available for women (apparently vinegar soaked sponges could be used as a form of Dutch Cap); if only for their own convenience. A wife who is constantly 'lying-in' after yet another exhausting and dangerous birth, is not going to want to have sex for some time; whereas a wife who is kept from becoming pregnant by the use of contraceptives, is going to be much more available to her husband.

Instead, men in Regency England denied their wives this security and condemned them to repeated pregnancies, each of which carried the risk of death either during birth, or post-partum, when infections were rife. One sure-fire way of avoiding pregnancy is celibacy, or abstinence; which doesn't seem to have occurred to Regency husbands either – but does make me wonder if the women in Austen's novels who have no children are infertile; or if their husbands are infertile, or they simply weren't having sex.

One thing which annoys me immensely in some Regency fan-fiction is the blithe disregard the authors have for contraception and pregnancy. Their characters fall into bed with each other without any thought; the authors seem to assume that contraception was widely practiced and easily available in Regency England. Or that by some miracle, their female characters won't get pregnant despite frequent, exhausting, and explicit sex-scenes. Until surprisingly recently, sex for women was fraught with danger – pregnancy could lead to death in child-birth, particularly as there was still a lot of ignorance and superstition around the process, and there were no anti-biotics, or reliable cures for post-partum infections. So, when a doctor tells a couple in a costume drama that there must be no more babies – what he really means is no more sex. For the woman at least. Men were much freer to go off and have sex with prostitutes, or other women (providing that no pregnancy ensued!), but would no longer be able to have sex with their wife.

It was not until women had access to reliable contraception that they were freed from the fear of constant pregnancy and child-birth; and the 1960's were considered a time of sexual liberation in England because of the advent of the contraceptive pill. This was ostensibly the liberation of women from unwanted pregnancy, but is actually the liberation of men into what I once read Germaine Greer describe as 'open season on the vagina'. Now that women had the Pill, all responsibility for avoiding pregnancy was cheerfully dumped on them by men, who ditched the clumsy condom, causing STIs to rise and continue to be spread around.

The women in Austen's novels who do not have children are possibly the lucky ones. Child-free couples in Austen's novels include, the Norrises and the Grants (in 'Mansfield Park'; both men are Vicars, which is interesting), the Phillips (Pride and Prejudice), Mrs Smith (Sense & Sensibility, and a second Mrs Smith in Persuasion), the Allens and the Squire (Northanger Abbey), Admiral and Mrs Croft in 'Persuasion', etc. The only time any regret over their child-free state is mentioned is Mrs Allen who is not able to compete with Mrs Thorpe in recounting the triumphs of her children, and has to be content with assuring herself that her own gowns are finer than those of her friend. Other women in the novels survived repeated child-birth; Mrs Morland had ten children, as did Mrs Price, Mrs Bennet had five, Mrs Thorpe at least six; even Lady Bertram exerted herself enough to give birth to four children. The mothers in Austen's novels who have fewer children have either been very lucky in not getting pregnant again, or they are not having sex with their husbands; in the case of the younger Mrs Dashwood (S&S), I would suspect the latter.

Regency England was a lot more rambunctious and a lot less outwardly repressed than Victorian England, and evidence for this is perhaps in the fact that the Government in 1773 had to pass an Act of Parliament to cope with the sheer quantity of babies being born out of wedlock. The rather wonderfully named 'Bastardy Act of 1773' meant that any unmarried woman who became pregnant could name the father, and he would be given the choice to marry her, support her and the child financially but not marry her, or go to prison. In some cases shot-gun weddings were performed; one such is recounted in his famous diary by the Vicar of Weston Longville, who was almost exactly contemporaneous with Austen. He did not like marrying two people who were in this situation, but as the local priest, he had no choice.

This is possibly what happened to Harriet Smith's 'decent' father (Emma); an indiscretion with a woman he couldn't marry resulted in Harriet, and he stepped up and paid for her education and upbringing.

For women in the genteel classes, sex before marriage was to be avoided – Lydia Bennet (P&P) is a good example of the panic that occurs if a woman did have sex before marriage. Georgiana Darcy's near elopement with Wickham is also nerve-shredding – if she had eloped, she would have been 'ruined' and either had to marry Wickham, or suffer a similar fate to Maria Bertram, and not be admitted back into polite society.

Despite that, there is pre- and extra-marital sex, in Austen's novels; Lydia lives with Wickham with no intention of marrying, but there is no suggestion that she is pregnant when they are forced to the altar by Darcy. Colonel Brandon's cousin leaves her husband, and Brandon knows she has passed from her 'first seducer' to 'sink deeper in a life of sin'. Finally, he finds her dying of consumption in a 'spunging-house' (debtor's prison), with a child from her first liaison. When this child grows up, she is in turn seduced by Willoughby, and is left with a baby of her own after he abandons her. Marianne has had a lucky escape.

In 'Mansfield Park' there are a number of young people; we meet most of the ten Price children, all of the four Bertram children, and the two Crawfords, as well as Mr Yates and Mr Rushworth (both unmarried men at the start of the novel). A large part of the novel is concerned with the manoeuvring of the various characters into and out of relationships with each other. Maria is the first to couple up with the unappealing Mr Rushworth. It is her Aunt Norris who brokers the match, and Maria goes along with it because she wants to leave home and have command of her husband's fortune, as well as the societally permitted freedoms of a married woman, which were far greater than those allowed to a single woman. Fanny is already in love with Edmund, but he doesn't know it, and then the Crawfords arrive to throw a very large spanner into the works.

Henry Crawford is not handsome, but he is engaging and flirtatious; he has a large fortune of his own, and an estate in Norfolk. His sister, Mary, is very handsome, intelligent, witty, and has a fortune of her own to boot. Maria immediately regrets being hustled so fast into an engagement with Rushworth, and transfers her affections to Crawford. While her sister, Julia, believing that Maria is sorted out and it's her turn to find a rich fiancé, also makes a play for Crawford. Tom

Bertram throws another contender into the ring by introducing his friend, the Honourable Mr John Yates, who sets the whole bonfire ablaze by suggesting that they all act out a play called, 'Lovers' Vows'.

When Mary Crawford arrives at Mansfield, she is convinced that she will fancy Tom Bertram, as he is the heir, and the more eligible brother. To her chagrin, however, she discovers that she fancies second son Edmund instead, and is further chagrined by discovering that he is to become a clergyman, that he is serious about his religion, and will not give it up even for her. Their roles in the play are as mother and son, but still involve a lot of physical contact, and much need for rehearsing their scenes away from the others.

Maria manoeuvres herself into playing the female lead opposite Henry, and their behaviour during rehearsals is blatant enough to arouse suspicions even in Rushworth's dim mind about her commitment to their union. To Maria's disappointment, Crawford leaves Mansfield Park without making an offer for her hand, so she goes ahead with her marriage to Rushworth. Later, she encounters Crawford again and leaves Rushworth for an extra-marital affair with Henry, hoping he will marry her this time, but he still doesn't. Julia elopes with Yates, but they do marry, and just about manage to retain their respectability, and be admitted back into society, and accepted by the family at Mansfield Park. Edmund is finally put off wanting to marry Mary by her careless attitude towards Henry and Maria's affair – as far as Mary is concerned, it can all be hushed up, and will soon be forgotten, oh, and it was all Fanny's fault for refusing to marry Henry in the first place and helping him to attain domestic bliss away from temptation.

Personally, I agree with Mary up to a point. Scandals break, are talked over, and then disappear as the next scandal rushes into the public's attention. Rushworth divorcing Maria would have re-ignited the scandal briefly, but if the Bertrams had laid low for a while, and then put Maria back on the market with her personal fortune, there would have been suitors lining up.

Fanny believes she has dodged the bullet by standing firm to her refusal to marry Henry on the grounds that he lacks moral principles – she feels her decision has been vindicated, and is further rewarded when Edmund finally marries her right at the very end of the novel. However, as I said earlier, I still think she would have been better off marrying Henry: she was definitely softening towards him when they met at Portsmouth. But there you are; Austen didn't agree, and so the whole debacle unfolded.

However, the sexual shenanigans don't end here – as we follow the characters from 'Mansfield Park' on into 'Return to Mansfield Park', they are still manoeuvring round each other, still forming and changing their relationships with each other. Some of what happens may seem quite shocking, and this is one sequel where I do diverge from the narrower range of actions in Austen's original novels; but given the context, and the characters, I assure you it is all within the bounds of possibility. Some of what happens is attested to have happened in Regency England; so there is a precedent.

The Slave-Trading Halletts of Lyme Regis and Axminster

Leafing idly through a copy of 'The Week' magazine during the First Great Lockdown of 2020, I was astonished to see an advert for the sale of Stedcombe House in Axmouth, formerly owned by the Hallett family.

I had not been aware that any branch of the Hallett family had ever been rich enough to build themselves such a sumptuous residence, and so I started to investigate further. What I discovered was shocking; the Hallett family of Lyme Regis and Axmouth were slave traders.

One Richard Hallett started off the dreadful trade in human bodies towards the end of the seventeenth century; and not only caused a sensation locally by bringing black servants back to Devon with him, but also made enough money to build Stedcombe House. It is not clear for how many more generations the Hallett family continued to profit from the slave trade; Richard passed his estate (and presumably business) on to his brother's son, helpfully also called Richard. Richard's son, John, died very soon after his father in 1747, leaving a wife, Jane Southcott Hallett, two school-age sons, and a daughter.

John's eldest son, Richard Hothersall Hallett became the Vicar and Squire of Axmouth and married one Sarah Cooke in 1760. They had nine children, most of whom did not live to adulthood; but two sons are mentioned: John Hothersall Hallett and the wonderfully named Southcott Hallett. Their father, Richard Hothersall, did not live at Stedcombe, but at Haven Cliff in Axmouth, described as an early 19th Century white stucco Gothic house with battlements, lancet and a clock face.

Richard Hothersall busied himself with improvements to the ancient port of Axmouth, making it suitable for modern shipping – which lends suspicion to his still being involved in the transatlantic slave trade. These improvements did not survive the coming of the railways, nor the severe winter storms which batter that coast line. John Hothersall inherited Stedcombe on the death of his father in 1800, and married, but did not seem to have had any children, or maybe none survived childhood.

John Hothersall's younger brother, Richard Southcott, became the Vicar of Axmouth when his father, Richard, died. He married a Miss Shaw of Bath in 1815, and they had two sons; William Trelawny Hallett (his heir), and Clements Thomas Hallett (who went on to become a Colonel in the Bengal Lancers and saw action in India). William Trelawny became a barrister, and married Ellen Whitehouse in 1850. He inherited the estate at Axminster on the death of his uncle, John Hothersall, but by then the family's fortunes were in severe decline, and Ellen had to sell the estate and move away after William's death in 1889.

As for the possibly impecunious cousins at the Vicarage – they are descended from Maria, the sister of Richard Hothersall and Southcott Hallett – who married a priest called John Comyns. Their son, George Thomas Comyns, became the absentee vicar Richard Southcott Hallett's curate, and eventually Vicar in his own right. A suitable residence for a gentleman was built to accommodate the Comyns family; it still stands and is now known as the 'Old Vicarage'. George Comyns, his wife and family were living here in 1841, through the 1850s, and into 1861, but by 1874 the living of Axmouth, in William Trelawny's 'gift' went to a Reverend Samuel Clement Davis, MA, of Caius College, Cambridge – so I don't know what happened to William's Comyn cousins. The living came with 41 acres of 'Glebe', and a residence, presumably the Vicarage.

For the purposes of 'Mansfield Revisited'; the nearest contemporaries of Tom Bertram are John Hothersall and Richard Southcott, so it is these two that he goes to visit, and stays at Haven Cliff with John, before joining Richard at Bath. Their cousins, the Comyns brothers and sisters, are living at the Vicarage in nearby Axmouth.

It looks as though Clements survived his time in the Bengal Lancers; he is mentioned as living at Haven Cliff in later life, while William Trelawny is listed as living at Stedcombe House.

Of course, I don't know if these Halletts are any relation of mine at all, and I can disclaim them still further by pointing out that Hallett is my married name. However, Halletts seem to have gone to live all over the globe during the eighteenth and nineteenth century: there are Halletts listed in America, Australia, Canada, New Zealand, etc.

One 'pioneering pastoralist and politician' called John Hallett, born in Woodford, Essex, emigrated to Australia in 1836. He did a land-grab on 'Willogoleechee' in Southern Australia, and in the true tradition of the Hallett family of Axmouth, participated in the massacre of Aborigines at Mount Bryan in South Australia in the 1840s, after they were accused of stealing sheep from his land. Willogoleechee was renamed 'Hallett' after John Hallett, and is still called that today. Hallett Cove is a coastal suburb of Adelaide, also named after this deeply unpleasant man.

There is also a town called 'Hallett' in Oklahoma, USA, named after Charles H Hallett, an officer in the Nineteenth Kansas Cavalry. After brief oil booms in the early Twentieth Century, it doesn't seem to have prospered. I know nothing more of Charles H, but given the reputation of the US Cavalry, I can't imagine he was someone I would have wanted to know either.

I was considerably more fascinated to discover that a John Hallett was one of the sailors set adrift with Captain Bligh from The Bounty; he was a mid-shipman, aged 17 at the time. He survived the marooning, but died on shore from unspecified causes at the age of 22.

Enough, already. I'm getting off the point. The point was, that I had found some slave-traders with my married surname and decided to include them in 'Return to Mansfield Park', and then got a bit carried away!

https://www.mansionglobal.com/articles/stedcombe-house-a-restoration-masterpiece-131538

https://www.lymeregismuseum.co.uk/related-article/the-slave-trade/

https://historicengland.org.uk/listing/the-list/list-entry/1333512

https://historicengland.org.uk/listing/the-list/list-entry/1306559

https://www.axmouthcommunity.org/history/nave/hallett-and-searle-monuments/

http://www.devonheritage.org/Places/Axmouth/AxmouthinKellysDirectoryof1889.htm

The Slave Trade and The Abolition

An excerpt from 'Emma' is one of the few direct mentions of a trade which was endemic in Austen's time; and which her own family participated in, albeit indirectly.

"There are places in town, offices, where inquiry would soon produce something — offices for the sale, not quite of human flesh, but of human intellect."

"Oh! my dear, human flesh! You quite shock me; if you mean a fling at the slave-trade, I assure you Mr. Suckling was always rather a friend to the abolition."

"I did not mean, I was not thinking of the slave-trade," replied Jane; *"governess-trade, I assure you, was all that I had in view; widely different certainly, as to the guilt of those who carry it on; but as to the greater misery of the victims, I do not know where it lies."*

Fanny Price appears to be the only person at Mansfield Park who acknowledges that much of the Bertram family's income derives from the slave trade, as her uncle owns a sugar plantation, which would have been worked by slaves. He may not have been in the business of shipping slaves across the Atlantic Ocean, but he was almost certainly in the business of buying those slaves which survived the crossing, and putting them to work in horrendous conditions on his sugar plantation. Sir Thomas was an absentee plantation owner, so employed a foreman who ran the plantation while Sir Thomas spent the money it made and lived in comfort in England. No matter how ethical a person Sir Thomas may have been, once he was no longer in Antigua himself, he had no real idea of how his slaves were being treated on his own plantation.

In Chapter 21 of Mansfield Park, Fanny says to Edmund,

"Did not you hear me ask him about the slave-trade last night?"

"I did—and was in hopes the question would be followed up by others. It would have pleased your uncle to be inquired of farther."

"And I longed to do it—but there was such a dead silence! And while my cousins were sitting by without speaking a word, or seeming at all interested in the subject .."

I have to wonder why Edmund himself did not take up the topic and enquire further; his doing so might have emboldened Fanny to continue, but he seems to have left her stranded in her other cousins' indifference.

The topic of slave trading is clearly a subject of debate in the country which has reached even the remote estate of Mansfield Park, and Fanny knew that it concerned her Uncle and his plantation, but the indifference of the rest of the family is very telling – it seems they were content to ignore the source of their wealth, and just spend the money earned from the cruel institution of slavery in their 'making artificial flowers or wasting gold paper.' (Chapter 2)

It is clear from the example of Richard Hallett (see above) that the trade in slaves from the continent of Africa was well under way in the late seventeenth century, and that trading in slaves by British companies continued until it was finally stopped by repeated Acts of Parliament. During Austen's life-time, the 'abolitionists' mentioned by Mrs Elton, were an increasingly vocal force, calling for the abolition of slavery.

In 1807, the first shots were fired when An Act for the Abolition of the Slave Trade was passed by the British Government. However, this did not end slavery; it just prevented British ships taking slaves across the Atlantic. Another Act was passed in 1833, The Slavery Abolition Act; and this did signal the end of slavery for British owned slaves – but again not of slavery itself. An estimate is that overall British ships took nearly 800,000 men, women and children from Africa across the Atlantic to sell as slaves; it was a hugely profitable enterprise.

Shockingly, there was another Act passed by the British Government to compensate slave owners for the loss of their slaves – I shall repeat that: the slave **owners** were compensated for the loss of their trade; the people who had been enslaved were not compensated. This was the Slave Compensation Act of 1837; the British Government borrowed a huge amount of money to pay the former slave owners, many of whom were wealthy people, like Sir Thomas Bertram.

The slaves on Antigua were among the first to be legally freed in August 1834, which means that Sir Thomas would have faced some labour issues at the very least. I don't suppose for a moment that the newly freed slaves on Antigua were suddenly given good working and living conditions, paid a decent wage, and had access to free healthcare, or education for their children. And, in fact, they remained economically dependent on their former masters for many generations to come. Free people generally do cost more to employ than the slaves which could be worked for nothing more than rudimentary housing, and just enough food to keep them alive long enough to work. However, so far from England, I would imagine that conditions for the former slaves changed very little after their emancipation. In one estimate I saw, slaves survived the conditions on the sugar plantations for an average of 3 years before dying.

Sir Thomas visits his plantations at some point close to the first Act for the Abolition of the Slave Trade was passed in 1807 – his reasons for going are left vague by Austen, but it's possible that news of the Act had caused some uneasiness in the absentee plantation owners, or that he had reason to believe his agent in Antigua was not maximising his profits on his behalf. There are hints that his plantations were not making as much money as formerly; and added to Tom's extravagances, the Bertrams' finances were suddenly looking precarious.

All of this feeds into the action of 'Mansfield Revisited'; which I hope you enjoy reading as much as I enjoyed writing.

On Rout Cakes

These tiny rich sweet cakes, which rather resemble modern scones, were endemic in Regency England at 'routs', or evening parties, and they are mentioned in numerous novels written by authors in Regency and Victorian England. I am not sure when they went out of fashion; or whether they simply morphed into drop scones, or rock cakes. They are still mentioned in recipe books into the Twentieth century, but certainly I've never been offered one, or seen one for sale in a café. Perhaps it's time to revive them?

Anyway, if you would like to have a go at making some, there are a number of competing recipes on the internet, some with quite scary amounts of ingredients, and very little on method or cooking temperatures and times.

Here's one from 1822:

ROUT CAKES: To make rout drop-cakes, mix two pounds of flour with one pound of butter, one pound of sugar, and one pound of currants, cleaned and dried. Moisten it into a stiff paste with two eggs, a large spoonful of orange-flower water, as much rose water, sweet wine, and brandy. Drop the paste on a tin plate floured, and a short time will bake them.

And another from 1914:

ROUT CAKES: Rub into two pounds of flour an ounce of fresh butter, washed in orange-flower water; then add half a pound of well beaten loaf sugar, the same weight of candied orange and lemon cut into strips, and a quarter of a pound of well-dried currants; mix all these ingredients well together with five eggs, well beaten, and half a glass of brandy or ratafia, or a little of both; drop this paste in small rough knobs upon floured tins, and bake in a quick oven; they will require but a very short time to bake, as they must not be high-coloured.

Good luck!

Foods of England - Rout Cakes

Printed in Great Britain
by Amazon